GIANTSLAYER

Felix ducked the sweep of a Chaos warrior's blade and lashed out a counter-blow against the cold black metal armour. His sword almost dropped from fingers numbed by the force of impact. The ancient magical blade cut through the enchanted vambrace and bit into the Chaos warrior's arm. Another stroke took him through the gorget and buried the blade deep in his throat.

Up ahead Gotrek and Teclis fought like daemons, chopping down anything that got in their path. Man or monster, beast or orc, nothing withstood them. The destruction they wrought was immense. They were almost halfway to their goal when it all went horribly wrong.

A WARHAMMER NOVEL

Gotrek and Felix

GIANTSLAYER

By William King

To Angela, for all her help

A BLACK LIBRARY PUBLICATION

First published in 2003.
This edition published in 2004 by
by BL Publishing,
Games Workshop Ltd.,
Willow Road, Nottingham,
NG7 2WS, UK.

10 9 8 7 6 5 4 3 2 1

Cover illustration by Geoff Taylor.

Map by Nuala Kennedy

A CIP record for this book is available from the British Library.

ISBN 1-84416-261-3

Distributed in the US by Simon & Schuster
1230 Avenue of the Americas, New York, NY 10020, US.

Printed and bound in Great Britain by
Bookmarque, Surrey, UK.

See the Black Library on the Internet at
www.blacklibrary.com

Find out more about Games Workshop
and the world of Warhammer 40,000 at
www.games-workshop.com

THIS IS A DARK age, a bloody age, an age of daemons
and of sorcery. It is an age of battle and death, and of the
world's ending. Amidst all of the fire, flame and fury
it is a time, too, of mighty heroes, of bold deeds
and great courage.

AT THE HEART of the Old World sprawls the Empire, the
largest and most powerful of the human realms. Known for
its engineers, sorcerers, traders and soldiers, it is
a land of great mountains, mighty rivers, dark forests
and vast cities. And from his throne in Altdorf reigns
the Emperor Karl-Franz, sacred descendant of the
founder of these lands, Sigmar, and wielder
of his magical warhammer.

BUT THESE ARE far from civilised times. Across the length
and breadth of the Old World, from the knightly palaces of
Bretonnia to ice-bound Kislev in the far north, come rum-
blings of war. In the towering World's Edge Mountains, the
orc tribes are gathering for another assault. Bandits and rene-
gades harry the wild southern lands of
the Border Princes. There are rumours of rat-things, the
skaven, emerging from the sewers and swamps across the
land. And from the northern wildernesses there is the
ever-present threat of Chaos, of daemons and beastmen corrupted by the foul powers of the Dark Gods.
As the time of battle draws ever near,
the Empire needs heroes
like never before.

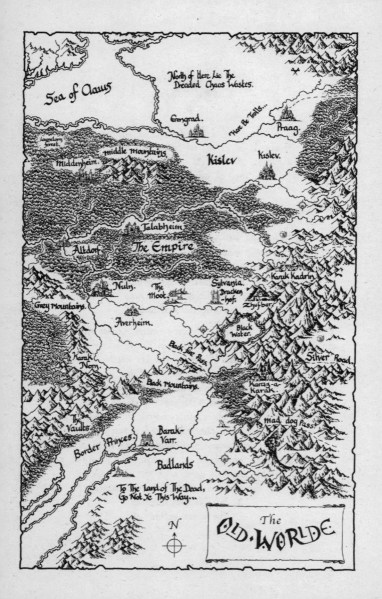

'Sylvania had proven to be a haunt of horror. The dire events at Drakenhof Castle left us filled us with sadness and fear. We had prevented the rising of a great terror but paid an awful price. And there was to be no respite from battle and dread. No sooner had we overcome our undead foe than we found ourselves thrown headlong into another even more desperate adventure, one that was to involve the titanic legacy of a long dead race and an encounter with the greatest living sorcerer of this age of the world, as well as battles with foes more horrible and deadly than almost anything we had faced before. During the course of these adventures I was to learn far more about the secret history of our world than I ever wanted to learn, and found my life and soul in the greatest of peril. Even now, looking back on these terrible events I am amazed that I survived. Many of my companions were not to prove so lucky...'

– From *My Travels With Gotrek*, Vol IV, by Herr Felix Jaeger (Altdorf Press, 2505)

PROLOGUE

THE EARTH SHOOK. All around him people screamed. Huge
buildings shuddered. The statues of the gods toppled from
their alcoves in the shrines of ancient temples, shattering
into a thousand pieces as the earth writhed like a dying serpent. He ran through the streets of the ancient city, seeing
the looks of horror on the faces of his people. He passed
decaying mansions where the desiccated ghosts of previous
owners gibbered thinly in their fear. Ahead of him the
mighty column of the Seafarer teetered and then collapsed.
The Phoenix King flew from his high perch, his outstretched
hand seeming to wave in terror as he tumbled earthward.

As he crested the high hills overlooking the mighty harbour, a glance at the peaks rimming the city told him the
worst. The mountains blazed with light as wild magic ran
out of control. He could sense its unbridled power even at
this distance, and knew without having to cast any divinations that something was deeply, deeply amiss with the old
spells that protected his land and his people.

Somehow, he was not sure how, he was atop the mighty
wall that had guarded the harbour for a dozen ages. Looking

out to sea, he saw the thing he had feared most of all. A towering wave, twice as high as the wall, driven by a force that would shatter the city, raced ever closer. Within it mighty leviathans, raised up from the deeps that surrounded the island continent, roared and bellowed and sought to break free. Strength that could shatter the largest ship in seconds was useless in the grip of that terrible tsunami.

Knowing that it was futile, that there was no way he could endure this, he prepared himself to resist, drawing on all his power, readying his mightiest warding magics, but somehow, as he had known it must be, nothing came. Power trickled into him where once it would have flooded.

A hundred times the height of the tallest man, the wave towered over his head, cresting, ready to break. For an instant he gazed into the eyes of a trapped sea monster, feeling a certain kinship with it; then its huge pink maw gaped, teeth the size of swords glinted in the shadows, and the mighty wave tumbled forward to break against the wall with awesome irresistible power.

It swept over him, crushing him, drowning him, smashing him down into the depths, and it rushed forward to sweep the last and greatest city of the elves from the face of the planet.

Suddenly he was elsewhere, in a place that was not a place, in a time that was outside time. There were presences there, not dead, not living, mighty mages all. Their faces were etched with aeons of pain, scarred from fighting a battle that no mortal should have been asked to fight. Even he, who was accounted mighty among the wizards of the world, was daunted by the power of the spells around him. More than that, he was frightened by where he knew himself to be, and when.

The shadowy presences danced around him, constantly performing a ritual that they must never stop, lest they bring disaster upon the world. They were wraith-like, and their movements were slow and pained, like the clockwork figures of the dwarfs whose mechanisms were slowly winding down. Once, he knew, they had been elves, the greatest wizards of their age, and they had sacrificed themselves to save their land and their people.

'Greetings, blood of Aenarion,' said an ancient voice, dry, dusty, but with the faint lilting accent of the mountains of Caledor still.

'Greetings, Lord of Dragons,' he replied, knowing who he faced, wondering if this was a dream, knowing it was not.

'We are remembered still among the living then?' said the voice.

'Remembered and honoured.'

'That is good. That is some repayment for our sacrifice.' There was more than a hint of self-pity in the voice. Understandable, he supposed. He would probably have felt sorry for himself if he had been trapped at the centre of the great vortex for five millennia, struggling to hold together the web of spells that kept the island continent afloat.

The scene shimmered, like a reflection on the surface of disturbed water. The ghastly, ghostly figures seemed to recede, and he was glad. He ought to let them go, but he knew he had been brought here for a purpose.

'Why am I here?' he shouted, and his words seemed to echo through infinite caverns, and resound into distant ages.

'The old barriers are falling. The Paths of the Old Ones are opened. We cannot hold the Weave against it.'

'What am I to do?'

'Seek the source of disorder. Find the Oracle of the Truthsayers. She will tell you what you need to know. Close the ancient pathways. Go swiftly and go alone. You will find the allies you need along the way and in the most unexpected forms. Go. There is little time left. Even this sending is weakening us and we must conserve the little strength we have left.'

Even as the words echoed up from the bottom of infinity, the voice was fading. A great fear came over him.

The Archmage Teclis sat bolt upright, pulling the silken sheets from the naked forms of his companions. Cold sweat covered him; he could smell it even through the musky scents worn by the two courtesans.

'What is it, my lord?' asked Shienara. Concern showed in her beautiful narrow face. 'What ails you?'

'Nothing,' he lied, rising from the bed and limping across the room. He reached for a goblet and a crystal decanter of wine cut in the shape of a dragon.

'Is it the dreams again, the nightmares?'

He shot her a cold glance. 'What do you know of nightmares?' he asked.

'You talk in your sleep, my lord, and lash out, and I guessed.'

He looked at her, long and hard. These were words his many enemies would pay much to hear.

'There were no nightmares,' he said, reaching out for the power. Unlike in the dream, it flowed strongly into him. 'There were no dreams. You should forget these things.'

A slight blankness came over her beautiful face as the spell took her. She looked at him and smiled quizzically. 'Sleep,' he told her, 'and when you wake remember nothing.'

Instantly she slumped next to the form of her twin. He shrugged, wishing that he could sleep so soundly, knowing that he never would again without the aid of magic, and that was something he could no longer afford. Momentary guilt afflicted him that he should treat a fellow elf so, but these were strange and evil times, and the need for security was paramount. Ancient enemies stirred. Old gods were awakening. Every oracle and soothsayer between here and far Cathay predicted doom. His own star charts spoke of as much. He took a sip of the bitter wine. It flowed down easily.

He gestured and his robe fluttered across the room, wrapping itself around his naked form. He pulled on a pair of slippers made from the finest Cathayan silk. He reached out and his staff leapt to his hand. He limped from the chamber, and down the cold echoing hallways of his ancestral home. He made his way to the workroom, knowing that he would do as he always did, and seek comfort in knowledge. The few aged servants still awake scurried away, knowing from his frown that it would be best not to interrupt his reverie.

Dark times were coming, he knew. The dreams were impossible to ignore now, and he had long ago learned the unwisdom of doing that anyway.

In the deepest cellars beneath the mansion, his workroom provided him with a haven. As he entered, he spoke the words of command. Immediately wards sprang into place. The air shimmered with their bridled power. Not even the mightiest daemon could penetrate them.

A trapped homunculus stirred slowly in a jar of preservative fluid. It gestured at him obscenely as he limped past. The creature was not best pleased with its home. Tiny gills pulsed in its neck. Its thin leathery wings stirred the liquid, turning it cloudy. He gave it a cold smile, and it froze in mid-gesticulation. Few things in this world or beyond had the courage to cross him when an evil mood was upon him.

He moved through the chamber, past the ordered alcoves containing mystical paraphernalia and the elaborately indexed series of volumes in a hundred languages, living and dead. Eventually he found what he sought, the strange apparatus he had unearthed in the ruins of the ancient Cathayan city nearly two centuries ago. A massive sphere of verdigrised bronze, engraved with strange runes that reminded him of the work of the decadent denizens of Lustria.

Teclis sat cross-legged before the Sphere of Destiny and contemplated his dream. It was the third time in less than a month it had come to him, each time more clear and vivid than the last. This was the first time the ancients had spoken to him, though. Had he really talked with ghosts of the ancestral wizards who protected his land? Had they reached out through the barriers that bound them and communicated with him? He smiled sourly. He knew that dreams could be sent to warn or to harm, but he knew equally that sometimes dreams were only his own deeper mind talking to him, giving shape to his fears and intuitions. Either some friendly power or his own deepest instincts were trying to warn him of something – it was irrelevant which. He needed to act.

You did not have to be a high wizard to know that something was amiss in the world. Reports from Eagle captains brought tales of disaster from the furthest lands. In Cathay, the warlords had risen in rebellion against the Mandate of Heaven. In Araby a fanatic who called himself the Prophet of Law was stirring up the natives to cleanse their land of evil… and his definition of evil included anyone who was not human. In the cities of their under-empire, the skaven stirred. The forces of the Witch King once more strode the soil of Ulthuan. Elven armies mustered to head northwards and oppose them, and elven fleets patrolled the northern seas constantly. But a month ago, he had been summoned here to Lothern and the court of the Phoenix King to discuss these matters, and having done so was told to prepare for war.

He passed his hands over the sphere. The casing of metal bands contracted in on themselves, revealing a milky white gem that pulsed with its own internal light. He spoke the words of the invocation he had found in a scroll from the reign of Bel Korhadris, near three thousand years old, and the lights danced over its surface. He snapped his fingers and the candles of hallucinogenic incense, concentrated from the leaves of the black lotus, sprang to life and began to burn. He breathed deeply of them, and opened his mage senses to the fullest, feeling his point of view being sucked into the depths of the crystal. For long moments, nothing happened. He saw only blackness, heard only the muted drumbeat of his heart. He continued the invocation, working effortlessly on a spell that it would have taken a lesser mage a lifetime to master.

Now his vision seemed to hover over Ulthuan. He could see perfectly even in the darkness, and he could view those things that would be visible only to a mage. He saw the flows of magic pinioned by the watchstones that kept the island continent above the waves. Raised by elder world magic millennia ago, it needed the same magic now to prevent it sinking beneath the surface of the sea. In his dreams he had spoken to those who maintained those spells. He knew that was significant. He saw the tiny glints that were his fellow wizards working magic, the intricate structures of spells as they were woven by masters of the most magical of all the world's peoples.

Sensing a disruption in the flows of power, he sent his consciousness racing in the direction from which it came. Far to the north he sensed the abomination that waited at the farthest pole. It pulsed with energy, no longer quiescent, promising the end of the world. Still, it had not fully woken, but yet…

Within heartbeats his spirit eyes soared over the Chaos Wastes, as close to the influence of the polar abomination as he dared go, taking in the vast hordes of black armoured warriors camped on the cold plains, and the hideous legions of horned beastmen who followed them. He saw the huge flows of Chaotic energy that the winds of magic blew over them, but he saw nothing there to cause any disturbance to his island home. All the same, it was disturbing, the size of that huge invasion force. It was larger than anything the diminished power of the elves could muster and he knew it was only a small fraction of what the dark powers were amassing.

He sent the sphere arcing through the sky towards the ancient city of Praag and saw that it was still in ruins, although its people were making valiant efforts to rebuild it. Interestingly, dwarfs were present. It seemed the ancient enemies of his own people had come to help the humans in this hour of need.

He let his eyes dwell on the massive citadel, wrapped as it was by spells that not even he could penetrate, and wondered what it was that was kept in the depths beneath that fortified pinnacle. What ancient secret brought the armies of Chaos back to this spot again and again? What ancient oaths bound the humans to rebuild their haunted city in the face of the unbreaking cycle of destruction? The speculation was interesting but it was getting him nowhere. It merely confirmed what he had heard: that the greatest invasion in centuries was taking place in the Old World, and he feared it would take more than the might of man and dwarf to repel it.

He raised his point of view higher until the curve of the sleeping world lay beneath him, the lines of power flowing through the night like an enormous web were visible to him even through the white turbulent spirals of the clouds. He inspected them closely, looking for clues, and found them. From the northern island of Albion the lines of power that would normally have flowed to Ulthuan did so weakly. Sometimes they flickered and faded. Sometimes they blazed brightly and massive pulses of energy raced out over the sea in the direction of the island continent. Out of the Chaos Wastes pulses of power rushed towards Albion and then diminished. From Albion, the flows raced onwards, rippling towards the Empire, Bretonnia, Ulthuan.

What was going on here? What magic was this? Those webs of energy dated back to the most ancient days – what could be using them for its own ends? Nothing good, he was certain. He sent the point of view of the sphere rushing towards Albion. It hurtled towards the magical barriers that surrounded the island, into the mists, and there it was stopped utterly and completely.

Not good, he thought. Albion had always been surrounded by spells of great potency intended to ward it from the eye of outsiders. Those spells obviously still held. No, he thought, that was not quite true. They felt different now. There was a subtle taint to them, of evil and something else.

Briefly he considered what he had seen, and a horrible suspicion began to grow in his mind. Fragments of certain ancient forbidden texts, written by mad elven wizards in the dawn ages of the world came back to him. Legends of the world's most ancient gods, that talked of things best forgotten. But apparently someone *had* remembered them. Someone had disturbed the things that were best left untouched. Fear clutched at his heart as he considered this. He needed to consult certain ancient sources, and he needed to do so now. If what he suspected was true, there was indeed not a moment to waste.

DAWN FOUND TECLIS on the balcony outside the library, a book spread on his lap, his face resting in his hands. The old mansion built on the side of the highest hills overlooking the city of Lothern gave him a fine view of the harbour. It was flat and serene as a pond; not the slightest hint of the enormous tidal wave of his nightmares menaced it.

Briefly, he wished he was back in the tower of Hoeth, with the greatest library in the world close at hand, and his fellow mages to consult with, but that was a foolish wish. Politics had brought him here. He did not like this place, the ownership of which he shared with his brother. He had not liked it when they were children, and he did not like it now. Too many old memories, he supposed, too many recollections of long evenings of illness and infirmity. It reminded him too much of a hospice or one of those temples of euthanasia where the old and the weary of life went to end their lives in peace and comfort.

He dismissed these thoughts. Even as he did so, the earth quivered. It was very mild. The wine in his goblet merely rippled. The walls of the old palace barely quivered. It might have been a natural earthquake, but he doubted it. All the signs were clear. Something was interfering with the ancient spells that bound the island continent of Ulthuan together, that stopped it from disappearing once more beneath the waves. And if something was not done, his nightmares would come true.

Aldreth, one of his oldest servants entered. Teclis knew it was important. The old elf had orders not to disturb him for anything less than a summons from the Phoenix King himself. 'Your brother wishes to speak with you,' he said.

Teclis smiled sourly. There was no way of denying he was at home. This place was as much Tyrion's as his own, and the servants were as loyal to his twin as they were to him. More loyal, he thought acidly. Of course, his brother would depart if he indicated a wish for privacy. His manners were as perfect as everything else about him. Teclis turned his gaze back to the sea. You are in a vile mood today, he told himself.

'Show my brother in,' he said. 'And prepare food if he wishes it.'

'It is a little early to be drinking that vintage,' said Tyrion as he strode out onto the balcony. There was a hint of reproof in his voice that was equivalent to a thunderous chorus of disapproval from anyone else. Teclis looked up at

his brother. So tall, so straight. The limbs so clean and so
unbent, the face so honest and open. The voice as beautiful
as a temple bell being rung to greet the dawn. Astonishing,
he thought, that this golden creature should be my twin. It
seemed that the gods had lavished all their gifts on him, and
left me an ill-made thing.

'I take it that means you won't be joining me, brother?'

He knew he was being unfair. The gods had given him a
gift for magic unequalled in this age of the world, and the
will necessary to use that power as it should be used. Still,
there were times when he would have gladly swapped all of
that for Tyrion's effortless popularity, his ease and courtesy,
his ability to be happy even in the unhappiest of times, and
his blazing good health.

'On the contrary, it is my brotherly duty to keep you from
drinking alone. The gods alone know what that might lead
to.' And there it was, the famous charm, the ability to change
the mood of the situation with a smile and a seemingly
thoughtless joke. Tyrion reached out for the decanter and
poured himself a full goblet. There was no formality there,
none of the endless empty ritual that Teclis so despised in
elvish social gatherings. It was the casual gesture of the warrior more at home in camp than the Phoenix King's court,
and yet it was exactly the thing his brother knew would put
him most at ease. Teclis could understand why there were
those at court who compared his brother to Malekith in
ancient times, before the Witch King revealed his true
colours. He had known his brother all their lives, and even
he was not sure how much art went into that carefully con-
trived artlessness.

Tyrion waved, and Teclis looked up. On the balcony above
them, Shienara and her sister, Malyria, waved back. They
looked at Tyrion with the mixture of open desire and admiration he had always commanded from women. Useless, of
course, as his brother had eyes only for his consort, the
Everqueen. He had not, unlike most elf males, ever been
unfaithful.

'What is this early morning toast in honour of?' Tyrion
asked.

'The end of the world,' said Teclis.

'That bad?' said Tyrion.

'The end of our world, at least.'

'I do not think the Dark One will overcome us this time,' said Tyrion. It was exactly what Teclis would have expected him to say, but there was a watchfulness about him now, a wariness. Suddenly he looked exactly like what he was, the deadliest elf warrior in twenty generations.

'It is not our dear kinsman and his lackeys I am worried about, it is Ulthuan itself. Someone, or something, is tampering with the watchstones or the power that underlies them.'

'These earthquakes and eruptions are not coincidence then? I had suspected as much.'

'No, they are not.'

'You will be leaving soon then.' It was not a question. Teclis smiled as he nodded. His brother had always understood him better than any other living being.

'Do you want some company on your journey? I am supposed to be leading the fleet northwards, to face the spawn of Naggaroth, but if what you say is true, I am sure the Phoenix King could spare my services.'

Teclis shook his head. 'The fleet needs you. Our armies need you. Where I am going, spells will be more useful than swords.'

Teclis slammed his drink down on the fine ivory table. It almost spilled over the parchments that sat there. He had spent most of the night writing them. 'Please see that these are copied and delivered to his majesty and the masters at Hoeth,' he told Aldreth. 'Now I must go. I have a long way to travel and a short time to do it in.'

CHAPTER ONE

WITH A HEAVY heart, Felix Jaeger watched the last of the remaining Kislevite warriors place the corpse of Ivan Petrovich on the pyre. The old warrior looked somehow smaller, shrunken in death. His face showed none of the peace that was supposed to belong to those who had entered the realm of Morr, God of Death, but then, Felix supposed, Ivan's last few moments had been anything but pleasant. He had witnessed his only child, Ulrika, transformed into a vampire, a soulless blood-sucking thing, and he himself had met his death at the hand of her undead master's minions. Felix shivered and drew his faded red Sudenland wool cloak about him. Once he had thought himself in love with Ivan's daughter. What was he supposed to feel now?

The answer was that he did not know. Even when she had still walked among the living he had been unsure. Now, he realised, he would never really have the chance to find out. Somewhere deep within him a slow, sullen, smouldering resentment against the gods was fanned to flame. He was starting to understand how Gotrek felt.

He looked over at the Slayer. The dwarf's brutal features were uncharacteristically thoughtful. His squat massive form, far broader than any human's, looked out of place among the Kislevite horse soldiers. He knuckled the patch covering his ruined eye with one massive hand, then scratched his shaved and tattooed head reflectively. His great crest of red dyed hair drooped in the cold and snow. He looked up and caught Felix's glance and shook his head. Felix guessed that in his own strange way Gotrek had liked the old march boyar. More than that, Ivan Petrovich had in some way been a link to the Slayer's mysterious past. He had known the dwarf since the time of his first expedition to the Chaos Wastes many years before.

The thought made Felix realise just how far from home Ivan had fallen. It must be three hundred leagues at least from here in the dark forests of Sylvania to the cold lands on the edge of Kislev that he had once ruled. Of course, the old boyar's realm was gone now, swept away by the vast Chaos invasion that had driven as far south as Praag.

'Snorri thinks Ivan died a good death,' said Snorri Nosebiter. He looked glum. Despite the cold, the second Slayer was no better dressed than Gotrek. Perhaps dwarfs simply did not feel discomfort like humans. More likely they were simply too stubborn to admit it. Snorri's normally stupidly cheerful features were masked by sadness. Perhaps he was not quite so insensitive as he seemed.

'There are no good deaths,' Felix muttered under his breath. When he realised what he had done, he offered up a silent prayer that neither of the dwarfs had heard him. He had, after all, sworn a vow to follow Gotrek and record the Slayer's doom in an epic poem what seemed like a lifetime ago. The dwarfs lived only to atone for some supposed sin or crime by meeting their doom at the hands of a mighty monster, or in the face of overwhelming odds.

The surviving Kislevites filed past and offered up their last respects to their former lord. Many of them made the sign of the wolf god Ulric with the fingers of their left hand, then cast a glance over their shoulder and made it again. Felix could understand that. They were still almost within the shadow of Drakenhof Castle, that mighty citadel of evil the vampire lord Adolphus Krieger had sought to make his own. He had possessed an ancient amulet and a plan to bring all the aristocracy of the night under his command. Instead he had succeeded only in bringing his own doom.

But at what cost? So many had lost their lives. There was another mass pyre nearby that the surviving Kislevites had hastily constructed for their own fallen. A second one contained the remains of the vampire's followers. Here in the cursed land of Sylvania these men were not about to leave any corpses unburned to face a possible dark resurrection at the hands of a necromancer.

Max Schreiber strode forward, leaning on his staff, looking every inch the imposing wizard in his golden robes. Not even the bloodstains and sword rips in the clothes detracted from the man's dignity, but there was something dead in his eyes and a bleakness to his features that matched Gotrek's. Max had loved Ulrika, probably more than Felix ever had, and now he too had lost her forever. Felix hoped that in his grief the wizard would not do something stupid.

Max waited until the last of the Kislevites had filed past the boyar's body, then he looked at Wulfgar, the ranking leader. The horse soldier nodded. Max spoke a word and banged the butt of his staff on the ground three times. With each strike, one of the pyres burst into flames. The sorcery was strong and obvious. Golden flames flickered into being around the damp wood and then settled on them. The nails driven into Snorri's skull reflected the light, making it look like he had a small blaze atop his shaven head.

Slowly smoke rose, the wood blackened and then burst into more natural flame. Felix was glad of the wizard's magic. There was no way under these conditions that even the dwarfs would have been able to light a fire.

Swiftly the fires spread and soon the sickly sweet smell of roasting flesh filled the air. Felix was not prepared to stay and watch Ivan be consumed. The man was a friend. He turned and strode out from the ruined hall into the cold air. The horses were waiting, and the wagons of the wounded. Snow covered the land. Somewhere out there was Ulrika and her new mentor, the Countess Gabriella, but they were out of his reach now.

War waited in the north. Chaos was coming, and it was there the Slayers expected to find their destiny.

THE OLD WOMAN looked weary. The children marching along beside her looked starved. They wore the usual rags common to Sylvanian peasantry. Their eyes were studies in hopeless misery. Beside them a few men in blood-spattered tunics grasped pitchforks in frozen fingers. Felix saw tiredness war with fear in their faces and slowly win out. They were scared of the riders and the dwarfs but they were too tired and too hungry to run.

'What happened to you?' asked Gotrek in a manner that was anything but reassuring. The massive axe he held in one fist made him even more threatening. 'Why do you wander these roads in winter?'

It was a good question. Any sensible peasant would be huddling in his hovel right now. Felix already knew the answer. These were refugees.

'Beasts came,' said the old woman eventually. 'Out of the woods. They burned our houses, burned the inn, burned everything, killed most and carried others off.'

'Most likely wanted breakfast,' said Gotrek. The expressions on the faces of the refugees told Felix that they had not needed to know that.

'Beastmen?' Snorri had perked up, as he always did at the prospect of a fight.

'Aye, scores of them,' said the old woman. 'Came out of nowhere in the middle of winter. Who would have thought it? Maybe the zealots are right. Maybe the end of the world is coming. They say the pale lords have returned and that Drakenhof Castle is inhabited once more.'

'That's something you don't need to worry about any more,' said Felix, then wished he hadn't. The hag was looking at him as if he were an idiot, which he supposed he was for saying such a thing. Of course, any Sylvanian peasant would worry about Drakenhof Castle and its inhabitants, no matter what some ragged stranger said.

'You say they burned down the inn?' said Max.

'Aye. Killed the innkeeper and most of the guests.'

'Snorri was looking forward to a bucket of vodka,' said Snorri. 'Snorri thinks those beastmen need to be taught a lesson.'

Gotrek nodded agreement. Felix had been afraid of that. The fact that there were less than a dozen unwounded Kislevite horse archers, the two Slayers, and Felix and Max to face what sounded like a mass of beastmen did not daunt either dwarf in the least. The Kislevites, hardened warriors from the march lands where human territories bordered Chaos, had sense enough to be worried, Felix could tell from their expressions.

'Don't go,' said the old woman. 'Ye'll just get yourselves killed. Best come with us. Stephansdorp is just a couple of days' walk south of here. It's less than a day without the snow.'

'If it has not been burned to the ground too,' said Gotrek, somewhat unhelpfully. A couple of the children whimpered. One or two of the men looked as if they were fighting back tears themselves. Felix could not blame them. Doubtless only the thought of sanctuary among their kin in the nearby village had kept them going. Even as Felix watched, one man collapsed onto his knees, letting his pitchfork fall from numbed fingers. He made the sign of Shallya on his breast and bowed his head. Two of the children went over to him and began to tug his sleeves, whispering, 'Da-da.'

'Best get going if we're going to overtake these beastmen,' said Gotrek. Snorri nodded agreement. Wulfgar shook his head. 'We will guard these folk en route to their kin,' he said. 'We must find a place for our wounded.'

He looked almost shame-faced as he said it. Felix did not blame him, though. The Kislevites had been sorely demoralised by the death of Ivan, and the events at Drakenhof had been enough to dent the courage of even the bravest. Gotrek stared at Wulfgar for a moment. Felix feared the Slayer was about to give the horse soldier the benefit of a few well-chosen words concerning the courage and hardiness of Kislevite humanity, but he just shrugged and shook his head.

'What about you, Max?' Felix asked. The wizard considered for a moment before saying, 'I will come with you. These beastmen should be cleansed from our land.'

The tone of the wizard's voice worried Felix. He seemed well nigh as bitter and full of rage as Gotrek. Felix hoped that he was not becoming unhinged by grief over what had happened with Ulrika. On the other hand, he was glad Max was coming with them. The wizard was worth a company of horse archers when it came to a fight.

Briefly, Felix considered sloping off with the horse archers himself, but decided against it. Not only would it have gone against the oath he had sworn to follow the Slayer, but Felix felt far safer in the company of Gotrek, Snorri and Max than he would in the company of the Kislevites, even if they were going hunting for beastmen.

'Best be getting on then,' he was surprised to hear himself saying, 'if we want to get there by nightfall.'

'THIS PLACE HAS certainly changed since we were last here,' said Felix, looking at the still smouldering ruins of what had once been a walled village. Nobody paid him the slightest attention. They were all too busy looking at the wreckage for themselves.

There was not much left. Most of the hovels had been made of wattle and daub with thatched roofs. Their walls had been kicked in, their roofs burned. Only the inn had been a more substantial structure, of timber and stone. It had taken a fair time to collapse, he guessed. The flames must have been fierce indeed to consume the structure. A pity it was gone, he thought, for the weather was already starting to worsen.

Even as he watched, shadowy figures moved within it. They were too big and too misshapen to be human. There was only one thing that looked like that. Beastmen! Snorri almost howled with joy when he realised what they were seeing and brandished his axe and his hammer in the air. Gotrek raised his axe, ran his thumb along the blade until it drew blood and then spat a curse.

If this intimidated the beastmen, they gave no sign. A group of them emerged from the ruins of the inn. Some of them possessed bovine heads, while others had the heads of goats or wolves or other beasts. All of them were massive and muscular. All of them were armed with crude spears, massive spiked clubs or hammers. They were an incongruous sight. The last time Felix had passed through this place, the Green Man had been occupied by humans and he had passed an evening in bizarre conversation with the vampiric countess. Now the whole small village surrounding the inn had been swept away. In his lifetime Felix had seen a great deal of slaughter and a number of villages razed, but he knew he would never get used to it. The senseless carnage fuelled his anger and his resentment.

The dozen beastmen swept forward. They obviously felt no fear at facing such a small group of opponents. Answering calls came from elsewhere, from the snow-girt woods around the sacked hamlet. Felix hoped he and the others had not bitten off more than they could chew.

As the beastmen loped forward, Gotrek and Snorri raced to meet them. Raced was probably the wrong word under the circumstances, Felix decided. The dwarfs' short legs carried them at what would have been a comfortable jog for Felix. In any case, the distance between them closed swiftly. Felix looked at Max to see if the wizard was going to cast a spell. Max scanned their surroundings looking for other attackers. He seemed confident that the Slayers could handle the beasts.

Gotrek hit the pack slightly ahead of Snorri. His axe hurtled through a tremendous arc, lopping off the arm of the nearest beastman, opening the stomach of another to send a wave of blood and bile spraying to the ground, and smashing through the raised club with which a third attempted to parry. A moment later Snorri took down the disarmed beastman with a stroke of the hammer he held in one hand, and buried his axe in the skull of another. There was a sickening crunch like rotten wood splintering as he drove it home.

Within a few heartbeats five of the beastmen were down. Gotrek and Snorri barely slowed. Gotrek leapt forward and chopped a wolf-headed creature clean in two, sending its upper body one way and its lower body another. Snorri whirled like an Arabian dervish and brought both his weapons smashing into another Chaos spawn. The hammer tenderised flesh even as the axe smashed ribs and bit deep into the creature's lungs. It stood for a moment, blowing bubbles of bloody froth from its chest before it collapsed.

The surviving beastmen had not even had time to realise the scale of the casualties they had taken. They swept forward, trying to overwhelm their foes. They obviously had confidence in the sheer brutal power of their blows, but they had reckoned without the strength of Gotrek and Snorri's stark ferocity. Gotrek whirled his axe in a massive double arc, driving them back. Snorri dived forward to land on his side and hit the snow rolling. He barrelled into the legs of one beastman, tripping it, while his axe took another behind the knee sending it stumbling to the ground. Without breaking stride, Gotrek brought his axe down twice with all the force of a thunderbolt. Felix knew that neither of the fallen beastmen would rise again, given the sickening power of those blows. A heartbeat later, the axe had risen again to behead another beastman.

Now the Chaos creatures were dismayed. They turned and fled. Gotrek's axe took another in the back. Snorri pulled himself to his feet and lobbed his hammer, catching another on the back of the skull, sending it tumbling forward into the snow. A few moments later, Snorri had reclaimed his hammer and turned the beastman's skull to jelly with it.

Felix glanced around. More groups of beastmen had emerged from the wood, just in time to witness the rout of their fellows. Felix could see that there were not nearly as many as he had feared. There were three groups with, at most, five members. It looked like the largest part of their force had emerged from the inn. Nonetheless they looked like they were considering a charge when Max raised his arms and began incanting a spell. In seconds a sphere of light brighter than the sun appeared in each of his clenched fists. When he opened his fingers bolts of pure blazing golden power lashed forward. They ravened among the brutes, charring flesh and melting bone. It was all too much for the Chaos creatures. They turned tail and fled into the woods.

Felix was amazed. Events had moved so swiftly, he had not even managed to bloody his sword. He felt almost embarrassed when he considered it. Seeing his expression, Gotrek spoke up.

'Don't worry, manling. You will get your chance to kill Chaos spawn when we follow these beasts to their lair!'

'I was afraid you were going to say that,' Felix said. He moved into the ruins of the inn. Butchered bodies were everywhere. Human bones lay in the snow, cracked for marrow and gnawed by powerful jaws. He felt like being sick but he controlled himself.

'Looks like they stopped here for a snack,' said Gotrek.

TWO HOURS LATER, massive trees loomed all around them. The snow was falling so heavily that Felix could barely see ten feet ahead of him. They had long ago lost all sight of the beastmen's tracks. Now it was only a matter of trudging forward through the storm, making sure to keep his eyes fixed firmly on Gotrek's broad back. The wind whined in his ears. The snowflakes melted in his hair. His breath emerged in frosty clouds. His fingers felt too numb to hold a sword. He was not sure that if he was attacked now, he would even be capable of fighting. He sincerely hoped the Slayers were in a better way. Right now he desperately wished he had gone off with the Kislevites. Now was not the time to be caught in the Sylvanian woods by a sudden blizzard.

They needed to find shelter soon, or they were doomed.

CHAPTER TWO

'I WANT TO KILL Gotrek Gurnisson myself,' said Grume of Night Fang. He loomed out of the shadows like a small mountain of metal and armour. The intricate net of potent enchantments on his armour was almost dazzling to Kelmain's mage sight. The warlord had been like a man demented ever since the defeated scouts had returned out of the blizzard, bearing word of the dwarf's presence. Kelmain wished he had never mentioned it now, but he had been at Praag and knew from the descriptions of their adversaries that only Gotrek Gurnisson and his associates matched the scouts' descriptions.

'Why?' asked the Chaos wizard, just to be contrary. Kelmain looked around the stone walls of the ancient antechamber, trying to gather his patience. The runes fascinated him and so did those bizarre carvings, but the smell was so distracting. He covered his mouth and his nose with one clawed hand. Grume stank of sweat and the old blood and congealed brains that covered his armour. Normally Kelmain did not consider himself fastidious, it was not something anyone in his line of work could afford to be, but this was the limit.

'Because his axe killed Arek Daemonclaw and I want it for
my own. Such a weapon would be worthy of me. All considered Arek's armour unbreachable,' Grume's deep voice
bellowed.

Outside, the wind and snow whirled past, deflected by the
spells Kelmain had woven around them.

Kelmain gazed into the hovering crystal and saw his identical twin, Lhoigor, reflected within. He might as well have
been standing in the room, not a thousand leagues away
within that dreary temple on the island of Albion. Tall, thin,
vulpine of features, pale of skin. The difference was that
Lhoigor was clad in gold instead of black, and had a
runestaff of gold as opposed to his own staff of ebony and
silver. Lhoigor flapped a hand beneath his nose and then
raised a hand to his mouth. Kelmain knew what he meant.
Why, of all the Chaos warlords gathered, did it have to be
Grume who accompanied him on this reconnaissance, he
wondered? Why could it not be Kestranor the Castrator? At
least the musky scent of the Slaanesh worshipper was pleasant. Even Tchulaz Khan, the festering follower of Nurgle,
was almost preferable to this. It was a pity he had drawn the
short straw and been forced to accompany this scouting mis-
sion. He would even have preferred the miserable wet
weather of that pestilential island to this. Still, he told himself, someone had to do it. Their acolytes were all busy
shepherding forces through the paths, and if truth be told,
the idea of using the ancient web of extra-dimensional roadways had excited him.

'That is a very dangerous weapon,' said Kelmain, and
immediately wished he had not opened his mouth. The
stench almost made him gag. Perhaps there was something
sorcerous to it. He was not normally so squeamish. Or perhaps it had something to do with that hideous weapon the
Khorne worshipper carried. Just looking at it with his mage
sight made the wizard squirm. That was not something he
wanted to be killed with. Death would be the least of his
worries then.

'All weapons are dangerous, but I am a follower of
Khorne,' said Grume with a grin of contempt. He was

every inch the great warlord, talking down to his wizardly minions.

Idiot! Kelmain thought. Why did they always have to work with these muscle-headed buffoons? He sometimes suspected that the Great Powers of Chaos chose their warrior champions for their stupidity – particularly the Blood God.

Indeed he is, murmured Lhoigor's voice within his head, and Kelmain knew his twin was thinking exactly the same as he was.

'I do not like working with you followers of the Changer of Ways, any more than you like working with me,' said Grume, 'but the Great Ones have spoken and daemons have brought me their words. The time has come for us to unite and overthrow the weak kingdoms of men.'

Indeed it has, thought Kelmain. And I wonder if you realise how much the place in which we stand has to do with this. He glanced around at the remains of the ancient arch that dominated the chamber. Here was spellwork of great cunning, god-like in its complexity, so intricate that even when dormant it threatened to overwhelm his mind. The Paths of the Old Ones, Kelmain marvelled. We have opened them, or rather our masters have, and we may use them as we will. Soon, he thought, they will put this entire ancient and corrupt world within our grasp, and we will reshape it to fit our dreams. But to do this we must work with idiots who want to use us only for their own stupid purposes.

Grume opened his visor to reveal his bloated and ugly features. A glint of feral cunning showed in the warlord's small pig-like eyes. Kelmain could almost read his thoughts. The Axe of Gotrek had become a legend among the followers of Chaos. At the Siege of Praag, it had breached the supposedly invincible armour of the great Chaos Warlord Arek Daemonclaw. The death of that mighty champion had led to the breaking of his army and the siege of the City of Heroes. Rumour whispered that the dwarf had even destroyed the physical form of one of the Great Daemons of Khorne in the lost city of Karag Dum.

Kelmain was one of the few in a position to know exactly how true those rumours were. Grume already had several powerful weapons forged with the imprisoned souls of mighty daemons and champions. It was obvious that he wanted to add the dwarf's axe to his collection. It was equally obvious that when the time came, after the forces of Chaos were triumphant, he fully intended to use the weapon against those who opposed him.

It was a plan admirably suited to one of his utter stupidity, but who prided himself on his cunning. It would hardly do, thought Kelmain, to explain to him the full perils of trying to use that axe. There, indeed, was a weapon that would take enormous power to pervert to the ways of Chaos, and a tremendous understanding of magic. Grume had absolutely no knowledge of such things. Kelmain did, although he was loath to risk using his powers in so dangerous a pursuit at so critical a time. They were needed to oversee the use of the Old Ones' devices and ensure that they served Chaos well. Still, perhaps Grume's ambition could be put to another use? He glanced into the crystal once more to see if his brother was following his thoughts. Lhoigor's answering smile showed that he was.

'Do you know what happened to the last wizard who mocked me?' Grume asked, his voice full of menace. He had the confidence of one who knows he has a small army of beastmen close at hand. The casualties the Slayer and his comrades had inflicted had reduced their numbers only by a fifth or so. Kelmain stifled a yawn.

'I believe his soul went to feed the daemon that resides in your bludgeon,' he said. 'Or did you not offer him up as a snack to your patron daemon prince? I forget. One meets so many mighty champions of Chaos these days, one simply cannot remember all the dreadful punishments they meted out to those who mocked them.'

'You play a dangerous game, wizard,' said Grume. Wrath twisted his bestial features. He loomed over the mage, nearly twice his height. His hand rested on the hilt of the odd magical mace that normally dangled from his wrist. 'By Khorne, you will pay the ultimate price.'

'You are showing the lack of intellect for which the followers of Khorne are so justly renowned,' said Kelmain in a tone of apology and abject grovelling that clearly confused the Chaos warrior. 'If you were to kill me or feed my soul to your mighty weapon, there would be no one to open the Paths of the Old Ones for you... or locate the Slayer on your behalf.'

'Then you will do what I command,' said Grume, self-satisfaction evident in his voice. He had chosen to listen to the tone, and not the words, as Kelmain had known he would. Here was a brute used to bullying his way forward over the objections of others.

'Why not? If you succeed, we will have one enemy less. I have no love for Gotrek Gurnisson and would be glad to see him dead.'

'I will give you enchantments to let you locate the Slayer and his axe,' said Kelmain. 'When you find him... kill him.'

'If you can,' he added, so quietly that Grume did not hear.

KELMAIN WATCHED GRUME'S force assemble within the antechamber. The carved heads of obscene toad-like gods seemed to watch them mockingly. Looking into the viewing crystal, he met the gaze of his brother. Lhoigor looked a little weak. Using the spell of speaking over so vast a distance was draining even to a mage of his power.

'You have found Gotrek Gurnisson,' said Lhoigor. It was not a question.

'Yes. My divinations show our fleeing beastmen were right. He is near where we are, at the Sylvanian nexus. One would almost think it was fate,' said Kelmain.

'Perhaps it is. Destiny seems to have marked that one. Or the powers that oppose us.'

'It will most likely prove unfortunate for that giant idiot,' he added, gesturing at Grume with his staff. The huge Chaos warrior ignored him and concentrated on bullying a score of his troops into position. 'I should close this portal and leave him to get cold feet treading through the winter snows of the Empire.'

'Call him back, brother, and you could always send him to Lustria, if you are worried about his health in the winter.' Lhoigor's smile was cold but there was an evil humour in it.

'Or to the gateway in sunken Melay – that would clean his armour for him,' said Kelmain.

'I don't think our last scouting team returned from testing the path we thought led into the heart of Firemount. Some lava might heat our large friend up nicely.'

'Or to Ulthuan, to teach the elves what happens to those who defy the champions of the Blood God,' said Lhoigor in an almost perfect copy of the Chaos champion's booming manner. Kelmain laughed, and so eerie was the sound of his mirth that the beastmen looked up and shuddered.

'Get on with it,' bellowed Grume. Kelmain shrugged and gestured expansively.

'I see you have another plan, brother,' said Lhoigor, a look of wicked mirth upon his face.

'As ever, you understand me perfectly. There is more than one way to doom a dwarf.' He picked up the orb of seeing he had taken from the ruins of ancient Lahmia. It felt cold as rock in his hands. The gem in the centre of the perfect sphere glittered with magical energy. He muttered the spell, and it rose into the air and swooped down to circle the Chaos warrior. Kelmain shut his eyes and concentrated on the link. His point of view shifted to that of the gem. It was his eye and he could see through it now.

'This will lead you to that accursed dwarf,' said Kelmain, and the spell allowed his voice to emerge from the Eye. 'And allow us to witness your great victory! Go kill Gotrek Gurnisson,' said Kelmain.

A little tired from the strain of the ritual, Kelmain yawned. His brother did likewise. A small significant feeling of triumph filled Kelmain as he prepared to shift his consciousness into the Eye. One way or another, Gotrek Gurnisson was as good as dead. And so was anybody with him.

Grume and his warriors were already heading out of the antechamber into snow.

'You do not think that Grume can overcome Gotrek Gurnisson?'

'He is tough and his force is very numerous, but even if he does not, it will serve our purposes. If they fail to overcome the Slayer, they will lure him here – there are things within the Paths of the Old Ones which can kill even him.'

CHAPTER THREE

THE SERVANTS LOOKED at him with awe as he entered the stable. Teclis was garbed for battle, wearing the war crown of Saphery and bearing the staff of Lileath. Ignoring their stares, he inspected the griffon. It was a magnificent beast, a winged eagle-headed lion, large enough for an elf to ride. It opened its mouth and let out an ear-piercing scream that caused the courtesans to shriek nervously and then giggle. It was a warcry that down through the ages had terrified the enemies of the elves. Now that the great dragons lay mostly dormant, these mighty magical creatures were the favoured aerial steeds of the elves. Of course, they were rare. This one, a champion racer, would have cost the ransom of a human king. The great breeder Ranagor had reared it with her own hand from an egg she had taken from the highest slopes of Mount Brood.

There were times Teclis wished he had learned to properly master a griffon, but he never had. It was a skill that only the strongest of elves could learn, and it was an art that had to be learned young. In his youth he had been too sickly. He would never be able to ride one of these magnificent creatures into battle without first paralysing its fierce will with magic, which would defeat the whole point. He would need to use a spell of stupefaction to make the thing docile enough to ride.

A spasm of dizziness passed through him. They were getting worse. He counted slowly to twenty and there was no surprise when the earth shook and the building quaked. His uncanny sensitivity to fluctuations in the level of magical energy around him, a side-effect of the spells he used to give himself normal health and energy, had forewarned him of the quake. He knew that he needed to get busy, that time was running out for his land and his people and, if the binding spells failed, for himself too, most likely.

He took a deep breath of the stable air. It held the overpowering stink of animal flesh and dung, and of feathers. His aged servants hooked the great saddle to the creature's back, all the while trying to be careful of its mighty claws and great scimitar-like beak. They checked the girth and the bridle and then looked at him. He shrugged and exerted his will, muttering the words of the charm. He felt the flow of energy round about him, warming him as it always did, and he sent tendrils of it out to touch the great beast, to calm its fierce heart and sooth its burning brain. The creature's eyelids drooped and its posture slumped as the spell took hold. It somehow looked smaller now, far less regal.

Teclis muttered an apology and limped forward, dragging himself wearily into the saddle and buckling himself in. Not for him the bravado of some young elves who rode bareback and unharnessed, and performed tricks on the backs of their steeds. He made sure all the buckles were in place, feeling slightly embarrassed as he did so. This was the way a child would ride, but he was taking no chances of falling from the saddle. Certainly, he knew spells of levitation, but were he to be stunned for a moment or distracted, or should the winds of magic simply not blow strong enough, a fall might prove fatal nonetheless.

His brother strode forward to look at him, ignoring the griffon's enormous beak and huge claws with a calm that Teclis envied. Even the bravest usually showed signs of nervousness around the beasts, but not Tyrion. He seemed as comfortable and at ease as he had done over the dinner table, and it was no false bravado either.

'Are you sure you do not wish me to accompany you?' he said.

'Your duties lie here, brother, with our fleet, and this is a task best accomplished by sorcery alone.'

'I bow to your superior knowledge, then, but it's been my experience that a well-honed blade can prove useful at the most unexpected of moments.'

Teclis tapped the blade that hung at his side with his left hand. 'I have a well-honed blade, and I was taught to use it by a master,' he said.

Tyrion grinned and shrugged. 'I hope you learned my lessons well, little brother.'

The affection and condescension in his tone irritated Teclis no end, but he hid them behind a sour smile. 'May you live a thousand years, brother.'

'And thee, Teclis of the White Tower.' With his usual impeccable timing, Tyrion stepped back out of the griffon's way and executed a perfect courtly bow.

He waved to the women and to his servants, drew back on the reins and waited. The griffon's haunches bunched beneath him as its muscles tensed for the spring. He felt a momentary dizzy lurch in his stomach as the creature bounded forward and launched itself into space through the opening in the balcony. For a brief giddy moment he saw the entire city spread out beneath him, from the palace-temple of the Phoenix King to the great statue of Aenarion that greeted the returning sailors in the harbour, all illuminated by the golden sunlight of Ulthuan.

His stomach lurched further as the griffon dropped earthward. He felt a momentary panic. The restraining harness that had seemed like such a good idea a few moments ago now felt like a death-trap. In the moments it would take to release it and cast a spell of levitation, he and his mount would be spattered on the hard marble below. He fought down the urge to close his eyes, and watched as the purple-tiled rooftops of the villas of the lesser nobles came closer.

Then, the griffon spread its enormous pinions with a
crack. They beat the air with the force of thunderbolts. For a
moment, the heart-stopping descent was arrested and the
creature seemed to float on the very air, caught for a heartbeat between the power of gravity and the force of its own
upward motion. For a second Teclis felt weightless, caught
between horror and exhilaration, then the griffon increased
the force of its wingbeats, and its gigantic, magical strength
triumphed over the earth's pull.

Beneath him, Teclis could feel its chest expand and contract as it breathed in time with its wing movements. He
could feel the metronome of its heart, driving blood to
muscles, powering sinews like some mighty engine. The griffon let out an ear-piercing shriek of pure triumph and Teclis
knew exactly how it felt. Looking down at the city stretched
beneath him like the model town in some elvish infant's
playroom, he was exultant. Perhaps this was how the gods
felt, he thought, when they looked down from the heavens
to see how their mortal pawns were behaving.

He saw the people in the street – the Tiranoci in their
chariots, proud dragonlords on their horses, scholar-slaves
from far Cathay, merchants from a dozen lands of men – all
look up at him. Did they recognise him, the premier wizard
of this land, going about his business? It did not really matter. They looked up in awe and wonder at the sight of an
elven lord passing overhead and they shouted and waved in
greeting. He waved back, letting the steed skim over the
rooftops out towards the harbour, to the thousands of towering masts that marked the position of the ships.

He passed over the decaying mansions, and the empty
houses, noticed the half-empty streets built to accommodate
ten times the current number of inhabitants and some of
the feeling of triumph drained out of him. The realisation
struck him with the force of a hammer blow, as it always did,
that his people were a dying race. No amount of pomp and
circumstance could conceal that. The endless parades and
ceremonies could not hide it. The towering genius that had
lined every avenue with mighty statues and soaring columns
was fading from this world. Slaves and outsiders inhabited

many of the buildings round the harbour, filling them with buzzing life that counterfeited the ancient glories of Lothern. But it was not elvish life. It was the life of outsiders, of people who had come to this island continent but recently, and who had never set foot outside the foreigners' quarter of this one city.

As it often did, a vision took form in his mind, of the inevitable death of all he held dear. One day, he knew, these streets, this city, this whole continent would be empty of elves. His people would be gone, leaving not even ghosts, and only the footsteps of those strangers would echo through the ruins of what had once been their homes.

He tried to dismiss the image but he could not. Like all elves he was prone to melancholy, but unlike his kindred, he did not revel in it. He despised it as a weakness, but now, leaving this ancient glorious city for what might prove to be the last time, he could not resist giving in to the impulse. Already, he could see that the number of human ships in the harbour near outnumbered the elvish ones.

True, there were many mighty Eagles, Falcons and Bloodhawks, their long lean lines designed to penetrate the waves like a spear. Driven by magical winds they were the fastest, most manoeuvrable craft on the sea, but even here in their home city, in the greatest of all elf ports they were hemmed in by the craft of others. Here were mighty galleons from Bretonnia and Marienburg. Below him he could see dhows from Araby, their sails like the fins of sharks, and junks from Far Cathay, with towering stern-castles and lateen rigs designed to catch the winds of distant seas. They had all come here to trade, to purchase the magical wares, and powerful drugs and medicines for which the elves were famous, and in return they had brought silk, exotic woods, perfumes, spices, and trained pleasure slaves; all the things required to make comfortable the twilight years of his people.

The salt tang of the sea caught his nostrils. He caught sight of a human gazing up at him with a spyglass from the crow's nest of one of the ships. He fought down the catlike malign urge to send his griffon flying close to the man's head to terrify him and pulled on the reins turning his mount upwards and northwards, towards the clouds and the distant mountains wreathed in the powerful aura of ancient and mighty spells. He realised for a moment he had been tempted by the old cruelty of his people, who saw the lives of other lesser races as nothing more than playthings, and he felt a surge of the sickness and self-hatred that made him so unlike the rest of his people.

There were times when he felt that the elves, in their arrogance, deserved to be replaced, to be superceded by the younger races. At least they still strove to build things, to learn, to make things anew, and in many ways they were succeeding. Instead his people lived in the past, in dreams of long-gone glories. To them all knowledge worth possessing was already known, all sorceries perfected to their highest level by elvish adepts. Teclis had studied the mysteries of magic long and hard, and he knew how deeply his people deceived themselves. In his youth, he had dreamed of uncovering new spells and recovering lost arts, and he had done so; but in recent years even that had lost its savour, and there were things he sometimes wished he had not learned.

He thought of the letter he had left with his brother to give to the Phoenix King explaining what was happening. He thought of the messages already dispatched by sorcerous means to the adepts of the White Tower. He had done what he could to forewarn those he was sworn to protect, and now he had to do his duty or die in the attempt. Considering the magnitude of the task that faced him, the latter eventuality seemed not unlikely.

He tugged the reins of the docile griffon and sent it arcing towards the distant mountains.

BENEATH HIM HE could see the carved peaks of Carillion. Ancient magic had reformed them into gigantic statues, a testimony to the power of the elves. Teclis shuddered to think how much magical energy, how many years of wizardly labour, had gone into carving those stones into the shapes of great beasts. Here two mighty pegasi flanked the valley, each a hundred times the height of an elf. Clouds gathered beneath their wings. Each was poised to take flight or strike with a massive hoof. It seemed like at any moment they might come to life and crush him like a small and pathetic insect.

They were not simply for show either. His mage sight showed him that they were wrapped around with spells of fantastic complexity, lattices of pure mystical energy that pulsed and crackled with power. They were part of the huge web of spells that covered the continent of Ulthuan and kept it stable. Without it to bleed off power and shape it to other uses, the entire land would become unstable and sink once more beneath the waves or be torn apart in immense volcanic convulsions. These huge statues were far from the mightiest works of his people. In the northlands entire mountains had been carved into the semblance of ever more fantastic and grotesque beasts.

There is a mad strain in us, he thought, it burns stronger in the hearts of our dark kindred of Naggaroth but it lurks in the heart of every elf. Pride, madness and a warped genius for art showed in those statues, just as it showed in every elf city. Perhaps the dwarfs are right about us, he thought. Perhaps we are indeed cursed. He dismissed the thoughts and concentrated on the task at hand.

He circled the griffon over the valley, seeking the thing he knew he would find in the shadow of those mighty wings. It blazed in his mage sight now, even more brightly than the flows of magic through the waypaths. This was new. It had not been so before, when last he had passed this way. Something was interfering with the work of the ancients here.

He dropped the griffon closer. An enormous standing stone stood there, and it was this which the pegasi had been set to guard. It was monolithic, eroded by millennia of strange weather, and yet it still stood.

In the side of the hill, in the shadow of the stone, was an entranceway. It led down into an antechamber that had been sealed for millennia, and with good reason. Behind it lay the work of those capable of challenging all the power and wisdom of the elves, artefacts of a people who had left these lands while his ancestors were still barbarians. This was the accursed place Tasirion had mentioned in his book, one of several to be found in ancient Ulthuan.

He dragged on the top rein giving the griffon the signal to land. He could see nothing threatening, but he was cautious. Many strange monsters were to be found in these lands, and sometimes, war parties of dark elves made it even this close to Lothern. It would not do to take every precaution against sorcery and find himself chopped down by some poisoned arrow.

Even as the beast descended, a wave of weakness passed through him again, and the earth shook. The stone danced. The mighty winged horses shivered as if afraid. In the distance, burning mountains spouted strange multi-coloured clouds into the sky. Teclis cursed. Whatever it was, it was getting stronger, either that or he was nearer the epicentre.

The griffon's claws touched earth. He felt the beast's muscles contract beneath him as it absorbed the force of impact. It paused there, uncertain as to what to do as the earth quivered beneath it. A moment later things had settled once more. Teclis descended from the saddle, struggling with the illusion that the earth would begin to shake once more or that he would somehow sink into it as if it were water. An earthquake was something that unsettled the senses in many ways, and made the brain doubt many things. He was almost surprised when the ground did not give way.

He strode closer to the entrance now, studying it. There was a stone arch and stone gates blocking the way forward. On the gate was inscribed the ancient edict forbidding any elf to proceed further. Teclis knew he was breaking laws made in the time of making itself by opening them. It was a crime punishable by death. This was one reason he had not wanted his brother with him.

Not that such things would have mattered to most elves. The spells to unlock these forbidden vaults were known to very few: the Everqueen, a few of the masters of the White Tower, and himself. Tasirion had read them and used them to his eternal regret centuries ago. His fate had been a warning to others who might disturb what lay here. Teclis considered this for a moment, and then spoke the spell. The wards laid by his forebears opened and the huge door slid silently inwards, leading down into a massive darkened antechamber. On the far side of the chamber was an archway, and through it he could see a road that led down into darkness.

The great arch was many times his height. It was carved in ancient-looking runes and the toad-like heads of an ancient race were carved in it. He could see the flow of powerful magic within it. It emanated a sense of evil that was almost palpable. Teclis shuddered and muttered a charm against Chaos even as he strode out of the balmy sunlight and into the cool shadows. The doorway slid shut behind him. He proceeded downwards under several more archways. The walls were huge blocks of dressed stone carved with odd linear runes. He sensed evil within them too.

No, he told himself, it was not the stones themselves that were evil; it was the stuff that seeped through them. Here was pure dark magic, the raw stuff of Chaos, a radiation that could twist mind and body in many ways. The spells built into the arch had been designed to contain it, but he could see now that they were ancient, flawed and unravelling, and that it was their weakness that allowed the sinister energy to flow through.

This was why ward spells were placed around this site, and his people were forbidden to enter. The whole area would eventually become tainted and corrupt, a cancer at the heart of Ulthuan, a stain of darkness that would slowly spread across the land. For now, though, he had other worries. If he did not solve the mystery of what was causing the quakes, there would be no need to worry about the corruption of anything but a few deep sea fishes, for his homeland would vanish beneath the cleansing waves. He must seek out the Oracle of the Truthsayers and find out what must be done.

He reached out and touched the surface of one of the stones. It was not smooth – strange angular runes had been carved on it, pictographic glyphs similar to those that elven explorers had brought back from the lost continent of Lustria and the steaming, jungle-girt cities of the lizard folk. Beneath them he could feel the magic flow, strong currents, powerful and deep. From his readings he knew this was not supposed to be the case. The ways were supposed to be dormant, sealed. This amount of power should not be passing through them.

He knew his suspicions were correct now. This place, and the others like it, were the source of the imbalance that threatened Ulthuan. Their activation was draining power from the watchstones, unsettling the precarious balance of the spells that protected the land. They were drawing massive amounts of magical energy out of the system and if they were not stopped, it would only be a matter of time before they caused a catastrophe.

Who could have done this thing, he wondered? It was always possible that it was all a colossal cosmic accident, or that the ancient wards had simply worn away. With a system so complex and ancient and fragile you could not rule such a thing out. Still, his instincts told him that such was not the case. He mistrusted anything to do with the dark power of Chaos. Too many other things were happening in the world for him to be happy with the thought that all of this was coincidence.

In the Old World, the armies of darkness swept across the land like a crimson tide, leaving red ruin in their wake. The seas had become dangerous, as monsters rose from the depths and the black ships of Chaos ravaged all they encountered. In the north, the ancient enemy stirred. War was coming to Ulthuan, just as it had already come to the rest of the world. At times like these, it was foolish to believe in coincidence.

He strode around the last and deepest arch buried deep below the earth, studying the runes, and the underlying pattern of magic that they channelled. He spoke a spell of divination that laid the entire intricate pattern bare. A work of breathtaking genius indeed, he thought, as he looked on the lines of magic. It was as if a million spiders had spent a thousand years spinning a web of near-inconceivable complexity. For all his centuries of study, this was a work that dazzled him.

He did not need to understand how the thing was created, any more than the drinker of a virility potion need understand the alchemical process by which it was made. He needed only to understand what the thing was used for, and that seemed clear enough.

Some of the spells were wards, designed to block passage through them. They were mostly frayed and gone now, no longer potent enough to fulfil their maker's purpose. It was what they guarded that interested him now. The wards guarded a doorway, an opening into somewhere else. Elf sorcerers had long known that these things existed but the ancients had closed them for their own incomprehensible reasons and the old elves had thought it best to leave them undisturbed. In these later ages they could only be opened at certain times, when the stars were right, when the flaws in the old spells were temporarily revealed. Until now, Teclis reminded himself. Now someone or something had clearly found a way to open them again.

He sat down cross-legged in the centre of the chamber. He considered the ancient network of spells his ancestors had built to keep the island continent stable. It was commonly assumed that they had been the creation of elves, a unique product of elvish genius. Was it possible those ancient mages had simply built on top of the work of the ancients, tapping its power for their own purposes? Now that someone had reactivated these artefacts of the Old Ones, they would draw power out of Ulthuan's magical wards. Yes, he thought, it was entirely possible that such was the case. It was a road to catastrophe.

There was only one thing to do now, he must find the source of all this and reverse it. He must find a way of passing through the gate, and shutting it down again. Teclis closed his eyes and began to meditate. He knew time was getting short.

CHAPTER FOUR

'I WISH THIS weather would ease up,' said Felix Jaeger, drawing his faded red Sudenland wool cloak tighter about himself, and leaning closer to the small sputtering fire. It just about lit the whole cave. Felix was glad of it. Another few minutes in the snowstorm would have done for him.

'It's winter, and it's Sylvania, manling, what do you expect? It's supposed to be as cold as an elvish heart.'

Felix looked over at the Slayer. If the massive dwarf felt any discomfort at the biting chill, he showed no sign of it. Snow clustered in his massive crest of bright orange hair, and covered the tattoos of his shaven skull, but he was still dressed as always only in his thick leather waistcoat, britches, and boots. His massive rune-covered axe lay close at hand. He drew a little further from the fire as if to emphasise his toughness. There were times when Felix hated travelling with dwarfs. He looked over at Max to see how the wizard was taking this display of rugged outdoor toughness, but he was lost in thought, staring into the fire as if he could discern some mystical pattern there.

He had been like this ever since they had discovered Ulrika's fate back at the keep. He had responded only to Felix's request to use his magic to light their fire when even the dwarfs' attempts with flint and tinder had failed. The wizard looked like a man caught in a particularly evil waking dream. Felix could understand that. Just the thought of Ulrika and what had happened to her drove a knife blade of conflicting emotions into his own heart. Whatever had once lay between them, it was over now, her transformation into one of the undead had seen to that. He tried to push the thought away. These were things he did not want to consider here in these dark woods in this ancient haunted land.

'Snorri was hoping there was a bear in this cave,' observed Snorri. He did look disappointed as well. An almost comic look of dismay passed over his broad, stupid face. He reached up with one massive paw and stroked the painted nails that had been driven into his skull. Like Gotrek, Snorri was almost as broad as he was tall and he was solid muscle, although in Snorri's case that included the space between his ears, thought Felix.

'Why?' Felix asked. 'Did you want to skin it and wear it for a cloak?'

'What would Snorri need a cloak for, young Felix? This is like a summer picnic compared to winter in the World's Edge Mountains.'

If I hear that line about summer picnics once more I will hammer some more nails into your head, thought Felix sourly. He had listened to the dwarfs' cheery comments on the worsening weather with increasing hostility for some days now.

'You think this is cold, manling?' said Gotrek. 'You should have been in the High Passes in the Grim Winter. Now that was cold!'

'I am sure you are going to tell me about it,' said Felix.

'Snorri remembers that,' said Snorri. 'Snorri was with Gurni Grimmson's warband chasing orcs. It was so cold that one night Forgast Gaptooth's fingers all turned black and dropped into the soup he was stirring. Good soup it was too.' He laughed as if at a fond memory. 'So cold that his beard froze solid and broke off in chunks like icicles.'

'You're making this up,' said Felix.

'No, Snorri isn't.'

Probably true, thought Felix. Snorri didn't have the imagination to make anything up.

'Very proud he was of that beard too; when he came home his wife didn't recognise him. He was so ashamed he shaved his head. A troll ate him at the end. Course, he choked it on the way down.'

'Now there was a Slayer,' said Snorri approvingly. Gotrek nodded. Felix was not surprised. The Slayers lived only to die in combat with the nastiest and largest monsters, to redeem themselves for crimes or sins they had committed. Felix was not sure that he would count choking a troll to death as it ate you a heroic death, but he was not about to mention that now.

'Wish there had been a bear in this cave,' said Snorri wistfully. 'A big one. Maybe two. Good eating in bears.'

'You would know,' said Felix.

'Better than squirrels, or rabbits, or hares,' said Snorri. 'Wish there was a bear in this cave.'

'Some say the caves about here are haunted,' said Max. It was his first contribution to the conversation in a long time, but it seemed to suit his gloomy mood.

'What do you mean?' Felix asked.

'In *Legends of Sylvania*, Neumann mentions that the caves around Drakenhof were meant to be haunted. The locals avoided them. Some claim that their roots went all the way down into Hell.'

'Perhaps you should have mentioned this before Snorri and Gotrek led us into these caves,' said Felix.

'It's only a story, Felix. And considering the alternative was freezing to death, would you really have let it put you off?'

Felix supposed not, but he still felt peeved. 'You think there is anything to these stories, Max?'

'Some stories contain hints of truth, Felix.'

'Is there anything else you forgot to tell us?'

'They say folk who went deep into the caves went missing, never to be seen again.'

'Maybe there was bears in them,' said Snorri. 'Bears could have eaten them.' He was glancing at the back of the cave hopefully, as if expecting to see it run deeper. Felix was glad he had already checked it earlier. The cave ran just a few more strides back under the hill.

'And there were lots of altered ones who sometimes used them for shelter.'

'The bears?' said Snorri, confused.

'The caves,' said Max.

Felix noticed that Gotrek had stopped listening, and was glancing over his shoulder out into the night. His fingers had tightened on his axe. Max was sitting up and glancing out into the darkness too.

'What is it?' Felix asked, already fearing the worst.

'Something is out there,' said Gotrek. 'I smell beasts. There is the taint of Chaos on the wind.'

Snorri cheered up at once. 'Let's go get them.'

'Yes,' said Felix sarcastically. 'Let's not worry about little things like how many of them there are, or whether they might be ready for us.'

'Course not,' said Snorri. 'Why would Snorri do that?'

'There is magic out there,' said Max, and his voice sounded sepulchral. 'Dark magic. The winds of Chaos blow strong this night.'

Felix groaned. Why was it, that just when he thought a situation could not get any worse, it always did? Sitting in a frozen cave by a sputtering fire with two death-seeking dwarfs and a gloomy wizard while a blizzard raged outside had been bad enough. Now, it seemed like the forces of Chaos and dark magic were about to take a hand. Why do the gods hate me so, Felix wondered?

'And there's something more,' said Max. His gaunt face looked strained and there was a feverish light in his eyes.

'I am no longer capable of being surprised,' sneered Felix. 'But do tell, anyway.'

'I don't know what it is. There is a power here the like of which I have not encountered before. There is a strange magic at work. I sensed it an hour ago.'

'Nice of you to mention that too,' said Felix. The two dwarfs stared at them impatiently.

'There was no sense in disturbing you while you rested, until I had a clearer idea of what it was. It might have had nothing to do with us.'

'Apparently it does.'

'Yes. Why else would the beastmen be coming this way? How could they have found us on a night like tonight?'

'You are saying they are coming for us?' said Felix, drawing his sword.

'They are already here, manling,' said Gotrek. Felix looked past the Slayer into the blizzard. He could see massive forms that bore only the vaguest resemblance to humans, and mighty black armoured warriors the likeness of which he knew only too well.

'Did they follow us all the way from Praag?' Felix asked, curling his lip.

'If so, then they've come a long way to die, manling.'

'Snorri thinks Snorri should go first,' said Snorri, suiting actions to words and charging out, brandishing his axe in one hand, and his hammer in the other. Within heartbeats he was amid the beastmen, cleaving through them like a thunderbolt, raising a tempest of snow around his booted feet. The look of glee on his simple, brutal face reminded Felix of children snowball fighting.

Gotrek moved in his wake, moving through the snow as if it was not there, no more slowed by the deep drifts than the beastmen or the Chaos warriors. Behind him, Felix heard Max begin to chant a spell. He knew better than to look around. A lapse of concentration in combat was often fatal, and he did not take his eyes from his opponents.

There were at least a score of beastmen. As always, they were shambling parodies of humanity, with the heads of goats or wolves or oxen. They clutched a variety of crudely made weapons in their mutated hands and talons. Their shields bore the symbol of Chaos, eight arrows radiating out from a huge cat-like eye. A monstrous Chaos warrior led them, quite the biggest Felix had ever seen. He was as huge as an ogre – perhaps he had once been one. He was more than half again as tall as Felix, and Felix was a tall man. Felix guessed the Chaos warrior outweighed him by a factor of four, and that was not counting the rune-encrusted armour that covered his massive form.

There was nothing else for it. He had put off entering the fray quite long enough. It was either fight or be cut down. And though a few minutes ago he might have thought that a mercy compared to the tedium of dwarfish conversation, he found that now his life was at risk, even Snorri's banalities were not without charm.

Howling like a madman, he charged at the nearest beast-man, swinging his dragon-hilted blade as hard as he could. The beastman raised his spear to parry. The sharp blade bit chunks from the shaft. Felix brought his boot up, catching the beastman between the legs. The thing howled in agony, and bent over. Felix's next strike separated its head from its shoulders.

He did not wait for another beastman to come to him, but lunged forward, hampered by the snow and the slickness of footing beneath it. He had learned his fighting in the arms houses of Altdorf's sword masters, on floors of hard wood and stone. I wonder why my fencing masters never bothered to tell me that most fights would not take place under those ideal circumstances, he thought bitterly.

Briefly, he wished he had a pistol, but then realised that in the damp and wet he would have been lucky to get one to work. He crossed blades with a massive beastman, a head shorter than he was but twice as wide. One of the creature's hands ended in a mass of slimy suckered tentacles. When it lashed out at his face, he could see a leech-like mouth in the middle of the palm. Once, the horror of the sight might have frozen him, but he had become used to such things over the past few years. In his time travelling with the Slayer, he had seen far worse things.

The tentacles slapped his face, and he felt something sting. The slime was corrosive, he thought, or worse – poisoned. Loathing and fear made him lash out all the harder. His blade took the creature in the wrist, shearing away its mutated paw. His next blow split the thing from breastbone to groin.

Something bright hissed and sputtered overhead. He knew enough to cover his eyes. There was a brilliant explosion of golden light. A blast of steaming snow scalded his face. He looked up to see that a crater had been cleared from the snow by Max's fireball, and many of the beastmen stood shaking their heads and blinking stupidly as they tried to clear their vision. A couple of roasted bodies lay in a pool of steaming meltwater at the centre of the crater.

Now was not the time for fighting honourably, Felix realised, particularly not since by the light of a few sputtering bushes he could see scores more beastmen approaching. He raced forward, lashing out with his blade, killing as many of the blinded beastmen as he could. Snorri and Gotrek moved among them doing the same as they headed towards the oncoming mass. Only the mighty black armoured giant held his ground. Overhead something strange moved, orbiting it. A magical gem of some sort, Felix guessed.

More fireballs arced overhead, bursting among the oncoming mass of beastmen, turning one or two into blazing torches of melting flesh, knocking others to the ground with the force of impact. Knowing it was madness but unable to think of anything else, Felix shouted, 'Follow me, Snorri. Let's get them!'

There was method in his madness. Snorri followed him with a will, ignoring the huge Chaos warrior, unable to allow a mere human to get ahead of him in the race to kill the beastmen. So far, so good, Felix thought. At least my back is covered. He knew that if anybody could take care of the huge Chaos warrior, it was Gotrek. The dwarf had yet to lose a fight, and Felix doubted that he intended to start now.

Felix aimed at the wounded and the fallen as he ploughed into the beastmen, picking off the easy targets, lashing out at any that were blinded. Snorri showed no such discrimination. He attacked whatever was closest, whether it was wounded, unwounded, sighted, blind or running away. He laughed as he killed, happy as a child with a new toy.

Max sent more fireballs arcing overhead. Their explosions turned night briefly to day, and snow to steam. Felix saw one beastman fall, his face a mass of blisters, skin falling away from flesh and flesh falling from bone like an overcooked ham-hock. He took a second to orientate himself and then threw himself forward, following Snorri into the deepest mass. Behind him, an enormous clanging sound told him that Gotrek's axe had met the blade of the huge Chaos warrior.

'Now, Slayer of Arek, prepare to die,' boomed a voice deeper than any human's by at least an octave. 'Your axe will be mine.'

'Do tell,' said Gotrek, his grating voice audible even over the roar of battle. Felix ducked the swipe of another beastman, and lunged forward, getting his blade beneath the creature's guard and through the wall of its stomach. He turned it upward, beneath the ribs, sending point to heart, and then withdrew it. Blood gouted and the creature fell forward, blood pouring from a wolf-like mouth, huge teeth snapping so close to Felix's throat that he could smell its foul breath. He lashed out again, clearing a circle around him, and found that the wild swirl of battle had brought him around facing Gotrek and his opponent.

The Chaos warrior was really huge, Felix realised grimly. Felix had not seen anything so big in human shape since he had fought Grey Seer Thanquol's mutated bodyguard back at the Lonely Tower. And in terms of combat prowess there was no comparison. This thing wore the glowing rune-encrusted armour of a Chaos warrior, the black metal surface etched with strange sigils and inlaid daemon heads. In its right hand was a monstrous shield, moulded to resemble the leering features of a bloodthirster, one of the greatest of daemons. In his left hand was a mace of some odd metal, its head shaped like the skull of some other enormous daemon. Perhaps it was one, burnished in black and gold. It radiated a strange power. The empty eyesockets glowed with an infernal light that made it seem as if the daemon was alive. As the Chaos warrior raised it, the mace emitted an eardrum-shattering shriek so loud it threatened to wake the dead.

'I am Grume of Night Fang and I will not grant you a swift death,' bellowed the Chaos warrior. 'I will break your knees and beat your joints to jelly and then I will throw your maimed body to my followers for their sport.'

'Did you come here to boast or to fight?' sneered Gotrek.

'Your death shall be long and terrible and your kin will wail and gnash their teeth when they hear of it.'

'I have no kin,' said Gotrek, and just uttering the words made his beard bristle with fury. He lashed forward with his axe. The blade clanged against the shield. The daemon's face seemed to twist and grimace in surprise as the axe bit home. Molten metal flowed forth like blood or tears. Strange sorcery was at work here, Felix thought, then ducked as another beastman tried to take his head off.

He whirled and brought the pommel of his sword down on the beastman's snout. There was a crunch as bone and cartilage gave way. He punched the creature on the newly sensitive spot with his free fist and was rewarded by a howl of anguish. As the beastman reeled backward, he sheared away half its face with his sword, leaving teeth and white bone momentarily visible before he put the thing out of its agony by severing its head.

More fireballs exploded around him, clearing the area. Felix stood blinking. Either Max had acquired pinpoint accuracy with his magic or he simply did not care whether he hit Felix or not. It was not a thought calculated to reassure.

Felix glanced around. The main force of beastmen were sweeping around the melee and avoiding the killing ground now, trying to get to Max before he could unleash more magic. For a moment, Felix and Snorri stood gazing at each other. The Slayer had killed everything within reach. He blinked and glared stupidly at Felix, unable to understand where all of his foes had suddenly gone. Felix saw Grume bring his howling mace smashing down at Gotrek. The move was incredibly swift and should have reduced the dwarf to a pulp, except that the Slayer was no longer there. With a shift of his footing, he had moved away from the point of impact.

Felix could tell from the look on Gotrek's face that he was having to concentrate ferociously on the fight. That was

hardly surprising since the unearthly shrieking of the daemonic mace was distracting enough from fifty strides away.
The gods alone knew what it must be like closer to the
source. Only someone who had seen the dwarf fight as often
as Felix had would have spotted that he seemed slower than
usual and that he did not move with quite his customary
blinding speed.

The monstrous Chaos warrior chuckled horribly, as if he
understood the effect his weapon was having and had seen
it often before. When he spoke his voice was full of confidence. 'The Skull Mace of Malarak is not to be opposed. It
freezes the limbs and chills the hearts of those who face it.
Prepare to greet your ancestors.'

Felix measured the distance between himself and the
Chaos warrior, taking aim at what looked like a weak point
in the backplate of his armour. Even as he did so, he knew
that he was too far away to get there in time. Had the hour
of the Slayer's doom finally arrived?

CHAPTER FIVE

As FELIX RUSHED forward he noticed a strange stink, like of rotting flesh and congealed blood. It came from the Chaos warrior, he was sure, and it was as nauseating as it was appropriate. Closing the distance revealed to him how huge Grume was – a veritable mountain of armoured flesh. The shrieking of his mace made Felix's head ache and his teeth grind. He felt like his ears were starting to bleed. How the Slayer withstood this, he could not guess.

Through the stinking fog he could see Gotrek still stood frozen as the mace descended. True to his word, Grume was not aiming for the Slayer's head but for his axe arm. He obviously did intend to capture and torture the Slayer. This did not bode well for the rest of them. Behind him, Felix could barely hear the sounds of carnage as Snorri fought with the beastmen.

Grume's insane booming laughter was barely audible over the daemonic shriek of his weapon. Gotrek's face looked pale and flinty. The mace descended like the hammer of some mad war god. At the last second, Gotrek's axe lashed out. The rune-covered blade bit into the daemonic skull.

Lines of fire flashed along the star-metal. The daemon's head shattered into a thousand pieces. The shrieking ceased instantly and the stinking cloud began to disperse.

'You will break my bones, will you?' said Gotrek, almost conversationally. The axe lashed out, catching the giant just behind the knee. The ornate armour buckled as if it were made from tin. Blood gouted. Grume began to topple backwards like a massive tree. Felix had to jump to one side to avoid being crushed.

'You will throw my battered form to your followers for their sport, will you?' The axe descended again on the giant's other leg, cutting through armour and tendons, paralysing it. Grume began to push himself upwards with both hands. The axe flickered out, taking off the left hand at the wrist. Another blow lopped off the right arm at the elbow. Gotrek spat on his recumbent form and turned to face the beastmen. There was an awful casual cruelty about the Slayer's actions that chilled Felix. The virtually limbless form of the Chaos warrior thrashed in the snow, bleeding to death.

Gotrek strode purposefully towards the beastmen, axe held ready. It was too much for them. They turned and fled in a mad rush. As they did so, Felix noticed the strange eye-like object still hovered there, almost invisible in the gloom. It swivelled backwards and forwards, like an eye tracking them.

What new evil was this, he wondered?

KELMAIN TURNED TO consult his brother's floating image. 'So much for the mighty Grume,' he said. The image of the dying Chaos warrior was still imprinted on his mind.

'It was predictable. The likes of Gotrek Gurnisson are not to be overcome by the Grumes of this world. That axe carries a mighty freight of destiny.'

'Best we should remove it from the gameboard of the world then,' said Kelmain smiling.

'Proceed with your plan,' said Lhoigor. 'Spring the trap.'

'No!' SHOUTED FELIX as Gotrek and Snorri disappeared into the gloom. 'Wait, we must have a plan!'

It was already too late, he knew. He turned and saw Max Schreiber walking closer. A glow surrounded him. The snow seemed to sizzle away at his feet, turning to steam. It was an eerie sight and made the magician seem somehow less than human.

'Too late, Felix,' he said. 'We'd best go after them.'

'Did you see that strange floating eye?' Felix asked.

Max nodded. 'A magical construct of considerable power – the focus of some sort of observation spell would be my guess.'

'You mean we are being watched by a wizard?'

'Aye – and a very powerful one too. Most likely the one who planned this attack, and led the Chaos worshippers to us.'

'A Chaos wizard as well as that monster, great,' said Felix sourly. 'Is there anything you can do about it?'

'We shall see when we find the others,' said Max Schreiber. 'Best get going, or we'll never catch up with them.'

'Don't worry,' said Felix. 'Dwarfs have short legs. There's no way they are going to outrun us.'

EVERY FEW HUNDRED strides, they found evidence of where the beastmen had turned at bay and sought to rend the dwarfs. Their lack of success was evident by the number of mutated corpses that lay in the snow. Now bigger, thicker flakes were starting to fall and fill the tracks and cover the corpses. Soon, he knew, there would only be odd-looking humps where once living, breathing beings had been. It was all rather depressing, he supposed.

Beside him, Max strode along, seemingly impervious to the cold. Felix was glad the mage was near. The aura surrounding him gave off enough heat to ward the worst of the chill. Perhaps Max was directing it that way, to help him. Felix did not feel like asking. It also provided enough light to see by.

'They went that way,' said Felix, pointing in the direction of Gotrek's tracks. The Slayer had a very recognisable print. His feet were larger and broader than a man's, and his stride was shorter.

'That does not surprise me,' said Max.

'I have the feeling you're about to tell me something I won't like,' said Felix, studying the gloom beyond the circle of light, looking for the reflected glint of beastmen's eyes. Without the Slayers, he and Max might be overcome. All it would take would be one lucky spear cast to incapacitate the wizard, and then he would be alone against the monsters.

A frown of concentration passed across Max's face. 'There is a massive source of magical energy in that direction. It blazes like a beacon. I can sense it even from here. It's powerful beyond belief and tainted by the power of Chaos.'

'Why did you not tell us this earlier? Didn't want to worry us, I suppose.'

'No, Felix, I did not tell you earlier because it was not there earlier.'

What new horror waits now, Felix wondered?

FROM UP AHEAD came the sound of fighting. Felix thought he recognised Gotrek's bellowing and Snorri's warcry. He raced up the slope through the snow and emerged into a clearing in the woods. Ahead of them lay what a great barrow or a small hill, incredibly weathered and ancient-looking. In its side was an arch, comprised of two massive uprights and a stone crossbar. All of the barrow except the arch was encrusted with newly fallen snow. It glowed oddly, and when the snow touched it, the flakes melted immediately. He guessed the stench of burning vegetation in the air came from incinerated moss.

'What the hell is going on here?' he asked.

'Magic,' said Max. 'Of a very powerful kind.'

Felix could see a battle was taking place at the entrance to the barrow. Snorri and Gotrek hacked and slew their way through a mass of beastmen. The retreating monsters fought a desperate rearguard action as they fled within. Felix and Max followed to the entrance. The way down was peculiar, unlike anything Felix had ever seen before. The walls were massive blocks of undressed stone covered in strange angular runes. Several more arches supported the ceiling, as the corridor descended down at an angle into the gloom.

Somewhere off in the darkness was another intensely glowing arch.

The mass of the beastmen raced through the glowing arch and simply disappeared. It was uncanny. One moment they were there, the next they were gone, leaving only a pattern of ripples in the glowing air. Looking closely, Felix could see that the glowing eye hovered over the scene, shifting its location with blurring speed as it moved to position itself for a better view of the combat.

Felix decided that he had better go do his part. He raced forward, feeling a strange shiver run down his spine as he passed underneath one of the stone arches. He did not need to be a powerful magician like Max to know there was something supernatural going on here.

Snorri slashed and whirled his way through the beastmen corpses, hacking limbs and crushing heads with merry abandon. As he got within range of the glowing arch something odd occurred. A massive tentacle, thick as the hawser cable on a moored ship, emerged from the glow and wrapped itself around him. Before Felix could shout a warning, the tentacle contracted, and Snorri was dragged through into the glow. In a heartbeat he had vanished.

Gotrek roared a curse, and redoubled his efforts, chopping down the last few beastmen. Felix strode up to his side. 'What was that thing that took Snorri?' he asked.

'A daemon, most likely, and soon to be a dead one, or my doom will be upon me,' replied the Slayer. Without a backward glance, he leapt forward into the glow. In a second he too was gone.

'Wait!' shouted Max. 'You have no idea where that portal leads.'

Felix stood before the glowing arch and wondered what to do. There was no trace of the Slayers, the beastmen or the tentacled monster. He could hear no sounds. Even as he watched, the shimmering began to vanish. Suddenly something blurred overhead. There was a sickening crunch. Looking back, he could see that Snorri had been cast out through the portal with the speed of a stone shot from a sling. Either by accident or design he had been thrown directly into Max. The two of them lay sprawled unconscious on the ground.

Instinct told Felix that he had mere moments to come to a decision. He knew that if he stood here until the light vanished, whatever portal the Slayer had passed through would be closed, and with it any chance of following him. Even as he stood there undecided, something small and round and hard smashed into his back, and propelled him forward into the light. Of course, he thought. I forgot all about the floating eye.

A wave of cold passed through him, and for a moment a dizzying sense of vertigo threatened to overwhelm his senses. He felt like he was falling down a huge mineshaft, accelerating at enormous velocity. He braced himself for an impact and was surprised to find himself stumbling along on solid ground. A moment later he wished he wasn't as a terrifying sight greeted his gaze.

Up ahead was a vast tentacled thing, a cross between a squid and a serpent, some hideous mutant daemon of Chaos. Its tentacles lashed out attempting to grasp Gotrek but the Slayer stood his ground and slashed away at them with his axe, severing the tips of some, drawing great gouts of gore from others. All around lay the shattered bodies of dozens of beastmen. A few more still fought, grasped in its giant tentacles. Obviously whatever this enormous brute was, it did not discriminate between its fellow Chaos worshippers and anybody else when it came to seeking its prey.

Something whizzed over Felix's head, and he saw the glittering eye hurtle past. For a second he could have sworn he heard chilling infernal laughter and then the thing flashed out of view. In the distance behind the daemonic thing, Felix thought he saw a black robed figure reach up and catch the gem, then race off into the gloom.

Felix felt a blaze of heat behind him, and the shimmering glow of light dimmed. He turned to look back the way he came, and was surprised to see nothing but a huge archway that seemed to look out onto infinite space. Blazing lights passed to and fro in the gloom. Not stars, he thought, but will-o'-the-wisps of sorcerous light.

Briefly he felt his sanity totter. Somehow, he had been transported to an entirely different location beyond his normal ken. There was no sign of the snow-covered forest, or the great barrow, or Max Schreiber or Snorri either. There was only an arch reminiscent in shape of the one he had passed through, but somehow newer-looking and carved with the gargoyle faces of some strange toad-like beings. This was indeed strong magic, he thought, wishing that he had paid more heed to what Max had said.

A howling war-cry behind him reminded him that battle still raged and he was part of it. Even as he watched, the last of the beastmen were raised high in the tentacles of the daemon and dropped into its huge gaping beak-like maw. There was a hideous crunching sound as bones were broken, and blood splattered the daemon's mouth. At the same time, more of the monstrous tentacles snaked past Gotrek and came looping towards him. He threw himself to one side, avoiding its suckered grasp, and lashed out with his sword. The blade bit deep into rubbery flesh. Black blood oozed slowly forth. He dodged and weaved forward, hacking at tentacles that came near him as he battled his way towards Gotrek's side. At times like this, it seemed like the safest place to be.

A rush of displaced air warned him, and he threw himself forward as a massive tentacle swept through where his head had been. He hit the ground rolling and noticed that the floor looked odd. It was made of old stone that looked as if it has been eaten away by something like acid. Set in each of the blocks were odd runes, straight lines and serpent-like squiggles. They were unlike anything he had ever seen before.

He let his momentum carry him to his feet, and found himself within a hairsbreadth of being decapitated. Gotrek's axe stopped mere fingerbreadths from his face. Felix felt a surge of relief that the Slayer had such control, otherwise he would surely be dead.

'I've seen better-looking creatures,' Felix said, gazing up at the thing. It was huge, the tentacled maw arched nearly four times his height overhead. He could see that it dripped slime. The eyes that looked down on him, though, were filled with a baleful and awfully human intelligence.

'It's probably thinking the same thing about you, manling,' said Gotrek, ducking the sweep of a massive tentacle, retreating step by step before the oncoming bulk of the thing. Felix realised that this was a hopeless battle. Even the Slayer's mighty axe was all but useless against a monster of such size and power. Gotrek's mighty hacks were like a small boy hitting a bull with a table-knife. They were causing the beast discomfort, but it was doubtful they would kill it.

Felix felt a surge of despair. How had it come to this? A few minutes ago they had been seated around a cheery fire in a comfortable cave, and now they were, well, the gods alone knew where, fighting some hideous daemonic thing.

Unless he did something desperate he could see no chance of surviving. Snarling, he drew back his sword and cast it like a spear directly into the one huge eye of the beast. It flew straight and true and embedded itself in the foul jelly of the great unwinking orb. The sword buried itself deep and Felix hoped it had lodged in the creature's brain.

A second later he regretted his actions. The monster let out an evil high-pitched shriek and began to lash the air blindly with its tentacles. Felix saw Gotrek sent tumbling head over heels to land on the floor by a convulsion of the thing's tentacles. Felix threw himself flat to keep himself from being swatted like a bug.

The huge monster began to retreat away from them, still lashing the air. A few seconds later a foul cloud of black inky gas billowed from orifices near its beak. Felix had just enough time to hold his breath before the cloud overwhelmed them, cutting off sight.

Felix noticed that his skin was stinging and tears billowed from his eyes. A foul stench filled his nostrils worse even than that of the giant Chaos warrior. That the gas was as poisonous as that from some vile Skaven weapon, he did not doubt. Desperately he launched himself backwards, hoping to get out of it before his lungs gave out and the fumes overcame him.

Even as he did so, he saw the blurred outline of something huge and snake-like emerge from the mist. He had only a second to recognise it as one of the daemon's tentacles before it made contact with his skull. The force of the impact of the great rope of muscle smashed him flat. Involuntarily he opened his mouth, and took a lungful of the foul polluted air.

Damn, he thought, as his chest felt like it was catching fire, and a wave of blackness sent him tumbling down into the darkness.

CHAPTER SIX

TECLIS THOUGHT HE had found the key to opening the ways now. He paused for a moment to check that all his defensive wards were in place, that all the manifold protective charms and amulets he wore were active. He murmured the spell of opening, then drew power to himself and sent tendrils of it out to touch the spells of the ancients. Ever so gently, like a master thief inserting a pick into a lock, he brought his magic into contact with theirs. For a moment, nothing happened. He stifled a curse, then faintly at first, and with ever-increasing force, he felt a tremor within the mystical structure of the spells. Light danced from stone to stone illuminating the archway. They swirled in a manner reminiscent of the auroras he had once seen in the uttermost north.

The way was open. He was free to enter the Paths of the Old Ones. Far off, he felt the faintest of tremors, as magical energy surged within the system. He could see nothing amiss. He had activated no traps – none that he could perceive anyway, although it was certain that those who had built this place would be capable of creating spells of the utmost subtlety. He wondered whether to proceed. This was useless. He could remain here until doomsday wondering about such things. Acting on instinct, he decided to follow it and strode through the archway.

The transition was instantaneous. One moment, he was standing in the vault in Ulthuan, the next he was somewhere else. It resembled nothing so much as a huge corridor carved from stone, every block of which bore runes of that ancient inhuman pattern. Closer examination revealed that the stonework was corroded in places, vilely tainted and mutated, and he knew at once that Chaos was loose within the paths. Overhead, strange gems set in the ceiling gave dim greenish illumination.

He looked back over his shoulder. Behind him, the way was still open. He stepped back through to the vault just to make sure he could. He considered returning to the surface for the griffon but he knew that attempting to compel it to follow him into this vast labyrinth would drive the creature to the brink of madness and perhaps beyond. He released it from the spell and set upon it a compulsion to return to Lothern.

What now, he wondered? Leaving this entrance open was not a good idea. Some innocent might wander in, or more importantly something might emerge into the land of Ulthuan. He shrugged, stepped through the portal once more and uttered the charm that would close the way. As swift as the dropping of a headsman's axe the gate closed. The vault vanished to be replaced by a view of a long stone corridor. He was committed now.

All around him he felt the surge of magical energies pulsing through the ancient network. They permeated the stonework and the runes. He thought of the few extant descriptions of this place, written by Tasirion and other sorcerers who had dared study it. Most claimed that it was dead; others that it was dormant, with the merest trickle of power. Such was not the case now. The place was alive with it.

Were these the forebears of the rune workings of the dwarfs, he wondered, or did they represent some parallel development? Perhaps they were not connected at all. He had no way of telling. The sorcerer in him was fascinated and he wished he had time to study these things and make sketches to show his fellow mages, but there were more urgent matters to consider, and he needed to push on into this vast magical maze.

He was in a halfway house, he realised, a place somewhere beyond the world he knew and close to the realm of Chaos though not yet part of it. He felt like he was standing on the edge of a great shaft that proceeded downwards to near infinite depths. Somewhere up ahead was another larger and more powerful portal.

Even as that thought came to him, he realised that he was not alone. He could sense other presences: vast, powerful and most likely daemonic. They had not yet sensed him, he realised, but it was only a matter of time. Wrapping himself in his most potent charms of concealment, he pushed on.

The corridor was strange. It seemed to become higher and wider as he strode through it, as if time and space were being distorted. He realised that this might actually be the case, for it was the only thing he could think of that would allow what should have been journeys of several months to be completed in several days. Or perhaps this was merely a trick being played on his mind by his senses? Such things were possible when a lot of magical energy was involved.

There had been hints in Tasirion's book that somehow these ancient roads ran through the daemonic realms of Chaos itself, although they constrained it in some way to make it manageable. That would be necessary, for the raw stuff of Chaos was a baneful thing, capable of warping the body and spirit of those who encountered it. Some claimed it was the very essence of magic, mutable, potent and destructive. It was not a thought calculated to reassure one whose chosen vocation was sorcery.

Of course, elves were more resistant to the baleful power of Chaos than most other forms of life. It was said that they had been created that way. Even so, resistant did not mean immune. Teclis had often suspected that the power of the Dark Gods had had more effect on the elves than they were prepared to admit. He sometimes suspected that the dark elves had been a product of Chaos's influence acting on the elvish spirit over a period of millennia. It was one of those things that could never be proven, but to him seemed all too likely.

He noticed as he walked that the walls were becoming higher and thinner. In places they seemed to have worn away, and bizarre patterns of light shone through. It appeared the further he walked this road, the more corrupt it was becoming. He was grateful now that he was wearing his most potent protective amulets. If anything, he only wished that they were more powerful. He sensed he was close now to the portal he sought.

He wondered whether the ancients had walked these paths this way. Certain texts had hinted otherwise. They claimed the Old Ones had ridden in fiery chariots traversing these paths at greater speeds, that they could pass between continents in hours rather than days. That must have been something. He considered other theories that he had read.

Some claimed that the skaven had dug great tunnel systems under the continents. He had seen some of their works in his time and knew the terrifying magnitude of the ratmen's delvings but tunnels that covered thousands of leagues seemed unlikely. Was it possible that the skaven had somehow gained entrance to this ancient network and used it for their own foul ends? All too possible, he decided, particularly since his nostrils had started to detect the faint but unmistakeable taint of warpstone in the air. There was nothing those vile creatures would not do to possess that evil substance, and no doubt if it was to be found here they would sniff it out.

Warpstone was not the only thing down here, he decided. The sense of presence he had felt earlier returned, redoubled. He cast a glance over his shoulder. He was not nervous, not yet anyway. He knew his own capabilities and there were few things in this world or the next that daunted him. Even so, he felt some need to be cautious. He reviewed all the deadly spells he knew, and prepared himself to unleash them instantly.

Whatever it was, it was coming closer. In the distance, by the light of the glowing runes, he could see things moving. He spoke a spell of perception and his point of view rocketed towards them. To his astonishment, he saw that they were beastmen, led by a black armoured Chaos warrior. There were at least a hundred of them moving through the Paths of the Old Ones, moving towards the gate that emerged in Ulthuan.

Immediately he realised the full horrific implications of what he was witnessing. One hundred beastmen were no threat to the realm of the elves, but these might simply be the first of many. Whole armies could move along these paths, and invade the kingdom long before any force could be marshalled to meet them. Elvish domination of the seas around Ulthuan would mean nothing under these circumstances, would in fact be merely a liability. All the warriors crewing ships would not be available to meet an invasion force on land. And if these beastmen were to share their secret with the Dark Ones of Naggaroth…

He told himself he was leaping to conclusions. He had no idea whether these Chaos worshippers were the vanguard of an advancing army or merely hapless fools who had somehow stumbled into this strange realm. Even if they did hold the key to entering the Paths of the Old Ones at will, perhaps no gates emerged in the land of the Witch King.

Teclis was not reassured. Tasirion's book had hinted at a vast network of gateways, and surely the Old Ones had been capable of building a system of such tunnels that would span the entire world.

The intensity of the threat posed to his homeland had doubled. Not only were these ancient ways threatening the stability of the continent by their very existence, they were an invasion route for the deadliest enemies of all sane people, the followers of Chaos. More than ever, he realised that he needed to track this threat to its source, and deal with it.

Briefly he considered turning back to warn his people of what was coming, but he realised that there was no time. Any moment wasted might prove critical if the gates were not returned to dormancy. A heartbeat later any decision was taken from his hands. The Chaos warrior looked up, as if sensing something, and gestured for his beastmen to move forward.

Too late, Teclis realised that this was no mere Chaos warrior but one gifted with sorcerous powers by the Changer of Ways. His spell had been sensed and now ruthless opponents sought him. The elf wizard considered standing and fighting, but realised that he could not afford to do so needlessly. He needed to conserve his power for greater challenges, not fritter it away in random conflicts with chance-met encounters in this vast extra-dimensional warren.

He wove a spell of levitation, feeling resistance to his spell as he did so. The corrupting influence of Chaos was interfering with his pure elven sorcery here. Even as he cast it he could see the beastmen come closer. He was not afraid... yet. He had overcome greater odds in the past. The spell took effect and he strode upward. The ceiling here was perhaps ten times the height of a man above him, and each step took him closer to it. If the beastmen chose to lob missiles at him there might be some problems, but he knew spells that would ward him against that. He was not too worried about any spells the Chaos warrior might possess. He had complete confidence in his own ability to deal with such things. He had long ago learned that there were few magicians in this world that he need fear.

Having achieved a position of safety he considered his offensive options. There were many spells capable of dealing with even such a huge crowd of beastmen. He could spray them with molten plasma or blast them with fireballs. He could send a rain of magical missiles showering down on them. He could surround them with mists and illusions that would set them at each other's throats. If worst came to worst he could simply reduce them to their component atoms, although that would require more power than he cared to expend.

So engrossed did he become in these calculations that it took him a few moments to realise that the beastmen were not charging towards him, but fleeing away from something.

Wonderful, he thought. That puts an entirely different complexion on things. As the sour moment passed, he smiled. There is a lesson here, he thought. The entire world does not rotate around you.

He strode higher and cloaked himself in refractory spells, bending light about him to conceal himself. Within ten heartbeats he was glad he had. The thing that pursued the beastmen was horrific, a titanic creature that looked like a cross between a slug and a dragon. Its huge armoured form slithered softly along the roadway leaving a trail of bubbling corrosive slime behind it. The thing was as large as a ship, and its long serpentine neck raised its huge head nearly as high as Teclis's present position.

There was something about it, an aura of menace and power that made even the elf wizard's stout spirit quail. He did not blame the beastmen and their leader for fleeing before it. Even as he watched, the creature opened its mouth. Teclis had seen the great dragons of Ulthuan, and he thought he knew what was coming. Once again he was surprised. Instead of a gout of flame, a foul festering mass of mucus vomited forth to splatter the beastmen. Where it touched them it hardened swiftly, immobilising them, holding them in place. It seemed to have some of the properties of a spider's web, and a butterfly's cocoon, and one thing more. When it touched the beastmen, they screamed like souls in torment.

The alchemist in Teclis was fascinated. Poison or corrosive, he wondered? Whatever it was, it seemed to cause a great deal of agony. Teclis felt no sympathy for the beastmen. They were vile creatures living only for killing, torture and rape. Whatever they got now, they doubtless deserved.

Even as he watched, the great head swooped down, and the monster began to feed. Tearing his gaze away, Teclis proceeded along the Paths of the Old Ones. He needed to follow this path to the source of the disturbance. Up ahead, the corridor ended in a ledge. It was through this that both beastmen and monster must have come. There was nothing else there save another glowing arch; beyond it, he sensed, the real danger began.

CHAPTER SEVEN

'WELL, MANLING, YOU are alive,' said Gotrek. He sounded neither pleased nor displeased. The expression on his face
could have been carved from stone.

Felix pulled himself to his feet. He felt a little dizzy and
the inside of his lungs felt rough. He coughed and noticed
that his phlegm was stained black when he spat. That was
probably not a good sign, he thought.

'What happened?'

'You blinded the beast, and it belched that noxious cloud
and then retreated.' Felix's hand felt for his empty scabbard.
The only weapon he had now was his knife. Realising what
he was thinking, Gotrek jabbed his thumb towards the floor.
Felix saw that his blade lay there glittering.

'Must have fallen out when the thing shook its head,'
Felix said, moving over to pick it up. Traces of a jelly-like
substance marred the blade. He wiped them off with a
strip cut from his cloak and then returned the blade to his
scabbard. He gave his attention to his surroundings once
more.

'Where are we?' he asked. The Slayer shook his head.

'I have no idea, manling. These tunnels are not dwarf work and they stink of sorcery.'

'Tunnels?' said Felix. He was thinking aloud. Of course, they were tunnels, they just did not feel like any tunnels he had ever been in before. It was more like being caught within some vast alien structure, a labyrinth or a maze. And mazes in legends were always full of monsters.

'Aye, tunnels, manling, although unlike any ever delved by dwarf. Still they have the feeling of runework to them. There is sorcery being channelled here, and no mistake.'

'You don't say,' said Felix ironically. 'I would never have suspected that from the way we passed through that arch and disappeared.'

Gotrek gave him a flat unreadable glance. Felix felt that perhaps he was amused. There was something about sarcasm that appealed to the dwarfish sense of humour, and Felix occasionally suspected that the Slayer possessed one. 'More to the point, how do we get back?'

'I don't think we can, manling. I think the way behind us is closed.'

Felix had an awful feeling he knew what Gotrek was going to say next, and sure enough, he was not disappointed. 'The only thing we can do is press on and hope to find a way out, or our doom.'

Wearily, Felix trudged after the dwarf, coughing unpleasant black stuff up with every second step.

'WHAT DO YOU think those monsters eat when they can't get beastmen?' Felix asked. The question was much on his mind. He was starting to feel very hungry. It had been a long time since he had eaten, and his rations were all in the packs they had left back in the cave. Come to think of it, so was his water flask. As soon as the thought hit him, his mouth felt dry.

'Curious humans,' grunted Gotrek. Felix wondered if he was making a joke.

'Perhaps they wander in through the stone arches.'

'Perhaps. I don't know, manling, I am not a wizard.'

'Speaking of wizards, where do you think our black-robed friend went?'

'As far away from me as possible, if he has any sense. Or maybe the monster ate him.'

'Somehow I doubt we should be that lucky.'

KELMAIN EMERGED FROM the Paths of the Old Ones and into the chamber of the temple. He was grateful to have avoided the Slayer's axe. He was even more thankful to be out, for no matter how great the protective power of the amulets his masters had showed him how to make, he always felt there was an element of terrible danger within the place. You could never be sure when some ancient protective device would spring to life or some rogue daemon of the Twisted Paths, unheedful of the warning runes on the talisman, would seek to gulp down your soul.

He was pleased to see that his acolyte's face showed the apprehension he kept so well concealed. Young Tzeshi was paler even than usual, despite the fact that he had at least a hundred beastmen and Chaos warriors at his back. He bowed on seeing Kelmain and sketched a gesture of deepest respect on the air. Kelmain nodded to him and indicated that he should continue. As he departed he could hear the youthful mage begin the chant that would extend the protective spells enfolding him to enclose all of his followers.

There was no reason why he should not. Their experiments so far had been successful and their scouting parties had covered half the globe. Soon, if all went according to plan, the armies of Chaos would be able to move swiftly from the Chaos Wastes to any nation on the surface of the planet, bypassing borders and fortifications, emerging deep within the territory of their foes.

Filled with a vision of glory, he strode through the ancient haunted hallways to speak with his brother.

FELIX SHUDDERED. THEY had walked for hours now, and the road had become stranger. The stones had a melted, fused look that he had come to associate with the warping influence of Chaos. Sometimes it looked like faces leered out of the walls or that bodies were trapped frozen within the stone. Sometimes he felt like they were moving very slowly whenever he took his eyes off them. The strange jewels in the ceiling overhead sometimes vanished, taking with them their illumination. When that happened, he had to move forward trusting in the dwarf's keen tunnel-bred senses, following the glow of the runes on the axe. They were lighted all the time now, and that was never a good sign. In the past it had always predicted the presence of evil magic or vile monsters.

Moving through the gloom was not reassuring. It felt like anything could be there, waiting. Sometimes he could imagine the presence of strange formless things in the dark, just behind him. He could picture huge jaws opening to snap at him. Even though he knew it was useless, he often turned and glared behind him. He had to fight down the urge to take out his sword and sweep the air all around. He told himself that had anything been there the Slayer would know, and would do something about it. The thought provided cold comfort.

'These tunnels do not run below the earth,' said Gotrek. He sounded almost thoughtful.

'What do you mean?'

'A dwarf can sense depth. Only a cripple would not know how deep below the mountains he was. All my life I have had this knowledge and never once had to think about it. Now, it is gone. It is like the loss of sight, almost.'

Felix could not quite picture it being that bad, but he realised that he was in no position to know. How would he feel if he suddenly lost all sense of up and down, he wondered, and then realised that he simply could not get his head around the idea.

'I really do wonder where that magician went to.' Felix said. It was not that he was keen to catch up with the Chaos sorcerer. He simply wondered how he had gotten away. Presumably there must be some way in or out of this strange place, and he must know it. If they could only find him, perhaps they could convince him to get them out of here. He doubted that even the wickedest of wizards could withstand the Slayer's powers of persuasion under the circumstances. Come to think of it, he would help Gotrek himself, if the need arose.

'Doubtless he is running as fast as his legs will carry him, manling. I never yet met a wizard who would stand and face cold steel, given any choice.'

Felix wondered about this. He could recall facing several magicians who had not run away from them. Still, this did not seem like the time to point this out to the Slayer. 'He might be our only way out of here.'

'We need place no reliance in the followers of Chaos.'

'We may have to. Otherwise your heroic doom will take the form of starving.'

Gotrek grunted. He did not sound impressed. 'If that be so, that be so.'

For the first time Felix was really forced to consider the fact that they might die here. There was no food and nothing to drink. Not unless they went back and ate the beastman corpses and drank their blood, and that was not a thing he could imagine the Slayer doing. They were probably poisonous anyway, and that was assuming they had not already been eaten by some other foul denizens of these supernatural ways.

Get a grip on yourself, he told himself. A dozen heartbeats after the thought occurs to you, and you are already considering eating beastmen and the gods alone know what other horrors. Things have not come to that pass yet, and you've been through worse. You've been through battles and sieges and treks through frozen mountains. You've fought dragons and daemons and monsters of all descriptions. You're not dead yet. In spite of himself, though, Felix could not help but feel they had never been so isolated or so far from home.

TECLIS FOLLOWED THE oddly glowing runes up to the ledge. Ahead of him the path ended at another archway within which flowed the strange polychromatic swirls of energy he had seen earlier. The sense of immense controlled energies contained within was awesome. He paused for a moment, knowing what he must do, but not quite prepared to do it.

This was the path Tasirion had written about. All he had to do was pass within it. All of these strange interdimensional corridors he had passed through so far had merely been a preparation for this. They were simply the approaches to the true Paths of the Old Ones. He had a feel for their structure now. They were like tunnels dug down through the surface of reality. What loomed before him was more like the entrance to an underground river.

The trail was clear. Why was he hesitating? He already knew the answer. Things had decayed since the time of the Old Ones. That much was obvious. Their works were potent but they had been infiltrated and corrupted by the powers of Chaos. Who could tell whether they would work the way they were supposed to, or even the way they had when Tasirion passed this way all those scores of years ago?

As it was he had two choices. He could turn and go back the way he came, and try to find another way to avert the doom of Ulthuan. If such were possible in the limited time he had available. Or he could press on, trusting to his knowledge and his spells as he had always done. He allowed himself a smile. Many had called him arrogant, and he supposed it was too late now to prove them wrong.

He stepped forward and touched the surface of the glowing substance. It felt cool and liquid and it flowed around his fingers, engulfing them. He took a deep breath and pushed through. In a heartbeat he was swept into the raging currents beyond. He had a brief glimpse of a huge corridor along which tumbled thousands upon thousands of glittering many-coloured spheres, hurtling along like asteroids through space. He sensed dark malign presences and prepared himself to meet them.

'AT LEAST THE lights are back on,' said Felix, realising that he was whining. They could see again. The path curved upward, or perhaps it was downward at a strange angle; he could no longer tell. All he knew was that even though it felt like they were walking on the flat, he could see the curve of the path. It was an effect that was most disorientating. Perhaps, after all, he could understand what Gotrek had been talking about earlier when he mentioned how confusing it was to no longer be able to sense depth. The cues that his eyes were giving him no longer matched the cues his body felt. It created an immense sense of dislocation.

'There is another source of light,' Gotrek said. Felix realised that he was right. The pathway ahead split into two, one going upwards, the other going downwards. Both ended after about fifty strides in glowing archways. No, he realised, it was not just the archways that glowed, it was what was within them. They appeared to be filled with some substance like mercury, except that it glowed and pulsed with all colours. Shimmering patches drifted over the surface like oil on water, pulsing as they went. The effect was eerie and definitely supernatural.

Even as the thought occurred to him, Felix heard an immense slithering sound behind him. Something huge was dragging itself from the dark tunnels through which they had passed. His forebodings had proven themselves to be true after all.

Out of the darkness a massive creature dragged its bloated body. Its head was draconic, but where its mouth should have been was a mass of squid-like tentacles. As they writhed, Felix saw a huge leech-like mouth the size of a manhole cover in its midst. If anything, it was worse than the first beast they had encountered.

It stank awfully and its skin seemed putrid. When he looked closely, enormous maggots writhed beneath it, sometimes biting their way through and inching away. It took Felix a moment to realise what they were: young. The thing was being eaten alive by its own progeny, although that did not appear to do anything to damp its own appetite. There was something about the look and the stench that was familiar, that reminded him of the followers of the Plague God Nurgle he had seen at the Siege of Praag. Was it possible that this thing was some sort of pestilential daemonic creature of the lord of pestilence? He did not suppose it would matter all that much if the creature ate him. Even as he watched he realised that something worse might happen. The maggots bursting forth from within it were crawling towards him.

Worse still, hideous high-pitched laughter emerged from somewhere high atop the beast's skull. When he looked he could see that one of the excrescences looked suspiciously like a human head. As the realisation struck he heard the creature speak. 'Once I was like you – soon you will be like me – ha ha! Lord Nurgle's gift will be yours, and you will be his – ha ha!'

Felix had once seen a caterpillar being eaten alive by the larvae of a wasp that had been implanted within it. He wondered if this was what would happen to him if those bloated, squelching sacs of foulness bit him. He braced himself for combat even as their foul parent loomed over him. Its shadow fell across him, bringing with it an awful stench. Then it leaned forward like an avalanche of flesh and pus.

I have fought some awful things, Felix thought, but surely this must be the worst.

THE CURRENTS OF magic swept Teclis down the endless corridor of many-coloured lights. He touched things, smashed through gossamer webs of energy and emerged on the other side. Before he could orientate himself, he tumbled headlong. Strange hallucinations overtook him. He passed through scenes he well remembered. His childhood, his first book of spells, the battles that had wracked Ulthuan when the Dark Kindred had invaded while he was still a youth. The mighty confrontation at Finuval Plain where he had fought with the Witch King and eventually triumphed. They flickered past. Between them were intervals where he hurtled down the long extra-dimensional corridor.

Sometimes the scenes were subtly different. In some, he looked into the book and saw there spells of convoluted evil that turned him to the darkness. In some of the battles he fought not against the Witch King but with him, clad in dark armour that was a reflection of Malekith's own. In others he saw himself standing over the body of his dying twin and laughing. Even as he felt horror he realised that these things reflected something within himself, some possibility. Were these his secret dreams and nightmares, or were they something else?

He touched the protective amulet on his breast and concentrated his mind, clearing the images from his thoughts.

As sanity returned, a phrase came to him, an expression from Tasirion's book: *The Paths of the Old Ones have been corrupted by Chaos, you must be wary of the Twisted Paths.*

He saw now what the mad mage had meant. Tasirion had claimed that the Twisted Paths were where the work of the Old Ones intersected with bubbles of pure Chaos. The stuff was malleable. It responded to the thoughts and dreams and sometimes the simple presence of sentient minds. He realised he had been falling through them and as he did so he had altered them.

In a way they were windows into other worlds, temporary things, bubbles rising through the seething extra-dimensional sea of Chaos, places that would exist for one heartbeat, or ten, or perhaps a lifetime or a millennium. He knew that he could, if he wished, guide himself towards them and enter them.

What would it be lik,e he wondered, to be caught in such a bubble, a miniature universe sculpted from his own innermost wishes, reflecting his own secret history? Could he make a paradise? Could he create a place where his illness had not struck him, where he was as strong and perfect as Tyrion, where the darkness within him would never have to come to light, where he would never need to feel jealousy or envy or bitter pain?

Was this the secret of the Old Ones' disappearance? Had they departed from our world to this place and created their own bubble universes, nestled within the sea of Chaos? Was such a thing even possible? It was a concept to boggle the mind. Even as it struck him, he accelerated faster through the corridors of this strange space. As he did so he saw that the bubbles of the Chaos stuff were travelling along like droplets of mercury dropped down the funnel of an alembic. Sometimes two would impact and merge, sometimes they would split and go their separate ways. It was like watching some primordial life forms. He moved to avoid any that came too close, fearing that they might be semi-sentient or drawn to him in some way and that they might consume him. The hallucinations stopped, as he had thought they would.

He studied his surroundings closely, noticing that the tumbling spheres were agitated by great pulses of energy, flowing first one way and then the other like seaweed being dragged about by the tides. He realised almost at once that the energy flows were linked to the disturbances in Ulthuan and elsewhere. By tracking them to their source, he could most likely find the cause of the disturbance.

There were other presences here too, none of them mortal. Some were alien and uninterested in him. Others were malign and followed in his wake like sharks following a ship. They were daemons who had somehow found their way into this colossal labyrinth. He knew that only his protective amulets kept them at bay, and that at the first touch of weakness they would take him.

Suddenly a strange intuition touched him, a feeling of dry ghostly presences such as there had been in his dreams. Was it a product of his imagination, he wondered, or had those trapped sorcerers really reached out for him? Or was it some subtle form of attack projected by the creatures following him? He willed himself to slow and as he did so, noticed an archway that glowed in a strangely familiar way. Moreover, he noticed a trace of an awesomely powerful magical resonance created by a thing that was not in itself Chaotic. It was in fact the resonance of a weapon or device that was powerfully resistant to Chaos, an artefact of near-godlike power. Was this some treasure lost long ago in the paths? Was this something he was supposed to seek?

Such a thing might prove very useful to him on his quest. By an effort of will, he pushed himself towards the archway. Within what seemed like heartbeats he hurtled through it and emerged to face horror.

FELIX DIVED TO one side as tendrils descended towards him. He lashed out, hacking the tips of a few and hit the ground rolling, just in time to see a mass of bloated white maggots moving towards him. He noticed that on each side of their leech-like mouths were small clusters of eyes that reminded him of a spider's, only these contained a strange intelligence and a glittering malice that was uncanny. Large as they were, though, he could not see what harm they could do him as long as they did not get close enough to bite. And he had no intention of allowing that to happen.

Gotrek was already amid the mass of maggot-things, hacking at them with the axe. Their jelly-like quivering flesh gave no resistance. The things burst under the impact, sending milky fluid that stank like rotten curdled milk everywhere. Overhead, the high-pitched laughter of the daemonic thing sounded anew. Felix wondered what it knew that he did not.

He threw himself forward, keeping behind the Slayer, guarding his back against anything that threatened to get past. Not that there was much danger of that with all the carnage the dwarf was wreaking. The huge monster leaned forward, tentacles stretching once more. Long rubbery limbs, suckered like a squid's, threatened to wrap around him. He cut at them, and his blade bit deep, causing more of the hideous milky fluid to surge forth. He noticed that the floor beneath his feet was becoming sticky, and his movements slower. The sheer nauseating stench was threatening to overwhelm him.

Gotrek showed no sign of slowing. Whenever a tentacle looped near him, he chopped it in two. The thing did not die, though. It hit the ground and began to writhe away like a snake, showing a life, if not an intelligence, independent of its original owner. Even as Felix watched, the severed tentacle began to heal and regrow, like the limbs of the fabled troll, or the heads of some daemonic hydra.

The huge bloated body of the monster had started to expand like a balloon as it sucked in air. Felix had the feeling that this was the prelude to nothing good, but he could not for the life of him predict what was going to happen. The thing was too alien, their circumstances beyond the ambit of all his previous experience. He was starting to wonder if they had somehow been cast into hell. At this moment, it seemed all too likely.

The monster exhaled, a gust of stinking, buzzing breath unlike anything Felix had ever quite experienced. It was a black gale that thundered around his ears, then he realised that the buzzing had nothing to do with the breath; it was the foul wingbeat of millions upon millions of flies. These were not any normal flies, either. They were huge things with fat glistening jewelled bodies, and eyes just as intelligent and malicious as that of the monster or the maggots. Perhaps they were all part of the same thing; perhaps they all shared the same intelligence.

That was the last conscious thought he had for a few moments as horror swept over him. Millions of fat buzzing bodies crept over him, their wings stroking his flesh softly and obscenely, the creatures battering against his eyes, and threatening to fill his mouth and his nostrils. He lashed out frantically, but it was like fighting with mist. He crushed hundreds, perhaps thousands as he rolled over but more and more of them came. He could imagine himself under a huge crawling mound of the creatures, covering every inch of his body. He felt them try to force their way through his lips, climbing into his ears. The smell intensified and the buzzing of the wings seemed to have a voice all of its own. He thought he heard the words *Nurgle* and *Praise* and *Pestilence* carried in that strange droning but could not tell if it was real or the product of his own terrified imagination.

Just when he thought things could not get any worse, he felt a massive rope of muscle encircle him. Suckers bit into his body. Something lifted him upwards as though he were weightless and he did not doubt that he was being carried towards the maw of the monstrous creature that was the lord of all these flies.

CHAPTER EIGHT

TECLIS EMERGED THROUGH the archway and found himself
looking down upon a scene of battle. Two humanoid figures
were engulfed within a carpet of flies, amid a vile white mist
that smelled worse than an orcish midden. One of the figures was quite plainly a dwarf. His outline was more visible
through the flies that carpeted him, and he held in one hand
an axe that could only be a dwarfish rune weapon, and one
of great power at that. No flies covered it. Where they
touched the blade they vanished and the runes blazed a little brighter.

This was the thing he had sensed. This was the thing he
had deludedly thought might help him. It could only be the
axe. There was another magical weapon present, one of
cruder make and lesser power. Its wielder was gripped by the
tentacle of the monster.

Teclis had studied all the grimoires of his ancestors who
had lived in age when daemons had walked the earth.
Moreover, he had personally as much experience of daemons as anyone not a follower of Chaos was likely to
have, and he could not recognise the thing. It bore some

resemblance to a beast of Nurgle, one of the lesser entities that followed the Lord of Disease, but grown almost as huge as a dragon, and mutated almost out of recognition. Moreover, it seemed to be spawning lesser beings at an appalling rate, and in his blinded state, Teclis realised that it was only a matter of time before one of them reached the dwarf. What would happen then would be interesting, for he guessed the maggots were infectors of some type, who would pass the taint of Chaos on through their venom, if they were not already doing so with their gore. Could even that appallingly powerful weapon protect the dwarf, if that happened, or would it use its power against him as it would another Chaos-tainted thing?

Tempted though he was to conduct the experiment, Teclis resisted. Two magical weapons, Teclis thought, borne by two heroes. Here were two allies who might prove invaluable in the quest to come, if they could be persuaded to see reason. Perhaps this was why they had been drawn to his attention. First of all, though, he had better deal with the daemon and its spawn.

Teclis drew on the powers stored within his staff, preferring to rely on it rather than the tainted but potent energies flowing through the Paths of the Old Ones. He chanted a spell of exorcism and banishment. The casting was sure and steady and bands of high magic danced from his outstretched hands, separating the weaves of power that bound the flies, reducing them at once to mindless insects, and he added a small incendiary component to the spell that caused the flies to combust. He shaped another spell to purify the foul air tainted by daemon effluvia, and then concentrated his efforts on the great beast itself, sending multiple lines of energy arcing and spinning towards its head. The magical fire passed through its body like so many red-hot wires through rancid lard. The creature screamed and its tittering stopped.

With his sight clear of the buzzing insects, the dwarf did not need any more encouragement to strike. He raced forward and the massive axe crashed through the slimy skin of the beast. The creature's wails intensified as the glowing rune-encrusted blade bit home. The massive tentacles uncoiled as the creature writhed in agony. The man in its grip was sent flying across the corridor as if flung from a catapult.

Teclis summoned a small pseudo-sylph to catch him and cushion his fall. It was a tiny air creature formed from magical energy to do his will, an extension of himself rather than a true elemental, but this was the shape in which he found it easiest to manifest his powers.

Such was the velocity with which the man was flung that Teclis was too slow. By the time he had commanded the sylph to act, he had already passed through the archway and vanished into the Paths of the Old Ones.

The dwarf seemed barely to have noticed. A quick glance was all he took. His one good eye narrowed when he saw Teclis, though, and then he returned to carving the massive Chaos creature. Now the daemon was in full retreat, slithering away into the darkness, its maggot children inching along after it. Teclis knew he must end this farce soon if he was to take advantage of the opportunity with which he had been presented. He sent another wave of magical power after the creature, incinerating the maggots and charring its flesh. The creature screamed as it died.

The dwarf spat on its smouldering remains and then turned to face the wizard.

'Now, elf, I will deal with you.'

FELIX FELT A sudden surge of heat around him, and then the buzzing stopped. He opened his eyes and saw a charred halo of dust falling away from him. The grip of the tentacle tightened painfully around his ribs, cutting off his breath. He felt as if his bones were about to break. Desperately he gripped his sword and tried to bring it to bear on the monstrous limb, but the angle was wrong.

He heard Gotrek's war cry ring out and axe bite home. A golden glow filled the air, and a swirling breeze dissipated the cloying stink of the beast. What was going on here, he wondered, as the glow intensified and lines of fire pierced the body of the daemon? Magic was at work – that was quite obvious. Had Max followed them?

Before he had time to consider things further, the creature's tentacles uncurled and he found himself hurtling through the air. Involuntarily, he closed his eyes. He knew that if he hit the ground or a wall from this height at this speed, at very best bones would be broken, at worst he would die a pulped gelatinous mass like the maggots. He braced himself for the impact that he knew could only be seconds in coming.

Instead, he felt himself engulfed in coolness. He opened his eyes, and saw that he was on the other side of the glowing barrier, caught amid swirling colours. He had but a few seconds to take this in, and then he felt himself gripped by acceleration. It was as if his velocity, already great, had increased by several orders of magnitude.

Desperately he looked around but what he saw was meaningless. He seemed to be hurtling though a breathable atmosphere along an infinite corridor whose walls changed colour every heartbeat. Strange glittering spheres moved through it as well, pulsing and changing, flowing into each other like droplets of quicksilver. Inside each seemed to be a shimmering vision. He had no idea where he was or where he was going. The sense of disorientation he had felt in the darkness of the corridors returned, increased tenfold.

Worse yet, he was alone and caught in some vast sorcerous trap from which he knew he would never escape.

TECLIS LOOKED AT the dwarf and considered the possibility of his own death. The more he looked at that axe the more his respect for its power increased. That it was an ancient rune weapon of the highest order, he had no doubt. The aura of antiquity surrounding it was clear. The runes were dazzling bright, more potent than any he had ever seen, and in his time, he had seen many.

Its wielder was no less frightening. He appeared to be a normal dwarf, albeit one of great size and physical power, but his aura told Teclis's keen and sensitive mage sight a different story. The dwarf had been changed in many ways. Magic permeated his being. Magic that flowed from the axe and changed him utterly. It was changing him still. He was far tougher and stronger than any dwarf had a right to be, and far more immune to the effects of magic as well. Fascination warred with fear. Here was a being in the process of transformation into something else, under the influence of a magic older than elven civilisation. Teclis would have given a king's ransom to be able to study this weapon, but at the moment he had other worries.

'I have no quarrel with you, dwarf,' he said.

'I can change that,' said the dwarf. He moved closer, the menacing axe held high.

Teclis considered his options. He had used much of the power stored in the staff, and the magical energies he could draw on here within the paths would all be tainted by Chaos, and thus most likely resisted by the axe. He would not have bet gold that under these circumstances he could overcome the protective runes on that blade. In Ulthuan things might have been different, but this was not Ulthuan.

Nor did drawing his sword and facing the dwarf seem like an acceptable option. He was a fair swordsman, but one look at this dwarf told him that even a magical blade in the hands of a competent fighter would not be nearly enough for victory.

'I saved your life and that of your companion,' he said, backing towards the archway. Under the circumstances, discretion seemed the better part of valour. Still, he was loath to simply run. He had the pride of all the line of Aenarion, and more, he felt that this dwarf was important to him somehow, that this meeting was not simply chance.

'I do not take kindly to that suggestion,' said the dwarf in a voice like stone grating on stone.

Of course not, thought Teclis, looking at the strange hairstyle and the tattoos, and the dwarf's generally morose demeanour – you are a Slayer, sworn to seek death in battle. I have done you no favours then. He kept backing away as the Slayer advanced, kept considering his options, looking for the key that would give him an advantage here. There was only one thing that sprang immediately to mind.

'If you wish to save your companion, you must work with me now,' said Teclis.

* * *

FELIX BEGAN TO see things as he tumbled headlong into the spheres. At first they seemed almost formless, but then he began to recognise pictures, fleeting glimpses of himself and others. Some of them were quite obviously memories. Others he did not recall. They might have been the dreams of another, save that he recognised those within them.

He saw himself as a youth in his father's house, quarrelling with the old man. He saw himself as a young radical student at the University of Altdorf, drinking and posturing and writing verses of no great worth in taverns of no great respectability. He saw the duel he fought with Wolfgang Krassner and the corpse at his feet, bloody foam still oozing from its lips. He saw the wild night when he had met Gotrek in the Axe and Hammer, and swore an oath to accompany him and record his doom. He saw their fatal encounter with the Emperor's cavalry during the window tax riots.

More images filled his eyes as his senses became somehow more real and more dream-like. What was going on here? What was this medium through which he moved? It seemed to respond to thought and memory with magical speed. He could not comprehend it. He was not a sorcerer and had no wish to be. He had read in some books of natural philosophy that the pure stuff of Chaos was supposed to be like this. He had heard of similar strange things happening during the first Siege of Praag before Magnus the Pious had intervened and saved the city. Stone had flowed like water, hideous monsters had been made flesh, nightmares had walked the street.

More scenes flickered around him. He saw an ancient castle in Sylvania where he and Gotrek confronted a vampire and rescued a girl. He recognised the vampire from a picture he had once seen in Drakenhof Castle. It was Mannfred von Carstein.

He saw a great battle in which the armies of the Empire confronted a horde of orcs, and Snorri Nosebiter fell in battle to be mourned by a regiment of Slayers. He saw a huge burning mountain on top of which Gotrek fought with a bat-winged daemon that looked like a combination of man and elf, only much larger. These things had never happened, he knew. Perhaps they were delusions given form by his feverish brain, prophesies of the future, glimpses of worlds that might have been if he had walked a different path?

He did not know, and he did not care. Already he felt his senses were about to be overwhelmed, that if this kept up his mind would collapse under the sheer rush of information, and he would be reduced to a mad gibbering thing. Then he saw that some of the other objects were coming closer and taking new forms. He sensed the presences around him, closing in, coming closer through the aether like sharks surrounding a thrashing swimmer. A tendril of thought, silky and malevolent and evil, reached out and infiltrated his brain.

We will feed soon, it said. *Your soul is ours.*

THE DWARF STOPPED his advance.

'Is this some elvish treachery?' he said. Teclis shook his head.

'Your friend has gone through the Portal of the Old Ones. He has no protective charms or amulets of spells. He has no idea of how to shield himself. He has no runes such as are to found on your formidable axe. If he is not found soon, he will die or be devoured by those who dwell beyond.'

The dwarf raised his axe once more, and advanced, a look of pure determination on his face. Teclis feared that he was going to have to fight. Instead the dwarf strode towards the gateway. 'I will find him. I do not need your help, elf.'

'It is not so simple. You are no sorcerer. You could not find him within the ways. Nor could you find your own way out without the correct key. You will be lost in there forever or until you meet something that not even your axe can slay.'

'But you will help me?' said the dwarf. There was harsh irony in his voice. 'Why do I feel there is a catch?'

'Because in return, you will help me to discharge my quest. A simple bargain. Something a dwarf should understand.'

The dwarf glared at him. 'Do not worry. I will require nothing that would compromise your dwarfish pride or your peculiar notions of honour.'

'What would an elf know of honour?'

Teclis smiled. 'Then after we have saved your friend I will leave it to you to decide whether what I ask of you is honourable.'

The dwarf cocked his head. He suspected a trap. So might I look, thought the wizard, if I were bargaining with a daemon. He smiled again, having just been given some insight into what was going on in the dwarf's head.

'Very well,' said the dwarf. 'But if this is a trick or you betray me, then you will most assuredly die, if I have to climb out of the pit of hell to kill you.'

The smile vanished from Teclis's lips. The dwarf sounded like he would do exactly what he said. He had the look of someone who could do it, too.

'If we are to travel together we should know each other's names. I am Teclis, of the line of Aenarion,' he said, giving a courtly bow as to one of uncertain status.

'I am Gotrek, son of Gurni,' said the dwarf. He did not bow.

'And if my rememberer is dead,' he said, 'you will soon join him.'

We'll see, thought Teclis, knowing that once they were within the Paths of the Old Ones, the balance of power would tip back into his favour.

FELIX WONDERED IF he were dead and passed within Morr's iron-gated halls. That seemed the one likely possibility, although if this was the afterlife it was a peculiarly hellish one.

Perhaps that was what had happened. Perhaps he had been condemned to one of the purgatories where evildoers were punished for their sins. He had not considered himself a particularly evil man in life, but perhaps the gods judged mortals by different standards.

He stood now in a strange dark place. Fire pits were everywhere. Suffering mortals were chained to walls and daemonic entities tortured them. The weight of his own chains was enormous, and their heat was uncomfortable against his limbs.

Worse yet, something large, horned and bat-winged was coming closer. It reminded him of daemons he had seen before. It had the same malicious eyes, and the same air of inhuman cruelty. It paused before him and looked up at where he hung.

'You are ours now,' it said. 'We will feast on your flesh and upon your soul. For us it will be a moment of mild diversion. For you, an eternity of pain.'

'WAIT,' SAID TECLIS. 'I must cast the spells of warding and tracking before we pass through this archway.'

The dwarf spat on the ground, and ran his thumb over the edge of the axe. A bead of bright blood appeared there. It was a disconcerting sight. Teclis reactivated the charms of protection woven into his amulets and extended their influence to an area about three strides from his body. The axe would most likely protect its wielder from the worst influences of Chaos within the paths, but he was taking no chances.

He next considered locating the man. Such divination was not easy at the best of times and he had barely caught a glimpse of the human. Still, the sword had a very distinctive magical pattern, and Teclis had the recall of an elvish sorcerer. In his youth he had performed thousands of exercises designed to increase the capacity of his memory. The application of such skills was invaluable to a sorcerer in countless ways, as he was just about to prove.

He visualised the man, freezing the instant in which he had been flung clear of the daemon-thing. He saw again the straw-blond hair, the scared blue eyes, the lined and tanned face with its horrified expression. He pictured the tall form wrapped in the ragged red cloak. He pictured the man's aura and the aura of the blade. The image of a great dragon sprang to his mind, and he realised as he contemplated the memory that a dragon's head had been the pattern on the hilt of the blade. Once he was certain he had the image as perfect as he was going to get it, he cast the spell of divination and location, sending tendrils of force through the gateway, relying on the principle of sympathetic magic to guide them to their source. For a moment, he feared he would find nothing, that the link was too tenuous, that even his skills were not equal to the task, then he felt something far off and receding.

As soon as he made contact, he wished he had not. The man was in great fear, and the shadow of another presence had fallen on his mind. Teclis suspected it was the shadow of a daemon.

'We must go now. Your friend is in grave danger,' said Teclis.

'Lead on,' said the dwarf as Teclis stepped through the glowing arch and into the nightmare reality of the Twisted Paths.

CHAPTER NINE

THE OTHER WORLD was different this time, Teclis realised. He was not seeing the same things at all. Maybe it was because he had increased the diameter of the weave of his protective spells, but he suspected it was the presence of that axe. The more time he spent in its presence, the more he realised how powerful it was. More than that, now that Gotrek Gurnisson was in the ambit of his spells, he could sense the strong magical links between the dwarf and the weapon.

He had heard of such phenomena before, but this was the first time he had seen it acted out so powerfully. Over time psychic links could be formed between any magical device and the person who wielded it. Such was an inevitable by-product of magical forces but this was something more. Power flowed down those links into the dwarf, power subtle enough to change even a creature so resistant to magic as a dwarf, and powerful enough to hold at bay the currents of Chaos here. He would have given a lot to know the history and provenance of that weapon, he thought. He doubted that the dwarf was going to share it with him though.

If the Slayer was daunted by the bizarre nature of their surroundings he gave no sign. Teclis wondered if they were seeing the same things. At the moment, they floated within a bubble of clear air defined by the boundaries of his spell. Outside, the magical currents of the Paths of the Old Ones flowed. Teclis sensed the inhabitants out there. Some were neutral spirits, elementals and other creatures who could feed on the direct flow of magic. Most were actively inimical, creatures of Chaos who had entered the pathways and been trapped there. Or perhaps they simply chose to live there. There were resonances of older things, spirits that had been hostile to Chaos, who had perhaps been set there as guardians by the Old Ones themselves, but who had been swamped and submerged and perhaps corrupted long ago.

Once again, he felt the fascination of the scholar. There was so much to learn and so little time to learn it in, even with the lifespan of an elf prince. There was material for a hundred studies contained within this place, if only he survived to write it. He fought to bring his thoughts back to the task at hand. First he needed to find the human, and then he needed to return to his quest. Had he not felt such a strong intuition about the dwarf and his axe he doubted that he would have even offered to help. Yet some instinct had told him that this was the right thing to do. You did not just encounter the wielder of such a weapon by chance. Their destinies had touched and intertwined at this point, of this he was sure. One thing had not changed, though; the great tidal swirl of energy still moved to and fro through the Twisted Paths, pushing the bubbles of reality hither and yon.

He reached out with the divination spell again, and sensed the human's pain and fear. If they did not reach him soon, it would be too late to do anything. He urged the sphere onwards through the aether, hoping that by sheer force of will, he could make it get there in time.

FELIX WATCHED AS another of the daemons came closer. He threw himself forward against the chains, knowing already that it was useless. They were strong enough to resist even

Gotrek's massive strength. His sword lay just out of reach, positioned there to add to his torment and his hopelessness.

The daemon leaned closer. He could see that its eyes were not like a human's. At first they appeared like pits of pure flame, but if you looked into them, you could see that a malign intelligence dwelt there. Instead of pupils, small flames danced in the ember pits that filled its sockets – sentient flames, flames of pure evil.

The daemon laughed, and the sound was chilling even in the heat. It was the laugh of a creature to whom the most unspeakable cruelty was the most natural of things, that found pleasure in the pain and fear of others, that somehow fed on them as an epicure might feast on pickled lark's tongues. Its mouth opened wider and he could see yellow teeth and a long snaky bifurcated tongue. It leaned forward, and he could feel the heat radiating from it. The thing emanated it like a furnace. The tongue snaked forward and licked his face.

This is not real, Felix thought. This is merely a horrible dream. But he knew it was not. The daemon knew it too.

'You are mine,' it said. 'By Tzeentch, you should not have come here.'

'It was not my idea,' he said. The creature backhanded him with its open palm. He could see that it had long talon-like nails.

'I do not like your human humour,' it said. 'I like your fear, and your pain.'

'Not many openings for a jester around here, then,' said Felix because he could think of nothing better. It was a weak joke, but it annoyed the daemon, and that was about all he could manage at the moment. The thing moved eye-blurringly swiftly again. His head smacked against the warm rocks. Small stars danced before his eyes. Pain blurred his vision. Felix lashed out with his foot, but the heavy chains slowed him, and the thing danced aside easily.

'I like it when my food struggles,' it said, in the sort of voice a cat might have used to a mouse, if it were capable of speech.

'I'll see what I can do to oblige,' said Felix, throwing himself forward against the chains once more, hoping to catch it with one of the links. It danced away and returned slashing with its claws.

TECLIS SAW THE glowing oval ahead, and the shapes that surged around it. He knew then that this was not going to be easy. The man had been sucked into one of the reality bubbles floating through the paths. Perhaps even one constructed by his own thoughts and fears. He was trapped within it, and there were daemons all around it. A few had entered already to feed. Teclis had no idea what was awaiting them within it, but he knew that in order to rescue the human, they were going to have to go in.

'There are daemons ahead,' he said to the dwarf.

'Bring them on,' said Gotrek Gurnisson. 'My axe has a thirst.'

FELIX BIT BACK a scream as the daemon's needle-like talons pierced his bicep. Blood stained his shirt. Blood filled his mouth. It was all his, too, despite his best efforts to hit the daemon.

'Giving up so soon,' it said, malicious humour filling its voice. 'I have barely started and my kindred have yet to have their turn. It's been an age since we had such sport, or so it feels to us. It's not often you humans are foolish enough to enter the Paths of the Old Ones unprotected.'

'Go to hell,' said Felix.

'We're already there, or hadn't you guessed?'

As SOON AS they contacted the bubble reality, Teclis knew it was going to be bad. Humans always had vivid imaginations and quaint superstitions about hell, and he guessed that he was now inside one of them. Still, he thought, it could be worse, we could be caught in a dark elf's dreams.

'I can smell daemons,' said the dwarf. 'Where are we?'

'You would know what a daemon smells like, would you?' sneered Teclis before he could stop himself. Clever, he thought, very diplomatic.

'Actually, elf, I would. And I can smell them now. Along with brimstone and sulphur.'

'I'll take your word for it,' said Teclis. 'We're in a bubble reality created from the stuff of Chaos. I am guessing it is one of the human hells.'

'A bubble what?' said the dwarf, stomping forward across the reddish stone between the fire pits. 'Never mind. I think we have found what we came for.'

A smiling daemonic figure looked up, and said, 'Oh good, more food.'

Teclis smiled back at it. The daemon's face froze and he looked closer at what he was seeing, and then the smile vanished from his face completely. Swiftly Teclis wove a low-level spell of interference which would prevent any of the creature's kindred from coming to its aid, at least for a time. He cast spells of inhibition over the area to restrict the creature's powers. He did not want to try anything more ambitious because he wanted to conserve his power against more pressing need. He did not want to have to draw on the tainted magical energies within the Paths of the Old Ones unless he was in the direst straits.

The daemon realised what he was doing and turned from the human. He threw himself at Teclis, his form changing in mid-air even as he did so. He became a creature much larger, far more ugly with scaly reptilian skin and huge jaws full of needle-like teeth. Teclis had his sword out instantly but before he could do anything the massive axe flashed forward. The daemon's wings opened with a snap, hurling it backward out of the way at the last instant. Still, despite its eye-blurring speed, the dwarf had managed to connect. Where the axe had hit, the daemon's flesh was scorched as if by flame. Its eyes widened with malice and hate. Anger and fear flickered over its expression. It opened its mouth and let out a long wailing howl, like a wolf summoning its pack to fight. From far off in the distance came the sound of response, and Teclis felt daemons press forward against the wards he had set. The spells were not intended to stop them, only slow them and cause them pain. He was gratified to realise that they were performing their work well, even here in this strange realm.

The daemon was less pleased. 'Soon, we shall feast upon your souls,' it said, but it sounded less than confident.

'I grow tired of endless bombast,' said the dwarf. 'Now you die.'

Teclis noted that their surroundings had changed. The crumbling cavernous walls now resembled well-dressed stone. There was even a hint of delicate elvish sculpting. He guessed that his presence and that of the dwarf was altering this bubble of reality subtly. It was only to be expected in a place so malleable.

The daemon looked at the dwarf and then at his axe. He was measuring himself against his opponent and quite obviously found himself wanting. He turned swiftly and lunged for the human, intent on killing him rather than letting him be rescued. Teclis could not allow that. He sent a bolt of energy surging towards the daemon. It was not enough to destroy it, but it was enough to cause it considerable pain. Using the lightning as a whip, he drove the creature away from its prey. It disappeared howling into the stone corridors.

'It will be back,' Teclis said. 'And it will bring friends.'

'I care not,' said the dwarf, moving over to the human. The axe flashed. The chains snapped, and the man slumped forward but recovered himself so that he did not fall. A moment later he reached down and picked up his sword. As soon as it was in his fist, he stood taller and straighter, and seemed ready for action.

'I am grateful for the rescue,' he said. 'Have you found an ally or is this another daemon of this foul place?'

'Worse than that, manling,' said Gotrek Gurnisson. 'It's an elf.'

Teclis ignored the jibe; he had other things to do. The daemons were coming closer, pushing into this bubble reality, in search of their prey. They were in sufficient number that he doubted that even he and the dwarf could stand against them all, at least in this place, and the daemons were trying a new strategy. Rather than trying to painfully push through his wards, they were collapsing the bubble reality, pricking its edges and allowing the magical energies to flow in and sweep away his delicate spell weave like the tide overwhelming a child's sandcastles on the beach.

'Elf or daemon, you have my gratitude, sir,' said the human. They exchanged names and introductions.

'You are very welcome, but now we must go,' said Teclis. The dwarf glared at him. Teclis felt that given the Slayer's avocation it would not be the cleverest of things to inform him that an overwhelming horde of opponents was about to descend upon them. He decided on telling the lesser, but still worrying enough, truth.

'This bubble reality is about to collapse, and a tide of wild magical energy flow in. I doubt this is the sort of doom you seek, Slayer. It would be a rather pointless death.'

The dwarf nodded. Teclis gathered his magical energies around him once more, cloaking himself and the dwarf and the human. Heartbeats later the bubble did indeed give way. He could feel the tide of magical energy smashing through his delicate weaves. A moment later, the walls glowed and vanished and they were back in the seething sea of magical energy. This was not a good place to attempt to fight the daemons. It was their natural home and their senses were far more attuned to such a place than any mortal being's, even his. He thought that perhaps he could impose his will on a bubble reality and create a place more suited to himself and his companions, but that would be a futile strategy in the end. He would have to maintain it against the combined efforts of the daemonic horde to tear it down, and en masse they would prove stronger than he, at least in this space and time. What they needed more than anything else at this moment was to get out of here, and there was only one way to do that.

He let the protective sphere of enchantments rush free into the currents. It hurtled forward like an inflated wine bladder thrown into a stream. He wove his most powerful and painful protective enchantments around its edges, and bound them as tight as he could. He applied the force of his will to sending them hurtling ever faster down the energy stream in the direction he wanted to go. For a moment they tumbled onwards faster and faster, and he thought they might outdistance the horde that pursued them, but then like sharks scenting blood the daemons set off in pursuit.

Teclis sensed them drawing closer. The runes on the dwarf's axe grew brighter. The human's face seemed strained, which given the circumstances they had just rescued him from was hardly surprising. They might all find themselves in similar circumstances soon, if he did not find a way out of here. Or they might find their flesh rent asunder and their souls the food of daemons.

FELIX LOOKED OUT beyond the confines of the strange shimmering spell-sphere in which they floated and wondered if what he was seeing was real. His experience with the daemon had left him doubting the evidence of his senses. Had Gotrek and this elf really shown up and rescued him, or was this all some sort of subtle torment dreamed up by the hell spawn? At any moment, was he likely to find himself back in that evil-smelling dungeon, in the clutches of that nightmarish creature? His heart beat faster and his palms grew sweatier at the mere thought of it. For a moment, he felt as if his sanity might be overthrown by the hideous prospect. He felt himself teeter on the edge of a vast abyss. What if he really was dead, and this really was some sort of hell?

Slowly, one step at a time, he stepped back from the edge. If this was a hell, it was a peculiar one indeed, and he doubted that even a daemon's imagination would extend so far as having Gotrek appear in the company of an elf. That was stretching probability entirely too far. To distract himself from his uncertain thoughts, he concentrated on his companions.

The Slayer looked deeply, deeply unhappy. He glared daggers at the elf and then at Felix and muttered to himself in dwarfish. Felix wondered what he had done to deserve such looks, but slowly it dawned on him that the elf was a wizard, and Gotrek must have made some sort of pact with him in order to win Felix's freedom. He could easily imagine that such a debt of honour was not the sort of obligation the dwarf cared to be under.

But who was this stranger and where had he come from? It seemed unlikely he had just been wandering about through these strange extra-dimensional passages. Felix studied the elf. He had never really had the opportunity to study one at such close range before although he had seen a few in the streets of Altdorf in his youth.

Teclis was taller than a man and much thinner. Indeed, he was quite feeble-looking, more so than any elf Felix could ever recall seeing before. He was extremely thin, and his flesh seemed almost translucent. His hands had long, extremely thin and fine fingers. His face was narrow and whatever physical weakness he might suffer from was not reflected there. It was a face that should have belonged to a fallen god, sculpted by centuries of pain. The almond-shaped eyes were clear and cold and cruel. The thin lips were curved in a malicious smile. Felix could understand why the dwarfs were so prejudiced against elves if they all looked like that. He seemed to be looking out on the world with a constant sneer, judging everything by the high standards of his race and finding it all unworthy.

Be careful, Felix told himself, you do not know this. You may simply be judging him in the light of Gotrek's attitude. He has done you no harm, indeed he helped rescue you, and at this moment seems to be doing his best to get us all out of this terrible place. As he thought this, Felix recognised another source of his prejudices.

Teclis was a mage and obviously a very powerful one. With a man like Max Schreiber he could accept this. He knew that he possessed a common humanity, a shared set of values with the wizard, but looking at this elf he was not at all sure he could say the same thing. There was something almost as alien about those coldly beautiful features as there was about an orc, or a vampire. Teclis might superficially look like a human, more so in some ways even than Gotrek, but Felix could not help but think that his point of view was even more remote from mankind's than the Slayer's.

He tried to recall all his tutors had told him of elves. He knew they were an ancient race, civilised when men had still been barbarians. They were mighty sailors and explorers and wizards without equal. They were said to be cruel and degenerate and given over entirely to pleasure. Elvish slavers often raided the coast of the Old World, and mortal man never saw those they took again. Some scholars claimed that there were two types of elves, some sworn to light, some sworn to darkness, and that it was the latter that enslaved mankind. Others claimed this was simply a convenient fiction that allowed elf traders to disclaim responsibility for their cruel corsair kindred. How was Felix to know what or who to believe? His own experience of such things was extremely limited.

Some said they were immortal, others only that they were extremely long-lived. This elvish wizard might well be the same Teclis who had fought against the last great Chaos incursion during the time of Magnus the Pious over two centuries ago. Was that possible? More likely he was simply named for that mighty wizard.

Felix shook his head. Looking at that ancient, smooth and ageless face, he could believe that this was the same mage. Perhaps if they got out of this, he would ask him. Then the implications of that thought struck him – was it possible that he had been rescued from daemons by a hero of ancient times, a being whose name he had read in books? Did legends still walk the earth by the light of day?

Suddenly he heard the wizard say: 'Beware! Danger is near!'

CHAPTER TEN

FELIX SAW THAT the shifting currents of the alien space around them were changing again. Hideous faces were pressing against the outside of the sphere. Some of them resembled people he had once known – Ulrika, Max, Snorri, Albrecht and many others – but their faces were hideously changed, fanged and malevolent. Some of them were like his father and brothers and others were completely unrecognisable, although all shared the same eerie and evil appearance.

Some had the faces of dwarfish women and children as well as males; some even bore a distinct family resemblance to the Slayer. Others were elven, beautiful and deadly-looking. There were handsome elf males and beautiful females, and a towering figure in black rune-encrusted armour. He heard his companions gasp as if they recognised some of the visages. Gotrek spat a curse and aimed his axe at the edge of the sphere.

It passed through and bit into one of the laughing faces. An eerie scream sounded as the sphere shuddered and appeared about to collapse. The elf let out a pained gasp and said, 'Do not do that! If you break the sphere then we will all drown in this vile stuff. It is the only thing that protects us at this moment.'

'I need no protection,' said Gotrek angrily.

'Do not be so sure, dwarf,' said the elf, and there was an edge to that musical voice that had not been there before. 'Even that axe can only protect you for so long in these mystical currents. Soon you would become like them – lost souls, daemons, a dishonour to your clan.'

The elf added the last as if it was an afterthought, but Felix thought he saw the subtle barb there. Gotrek grimaced. 'I am already a dishonour to my clan.'

'Then you will have no chance of redemption, only a chance to deepen their dishonour.' Elf though he might be, the wizard obviously knew something of dwarfs. Gotrek fell silent, save for the occasional muttered curse.

Before Felix had a chance to say anything, an eerie high-pitched sound penetrated the sphere. It was a sound such as souls in rapture might make – calm, peaceful and wonderful. It promised everything your heart might desire. Peace if you were weary of struggle, happiness if you were tired of melancholy, outright joy even seemed possible now and forever.

At first, it seemed ludicrous that those faces should sing such a song, and he realised that this was just some subtle spell, used by the daemons to try and ensnare him. It was a pathetic trick, an obvious lure, and it was as easy to ignore as to see through. Then he looked closer and he could see that the faces had altered. They were friendlier now, and smiled at him as one might at a long-departed loved one who had just returned.

'They cannot yet break through my shield, unless your companion aids them with his axe,' said Teclis. 'But it is only a matter of time. Pray to your human gods that we can escape before they do so. In this place none of us will have the strength to resist them for long.'

What did the wizard mean, Felix thought? It was becoming increasingly obvious that the beings out there meant them no harm. They were friendly, welcoming – all of what had happened earlier had merely been a misunderstanding. They were willing to share with them the secret of eternal happiness. All you had to do was to be willing to listen.

Part of Felix knew this was simply not true. These were the false promises of daemons, but the part of him that was frightened and tired wanted desperately to believe that what they said was true, to put an end to this suffering and anxiety forever. He offered up a prayer to Sigmar. These were the ways the subtlest of daemons worked on men, tempting them when they were at their lowest ebb, promising them a surcease from their travails. He knew he should not want to believe them, but still he did. Worse yet, he knew that as his desire increased, so the spells protecting him weakened. His own connection to the daemons was weakening the wards.

He saw another face he recognised. It was that of the creature that had tormented him. It no longer looked so wicked. It looked ashamed, apologetic. It beckoned to him to come closer, so that it might apologise. In spite of himself, Felix felt the urge to respond.

Outside the sphere, the Paths of the Old Ones flickered past. All around the daemons crowded in, preparing for the moment when the protective spells would give way.

TECLIS KNEW IT was only a matter of time now before his wards eroded. The dwarf's axe had severed the weave. Given the chance, he might have resealed them, but at the moment it was all he could do to hold them closed. Worse yet, Felix Jaeger was faltering. He already had a connection with the daemons out there, having once fallen into their clutches. If they got out of this alive, Teclis knew he might eventually have to perform some rituals of exorcism to remove the taint from the man's soul and sever any residual link to the creatures of hell. If they survived… Right now, he needed to find a way to ensure that they did.

A glance at the dwarf showed no weakness there. If anything, the dwarfish kind were even more resistant to the lures of Chaos than elves – a certain stubbornness had been bred into them early in creation. And even if that were not the case, the weapon Gotrek Gurnisson bore would have protected him from any of their wiles. Doubtless the first few of the creatures to break through his defences would die the final death, but after that Teclis did not see how even the mighty dwarf could survive in this place.

Frustratingly, he could sense that they were getting close to the source of the disturbances he had been tracking. With every heartbeat, they were nearer to the great pulses of power that threatened to destroy this ancient network. If only they had the time, he felt certain he could locate the source of the disturbance and neutralise it. In terms of the distances within the paths, they did not have much further to go. Unfortunately, it was only a matter of heartbeats before his defences were overwhelmed and they were thrown into the current to deal with the daemons as best they could.

Even as this thought passed through his mind, he noticed a swirling vortex of force nearby. It was an exit path, of that he was sure. Given a few seconds they could reach it, and return to the world of men and elves and dwarfs. The siren song grew louder, and a taloned hand reached through the protective sphere. He sensed the presence of the daemons all around them. There was no other choice – if they were going to escape they were going to have to do it now, and face the consequences of his decision later.

'Prepare to do battle,' he said and sent them tumbling headlong towards the portal.

FELIX HEARD THE elf speak and braced himself. He had no idea what was about to happen, but he guessed that it was not going to be good. He was almost sorry that the elf had interrupted his reverie, for he felt he had come closer to understanding the inhabitants of this strange and wonderful place than any man ever had before. He knew that if only he could communicate with those strange intelligences, he might achieve wonderful things, far beyond the dreams of normal mortals.

All such thoughts were swept aside as he felt a sudden tremendous burst of acceleration. They tore free from the pursuing beings and headed towards a swirling whirlpool of light. Moments later they were flung through what felt like a normal atmosphere, and landed on hard stone. Felix felt all the air being blasted from his lungs by the force of the impact. He hit the ground rolling, doing his best to kill his velocity. He knew he had acquired a few more scrapes as he did so.

Quickly he pulled himself to his feet. They were once more in a long stone corridor like the one he and Gotrek had been in before he had been cast into the maelstrom of alien energy. Behind them was a glowing archway, the like of which he had seen before although this one was marked with different runes. Gotrek was already on his feet, quick as a cat, and had turned to face the archway. The elf somehow remained floating in the air at about shoulder height, surrounded by a strange mystical glow. Chained lightning circled his staff, the gems set in his armlets and towering headpiece gave forth an eerie light. The look on his face was as grim as Gotrek's. Both of them seemed prepared to fight.

Felix took in a lungful of air, grateful for the substantial feel of it even though it was damp and smelled musty. Whatever he had been breathing in the paths had been much rarer stuff. He felt slightly dizzy now but held himself upright and waited for whatever it was his companions expected.

Nor did he have to wait long. Within moments daemonic shapes, humanoid, but winged and fanged and taloned, had taken shape in the glowing light of the archway, emerging from it like swimmers from water. The sight of them in no way reassured Felix. Some of them were feminine but with shaven heads and massive crab-like claws. They gave forth a strange musk. Along with them were hounds with long, pre-hensile tongues and soft doe-like eyes that held the glitter of evil humour. Felix had seen their like before, during the Siege of Praag. The thought that he could recognise such things was a profoundly disturbing one.

Their leader was the batwinged humanoid that reminded him of the creature who had tortured him, but who here seemed at once more beautiful and more horrible. Behind him he could see more of the creatures trying to push through. The runes on the gateway glowed, and ruddy lightning bolts flickered over the surface of the light. The daemons and their hounds screamed but kept coming. It was obvious they had triggered some ancient device set to defend against their kind, but whatever it was, it was too enfeebled now to hold them for long.

Gotrek laughed and threw himself forward. The great axe cleaved through the daemons, rending them asunder. They disintegrated into a shower of sparks and a sickly sweet odour. They left no corpses. As Felix watched, some of the sparks tried to return through the archway, but they were met by the red lightning and overwhelmed.

Despite seeing the fate of their comrades, more of the daemons and their long snouted beasts pushed forward. By sheer weight of numbers they drove the Slayer away from the portal. Gotrek continued to hack and cleave, destroying them as they came at him. A few decided to seek easier prey and swept around the edges, flanking the Slayer and coming towards Felix and the elf.

Felix met the first of the daemon women head on. She aimed a claw at his head. The huge lobster-like pincer looked as if it would snap his neck like a twig. He ducked beneath it, aiming a blow upward and taking her through the throat. She disappeared into a cloud of sparks leaving only that peculiar musky perfume behind.

Felix had fought these creatures before, and they had seemed much tougher then. He doubted that he himself had become any stronger, so he could only conclude that something about the sorcery in this place was weakening them and leaving them vulnerable. It seemed that if he and his companions had been at a disadvantage within the sorcerous web of the paths, then the shoe was quite definitely on the other foot here.

The winged creature that had tortured him was hurtling over the Slayer's head towards Teclis. It hit the glow surrounding him and bounced away screaming. Filled with rage and a lust for revenge, Felix leapt upward, jabbing his blade through the creature's crotch and twisting. It too vanished, its essence trying futilely to return to the place beyond the portal.

Felix smiled grimly and moved to aid Gotrek, although the Slayer did not appear to need his help. He had already carved his way through the daemons opposing him. The onslaught from beyond slackened, and at that point the elf began to chant a spell. Instantly the remaining creatures were sucked backwards towards the void, coming apart as if sliced by fine invisible wires when they hit the red light web of the ancients. In seconds the corridor was clear although the howling mass of the mob was visible beyond. Even as Felix watched, the ruddy light seemed to thicken and congeal forming first a translucent film and then a hard opaque layer over the portal. He shook his head, not quite understanding what was going on.

'It seems that this incursion has activated some ancient ward,' said the elf. 'Unfortunately, it will prevent us from using this portal again ourselves for quite some time, although I doubt that using it would be quite such a good idea. Doubtless the daemons are waiting beyond, hoping we are foolish enough to stumble back through and allow them to take their revenge.'

Gotrek sucked his teeth loudly but said nothing. The elf's presence was something of a strain for him. He looked as if he would like nothing more than to take his axe and start hewing. Felix was glad that he restrained himself. It was obvious that they owed a debt of honour to the wizard.

'Where are we? What is this place? How do we get out?' he asked.

'We are within an artefact of the Old Ones, and this is not the time or place to discuss it. As to how we get out – follow me. If you please, sir dwarf,' the elf added with exaggerated politeness. Gotrek's fingers tightened around the haft of his axe. Felix could see his knuckles whitening. A sensible man would have fled at that point, but the elf seemed oblivious. Felix was wondering whether his own nerves could stand the strain of this for much longer.

He fell into step behind the elf, and considered his words. The Old Ones were a legend, a race of god-like beings that had vanished from the world long ago. Some scholars claimed that they were the fathers of the present gods banished by their rebellious children. Others wrote that they had brought some cosmic doom upon themselves and fled. Most tomes said nothing about them at all. Only the vaguest of hints could be found in even the most ancient texts.

In spite of this, the elf seemed certain of what he had said, and he, of all people, ought to know. Felix paid more attention to his surroundings now, looking for clues about the beings that had made these things. The stonework was rough-hewn but marked by glyphs of some oddly reptilian design. Felix was not quite sure how he got that impression, but get it he did. Perhaps they were mere decoration, perhaps they were protective wards. How could he tell? Max Schreiber would doubtless have had a theory about this, he thought. Why was he never around when you needed him?

Suddenly, a thought struck him. These corridors were obviously a link between the real world and the odd world beyond the portal. 'An antechamber,' he said aloud.

'A good guess, Felix Jaeger,' said the elf. 'Yes. Doubtless this place is a bridge between our world and the place through which those paths run. It is neither here nor there, caught between the two worlds.

'And that would mean at the far end of this corridor, we will find a way back into our world,' said Felix.

'I most certainly hope so,' said Teclis. 'Otherwise we may well prove to be stuck here forever.'

'Entombed forever with an elf,' muttered Gotrek. 'Truly this is the gateway to hell.'

CHAPTER ELEVEN

ALTHOUGH HE DID his best to hide it, Teclis was desperate. The way back into the Paths of the Old Ones was effectively sealed from this point. Even if he could break through the ancients' protective spells, doubtless the daemons would still wait beyond. They were immortal and malicious and could take as much time as they liked. He could not risk waiting for them to depart.

Inwardly he cursed his decision to rescue the human and the dwarf. They had cost him valuable time and energy on his quest, and what had he got for his trouble? An ungrateful surly wretch of a Slayer, and a human who appeared on the verge of madness, or giving way to Chaos. He knew he would have to check later for the possibility of daemonic possession. Certainly once they were out of the paths an exorcism would have to be performed.

He matched his breathing to his stride and performed the calming mental exercises he had learned as an apprentice. What was done was done. There was no sense in regretting it. And he could not believe it was simple chance that brought the dwarf and that axe into his path. The gods were taking a hand here, he felt. The question was – which gods? Not the powers of Chaos as far as he could tell, not with that weapon. Perhaps the Ancestor Gods of the dwarfs, perhaps those of his own people. A meeting between the bearer of that axe and the mightiest elven wizard of the age, bearer of the staff of Lileath and the war crown of Saphery, had to hold a deeper significance.

Calmness returned. He took in his surroundings. The stones here appeared to be less worn and less corrupted by Chaos than the ones in Ulthuan. He asked a question that had been nagging at the back of his mind for some time. 'How did you come to be within the Paths of the Old Ones?'

'It was an accident,' said Felix Jaeger. 'We were pursuing a Chaos sorcerer and his minions when a large daemon appeared and...'

Teclis laughed softly. The man's manner was quite matter of fact, even though he was discussing things that would have terrified many an ancient elf.

'Something funny, elf?' asked the dwarf. Teclis shook his head.

'I find your composure in the face of such things... refreshing.'

'I was not very composed at the time,' said the man. 'But things happened so suddenly once we entered the chamber...'

Doubtless it was a chamber just like the one in Ulthuan. The Chaos sorcerer must have been the one to open it. That meant the beastmen he had seen had not simply wandered into the paths by accident. It seemed that followers of darkness had indeed gained access to the Paths of the Old Ones. They must be using them to move swiftly between various places. The question was, were they aware or unaware of the other consequences of what they were doing? Did it matter? The followers of the Four Powers of Destruction were insane enough to keep using the paths anyway, regardless if it meant the destruction of Ulthuan, perhaps particularly if it meant the sinking of the island continent.

'The strange thing is that I believe I have seen the wizard before,' said Felix Jaeger.

'Yes?'

'At Praag, during the siege. He was one of those who summoned daemons, but was also doing other worse things.'

'Worse things?'

'Max Schreiber claimed the Chaos wizards were drawing the powers of dark magic down from the North.'

'Max Schreiber? Who is he?'

'A wizard of our acquaintance.'

'He knows what he is talking about. If daemons were summoned at Praag, something would have to increase the level of ambient magical energy for them to be able to manifest.'

'Max said something similar. He knows more about such things than I.'

'You already know as much as many wizards, Felix Jaeger.'

'And much good it has done me.'

Teclis considered this. These men had been at Praag, and so had the wizard they pursued. He considered Praag and its ancient hidden secret, and the way the forces of Chaos attacked the place so constantly and the rulers of Kislev constantly rebuilt it again. Oblivious to his dark thoughts, the man continued to speak, recounting their adventures within the great extra-dimensional labyrinth. Teclis nodded and encouraged him as they neared what he sensed was the exit.

He paused before the stone archway and studied the runes, then uttered the spell of opening. They emerged into what appeared to be another stone corridor running upwards and moved onwards in silence towards the light. Up ahead was another sealed doorway. He opened it with a spell. A moment later he was hit in the face with a gust of cold wet air and a flurry of driving rain. He stepped through into a puddle and looked around, pursing his lips in distaste.

The wind drove a lock of his hair into his eyes, and he pushed it back into place. In the distance he could smell marsh. The skies overhead were leaden, and full of clouds. All around were dark gloomy trees. Somewhere in the distance, thunder rumbled and the brief intense flash of lightning flickered across the sky. There was something odd about the way the winds of magic blew here. Their energies flowed turbulently through the sky. He would need to be careful with his spell casting. Still, it helped him evaluate where they were.

'As I suspected,' he said. 'We are in Albion.'

FELIX GROANED AT the elf's words. 'That's not possible,' he said.

'You have just come through the Paths of the Old Ones, fought with daemons and witnessed the creation of a bubble reality, and you are telling me that this is impossible?' said Teclis sardonically.

'But Albion is a thousand leagues to the north of the Old World, a place of mists and giants and fog...' Felix looked around him. The place was certainly cold and wet enough to be Albion.

'Albion is perhaps a hundred leagues at most north of your land, Felix Jaeger,' said Teclis. 'Elf ships pass its coast all the time.'

'Elf ships!' The words burst explosively from Gotrek's mouth. They had all the ring of an obscenity. Given how the Slayer felt about elves and ships, Felix supposed that was understandable. He was still surprised that the Slayer had not buried his axe in the wizard's skull.

'But Albion...' he said. Suddenly he realised how far he was from home. Even if what the elf said was correct, they had been in Sylvania – scores, if not hundreds of leagues from the coast. In what seemed like a matter of a day at most, they had crossed a huge chunk of the continent and passed over the sea. This was magic to stun the mind. He looked around again, searching the forests for monsters. Nothing seemed inclined to emerge, but that might change at any moment.

Felix shook his head, and pulled up the hood of his cloak against the rain. Guiltily he realised that he had no idea what had happened to Snorri or Max, or if they were even still alive. Now there would be no way of finding out for months, if they could even find a way back home. Felix was not at all keen on the idea of re-entering the Paths of the Old Ones. Once had been quite enough for this lifetime.

'How are we going to get home?' he asked. The portal was already closed. Briefly, very briefly, he considered asking the elf to open the way and stepping back through it, then dismissed the thought out of hand. He would rather swim home than return the way they had come.

'We have other things to do first,' said the elf.

'*We?*' said Felix. He felt indebted to the elf but he was not sure he liked the assumption that he would automatically do his bidding. He liked even less the thought of the wizard implying such a thing to Gotrek. Dwarfs were a proud race, and touchy as impoverished noblemen with a string of debts. To his surprise, the Slayer said nothing. He merely shrugged and said; 'What would you have us do? I am in a hurry to pay off my debt.'

'It will take some time to explain,' said the elf. 'And first we should get away from this place. Who knows what might stumble through those portals.'

'I do not care,' said Gotrek.

'Alas, I do. It is difficult to explain such things as the Paths of the Old Ones while you are trying to beat off the onslaught of daemons. I do not think it likely they will find a way through, but I am loath to take the chance.'

'I see your point,' said Felix, who was, if anything, even less keen than the elf to confront any monsters that might materialise. 'Let's see if we can find some place to shelter. You can explain things to us as we walk.'

They strode downhill away from the stone ring. The rain fell harder. The lightning flashed closer. The thunder rumbled louder.

To HIS SURPRISE, Teclis found that his two companions grasped his explanation of events on Ulthuan quickly. Whatever else they might be, Felix Jaeger and Gotrek Gurnisson were not stupid. They listened and they absorbed what he said.

'You are telling me that if we do nothing Ulthuan will fall beneath the waves,' said the dwarf. 'I don't see the problem.'

'I might expect a dwarf to say something like that,' said Teclis, unexpectedly touchy. The dwarf's surliness was getting on his nerves, and he was not used to having to be cautious around anyone.

'All of elvenkind would be destroyed,' said Felix Jaeger.

'Not all, but most,' said Teclis.

'I still don't see the problem.'

'Then perhaps I can explain,' said Teclis trying to keep the sneer from his voice, and not entirely succeeding. 'What do you know of the Old Ones?'

'They are a legend,' said Gotrek Gurnisson. 'A race of gods older than the gods. Some claim they created this world. Others that they never existed at all.'

'They existed.'

'If you say so, elf.'

'I have consulted the Book of Isha within the Library of the Phoenix Kings. It was written in the time before Aenarion. A record of the golden age when elves and dwarfs were at peace, and the Old Ones still watched over the world. I have read the *Book of Valaya*…'

'You have what?' sputtered the dwarf.

'I have read the *Book of Valaya*.'

'An elf has read one of the sacred books…'

'There is a copy of the book in the Library at Hoeth.'

'The world has changed. Now only the Priestesses of Valaya consult those iron-bound tomes.' Another thought seemed to occur to the Slayer.

'You have read a book written in the High Tongue of the dwarfs?'

'Elves and dwarfs were not always enemies, Gotrek Gurnisson. In times gone past there were grammars and dictionaries written. Old Dwarfish is not a language much studied now among the elves, but I have an interest in such things…'

The dwarf glared at Teclis but did not speak further. He seemed on the verge of exploding.

'Both books claim the same thing. The Old Ones possessed powers greater even than our gods in many ways. They not only altered our world's climate, they did so by moving its position in space. They altered the seasons and the shape of the continents themselves. They raised

Ulthuan up out of the sea, and made it a home for the elves.'

'Spare me the lessons in elvish mythology,' sneered the dwarf.

'These are not myths, they are truths. They used magic that almost beggars imagination to fix the continents in place and to keep Ulthuan above the waves. They span a web of magic from pole to pole, a lattice of forces that encircles the planet. The Paths of the Old Ones are part of that.'

'Why?' asked the man. He seemed to have no trouble believing this, but he possessed a very human curiosity.

'I do not know. Who can guess the motives of such beings? Not I!' Teclis wondered if he should avoid telling them his suspicions. All of the events of the past few hours tended to confirm his theories. He decided that he needed these two on his side. They were his only allies here, and they were potentially very powerful ones. 'It may be that the whole project, the shifting of the planet, the raising of continents, the lifting of both our peoples out of the mire of barbarism, was nothing more than a tiny part of some great cosmic scheme, the purpose of which I do not know.

'I do know that when the Old Ones left our world, Chaos came. The two things are connected, I am sure. The Old Ones built this whole system so that it connected with a mighty portal at the Northern Pole, a gateway on a size and scale that makes the portals we have passed through seem like a child's plaything. I suspect the Old Ones may have used it to pass to another world unimaginably remote. Perhaps they were like sailors shipwrecked here and what they built was a beacon or a lifeboat.

'Whatever its purpose, as they departed they worked some mighty ritual and it failed at least in part. Something went wrong with the portal. It opened a way to somewhere else. The dark powers of Chaos used it to enter our world and almost overran it. To this day, it remains there in the north, mostly quiescent but sometimes erupting like a volcano.'

'The god Grimnir passed into the North in search of it, and to find a way to close it. So much is written in the *Book of Stone and Pain*, in the time when the skies rained fire and the world was changed forever,' said Gotrek. It sounded like the words were torn out of him unwillingly.

'Then our myths agree on something, Gotrek Gurnisson, for so it is written in the *Book of Isha* as well.'

'I still do not see what this has to do with the Paths of the Old Ones.'

'All of these things are interlinked. Before I can tell you more I must have your word that you will tell no one of this.'

Felix nodded. Gotrek considered, as if wondering if the words contained some sort of snare, and then said, 'You have it.'

'Ages ago, evil mages attempted to destroy Ulthuan. They did so by unravelling the network of energies used to keep it above the sea. The attempt failed thanks to the effort of many heroic elven mages who gave their lives to prevent it. They stabilised the system and rewove the great net as best they could but they discovered that the work of the Old Ones was more damaged than they had imagined. Chaos was using the Paths of the Old Ones as a way to invade our world, and as a source of corruption. The places where they touched the earth became tainted places. My ancestors needed the power within the paths to stabilise Ulthuan. I suspect they got it by draining energy from the paths.'

'And now someone has opened the paths again,' said the man.

'The magical energy needed to maintain my homeland is being bled off and if something is not done soon, it will be destroyed.'

Gotrek Gurnisson cursed. He turned to a tree, lifted his axe. There was an awful crack as with one blow he sheared through it. Splinters flew everywhere. The tree began to topple. Teclis gasped; it was the most awesome feat of strength he had ever seen. The oak had been almost as thick through as his body, and solid. The tree's branches made a terrible noise as they impacted on those of other trees as it fell. The sound was like a mastodon stampeding through the forest.

'I hate trees almost as much as I hate elves,' said Gotrek Gurnisson.

'What has got into you, dwarf?' said Teclis.

'You have just given me the means to avenge the Beard,' said the Slayer.

'The what?' said Felix.

'It is an old tale,' said Teclis, 'and one best not dwelt on. An elven king insulted a dwarf ambassador in a shameful way. Suffice to say that because of it, the elves and dwarfs fought the bloodiest war in history. It's an insult the dwarfs still wish to avenge to this day.'

'You mean to say you would let a continent full of people be slain to avenge a beard?' Felix Jaeger asked the dwarf. He sounded incredulous.

'A land full of elves,' said the dwarf, in a grating voice. 'And not merely to avenge the clipping of the beard, but to right the many wrongs that are set to the elven account in the *Great Book of Grudges*.'

'Well, that's different, then,' said Felix Jaeger sarcastically. Teclis was pleased to see that the man was on his side, for it occurred to him that the simplest way for Gotrek Gurnisson to ensure the doom of Ulthuan was for him to use the axe and take Teclis's head. After that there would be no one capable of stopping the impending catastrophe in time. Perhaps, thought Teclis, now would be the time to use his most destructive spells. Best to slay the dwarf before the dwarf slew him. Still, he had one last throw of the dice.

'You swore to aid me,' he said.

'If it was not dishonourable,' said Gotrek Gurnisson. 'And you left that decision up to me.'

Teclis cursed inwardly. 'It is said dwarfs would haggle over a contract while the world burned.'

'It is said the words of an elf are as slippery as machine oil.'

'This is foolish,' said the man. 'You two stand and argue while the lives of a nation are at stake.'

'More than a nation,' said Teclis. 'If that will make any difference.'

'What do you mean by that?'

'The old ley lines do not just underpin Ulthuan. They run through other places – the World's Edge Mountains, for instance.'

'I do not believe you,' said the dwarf.

'Was there not a time when the mountains shook and many dwarfish cities suffered? Did not the skaven emerge to take one of your holds?'

'Karag Eight Peaks,' said the man.

'The skaven once experimented with machines that tapped the power of the ley lines. I do not know if they did this deliberately or unknowing. I would guess the latter, knowing the ratmen. In any case, the devices proved too deadly even for them...'

'Unless they are the ones behind our present troubles,' said the man.

'How would you know what the skaven do? Unless you consort with rats, which is not a thing I would put past elves.'

'We intervened when we sensed their sorceries, and sent a force of mages and warriors to destroy them. A few returned to tell us of the battle.'

'It must be a famous one, to be so well renowned,' sneered Gotrek Gurnisson.

'Not all who fight seek glory,' said Teclis, feeling his patience coming to an end. 'Nor do their names live forever afterwards. Some give their lives willingly so others might live on, and ask no reward.'

'And you would be one of those, would you, elf?'

Teclis smiled nastily. 'I have no intention of dying at all if I can help it,' he said.

'Sensible man,' he heard the human mutter under his breath.

'Are you with me? Or do you wish to go back on your word? Surely not even a dwarf can see something dishonourable in staving off a disaster that might engulf the mountain halls themselves.'

'Aye, if what you say is true.'

'If I am lying to you, kill me,' said Teclis.

'That goes without saying,' said the dwarf.

'What do you want us to do?' asked the human. He was visibly reluctant, caution and a desire for self-preservation obviously warring with the urge to help.

'Whatever I am doing, two such mighty warriors could be of help,' said Teclis. 'I fear I shall need swords and axes before this all ends.'

'I thought as much,' said the man. 'What I meant was – what do you want us to do now?'

'We need to find the source of the trouble and eliminate it. I must locate the Oracle of the Truthsayers, whoever she is. If we cannot now... well, we are on Albion, and perhaps close to our goal, for the records say that this is where the greatest temples of the Old Ones were in the ancient times. The main nexus of the ley lines is here, the grand confluence of all their magical energies. We must find it, and from there we must find a way to close the paths.'

'You are the wizard,' said Felix Jaeger. 'You know more of these things than us. Lead us to the temple and we will help you get in. After that, it's up to you.'

The man looked at the dwarf as if expecting disagreement, and was obviously surprised to find none.

'Very well,' said Teclis. 'But first we must rest and there are rituals that need to be performed.'

'Rituals?' said the man.

'First we must make sure the daemons cannot take you once more.'

'That sounds like a good idea to me. How will you ensure that?'

'There are spells I can perform that will secure your soul and your body, and break any links that might remain.'

'Links? You're telling me that those things in that weird other world might be able to find me again?'

'Unless I do something, it's almost certain. They will come to you in your dreams... at first.'

The man fell silent. He looked thoughtful and scared. The dwarf just looked angry, but that seemed to be the natural state of things.

'Best cast your spells then,' said the man.

'This will hurt somewhat,' said the elf.

'I suspected as much,' said the man. 'Let's get it over with.'

* * *

TECLIS LED THE way along the forest path, hoping that the two would follow him. He was impressed by the human's courage. He had endured the spells of exorcism with very little complaint and Teclis knew how painful they could be. The process had left its mark, though. The man's fingers constantly sought out the amulet Teclis had given him. Teclis considered the wisdom of that decision. It was worth parting with some of his own protections in order to ensure that his companion was not possessed. He was fairly certain that his spells had been successful, but with the strange flow of magic in Albion, it was best to take no chances. And there were other reasons for giving the human the talisman. If the dwarf turned against him, it would be as well to have an ally, willing or unwilling.

Even now he could sense the dwarf bubbling with rage, and the man's anxiety about their future peril. Felix Jaeger was right to be anxious, he thought. Whoever or whatever could open the Paths of the Old Ones would be a mighty foe indeed.

He let out a long sigh. He would face that peril when he came to it. Right now, his greatest worry was an axe in the back from a demented dwarf. His brother could have handled this situation so much better, he thought.

CHAPTER TWELVE

FELIX PULLED HIS sodden cloak tighter about him, and watched the air mist as he breathed. It was winter here, he thought, but winter was different from back in the Empire. In the Empire, snow lay thickly on the ground. Here it merely rained, although the rain was so cold it was like a thousand icy knives biting into your flesh. The ground squelched below his feet. The sky was the colour of lead. Stones erupted through the turf. He would almost have preferred the snow, he thought. Here it seemed like the skies wept along with the land.

For all that, the scenery was not without beauty. Occasionally when they came to gaps in the trees, he caught glimpses of rolling rugged hills, down whose sides streams scampered and played. Now and again, he thought he managed a glimpse of a stag or some roe deer moving through the forest. At the moment, in the distance he caught sight of a thin column of smoke rising into the sky. At first he was not certain, for it blended into the sky in such a way as to be almost invisible, but after a few more leagues of weary trudging, he knew that they were approaching habitation, and that it was towards this the elf had been guiding them all this time. His eyes are much, much keener than mine, Felix realised.

He wondered at the confidence of the elf. He could not have maintained the elf's air of supreme self-possession with Gotrek muttering at his back. The elf, however, gave no impression of caring. He moved calmly and fastidiously down the slope, never missing a stride no matter how slippery the turf. For all his enfeebled appearance, he seemed tireless. Studying him, Felix noticed other things. His own boots were sodden with mud, and some of it spattered his cloak and britches. Gotrek's boots were filthy and streaks of red clay marked his bare arms. Yet Teclis was as clean as when they had started. His boots gleamed. His blue robes shimmered. Not even the tip of his staff was stained where it hit the ground.

How was this possible, Felix wondered? Were his clothes enchanted in such a way as to repel dirt, or was there some spell at work here? From listening to Max Schreiber, Felix knew that it cost a wizard some of his personal strength and endurance each time he used magic, that it tired them out the way running a race might tire any normal man. Surely not even a wizard as powerful as the elf appeared to be would waste his strength merely on keeping clean? Or perhaps he would, Felix thought; there was a cat-like fastidiousness about Teclis that Felix guessed was typical of elves. Not only that, at any time he got downwind of the elf, he caught the scent of a faint musky perfume such as a woman might wear. Nobles of the Empire carried pomanders to ward of the stinks of the street, but he had heard of few of them wearing perfumes. Another area in which elves differed from men, he thought.

Even in the elaborate headgear and jewellery, and the fine silk robes, there was nothing effeminate about the elf. He was dressed to a different standard than a man, that was all. Human nobles dressed like peacocks for show, to display their wealth. Perhaps it was the same for elves. There was something very aristocratic about the elf, an air of hauteur and languor that Felix would have found infuriating in a nobleman, but which somehow he did not mind in the elf. He did not feel as if the elf were behaving like this to put him in his place, as the son of an uppity merchant mingling with the upper classes, but that it was just the natural air of the Elder Race.

A thought occurred to Felix – was it possible that much of the pose of the human aristocracy was modelled on the behaviour of the older and more cultured race? He would never be in a position to know anyway. Nor did it matter all that much in their present situation.

He looked at the rising column of smoke again and felt a shiver of vague apprehension. They were strangers here, and he had heard rumours that all the folk of Albion were cannibals. Perhaps they were merely seamen's stories. There were other tales of human sacrifice and strange monsters in the swamps. The whole land was cloaked in impenetrable mists and ringed round by sharp savage rocks so that sailors rarely made landfall there save by shipwreck, and fewer still returned to tell of the treacherous voyage. And who knew if the tales could be trusted anyway? Sailors were not known for their honesty when speaking of their travels in taverns.

Looking back, the nightmarish trip through the Paths of the Old Ones was already starting to take on the quality of a dream. He doubted that the human mind could really absorb what he had seen there. It all seemed so unreal, particularly now that he was soaking in the all too real rain of Albion. He pushed his dark thoughts aside.

Albion! Were they really in Albion? Teclis seemed certain and he was in the best position of all to know. And what of his other claims, that the daemons could sense Felix and might even come looking for him? That part of his experience was all too easy to accept. He had encountered such creatures before in Praag, and in Karag Dum. He had no doubt of their malice or the fact that they might take his escape from their clutches personally. He offered up a prayer to Sigmar, for the safety of his soul, but given how effective his prayers had been in the past, he did not expect any help from the hammer wielder now. His hand strayed once more to the protective amulet the elf had given him, along with a warning never to remove it, even when he slept. It was a beautiful thing of elven workmanship. The chain was of some silvery alloy and the amulet itself was a disc of ivory inlaid with the curved elf runes, all of silver. Felix hoped that it was as powerful as it was beautiful. The thought of having his soul devoured by daemons was not a pleasant one.

He gave his attention back to Gotrek. The Slayer was being even more than usually surly. His one good eye was fixed on the elf's back as if he were contemplating using it for axe practice. Remembering the way Gotrek had casually chopped through that tree, Felix was more impressed than ever by the elf's composure. Still, he did not expect Gotrek to go for the elf, not without any warning anyway. Hacking an unarmed opponent down from behind was not the Slayer's way.

He fell into step beside the Slayer, but Gotrek merely glared at him, and looked away. Felix shrugged and strode forward to talk with the elf. Anything to distract himself from this freezing, constant rain.

'Are you related to the Teclis who fought alongside Magnus the Pious?'

'I am he.'

It was all Felix could do to keep his jaw from dropping. It was one thing to speculate about such a thing, but another entirely to have it confirmed. The elf gave him a look of malicious amusement.

'Long are the lives of elves,' he said.

'Short are the tempers of dwarfs,' Gotrek muttered, just loud enough to be heard.

Felix did not quite know what to say next. What did you say when you met a character you had once read about in your history books as a child, one who had mingled with the contemporaries of your great-great-great-great-grandfather? He supposed there were many questions his old professors would have killed to have him ask, but right now his mind was blank. 'So what was it like?' he said.

'Desperate, dirty, bloody and vile,' said the wizard. 'Like most battles. I saw friends die before they should have. There are few elves now, and every one lost is a tragedy.'

'That's a matter of opinion,' grumbled the Slayer. The elf ignored him with admirable composure. Felix knew that he could not have.

'Did you really fight the Witch King of Naggaroth?'

'I am surprised that you have heard of such matters,' said Teclis.

'My father is a merchant. He often does business in Marienburg. There is a colony of elves there even to this day. Word gets out. Stories get told.'

'I can imagine. Merchants are forever gossiping. I suppose it must be part of their trade.' Felix realised something else about the elf. His speech had the same sort of accent he had once heard his grandfather use back when he was a very small child. There was an archaic lilt to the tone of his words that suggested a being of great age, a fact that was singularly at odds with the elf's youthful appearance. He was suddenly reminded of the Countess, the ancient vampire he had encountered back in Sylvania, and he shivered. This time it was not from the cold.

'Is there something wrong?' asked the elf politely. 'Did my words upset you?'

'No. You just remind me of someone I once met.'

'From your expression, it was not a pleasant memory.' Felix was surprised that the elf was so perceptive about humans; then again, he supposed that after several centuries of meeting them you might have insights that few others would have. Once again, his thoughts drifted back to vampires, and from there to Ulrika, and that was not pleasant either.

'It was a vampire,' Felix blurted out.

Gotrek gave a short bark of laughter. Felix guessed that he found the comparison all too apt.

'You have encountered one of the arisen?' Teclis asked. Felix saw that he was interested.

'Several, actually.'

'You seem to have had an interesting career, Felix Jaeger. I am constantly surprised at how much you humans manage to cram into your short lives.' Felix could tell that Teclis did not mean to be offensive, but he was starting to understand what it was that dwarfs disliked about elves. He was starting to revise his earlier opinion about the elf's manner. The tone was faintly patronising without intending to be, and that just made it worse.

'I can see that I have offended you somehow,' said the elf. His tone made it clear that he did not care in the slightest. Perhaps the feelings and opinions of lesser beings were of no relevance if you were a powerful wizard, centuries old. Felix forced himself to smile blandly. Two could play this game, he thought.

'Not at all. It was I who offended you, perhaps, by inadvertently comparing you to one of the undead. If I gave offence, I apologise.'

'No apology is necessary, Felix Jaeger. I have taken no offence.'

Which was probably just as well, thought Felix. The last thing he wanted was to have this powerful mage angry with him. The current situation was potentially explosive enough without him adding to it.

'What did you think of the arisen?' The elf's tone was genuinely curious. 'Why do I remind you of one of them?'

'It's not exactly that you remind me of them,' said Felix, choosing his words carefully. 'It's merely that I was thinking that being so long-lived you might have similar attitudes and insights into the human mind.'

'No. The arisen regard your kind as their prey,' said Teclis. 'There are several fascinating monographs from the period of your Vampire Counts which expound their point of view quite cogently. Manheim's *Reflections on Mortality, Immortality and Immorality*, for example.'

'Never heard of it,' said Felix. He was quite surprised. He considered himself quite the scholar, and yet he had never heard of either the author or the book.

'The author was one of the arisen, a lackey of one of the von Carsteins. He fancied himself as something of a philosopher. His books were privately printed and distributed among his kind. Some of them fell into the hands of Finreir after the wars of the Vampire Counts. He brought them back to Ulthuan with him.'

'Any others that were found were most likely burned by the witch hunters,' said Felix.

'I know,' said the elf. 'Now there was a heinous crime.'

'A heinous crime? I do not think so. What could be so heinous about destroying a work by one of those evil creatures?'

'Destroying knowledge is never good,' said Teclis. 'And who is to say what is good and evil? Manheim regarded himself as no more evil than a human farmer. Indeed he regarded himself as less evil, for he did not kill his cattle but rather did his best to look out for their welfare.'

'That is something only an elf would say,' said Gotrek.

'Manheim said it, not me. He was not an elf.'

'Comparing people to cattle implies ownership,' said Felix. 'Is it right to own people?'

'Elves have done so in the past. Humans still do.'

'Dwarfs never have,' said Gotrek.

'Yes, yes,' said Teclis. 'Shall we take it as given that your race enjoys moral superiority over all others? That way we will be in agreement with the dwarfs themselves.'

'Elves still own people. Humans, dwarfs, elves,' said Gotrek. 'Slavers still attack the coasts.'

'This is true,' said Felix.

'Dark elves,' said Teclis.

'Are there any other kind?' asked Gotrek.

Teclis halted for a moment and turned to look at the Slayer. He seemed on the verge of losing his temper. Gotrek grinned in anticipation.

'There are dwarfs who worship Chaos. Does that mean all dwarfs are Chaos worshippers?'

Gotrek's knuckles whitened as he gripped his axe tight. He reached up and ran his thumb along the edge of the blade. A drop of bright blood showed. Felix knew he had to do something before violence inevitably erupted.

'Surely only the followers of Chaos will benefit if we fall out among ourselves now. We have a quest to fulfil that is more important than petty bickering.'

'There is nothing petty about such accusations, manling,' said Gotrek. There was a very hard edge to his voice.

'I was merely pointing out the flaw in your logic, not making an accusation,' said Teclis.

'And once again is proven the old saying: an elf will twist the meaning of his words to suit any purpose.'

'That is a dwarf saying, I imagine. I could reply with an elvish saying…'

What was it about these two, Felix wondered? Gotrek was rarely particularly rational but he was not stupid. Surely he could see the need for cooperation here? Teclis seemed like a very intelligent being but there was obviously something about the dwarf that goaded him to cold fury. It was like watching a cat and a dog eying each other. To tell the truth, he felt his own temper starting to fray.

'Cats and dogs, elves and dwarfs, men and Bretonnians,' he said.

'What?' said Teclis. Gotrek merely glared.

'It's an old joke,' said Felix. 'In the Empire, where I come from. I thought while we were all exhibiting our prejudices I might as well exhibit mine.'

'Has your trip through that hell damaged your mind, manling?' asked Gotrek.

'A fine example of your human humour, I am sure,' said Teclis. His tone of voice was a good deal chillier than the wind. Wonderful, thought Felix. I managed to distract them from each other by getting them angry with me. He could see it was an effective strategy, but he was not sure he could survive it for many days.

Felix shrugged. The sopping wet cloak shifted uncomfortably on his shoulders. He felt like comparing their behaviour to that of children but he was fairly certain it would not be good for his health. Instead he said, 'Perhaps we should concentrate on the matter at hand. I thought you wanted to save your people, Teclis of Ulthuan. And I believed that you had made a pledge to aid him, Gotrek.'

The dwarf bristled for a moment, and Felix feared for his life, but then like an attack dog deciding not to go for the throat, Gotrek settled back and lowered his axe. 'It has come to something when a dwarf needs to be reminded of his word by a human,' he said.

He actually sounded slightly ashamed. Felix was glad that
Teclis had the good grace not to gloat. Indeed the elf looked
a little abashed himself. Perhaps I might survive this after
all, Felix thought. He considered the volatile nature of his
companions and the situation – then again, perhaps not.

THEY STOOD ON a rise looking down on a most unusual village. Even in the gathering misty twilight, its strangeness was
evident. It was built in the middle of a lake, amid a mass of
reeds, and the houses appeared to either be on stilts or situ-
ated atop small artificial islands. Actually, houses was the
wrong word for them. They looked far more primitive even
than Sylvanian peasant dwellings. Causeways of mud and
logs linked them. Fires glowed within. A few people were
still abroad. Some sat on the causeways fishing. Others
drifted on the lake in coracles. A few appeared to be walking
on the surface of the fen, and Felix suspected magic until a
closer look revealed that they were wearing stilts.

Felix looked at Teclis. 'What now?' he asked.

'We may as well seek shelter here for the night. There will
be food and warmth and perhaps sanctuary where I can perform the needed rituals.'

'And what rituals would those be?' asked a voice from near
at hand. Both the elf and the dwarf reacted instantly. Gotrek
raised his axe and whirled. Teclis raised his staff and a nim-
bus of light played around it. Felix was impressed. He had
never known anybody to take the Slayer off guard before.
Nor did the elf look like one who could easily be ambushed.

He moved his hand to the hilt of his sword but did not
draw it. 'Peace,' said the voice. It had a soft lilting accent but
there was nothing weak in it. 'There is no need for violence
between us. I merely asked a civil question.'

'Where I come from,' said Felix, 'it is customary for a man
to introduce himself before questioning others.'

'And where would that be, my young friend?' Felix peered
into the darkness to see who this suicidal maniac might be.
He had given the man an excuse to make a civil introduction
to two of the most dangerous beings Felix had ever met, and
he seemed hell-bent on not taking it.

He could just see the figure of an old man, gnarled as an oak branch and just as tough-looking. He was wearing trews and a pleated cloak of a tartan pattern that blended into the undergrowth. A long sword was slung across his back. He leaned on a long spear as if it were a staff. His nose was small and snub, his smile wide, his teeth yellow and feral-looking. There was a malicious glint in his bright blue eyes as he returned Felix's inspection. Strange angular tattoos blotched his cheek and brow. 'The Empire,' said Felix. The old man laughed.

'No one from the Empire has made it through the mists in a long time, not since my grandfather's time, when those hell-spawned greenskins arrived.'

'You mean orcs – they are not from the Empire,' said Felix.

'They occupy the same clanlands,' said the old man.

'And men from the Empire arrived at the same time?' asked Teclis. The old man gave him a look of studied contempt.

'Only your folk come and go as they please, spawn of Naggaroth,' said the old man. 'And by the time this night is out, there will be one less of those unless you surrender your weapons.'

Gotrek simply gave him an incredulous look. The stranger raised his hand and gave a piercing whistle.

From out of the long grass a score of archers appeared. Most astonishingly of all for Felix, from out of the mere more spearmen appeared, their long harpoons like spears drawn back to cast.

'There's no need for violence,' said Teclis.

'I'm afraid there is,' said the old man. 'Unless you surrender your weapons now.'

'You will take this axe from my cold dead hand,' said Gotrek. 'Though it pains me to have to defend an elf.'

Felix flinched, expecting at any moment to feel an arrow bury itself in his back or his eye. Things were certainly not looking good, he thought. Just then the rain started again.

CHAPTER THIRTEEN

THE OLD MAN gestured again, and suddenly arrows flashed through the air. Felix threw himself flat, aiming for the oldster, but with surprising agility for a man his age, he had already rolled behind the rock, out of sight. Felix cursed and glanced back to see if Gotrek or the elf had been hit. He was astounded by what he saw.

The arrows bounced away from the area around them, repelled by a glowing sphere centred on the elf mage. Teclis gestured again and the men of Albion all stood frozen. A few gave gasps of fear, but they stood still as stone. Felix looked at the ones who had seemingly emerged from the water like mermen. He could see that each of them held a cut reed in his mouth, most likely as a tube to breathe through. It was a trick he had heard of, but it spoke of enormous patience, not to mention courage, to actually be able to use it.

Felix looked behind the rock and saw that the old man stood there. Frozen. Beads of sweat ran down his forehead, as he tried to resist the spell. Felix considered very briefly running him through with his sword, but resisted the impulse. He was tired and scared but there was no need for killing just on that account. Yet.

'Your magic is strong, servant of Malekith, but the Light will overcome.'

Felix glanced at the elf, expecting him to look angry. Instead he looked amused. 'It seems that we have another who shares your opinion of elves, Gotrek Gurnisson.'

'A sensible man,' said Gotrek. 'It would pain me to have to slay him. And there's no honour in taking an axe to men who stand like sheep for the slaughter.'

'Your familiar speaks truth,' said the old man. 'Free us and let us settle this like warriors.'

Wrath clouded Gotrek's face. He looked as if he was going to take his axe to the old man there and then. 'I have never been familiar with an elf,' he said.

Felix shook his head. Diplomacy was obviously not the strong suit of anybody around here. He looked closer at the old man. His face was tattooed in odd geometric patterns that reminded Felix of something. Of course, he thought, the runes on the standing stones. 'Are you really so tired of living, old man?' he said. 'Not content with ordering an attack on a powerful wizard, you must insult a dwarf Slayer. There is a fine line between courage and stupidity, and you have crossed it.'

'And you are obviously enthralled by elvish magic. I have seen it often. Good men often return as slaves in the service of the Dark Ones.'

'That makes all three of us now,' said Felix. He looked at the elf for a lead. Max Schreiber had told him how draining magic could be, but the elf showed no sign of any strain at holding a score of warriors immobile. What were they to do, Felix wondered? *We can't just slit these men's throats, can we?*

'I am not what you think I am,' said Teclis. 'I am no servant of the Witch King. Indeed I have been his enemy for many years.'

'So you say,' said the old man. 'But I have only your word for that.'

'Tell me, does it mean nothing to you that I hold you in my power, and yet have spared your lives, despite your insults to myself and my companions?'

'This could just be some elvish trick. You may wish to enthral us or bring doom on us in some dark and terrible way...'

Fire entered the wizard's eyes and when he spoke his words were full of menace. He became a figure of immense power, suddenly cloaked in a strange majesty. His face looked carved from stone.

'I am Teclis, of the line of Aenarion, of the firstborn of Ulthuan. If I wished to destroy you or enthral you or bring doom down upon your pitiful barbarian village, it would already be done and there is nothing that you or your followers or your childish magic could do to stop me, old man.'

Felix believed him. At that moment, he was as menacing as anything Felix had ever seen, and he had looked upon powerful daemons in his time. At that moment there was something almost daemonic about the elf himself. Then Teclis shrugged and the spell was broken. Suddenly the old man and his followers were free to move. They slumped to the ground, weapons slipping from nerveless fingers.

'Fortunately for you, I do not,' said Teclis. 'We require food and shelter and a place to sleep for the night. You will give it to us, and in the morning we will be on our way. You will be recompensed for your trouble.'

Almost as if the words were torn from his throat unwillingly, the old man said, 'Aye, as you wish. For this night and this night only you will be guests in Crannog Mere.'

Felix had heard heartier welcomes. He wondered if the elf knew what he was doing. Maybe they would wake up in the night to find knives buried in their throats. He looked at the elf and then at Gotrek and decided no, that was not going to happen. Whatever doom might lie in wait for this pair, it would not be a knife in the dark from some barbarian tribesman.

* * *

THEY FOLLOWED THE barbarians down to the edge of the water. Felix never took his eyes off them, for he feared that at any moment, despite their leader's words, they might turn and attack. If that happened, he knew there would be carnage.

At the water's edge the men walked straight in. Felix gasped, for they seemed to be walking on water. Their feet barely sank below the surface even though the water had been deep enough to conceal spearmen. Was this some new form of magic, he wondered?

Teclis followed them and so did Gotrek with barely a shrug and a sniff. Knowing that the others were waiting for him, Felix put his feet in the water and the answer to the mystery became clear. Just below the surface was a narrow causeway, cunningly concealed so that it could only be seen from close at hand. The men of Crannog Mere obviously knew the way by heart for they did not need to look down. Nor did Gotrek, who always seemed sure-footed in these situations. Close inspection revealed that the elf really was floating just slightly above the surface of the water, effortlessly and doubtless by the use of magic. Felix had to keep his eyes down as he moved for the causeway wound about like a snake, to confuse attackers. It was a simple and effective system, as simple as using this fen as a moat.

As they approached the gate, women armed with bows and spears hailed them. They were mounted on the low wooden parapet that surrounded the main island, certainly the central fortification for the community. It was obvious they had been hiding while their menfolk waited. It was equally obvious that at least some of the women here were prepared to fight alongside their men.

'They are guests, Klara,' said the old man. 'They are not enemies for this night at least.'

'But one of them is a Dark One…'

Gotrek cackled.

'And the other appears to be some form of squat daemon.' The dwarf's laughter stopped abruptly and he stroked his axe-blade meaningfully.

'I am a dwarf of the World's Edge Mountains,' he said.

'Och, and what might they be?' the woman enquired. Gotrek did not deign to reply, although he looked like he was considering taking an axe to the gate. Felix wondered at the isolation of this place. He had grown up in a city where elves and dwarfs could oft times be seen walking the streets. He supposed that a tiny village in the middle of a bog was slightly less cosmopolitan.

'Nonetheless they are our guests,' said the old man. 'They had us in their power and they did not kill us. They say they are not our foes and until they prove differently we will take them at their word.'

'I wondered why ye were standing there like big glaked nambies,' said the woman. 'Magicians, are they?'

'One of them is, and very powerful too. More so even than the Wise One, unless I miss my guess.'

'She'll no thank ye tae be saying that,' said the woman.

'Are we going to stand here all night discussing this, woman, or shall you open the gate?' The old man asked.

'I suppose we shall be opening the gate then.' It creaked open and they strode within, to be greeted by the smell of peatsmoke and middens and fish, and the barking of dogs and the crying of children. Teclis raised his hands to his nose and coughed delicately.

'I've smelled worse,' said Gotrek.

'I doubt you ever bathe,' said the elf. It took some time for Felix to realise that he was making a joke. He suspected that Gotrek ever would. He glanced around as they walked through the street. One small boy, cheeks stained with soot, looked at him and burst into tears. Other children were hustled away by their mothers. They moved to the huge turf-roofed hall that dominated the central mound. The eyes that watched them were hostile. If Felix had had to guess he would have said most of the hostility and fear were aimed at Gotrek and Teclis, but still the villagers managed to reserve a small portion for him too. It looked like it was going to be an uncomfortable night.

THE HALL WAS long and low and dimly lit by torches soaked in pitch and lamps that contained some sort of scented oil.

The place was obviously some sort of communal feasting and living chamber. A massive fireplace dominated one wall. Another was covered in what appeared to be small kegs of spirit. The men tossed off their cloaks and threw themselves down where they could, to sit cross-legged or squat as they saw fit. Their weapons never left them, though, and Felix noticed that there were still sentries at the gate.

'I am Murdo Mac Baldoch, welcome to this hall,' said the old man.

'I am Teclis of Ulthuan, I thank you for your welcome.'

'Gotrek, son of Gurni.'

'Felix Jaeger of Altdorf. I thank you for your welcome.'

Murdo went round the room and introduced each of the men in turn. From outside he could see the women peering in. They looked curious and frightened in equal measure. Felix guessed that they did not see too many strangers in these parts, and those that they did were most likely enemies. The fortifications gave that much away about this place. Men did not build such things without good need for them.

The old man picked up a goblet from the stands and tapped one of the kegs. The smell of strong alcohol became obvious as some form of golden spirit emerged. He took the goblet, sampled it himself, and then handed it to Teclis. The elf looked at it, sniffed it, and said; 'The fabled whisky of Albion. I thank you.'

He drank a sip and held the goblet. Murdo repeated the process with Gotrek who gave the elf a contemptuous glance and then tossed it back in one. The feat drew gasps of what Felix took to be admiration from the tribesmen.

'Och, you are a drinking man, Gotrek Gurnisson,' said Murdo.

'I am a dwarf,' said Gotrek. 'The whisky is good – for a human brew.'

'You'll be having another then?'

'Aye.'

Murdo refilled Gotrek's goblet and brought one to Felix. He sniffed it. The smell of the alcohol was very powerful. He took a sip and almost spluttered. It burned his tongue and sent powerful fumes racing up the back of his throat and into his nostrils. The taste was slightly smoky but not unpleasant if you were used to it. It was certainly no worse than Kislevite potato vodka.

'Very good,' he said, noting that Gotrek had drained the second goblet and looked no worse for wear. This time there was general applause from the tribesmen. Whatever else they might think of strangers, the men of Albion obviously appreciated a good drinker. As if this were a signal, each of the men took up a goblet and tapped a cask. It seemed like each had his own separate one, or perhaps it was that each family had one. He noticed that groups of men all drank from the same cask, but that was the only pattern he could put to it.

All of them took up places by the walls, sitting with their backs to it, looking inwards into the circle. Someone produced a set of small windpipes and what appeared to be a fiddle, and music began to play. The scent of cooking food began to overcome the midden murk.

'And what brings you to Albion, wizard of Ulthuan?' Murdo asked. His face was bland but keen interest showed in his eyes. Felix noticed that he only sipped at his whisky while others attempted to repeat Gotrek's feat. Felix could tell the Slayer was listening even though he appeared to be doing nothing more than staring into the fire.

'I am on a quest,' said Teclis. 'As are my companions.'

'A quest is it? The work of wizards and wise ones, no doubt. I shall not pry.'

'You are not prying, friend Murdo. Perhaps you can be of assistance. I seek the Oracle of the Truthsayers, or failing that, an ancient temple perhaps recently occupied by the forces of darkness.'

Felix could have sworn that the glint in the old man's eyes grew brighter. He nodded. 'And what would you do if you found her?'

'I would ask her help. I have great need of it.'

'It is not often one of your kind would admit that.'

'These are dark times.'

'Aye, the world over, it seems. You spoke of a temple – what do you know of this?'

'It is said to be the work of the Old Ones. Do you know ought of them?'

This time the old man definitely flinched. Felix could see his fingers toy with an amulet on his breast. For the first time, Felix noticed there were runes on the stone tip of the old man's spear. He was undoubtedly a wizard of some sort.

'I know of them, although these are not the sort of things a wise man speaks of in public. There are sacred mysteries involved.'

'It is a matter for the Truthsayers then?' The old man looked a little shocked now.

'You are very learned.'

The elf smiled with what Felix took to be mock self-depreciation.

'What would you do if you found a temple like the one you seek and it was occupied by dark powers?'

'I would cast them out, or failing that make sure they could not use the power that lies within the temple for their own evil purposes.'

'You and your two companions are going to do this? You have set yourself no easy task.'

'You know of the things of which I speak then?'

'I know of such things.'

'Will you tell me of them? I cannot reveal all of my reasons but I believe that my quest will also help your people.'

'In what way?'

'Has the earth recently shook? Has the weather gotten worse?'

'The weather is always bad in Albion but recently it has seemed particularly so. Great storms lash the lands. Rivers flood. Villages are swept away. A great curse has settled on our land, Teclis of Ulthuan. First the greenskins descended from the mountains in their hordes and then all of the things you have described have happened. Some say the Gods of Light have turned their faces from Albion and that the Seven watch over us no longer.'

'All of these things are linked, I am sure,' said the elf. 'Old magics have been woken by evil men. These spells are centred on Albion. If there is a curse, it has a source, and that source can be cleansed.'

'So the Oracle claims and I believe her. She says the old paths have been opened and daemons are creeping through them. Some claim she is senile and that the sight has left her, but I myself am not so sure.'

'Your people are divided in this matter?'

'The Truthsayers are.'

'Again you speak of the order of wizards of Albion…'

'Aye, how came you to be familiar with such things?'

'There are texts in my library in… but you are the first I have met.'

'First and least, Teclis of Ulthuan. I am not a great wizard, so do not judge the power of my brotherhood by my own.'

'You are not the least of mortal wizards I have faced, Murdo, and there is no shame in being bested by me. In my time I have faced down the Witch King himself.'

'That is a boast that few would ever dare make lest it bring the anger of the Dark One down on them.'

'It is nothing short of the truth.' Such was the elf's manner that Felix could see the old man was swayed.

'They say the elves have silver tongues,' he said.

'It was yellow livers I always heard,' muttered Gotrek. A massive tattooed man was staring at him. Gotrek looked up and downed another goblet of whisky.

'What are you looking at?' the man asked.

'I don't know,' said Gotrek, 'but it's looking back.'

Felix studied the warrior. He was as broad as Gotrek and near as brutal-looking. His nose had been mashed several times by the look of things, and his ears were as cauliflowered as those of a prize fighter. His head was bald and he had a long ginger beard. He was muscled like a blacksmith. He was soon to be a dead man if he provoked the dwarf, Felix thought.

If a fight broke out here in this enclosed space there would be carnage, thought Felix. If the wizard joined in, the village would most likely be levelled and these people so far had

done them no harm. They seemed more scared by their own
troubles than anything else, and Felix could understand
their mistrust of outsiders. It had to be said that after the
rigours of the past few days, he was not keen on fighting
himself at the moment.

'You think you're strong, wee man,' said the stranger, grin-
ning. He interlinked his fingers and cracked his knuckles.

'I am a dwarf, but can see you are too thick-skulled to
remember that.'

The whole place had fallen silent. 'Now, Culum,' said
Murdo. 'These folk are our guests and we be wanting no
trouble.'

'I was thinking more of some sport,' said the bruiser.

'And what sort of sport would that be?' said Gotrek.

'Can ye arm-wrestle?'

Gotrek laughed. 'Can you ask stupid questions?' he
retorted. Felix was pleased to see that the whisky had apparently mellowed the Slayer enough so that he did not reach
for the axe. He stood and flexed his fingers. Both of them
leaned forward over the table and grasped hands. The tribesmen had begun to chant Culum's name. 'He has never lost
a bout,' said Murdo proudly. Felix could see that there was
some family resemblance between the two.

Huge muscles flexed. Felix studied the pair. Culum was
even more massive than Gotrek and his shoulders were
huge but his arms were not as thick, and there was something about dwarfs, Felix knew, that made them stronger
than humans of comparable mass. He had never worked
out quite what it was. And Gotrek was strong, even for a
dwarf.

Watching them Felix was aware that enormous power was
at war here. Culum looked capable of uprooting treestumps
with his bare hands. His muscles bulged, sweat beaded his
brow. Slowly but surely, the Slayer's arm was forced backward. The tribesmen cheered louder. The smile on the
human's face widened. Gotrek took a slug of whisky with
his free hand, and grinned, showing his rotten teeth. The
movement of his arm towards the table slowed and stopped.
Felix was amazed that he could hold it at that angle. Culum

grinned back and pushed harder. Great cables of sinew writhed in his arm and neck.

And yet, Gotrek's arm did not move. Culum's grin became sicklier as he pushed harder and harder. Veins bulged in his forehead and he looked as pop-eyed as a fish. Gotrek began to exert his strength. The human's arm quivered and then was pushed back. The tribesmen's cheering stopped. A hairsbreadth at a time, his arm was pushed back to the upright position, then slowly, inexorably, the human's arm was forced back to the tabletop. It hit the wood with a slamming sound, and there was for a moment total silence. Then the tribesmen began to cheer and applaud. Gotrek glared at them, but it did not stop them from beating their goblets on the table or praising his strength.

'That's a feat of which the harpers will sing for many a moon,' said Murdo. 'I would not have believed it if I had not seen it myself.'

After the initial shock even Culum seemed to be taking it well. He grinned ruefully and offered Gotrek his hand. The Slayer grasped it briefly and then returned to his drinking.

Food was brought, soup and coarse bread and cheese and cooked ham. The folk seemed friendlier now, but that might just have been the whisky. Felix noticed that the elf sipped his, and his goblet did not seem to empty by much after each sip. Felix decided that he had better emulate the elf. While the people were friendly enough now, he did not want to wake with his throat cut.

As these dark thoughts raced through his mind, he noticed that the elf and the old man had been talking and seemed to have reached some sort of agreement. He glanced over at the Slayer, who helped himself to the food with melancholy relish. He noticed that Gotrek's axe was within easy reach. Drunk or not, the dwarf was taking no chances. Felix wondered what was going on in the minds of their putative hosts.

CHAPTER FOURTEEN

FELIX WOKE THE next day to the sound of water washing against the walls of the village and the patter of rain on the roof. He felt quite warm and threw off his cloak, noticing that his sword lay within easy reach where he had left it. He glanced around the hall, and noticed that most of the men were still asleep, snoring loudly. Teclis sat on a wooden chair, his eyes open and fixed on the middle distance. He appeared to be in a trance. The Slayer was nowhere to be seen.

Felix got up and rubbed his back. There was an ache there that lying on a straw pallet had done nothing to improve. He shrugged and reached down and fastened his sword belt to his waist. Somewhere in the distance he could smell fish cooking. He stepped outside into the mist and the rain. The chill bit him immediately and began to clear his head. He stretched and shrugged and did his best to loosen up.

Strange dreams had troubled him the night before – dreams of daemons and the things he had seen within the Paths of the Old Ones. He touched the elvish amulet for reassurance and wondered what would happen if he slept without it. Was it really possible that he might become a victim of daemonic possession, or had the elf only said that to frighten him? It was one of those things that he was in no position to judge. Teclis was a wizard and he was not. More than that, he was an elf, and Felix had no way of guessing his motives. He had no idea what went on behind those cold slanted eyes. The thoughts might be as alien as those of a spider or a skaven for all he knew.

'Good morning, bonnie lad,' said a clear voice behind him.

'Good morning, Klara,' said Felix, turning to look at the wench who had greeted them at the gates yester eve.

'You remembered my name,' she said. 'That be good.'

'I am Felix Jaeger,' he said, bowing and feeling stupid when she laughed.

'An unusual name.'

'Not where I come from,' he said.

'Och, and that would be the Empire.'

'It seems word spreads fast around here.'

'Fast as a dugout in a stream,' she said. 'This is a small village, and we are a small clan and to tell the truth, the men were bellowing so loudly about all manner of things that the womenfolk find them out whether they will it or no.'

Felix laughed, amused more by her expression than her words. She seemed good-humoured and she was pretty. Her complexion was fair and freckled, her hair a deep reddish brown. Her lips were wide and her eyes clear blue. 'And you'll be going to see the Oracle,' she said. 'And she'll decide what's to be done with your elvish friend and his wee familiar.'

'I would not let Gotrek hear you say that if I were you.'

'Why no?'

'He's not a familiar, he's a dwarf, and they have no liking to be associated with elves in any way, shape or form.'

'And yet you are all travelling together…'

'Circumstances are unusual,' he said.

'Must be. Must be. It's been a strange year and your appearance no the least strange thing.'

Felix felt his curiosity being piqued. 'Is that so?' he said, letting the words hang in the air.

'Aye,' she said. 'That is so. There have been great storms and strange portents. Lightning dancing on the hilltops and horned men walking the marshes and the greenskins every-where – a pox upon them all.'

'Orcs, you mean?'

'Yrki, orcs, greenskins, whatever word you wish to use. They be as bad as the Dark Ones – only 'tis said they herd folk for eating instead of for slaves.'

'I have heard that is so, though I have never seen it.'

'And how would you know, pretty boy? You look more like a candidate for the Bardic college and you have not a scar upon ye, save for that wee scratch on your face.'

Felix was not offended. He realised that he did not look or sound like most people's idea of a warrior and he did not think of himself as one. 'Nonetheless I have killed my share of greenskins,' he said. 'And maybe a few more.'

'Och, away wi' ye.'

'It's true, though if truth be told, Gotrek did most of the killing.'

'The familiar? He has the look of a fell-handed one right enough, and that axe looks like it could dae some damage.'

'It has,' said Felix, and resisted the temptation to tell her a few stories. He realised that he was being pumped for infor-mation in exactly the same way as he was hoping to obtain knowledge from her. 'But you were telling me of the strange-ness of the year.'

'Aye. 'T'as been a bad one. The fishing has no been good, and the barley barely sprouted in the hills. They say the clans in the mountains be starving and the swamp beasts be on the prowl once more.'

'Swamp beasts?'

'Big bad things all covered in moss-like stuff and strong enough tae uproot trees if they have the mind.'

'Like treemen?' Felix asked, trying to relate them to some-thing within his knowledge. Although, if truth be told, all he knew of treemen was what he had read in books. They were supposed to be allies of the elves, living beings half man, half tree and stronger than trolls, capable of crushing boul-ders within their gnarly fists.

'I hae never seen a treeman, so I couldnae tell ye.'

Felix shrugged and told her what he knew. 'And you'll be telling me you have fought these as well, I suppose,' she said.

'No. Not yet anyway, although the way my life has been going it's only a matter of time.'

'What do ye mean by that?'

'It sometimes seems like I have fought just about half the monsters out of the old tales,' he said.

'Och, you're just saying that tae impress me.'

Felix laughed. 'No, it's true. Although to be honest, Gotrek did most of the fighting. I was really just there to watch.'

'What do you mean?'

'I swore an oath to follow him and record his doom. He swore an oath to seek death in battle against the mightiest and most monstrous of foes.'

'He disnae seem to have kept his oath very well then.'

'It's not for lack of trying.'

'Aye, he has that driven look. I've seen it before on the faces of those who think they've heard their death spirits a-wailin' although he has a face that would frighten even one of the Deaths.'

'That he does.'

'Perhaps he'll be wanting to seek out one of the swamp beasts then, to try his luck against them.'

'Don't say that too loud, he might hear you.'

'I take it you're no too keen on seeing his doom then.'

'I've always thought that anything tough enough to bring Gotrek's doom about would bring mine about very soon afterwards.'

'You're saying you're a-feared o' death then.'

'Isn't any sensible person?'

'You will not hear too many o' the menfolk around here admit such a thing. And I would not say it too loudly if I were you, lest they think you less than a man.'

'Is that so?'

'A man here is proud of courage and of his deeds. He tells them at every opportunity. A boastful bunch they are, but they have much to boast about.'

Felix was suddenly reminded of Teclis. Perhaps the elf would fit in here better than they. She misread his smile.

'Don't misjudge them,' she said. 'They are a fell-handed bunch of men.'

'I better hope they don't misjudge me then.'

'I would not worry if I were you, Felix Jaeger. There are few around here who would make that mistake.'

'I worry that there will be a misunderstanding. We did not come here looking for trouble. We came here on a quest of our own.'

'This is Albion, bonnie laddie, trouble always finds you soon enough. And speaking of which, here is my husband…'

Felix looked up to see Culum striding towards them. There was a scowl on his face when he looked at them. Felix suddenly regretted his easy manner. It had never occurred to him that anybody as free-spoken and flirtatious as Klara would be anything other than unmarried. The look on Culum's face told him that it might be a fatal mistake if he made it again. Felix strode off quickly. Gotrek was the one who was seeking his doom here, not him.

THE SLAYER LOOKED out from the wooden ramparts into the gathering mists. He seemed unbothered by the rain and untroubled by the cold. Felix wished him a good morning.

'What's good about it, manling?'

'We're still alive,' Felix was about to say, and then realised it was the wrong thing. 'What's so bad about it?' he countered.

'I have sworn an oath to aid a pox-ridden elf,' he said.

'And why would you do that?' Felix asked. Gotrek merely glared at him. Of course, Felix thought, he did it to help me. Gotrek's no sorcerer. There was no chance he could have found me without the elf's help, was there? Felix was actually quite astonished and more than a little grateful. 'I am sure it will not reflect to your discredit,' he said eventually.

'I am aiding one of the beard-clippers,' he said.

'What do you mean by that?'

'The locks of a dwarf were once shorn like those of a sheep by those elves.'

'Is that such a bad thing?'

'There is no greater insult to a dwarf.' Felix considered this. He knew nothing of the religious taboos of the dwarfs, but he was quite prepared to believe that there were many connected with facial hair.

'Even so, is that really reason enough for the long feud between the Elder Races?'

'Aye, manling, it is. Not least because the beard belonged to the brother of a dwarfish king. No dwarf may rest until such an insult is avenged. And if the grudge is not settled in his lifetime, it passes to his descendants.'

'Remind me never to get on a dwarf's bad side,' said Felix. Gotrek ignored him, lost in his own gloomy thoughts.

'But it's not the only reason. Ever the elves have betrayed us, slaughtered our people in sneak attacks, used their foul sorceries to ambush us. They betrayed our trusts and our ancient treaties. They took slaves and sacrifices to their dark gods.'

'Teclis does not seem to want to sacrifice anybody to the Dark Gods.'

'Who can tell what an elf thinks? Who can tell if they lie or are simply bending the truth the way a blacksmith works hot metal?'

Felix studied his companion. 'You are troubled because he may be telling the truth?'

'Aye manling, I am. I care not whether the island of the elves sinks or floats. The world would best be rid of the primping, perfumed, pointed-eared...'

'But?'

'But what if he is telling the truth about what may befall the World's Edge Mountains and the lands of men? My people swore an ancient oath of allegiance to yours and we do not forget our oaths...'

Gotrek sounded almost embarrassed. Felix guessed it was because of the oath he had sworn to the elf, and which he had threatened to go back on.

'Gotrek – if there is even a chance he is correct, we must help him. It is a risk we cannot take.'

'Aye, manling, that is the conclusion that I have come to. Although when that matter is settled, there may yet be a reckoning.'

'Great,' murmured Felix so low that he hoped not even the Slayer could hear. 'That will give us something to look forward to.'

'Aye,' said Gotrek. 'It will.'

Felix drew his cloak tighter about him, and studied the mist. It seemed to him that huge menacing shapes moved in it, but he hoped they were merely the outlines of the trees.

When they had returned to the hall, Teclis greeted them. 'I have talked with Murdo. He has agreed to take us to see the Wise One.'

Felix stared at the old wizard. 'You have changed your tune,' he said. 'Yesterday we were the spawn of the Dark Ones. Today you are prepared to help us.'

'Let's just say that there is nothing like drinking with a man – or an elf or a dwarf for that matter – to give you a better idea of their character.'

Felix wondered about that. He was not sure he trusted the old man. On the other hand, it did not look like he had much choice.

'I HATE BOATS almost as much as I hate elves,' said Gotrek as they clambered aboard the barge.

'I am glad you shared that with us,' said Felix looking around to see how Teclis and the boat owners of Crannog Mere were taking the statement. He was pleased that they appeared to be diplomatically ignoring it. 'I suppose you would prefer to walk to where we have to go?'

'Aye, given a choice, manling.'

'The water would be above your head if you tried,' said Murdo, then seeing the Slayer's black look added, 'Mine too.'

He was surprised to see Murdo and twenty warriors clamber aboard behind them. It looked like the men of Crannog Mere were giving them an honour guard. He was less pleased to see that Culum was one of them. He glared at Felix suspiciously as he passed. Surely the man could not be that jealous, he thought, but common sense told him otherwise.

He studied the boat. The construction was strange. It was flat-bottomed with a very shallow draft, not at all like the ships that sailed the Reik, more like a barge in fact. Felix supposed that it was because the waters here were comparatively shallow. They were in a huge marsh after all, not the open sea or a mighty river. Some of the men had taken up long poles and begun to push the ship out into the water away from the island. On the walls, the women watched quietly, a few children waved goodbye. Somewhere in the distance a piper played what sounded like a lament. It was not a cheery farewell.

'Why does everybody look so happy?' Gotrek asked sarcastically.

'No trip through the great swamp is ever taken lightly, Gotrek Gurnisson,' said Murdo. 'There are many strange perils – the swamp fiends, the marsh daemons, the walking dead, all manner of curses lie on this land. Who knows when or if we will see our homes again?'

Felix did not like the look of interest that appeared on the Slayer's face. 'If any of your swamp fiends show up, leave them to me,' he said. 'They will taste my axe.'

'Well spoken,' said Murdo.

Some of the men had taken up bows and spears and stood watchful. They seemed to be more interested in what they could hear than what they could see. Felix supposed it was because the mist limited their vision.

Old Murdo stood on a platform at the front of the ship, guiding them, making the choice whenever they came to a fork in the channel. As they rode along, Felix realised that in addition to everything else, the swamp was a huge labyrinth of murky water and unstable land. He doubted that he would ever be able to find his way back to Crannog Mere even if he wanted to. Perhaps that was part of the plan.

'What is the matter, Felix Jaeger?' Teclis asked. 'You look pensive.'

An open boat where everybody could hear was no place to go voicing his suspicions, Felix knew. Matters were delicate enough between them and the men of Albion. Right now they were dependent on them to get where they wanted to go.

'I was thinking about how we are going to get home after this,' he said. The elf laughed.

'It is good that you look on the bright side of things, Felix Jaeger.'

'What do you mean?'

'Who says we will be going home afterwards?'

'It's always good to have a plan.'

'Let us cross that bridge when we come to it,' said the elf and gave his attention back to the waterways. He looked as if he intended to memorise them. Perhaps he could, Felix thought, and cursed the mist and rain.

'Is it always like this?' he asked Murdo.

'It's no usually so nice,' said Dugal, one of the Crannogmen, with a cheery grin. Felix laughed until he realised that the fellow was not joking.

AT FIRST AS they travelled, Felix only noticed the sound of the water lapping against the side of the boat, and the swishing of the poles through the water. Occasionally a man would grumble something and then fall silent as if realising what he had just done. After a time, he began to notice other noises – the calls of birds, the growls of animals, distant furtive splashings as something big entered the water. The air was dank and damp and smelled of rot. There was something about the swamp that reminded him of an old half-ruined house by the river he and his brother had once gone into as a dare when they were children. There was the same air of abandonment and chill gloom, and a sense that things were stirring just out of sight. Looking back on that long ago adventure, Felix was certain that the worst things in the place had been merely the phantoms produced by their own imagination. He was not so sure here.

Albion was a haunted land. You did not have to be a magician like Teclis or Max Schreiber to know this. You could sense it. Old powers stirred here, strong magic was in the very air you breathed. He thought of Teclis's tale of how the island was integral to the magical fabric of the world, and he could now believe it.

All around he could see the twisted trees rising out of the murky water. They looked trollish and menacing, more like twisted evil giants than plants. Things scuttled along their branches. Once something dropped onto the deck of the boat in front of him, and began to slither across the floor. At first Felix thought it was a snake, but then he realised that it was segmented and insect-like. Culum brought a heavy sandaled foot down on it, and glared at Felix as if he wished the thing were his throat.

Murdo came back to study it. Felix examined the remains with him. It resembled a giant millipede but its jaws were enormous and ant-like. 'Treescuttle,' said the old man. 'Lucky it did not bite you.'

'Poisonous?' Felix asked.

'Aye – saw a man bit once. Before he could be treated his arm had swelled and turned black and bloated with the venom. We had to amputate. Still he died, raving about daemons and fiends. Some of the other shamans and wizards collect the venom, and use it in small quantities to bring on visions. That way lies madness, I think.'

Teclis strode over and looked down on the scuttler's corpse. His eyes were bright with curiosity. 'Interesting,' he said, tipping the thing onto its back with his dagger. 'I have never seen one this big before.'

Felix wondered how he could be so cold about the thing. Just the sight of the creature made him shudder. Its legs were moving despite the fact that its body was crushed in the middle. Teclis produced a small sack from within his robes and carefully sliced open the head, revealing the venom sacs. He took them out on the knifepoint and placed them in the sack. A gesture and a word and the sack was sealed.

'You never know, I may have the chance to sample this at some later date.'

'Decadent beard-clipper,' came a voice from the back of the ship. Felix felt sure that it belonged to Gotrek.

* * *

FELIX SAT AT the back of the ship and listened to the sounds of the twilight. They had taken on a different quality. The bird songs were lower and less musical. Something large and winged sometimes flapped overhead hooting. Glowing bugs emerged from out of the water and swirled around them like lost souls. The shadows lengthened. There was a strange and rather frightening beauty about the whole thing.

'How much further?' he asked Murdo. The old man stood rock-still, showing no fatigue although he had been there most of the day.

'Such impatience, laddie. It will take more than a day's poling to get us to the Wise One, but our journey is almost done for the day. We will tie up near the Haunted Citadel.'

'That sounds inviting,' said Felix sarcastically.

'There's nae need to be afeared – the place has been deserted for a dozen lifetimes.'

'Let's hope so,' said Felix, as a gigantic ominous stone shape rose out of the mists.

CHAPTER FIFTEEN

THE MEN OF Crannog Mere brought the barge coasting to a halt just out of bowshot of the island. They did it by the simple expedient of driving the poles down into the water and tying the ship to them with long hempen ropes. One man apiece stood watch at prow and stern. The others broke out meat and bread and cheese from the knapsacks and began to sip whisky from their flasks, mixing it with what smelled like beer from huge leather skins. Murdo offered Felix some.

'Best take it, the water here is oft undrinkable and haunted by the foul spirits of plague.'

Felix helped himself. It was small beer, malty and watered. He had heard some claim that the process of brewing purified water. He was quite glad to have it anyway. Teclis stood at the prow examining the ruins. The mist had parted slightly and the moons were wanly visible overhead. Just looking at the stonework, Felix could tell that the structure had not been built by men. There was something about the construction he could not quite put his finger on.

'The gates are too low and square,' said Gotrek, as if reading his thoughts. 'The stonework is carved with runes. You can see them near-buried beneath the moss.'

'If you can see in this gloom like a dwarf,' said Felix, although he did not doubt the Slayer was correct.

'This place was not built by my people or yours,' said Gotrek. 'Nor by the elves. I have never seen anything like it.'

'I have,' said Teclis. 'On the coasts of Lustria. One of the abandoned cities of the slann, overgrown by the steaming jungle.'

'I thought the slann naught but a legend,' said Felix.

'You will find that there are truths behind many legends, Felix Jaeger.'

'I was taught they became extinct long ago. Scourged from the earth by the gods, wiped out by fire and flood and plague for their sins.'

'I believe they still live,' said the elf carefully, as if considering his words. 'I believe that in the heart of Lustria there are still cities where they practise their ancient rituals.'

'Why would there be a slann fortress here? We are a long way from Lustria.'

'I do not know. The slann prefer places that are warm. They are a cold-blooded race and chill makes them sluggish. This place is very old – perhaps when it was built the climate was different. Or perhaps there are other reasons.' The elf looked as if he might have some idea of what those reasons were, but did not want to discuss them. 'I would never have guessed we would have found such a thing here in the heart of Albion.'

'You did not find it,' said Murdo. 'We have known about it for centuries.'

'I wish to take a closer look at this,' said the elf.

'In the morning,' said Murdo. 'There will be more light and it will be safer.'

'I do not need light,' said Teclis. 'And I do not fear anything we might find here. And tomorrow we need to start moving again.'

'You propose going ashore then?'

'I do.'

'Then I will accompany you and so will Culum and Dugal. I have sworn to help you, and it would shame me if any harm came tae ye.'

Felix looked at Gotrek knowing what the Slayer was going to say already. 'Anywhere the elf can go, a dwarf can go too.'

Felix shrugged. There was something about this place he did not like, an eeriness that had nothing to do with it being deserted but rather suggested some strange inhuman presence brooding over the ruins. It's just your imagination, he told himself, affected by the hour, the mist and the talk of the pre-human slann.

Part of him knew it was more than that.

THE MEN OF Crannog Mere poled the barge close to the shore, to where a great tree root ran through a broken wall and disappeared beneath the water like the finger of some giant clutching the island's edge. Teclis bounded up from the boat and onto it effortlessly, running along the bark until he had vanished through the walls.

Gotrek went next. His axe bit into the wood easily and he pulled himself up its haft. As cat-footed as the elf, he too vanished silently through the gap in the walls. The luminescent insects swirled around them.

'Some say they are the souls of the dead drowned in the swamp,' said Dugal. 'The fireflies, I mean.'

No one seemed inclined to disagree with him. He sprang up, scrambled onto the branch and away. Murdo and Culum followed. Some more of the tribesmen passed them torches. Felix threw himself upwards and was surprised by how wet, slick and slimy the surface was. He felt his fingers begin to slip, and frantically and ungracefully pulled himself up. The surface of the branch seemed slick and slippery as well. How did Teclis and Gotrek make this look so easy, he wondered, as he reached down for the torch offered to him? Arms wide, torch in one hand, sword in the other, he moved cautiously along the branch and into the ruins of a structure built by an Elder Race.

* * *

'WOULD YE LOOK at that?' said Dugal, swearing softly.

'No wonder men avoid this place,' said Teclis. Felix could see what he meant looking down onto the ruins. There were many smaller buildings within the walls. What might have been streets between them were now canals, or at the very least sluggish channels of brackish water. Huge webs hung between some of the buildings. In some of them dangled bodies the size of large animals or men.

'I would not want to meet the spider that spun those,' said Felix.

'I would,' said Gotrek, running his finger along the blade of his axe meaningfully.

'Seen enough?' Felix asked the elf. He was half hoping that the mage would be discouraged and retreat. He might have guessed he could no more expect common sense from Teclis than he could from Gotrek.

'There is something about this place,' said Teclis. 'I sense power here, like the power at the stone ring. Perhaps we have found another entrance to the Paths of the Old Ones.'

'Excellent,' said Felix sardonically. 'Is that why you wanted to explore this place – you had already sensed something?'

'In part, yes. But I am genuinely interested in this place.'

'I'll bet you are.'

Somewhere in the distance, Felix could have sworn he saw something large moving. He pointed it out to the others. 'It's a spider,' said Teclis. 'A big one. I am starting to understand something about this swamp. These twisted trees and luminous mutated insects are all of a piece. They are being warped by the power buried within these ruins. Its evil influence must contaminate everything for leagues around.'

'That would be why it is unhealthy to drink the waters in these parts then,' said Murdo, as if what the elf said jibed with something he already knew.

'Certainly. Drink nothing and eat nothing found anywhere near here.'

'Thanks for mentioning that,' said Gotrek. 'I was planning a feast.'

'You can never tell with dwarfs,' said Teclis. 'I have heard you feast on blind fish and fungus found in the darkest depths beneath the mountains.'

'And your point is?'

'There's no telling what a dwarf will eat.'

'That's good coming from someone who eats larks' tongues pickled in sheep vomit.'

'In aspic,' said Teclis.

'Same thing, isn't it?'

'Are we going to stand here all night discussing culinary matters or shall we proceed?' asked Felix. The elf and dwarf glared at him. Felix was starting to suspect that in some sick way the two of them enjoyed baiting each other.

They moved along the wall. Ancient slippery stairs carried them down to the water's edge. Murdo tested the depth with a spear, and they found out it came only waist high. The glittering bugs swirled around them.

Felix looked at them. 'You can't seriously intend to walk through this, can you? Who knows what lurks beneath this muck?'

'Only one way to find out, manling,' said Gotrek, splashing down into the water. It came up to about half the height of the dwarf's chest. He carefully held the axe above the water as he proceeded. Teclis followed, but his feet did not descend below the surface. Instead he seemed to walk smoothly along the top of it. His fine footwear did not even appear to be slightly wet.

The others followed Gotrek, holding the torches high so that they would not be extinguished. Briefly Felix considered offering to wait here until they returned. There was something about this stinking, stagnant water that he did not like. He felt that at any second something might emerge from beneath its surface and seize him. He halted for half a heartbeat and then gritted his teeth as he entered the water. Wetness sloshed around him. It was warmer than he expected. The smell of rottenness increased.

Slowed by the water's clammy grip he pushed onwards in the wake of the others. Wonderful, he thought. Surrounded by barbarians and giant mutated insects, up to my waist in slime, in a misty haunted swamp in a land hundreds of leagues from home – how could it get worse?

At that moment he noticed an insect had bitten him and the bite was beginning to swell. I suppose the gods had to give me that answer, he thought. He looked at Teclis with something like hate. It was very annoying that the elf could look so calm and clean and in control while all of the rest of them suffered. He felt an irrational urge to splash him with muck or tug his cloak until he too was pulled down into the slime. And he knew at least one person here would support him if he did it too.

Get a grip, he told himself. You are just tired and scared and focusing all your aggression on the nearest easy target. If events run true to form there will soon be other things to worry about. And he knew that was what really scared him.

Ahead of them, the others had come to something. A fallen tree branch had been run between two buildings over the stagnant water. It looked for all the world like a crude bridge. Was there some sort of intelligence at work here, he wondered? That is all we need – smart giant spiders. Although why a spider would need a bridge eluded him.

'This looks like the work of men,' he heard Teclis say.

'I have heard tales of mutants and other degenerates dwelling deep in the swamp. Perhaps they had sought this shunned place as a refuge.'

'Why did we come here again?' Felix asked, but no one paid any attention to him. They were too busy climbing up onto the log and striding into the opening in the nearby building. Felix decided to follow.

Inside, the structure was massive, hewn from great cyclopean blocks of stone. The stone was unmortared but fitted into place so cunningly that it seemed immovable, an illusion that the creepers and branches and roots running through the gaps did little to dispel. They seemed almost like organic parts of the place, part of a great design, rather than a random intrusion of nature. Felix told himself he was imagining things.

He noticed Gotrek running his massive stubby fingers over the stonework. A closer look showed him the Slayer was tracing more of those odd runic patterns. Once again they were all right angles, and they reminded him of the tattoos of the men of Crannog Mere. What is the significance of those things, he wondered?

Water dripped from the ceiling above them, forming puddles on the floor. Things with glittering eyes retreated before their torches, and Felix was glad that he only got the slightest glimpse of them. He was not fond of things so big that scuttled. They entered a chamber, and saw bones scattered all over the floor. They had been cracked open for the marrow. The Slayer inspected these too. 'Human,' he said. 'Or my mother was a troll.'

Murdo and Dugal nodded agreement. 'And they ate them raw,' said Teclis shuddering slightly. As if that made a great deal of difference, Felix thought. He doubted that the inhabitants of this place found it easy to light fires. A moment later he asked himself: what has become of me? I am speculating on the difficulties of lighting a fire to cook people over. Once there was a time when the mere thought would have had me run screaming from this place. Now noticing my own reaction just leaves me amused and a little scared. He knew then that he had come a long way from home in more ways than one.

'Looks like there's nobody home now,' said Gotrek.

'Maybe they went shopping,' said Felix. The elf lifted his hand and a glow surrounded it, brightening until it was almost the intensity of the sun. The whole chamber was thrown into relief. At first Felix flinched, expecting to see some huge monster about to attack them, but then he noticed the elf's attention had been drawn to a massive stone table set in the middle of the floor. Teclis laid his hand on it, and fire spread, burning the moss and lichen causing it to shrivel and vanish in wisps of strange-smelling smoke. As it did so, Felix noticed that it revealed a pattern on the table top, one that was oddly familiar although for the life of him he could not quite work out why.

'What is it?' he asked. The elf continued to stare at the tabletop.

'Unless I am much mistaken, and I doubt I am, this is a map.'

The lines graved on the stone certainly looked that way. 'What of?' Felix asked.

'The world.'

Felix laughed, realising what had looked familiar. Parts of the pattern resembled the maps his father possessed of the Old World. Only parts, though.

'It can't be. There is no land so close to the coast of Estalia,' he said. 'If there was our mariners would have found it.'

Teclis traced part of the pattern with his finger. It was a ring of islands surrounding a central sea. 'This looks like Ulthuan,' he said, 'but it is not. Quite.'

He moved his hand again. 'This is the coastline of Northern Lustria, but it's in the wrong place. And this is the cold hell of Naggaroth but its relationship to the area that should be Ulthuan is wrong.'

'Maybe the mapmaker did not have eyes quite like ours,' suggested Gotrek. Felix was not entirely sure he was being sarcastic.

'Possibly,' said Teclis. 'Or maybe it was a map of the world in a different time. When the continents were different. It is said the Old Ones shifted the lands and pinned them in new places as part of their great design.'

'Or maybe,' suggested Felix, 'it's a map of the world as it was intended to be.'

'That, Felix Jaeger, is a terrifying thought,' said Teclis.

'Why?'

'Because perhaps someone still intends to make it so?'

Felix looked at the elf, not quite knowing how to respond. Teclis seemed lost in thought.

'Perhaps the Old Ones' plans were never completed. Perhaps they were interrupted. Perhaps the opening of the paths is a sign that other things have reactivated.'

'That is insane,' said Felix, unable to contain his thoughts.

'Is it, Felix Jaeger? We are dealing with the work of beings as far beyond you and I as we are above an insect. How would we qualify to judge what is sane or not for them? We might as well judge the sanity of gods.'

'The Chaos Gods are insane,' said Gotrek.

'Perhaps not from their point of view, Gotrek Gurnisson.'

'Only an elf could say something like that.'

'Perhaps because we are not as rigid in our thinking as dwarfs.'

'Or your morals.'

'Only an elf and a dwarf would argue about such things while they discussed the end of the world,' said Felix. Both of them looked at him dangerously. 'If the continents are intended to shift like carpets, our people and our cities will be so much dust.'

'If,' said Gotrek. 'So far all we have heard are some long-winded speculations from a pointy-eared, tree-loving, spellsinging...'

'If there is even the possibility he is correct, something must be done,' said Felix quickly before the argument could erupt in its full glory. 'The earth would shake, the mountains would rain fire, foul warpstone dust would fall from the skies...'

Even as he said the words, Felix realised that he was describing events from the legendary age before Sigmar and the rise of the Empire. He could see that the thought had struck the elf too. 'Perhaps all of this has happened before,' said Teclis. 'During the Dawn Ages, before even the War of the Beard, when elf and dwarf were allies against a common foe.'

'It was not the dwarfs who betrayed their sworn oaths,' said Gotrek testily.

'Quite,' said the elf. 'But putting that predictable interruption to one side for a moment, I believe Felix Jaeger is right. If there is even the remotest possibility of something like this happening, then our ancient animosities must be put aside... until a better time, for I know how unlikely it is that a dwarf will ever lay down a grudge.'

'It seems to me that you are engaging in a mighty load of speculation on the basis of one old map. Who says this has anything to do with the Old Ones and their works?' asked Murdo. There was something odd in the old man's manner, Felix thought. He wondered if the others had noticed this.

'All of Albion is connected with them,' said Teclis. 'It is the nexus of their work. It formed some mighty part in their great scheme of things, no less so than Ulthuan. This fortress is part of some greater design, I am sure of it.'

Murdo looked troubled, as if the elf was touching on matters that he felt were best left unspoken.

How much does Murdo really know about such things, Felix wondered? He is more familiar with these ancient secrets than he lets on.

'Perhaps we should be getting back now,' said Felix.

'Not yet,' said the mage. 'We are close to the mouth of another portal. I can sense it. We must investigate it before we leave. We must get closer to the heart of this structure.'

'I was afraid you were going to say something like that,' said Felix. The elf laughed as if he were joking.

The mists closed in as they left the hall. Somehow they were coming through the walls. Luminescent insects drifted among them. Their buzzing whines keened in Felix's ears. Their bites blotched his skin. He noticed that not one of them ever seemed to close with the elf, even though the others were all troubled by them. Infuriating, Felix thought. The elf led them deeper into the ancient structure, through a labyrinth of stonework that made Felix's head spin. Sometimes they came to dead ends and were forced to retrace their steps. At others, the passageways would take ninety-degree turns for no foreseeable reason. The elf did not seem discouraged. He merely nodded his head, as if this confirmed something.

He strode over to Gotrek, who was far more at home in such places than he could ever be.

'Can you find your way out of here?' he asked in a whisper.

'Aye, manling, no dwarf ever got lost in such a simple maze as this. I could find my way out blindfolded if need be.'

'I don't think that will be necessary. Impressive as it would be.'

'There is something odd about this place.'

'What?'

'This maze is laid out seemingly without rhyme or reason. Look to your left and you will see a dead end. To the right if we went that way, I have no doubt that once that corridor turns it too would reach a dead end.'

'Why are you so certain?'

'There is a pattern here. It's obvious.'

'Not to me,' said Felix.

'You are not a dwarf brought up in the endless corridors of Karaz-a-Karak.'

'True. What is this pattern you see?'

'Unless I miss my guess, it is the same as one of the ones we have seen on the stones in the Paths of the Old Ones, and inscribed on the rock walls of the barrow in Sylvania, and on the walls of this place. Similar even to the ones tattooed on the faces of our friends.'

'You can remember all of these?' said Felix, amazed.

'Dwarfs have a good memory for more things than grudges.' Felix thought about this and decided that it was most likely true. He had never known the Slayer to lie. But if it were, then somehow this was all part of a vast puzzle, one that Felix did not quite understand. And if the elf was right, he most likely never would. His mind was not equipped to grasp what creatures that were close to gods might have been about when creating such a thing.

The maze continued until they found themselves standing in a huge chamber, gazing down into a vast pit. The ceiling had collapsed above and tons of rock had fallen downward, crushing whatever was below. Massive webs formed a new roof overhead and blocked out part of the moonlight. Rain dripped through and the wet droplets made Felix shiver.

'We are in the centre of this place. The entrance to the paths is directly below us,' said Teclis.

Gotrek's bitter mad laughter rang out. 'Then you will go no further. Give me a hundred dwarfish miners and a month and we might get through those rocks. Might. Unless you can use magic there is no way through.'

'The stones here are still partially protected by runework,' said Teclis. 'With ten mages and ten days we might clear this, but now is not the time.'

'So what now?' Felix asked.

'We go back and seek another way to our goal,' said Teclis, looking at Gotrek as if daring him to say something.

The dwarf stiffened and glanced around, head cocked as if listening. His stance bespoke the utmost wariness and preparation to do violence.

'Something is approaching,' said Gotrek, raising his axe. 'And I doubt it's friendly.'

CHAPTER SIXTEEN

'What is it?' Felix asked.

'Nothing natural,' said the Slayer. The humans had already readied their weapons. Dugal and Murdo stood with spears raised. Culum had produced a huge hammer with a stone head. Teclis had his hand on his sword. Quicksilver runes flowed along the blade.

The things emerging from the other entrances were not entirely spider-like. They pranced along the edge of the great pit on only six long spidery legs for one thing – it was funny how you could notice such details at a time like this, Felix thought – and they had faces that looked sinisterly human mounted high on their abdomens. Their eyes burned with an intelligence that no spider had ever possessed. Luminous fungus blotched their sides. A wild ululating wail emerged from their mouths. There were perhaps a dozen of them. Felix noticed that they had two smaller manipulative arms at the front of their bodies. Perhaps they were the ones who had crunched the bones after all. Several of them scuttled up and along the walls, magically attached. Behind the spiders came a host of human mutants. Twisted beings marked by the stigmata of Chaos who looked on the spiders with a mixture of fear and reverence emerged from every entrance to the huge hall. They were armed with spears and slings and clubs.

'Perhaps we should leave here,' said Felix. Gotrek charged along the pit edge towards the leading spider thing. Teclis raised his arms and sent a wave of golden fire lancing towards the humans. A few cast spears which ignited as they arced towards him, shrivelling to black ash in flight. Screams echoed around the ancient walls as flesh melted and ran like wax. Through it all, the spiders kept coming. When the magical flames touched them the blotched patterns on their sides blazed brighter and they seemed to move faster. Are they immune to spells, Felix wondered?

Teclis strode into the air, taking up a position above the centre of the great pit, and gestured. Lightning lashed from his hands, whipping the stone. Sparks arced up from the puddles of water. Felix saw a reptile-faced mutant flung into the air on a pillar of lightning. The spiders ignored it and kept on coming.

'They are ancient guardian daemons,' shouted Murdo. 'Save your spells.'

Gotrek meanwhile had met the leading spider. His axe thunked into its armoured side. Instead of cleaving straight through as it normally would, it bit deep into the chitin and stuck. Felix shuddered to think at how resistant the creatures must be to withstand the appalling force of the Slayer's blows. Was it possible that their end was in sight, here in this god-forsaken pesthole in the backwaters of Albion?

He had no more time for such thoughts. A flicker of movement caught from the corner of his eye caused him to duck. A slingstone shattered against the rock walls behind him. He cursed and kept moving, looking for cover, wondering if he dared ditch the torch that made him such an obvious target. There was enough light here to see by but he had to get back through the stone corridors. If any of the others were present there would be no problem but if they were separated…

Above him he saw a huge daemon spider moving along the walls. A spray of webbing spurted from its bulbous rear and hit the ground near Felix. He leapt back to avoid the sticky stuff and saw another spider closing the ground between them with appalling speed. It sprang down from the wall and landed amid the men of Albion, scattering them. With unerring instinct it came straight at Felix.

'Do not let them take you alive!' shouted Murdo. 'They will implant their eggs within you, make you into one of them.'

Now that is a disgusting idea, thought Felix, whirling the torch so that it flared brighter. As the creature neared him, he struck it in the face with his torch, hoping to blind it. Moments later his blade bit into the tough chitin of its leg. He aimed for the weakest point, shearing through the joint. The thing squealed with pain as its leg separated. Black stuff oozed from the wound, sealing it. Another leg flicked forward. It hit Felix with the force of a hammer blow, knocking him onto his back. The torch left his numbed fingers. He only just managed to keep his grip on his sword.

He rolled aside as the thing moved its bulk above him, and brought its foreleg down again. He could see there were hooks on it that could slash skin to the bone. He barely managed to evade it, but it snagged his cloak pinning him to the ground. Using his left hand, Felix desperately attempted to free the clasp of the cloak, while stabbing upward with his sword. The blade pierced the thing's underbelly, and dark stuff dropped from the wounds. It burned where it touched his skin. Perhaps that was not such a good idea, he thought, noticing the legs of the approaching mutants as they came ever closer.

The stench was near overpowering, of rot and mould and something old and fusty, mingled with a smell like rotten eggs and curdled milk. It made him want to gag. Instead he gritted his teeth and grabbed the hilt with both hands, twisted the sword, and proceeded to saw into the wound. The burning blood boiled over his hands. The spider-thing screamed louder. Felix felt like joining in, but did not.

Lightning flashed and flames danced. Whirlwinds of golden fire swept across the room. Felix found himself being dragged along beneath the spider as it headed up the wall once more. He tucked his head into his chest to avoid having it bumping on the stone. The strain made his neck ache and the muscles bulge until they felt like taut wire beneath his skin. Slowly his blade was dragged from the wound. He glanced down and saw that most of the mutants were in retreat, unable to cope with the blazing energies that the elf wizard sent ravening across the chamber. Felix pulled his blade clear and dropped to the floor. Overhead the thing he had wounded seemed to be deflating like a punctured sac of bile as it limped and scurried upwards towards the shadows.

Elsewhere things were not going well for his party. Gotrek had overcome his beast by the simple expedient of chopping it to pieces. No matter how tough the spiders were, they were not tough enough to withstand that terrible axe for long. However, even as Felix watched, three more of the creatures began to surround the Slayer, spurting sticky web stuff from their abdomens that was slowing the dwarf down. Two more pressed on the men of Crannog Mere. If there were any more to be dealt with, they were hidden from view.

Felix raced over towards Gotrek. A flying leap took him onto the back of the spider. His fingers caught on the fine mesh of hair that covered its back and he pulled himself up. The thing roared as it realised what he was about. It tried to reach back with its small forearms to get him but they were not long enough, and its other legs were not positioned to enable it to dislodge him. He gritted his teeth and brought his sword down onto the back of the thing's humanoid face. His fingers were numb now from the poison that had spilled on them earlier, and he was desperate to do damage before they froze completely.

As the blade bit home, the face screamed, a sound oddly like a human child. The daemon spider began to buck and shake itself from side to side, hoping to throw its burden clear. Felix held grimly on and kept stabbing away, and the thing's struggles eventually grew weaker and weaker. As the spider jigged backwards and forwards he caught glimpses of the others.

Culum had partially pulped one of the spiders with his massive hammer and Murdo was jabbing his spear into its vulnerable eyes. Dugal, though, shrieked as he was lifted up by a set of fiendish mandibles. The spider carrying him backed away towards the exit. Felix wanted to help but there was nothing he could do.

A wave of fire descended from the elf wizard and engulfed Gotrek. What treachery was this, Felix wondered? Was Teclis mad to strike down their mightiest warrior in the midst of this desperate affray? Or had he been in league with these foul daemons all along? Had his mind been poisoned by some evil magic? Felix felt a wave of despair pass through his numbed and pain-wracked frame. If the elf was against them all hope was gone.

Heartbeats later, though, the method behind the wizard's madness became clear. The flames flickered around Gotrek shrivelling away the sticky webs that threatened to immobilise him. A second later, a mighty blow from the axe chopped through the thorax of one of the creatures. Both halves kept moving for a moment before collapsing to the floor. The struggles of the thing beneath Felix were subsiding, which was just as well since his numbed fingers were finding it increasingly difficult to maintain their grip. He stabbed one last time for good measure and then let go, rolling to absorb the impact as he hit the floor.

Swiftly he pulled himself to his feet and went to aid Dugal. Thinking he spied a weakness in the things, he aimed at the place where the leg merged with body and the armour seemed less substantial. It was a difficult strike to place and his first blow went awry. His second bit home and he was rewarded. The blade found a weak spot in the armour and slid home easily. Once more he twisted it. The thing bucked and writhed in agony, dropping Dugal. A moment later, Culum and Murdo were on it hammering and stabbing with a vengeance. It swiftly retreated backwards into the gloom, leaving them alone to watch Gotrek dismember his foe.

Felix inspected Dugal. The screaming had stopped. He lay still and cold as a corpse. Felix could see there were punctures in his tunic. He took out his knife and cut it away. The flesh beneath was bruised and bled slowly where the mandibles had penetrated flesh. He could tell by the look of horror in the man's eyes that he was still conscious and aware of what was happening to him.

Murdo dropped to his haunches beside Dugal. His ran his hands over the wound and muttered an incantation. A light passed from his tattooed fingers to the wound. Dugal's eyes closed and his breathing became even shallower. The old man shook his head.

Teclis drifted down to earth like a falling leaf and knelt beside Murdo. 'A fine casting. There's not much more I can do at the moment – without the right herbs or access to an alchemical laboratory. All I can do is slow the spread of the poison.'

'It might be enough,' said Murdo. 'If we can get him to the Oracle in time. There is no one quite as skilled at healing as she.'

A slightly sullen expression passed over the elf's face. Surely he was not so vain, Felix thought. He held up his own hands and looked at them, wondering if there was any chance that the bile of the spider thing could have poisoned him too. They were dyed bluish and hurt very badly.

The elf looked at them, and spoke a word. A spark passed from his hand to Felix's. The blue colouring hardened, cracked and flaked away, taking what looked like the top layer of skin with it. Felix's hands now looked pinkish and raw, and felt even more painful, like a graze swabbed with alcohol. Liquid fire coursed through the veins on the back of his hands. The tendons jumped and spasmed and were still.

'If there was any poison, it is cleansed now, Felix Jaeger,' said the elf.

'Thanks, I think,' said Felix. His hands still stung and it was painful for him to hold a sword. Still if the alternative was death, this was preferable.

'There is nothing here for us now,' said Teclis, glancing backwards into the pit. 'We'd best be going. Quickly.'

Gotrek looked wistfully after the spiders, and Felix could tell he was considering hunting them down. At this point, it was not something he felt like doing. Eventually, though, the dwarf shook his head and turned to follow them. Culum carried Dugal as easily as a baby. His expression managed to tell Felix that somehow this was all his fault.

THEY EMERGED INTO the moonlight. It gleamed in the dark oily waters covering the semi-sunken structures. The remaining tribesmen greeted them worriedly.

'We wondered if the daemons had taken you,' said a short squat man even more tattooed than the others. 'I was going to come looking for you.'

'No need, Logi,' said Murdo gently. 'We're back.'

'Dugal disnae look well,' said Logi.

'Bitten by one of the lurkers within.'

'That isnae good.'

'No.'

Felix saw that the tribesmen were all staring hard at him, as if they too blamed him for what had happened to their kinsman. It took him a few fraught seconds to realise that they were actually looking past him at the elf. The wizard gave no sign of either noticing or caring, although he could not have been unaware of the hostile crowd. Felix envied him his self-possession, or perhaps it was simply arrogance.

Without saying a word, the elf moved over to Dugal, who now lay on the soaking wooden boards at the foot of the barge. He cocked his head to one side as if considering something, and then began to slowly chant what sounded like a dirge. At first nothing happened, then Felix noticed that the beams of the greater moon all appeared to be drawn to his staff. Slowly it grew brighter with a gentle radiance. He noticed that over and over again the elf invoked the name of Lileath, doubtless some god or goddess of his pantheon. The others watched, hands on weapons, not quite sure what was happening. Despite the stinging in his hands, Felix did the same. He noticed that his skin was starting to tingle, and felt the hair stand on the nape of his neck. He sensed strange presences, hovering just outside the line of his vision, but whenever he turned his head, he could see nothing, and merely got the maddening feeling that whatever it was, it was still there, just out of sight.

Eventually a web of light spun itself out from the elvish staff. Long silver threads, seemingly woven from moonbeams, unravelled away from it, as from a spindle. They leapt from the staff to Dugal's twitching, moaning form, and entwined it, until he shimmered like the moon reflected on water, then slowly they began to fade, leaving him seemingly unchanged. Felix wondered if he was the only one who had noticed that the man's chest had ceased to rise or fall. He did not have long to wait.

'You've killed him,' said Culum, lifting his hammer menacingly.

The elf shook his head. The big man reached down and touched Dugal's chest. 'There is no heartbeat,' he said.

'Wait,' said Teclis. An expression of baffled concentration clouded Culum's features. The silence deepened as the long moment dragged on.

'I felt a heartbeat,' said Culum. 'But now it is gone.'

'Keep waiting.' Felix counted thirty more of his own quickening heartbeats before Culum nodded again.

'It's a spell of stasis,' Teclis said. 'I have slowed down his life functions – breathing, heartbeat, everything. For him time passes at a fraction of the speed as the rest of us. The spread of the poison has been slowed, and the time before death increased.'

'His pain has been somewhat decreased as well,' the elf added, almost as an afterthought.

'But he will still die,' said Murdo softly.

'Unless this Oracle of yours can do something for him, yes,' said Teclis.

'Then we had best make speed.'

'You wish to go now?'

'In this light and fog? I do not see how.'

'If you need light, I can give it to you,' said Teclis.

Murdo nodded. A huge flash lit the night. For a moment, Felix wondered if Mannsleib had come to earth and settled on the end of the elf's staff, then he saw it was only the chilly glow of another spell. He flexed his fingers, noticing that the pain was already starting to fade, and the healing had begun at what seemed an unnatural rate.

The tribesmen settled down at their poles and pushed the boat on through the misty channels. From the ancient, haunted city behind them came the sound of drumming. Felix wondered what it meant, and feared that it boded no good whatsoever.

'Perhaps we will be pursued,' he said.

'If it's by those altered things, we have nothing to fear,' grated Gotrek.

'I suspect there are worse things waiting in this swamp,' said Felix. The Slayer looked unusually thoughtful. He sniffed the sour air and then ran his thick fingers through the massive crest of dyed hair.

'Aye, manling, I think you might be right,' he said almost cheerfully. For Felix, that was the worst portent of all.

CHAPTER SEVENTEEN

DAWN CAME SLOWLY. The wan sunlight had a hazy quality as it shone through the thinning mist. Felix sat slumped in the back of the boat, listening to the slosh of water against bow and pole and the chirruping of the early morning birds. Behind them the drums were fading, but were still evident. To Felix they sounded like the heartbeat of the great monster that was the swamp.

He ran his fingers through his stubble and rubbed his reddened eyes. He had slept fitfully at best on the hard wet boards of the boat, all too aware that nearby Dugal lay dying. Even though the man's silence was eerie, he still cast a pall over the entire crew. They all knew how close he was to death too, and it was affecting them. Probably more than it does me, Felix thought. After all, he is virtually a stranger to me, they grew up with him.

He shook his head and offered up a prayer to Shallya. Even though he no longer believed in her mercy, it seemed old habits died hard. How often have I done this now, Felix wondered. How often have I sat and watched a not-quite-stranger die? It felt like a hundred times. He felt like he was a thousand years old. He felt like he was being worn thin by the constant friction of events. He asked himself, if he had known it would be like this on that drunken night, would he have still sworn to follow Gotrek? Sadly, he knew the answer was yes.

Dugal might be dying, but Felix was still very much among the living, and keenly aware of it. Even this sour, reeking air tasted sweeter and he could see hints of the strange beauty amid the swamplands. Monstrous flowers blossomed on long creepers hanging from the branches overhead. Huge lilies floated on massive pads in the channels. Even the weeds that clogged the waterway and impeded their passage gave forth an odd narcotic perfume.

Ahead on the prow, Teclis stood, immobile as the figurehead of a sailing ship. His strange chiselled features held no human expression, and he showed no more sign of weariness than a wooden carving. As the dawn light filtered through the canopy, he had let his spell dim, and now simply watched as Murdo guided the ship with soft commands, telling the men with the poles to go left or right as their route dictated.

There was nothing about the elf's physical appearance to suggest his great age. He looked as fit and fair as a youth of eighteen summers. And yet there was something there that spoke of his years; Felix could not quite tell what. Perhaps it was the controlled expression of his face. Perhaps the aura of wisdom he projected or perhaps, Felix thought, it is simply his imagination.

Gotrek slumped with his back to the wood of the hull, as immobile as the elf, and as watchful. Whatever he had sensed the night before had not shown up, but that had not reduced his wariness. Rather, it seemed to have increased it. His coarse rough-hewn features might have belonged to some primordial statue. He looked aged and powerful as some warrior god from the morning of the world. The axe looked older still. What stories might it not be able to tell if it had a voice, Felix wondered?

He rose slowly and walked the length of the ship, carefully avoiding the men sprawled in sleep. The men of Crannog

Mere had taken watches and rested in shifts. They seemed determined to keep the barge moving until they reached their final destination, and perhaps succoured their comrade. Felix could almost feel Culum's eyes boring into his back. It was starting to get on his nerves. He felt like saying, 'All I did was talk to her', but he knew that it would not help. He had met Culum's type before. The big man had made up his mind to dislike him, and nothing Felix could say would change his mind.

Well, he thought, if there's going to be violence between us, then there will be violence. There was nothing he could do about it at the moment. Still, in that instant, he could not help envying the elf his magical powers.

TECLIS STOOD IN the prow and drank in everything he saw. He knew he might never pass this way again, and he wanted to fix it in his memory. It was rare these days for him to experience a completely novel situation, and he wanted to milk it for everything it was worth.

He looked at the slippery branches dripping with creepers and large evil-looking blooms. His eyes were keen enough to pick out the lurking millipedes and the noxious spiders as well as the glittering jewel-eyed dragonflies resting on the leaves. He could see the shadow and silver shapes of the fish moving in the murky mere. He could smell at least seven different kinds of narcotic bloom, and vowed that if he got the chance he would come back here, and sample and catalogue them. If he lived, there would be plenty of time.

He could feel the resentful gaze of the humans on him, and it amused him. He felt like an adult surrounded by a pack of angry children. They might bristle and look surly but there was nothing they could do to hurt him. He fought to keep a smile off his face. He knew he was starting to behave like all the elves he so despised, in the way they looked down on all the younger races. How easily it crept up on you, he thought.

Perhaps it was merely a response to the events of the night before. He had been shocked to encounter creatures so resistant to his magic. They had obviously been intended to be

so. Doubtless guardians left by the Old Ones to deal with
any intruders in their temple-fortress. It had been a long
time since Teclis had encountered anything against which
his magic could not protect him, and it had left him feeling
more unbalanced than he would have believed.

Still, in a way, he welcomed it. There had been a thrill to
that combat he had not experienced in some time, a sense
of having laid his life on the line that had become rare in his
life. It almost made him feel young again. Almost.

He considered the nature of last night's foe. His theory
was not quite pure speculation on his part. Certain hidden
books had hinted that the Old Ones had left guardians, but
those things had been tainted by Chaos. Was it possible that
millennia of exposure to the energies seeping through the
portal beneath the tower could have changed them? Yes, he
supposed it was. No matter how resistant the Old Ones had
made their creations, they were no less likely than the paths
to be tainted. Chaos warped living things far more easily
than it warped unliving matter. He supposed the same thing
might happen to elves, given time. After all, Ulthuan had a
heavier density of magical portals, gates and ways than
almost any other place on the planet, as well as a higher
concentration of magical energy.

Perhaps, he thought, the change has already happened.
Perhaps the split between the dark elves and his own people
was rooted in a simple physical cause. Or perhaps, his own
people had been changed as well. Perhaps over the millennia they had altered too. Certainly in some ways this was the
case. Fewer elves were born now. Were there other changes?
Only Malekith and his dreadful mother would be in a position to know for certain, and somehow he doubted he
would ever get the truth from them, even if they met somewhere other than on a battlefield.

Not for the first time, he felt the temptation of the darker
side of his nature tug him. Perhaps he could arrange such a
visit sometime. Perhaps knowledge might be exchanged. He
almost laughed at his own folly. The only knowledge he
would ever be able to extract from a visit to Naggaroth
would be the intimate knowledge of pain inflicted on him

by the dark elf torturers. No, that was a path that was closed for all time.

He could feel the dwarf's eyes boring into his back. He considered Gotrek Gurnisson. There was an enigma there that would need solving some day. The axe he bore was a weapon of awesome power, and it had changed the dwarf in many ways. The signs written all over his aura had become far clearer last night during the battle when dwarf and weapon had seemed to become almost as one. Power had flowed both ways during that conflict, he was certain, although the manner in which it had done so had baffled even him. The knowledge of those ancient dwarven rune-smiths had been enormous. The Old Ones had revealed mysteries to them they had kept even from the elves. Oh, for a year to study that weapon. He smiled. That was an eventuality as likely as him gaining knowledge from the Witch King of the dark elves, and only marginally less dangerous.

Still, the dwarf would make a mighty ally in whatever trials lay ahead. The encounter with the spider daemons had shown Teclis that there were areas where an axe might come in handy. Nor was the human, Felix Jaeger, to be discounted. The man was brave and resourceful. Perhaps the gods had sent them to aid him.

He considered the dying man, for so Teclis thought of him. Unless this Oracle was skilled beyond all reason, Dugal's fate was already sealed. All Teclis had done was delay it, and that had been as much a matter of political expediency as charity. He had needed to be seen to help the man, otherwise the blame for his fate could quite easily have fallen on Teclis and he still needed the men of Crannog Mere as allies, at least for the present. And it would not do any harm for the tribesmen to think that the fate of their companion was linked to the wizard's under the present strained circumstances.

Of course, should Dugal die, that would change. It was a hurdle he would leap when he came to it. He did not wish Dugal or the tribesmen any harm, but if it came to a choice between survival for himself and Ulthuan, or their lives, then there was no choice at all. Teclis knew he would sacrifice all of those present, including himself, and ten thousand times more if need be to preserve the kingdom of the elves.

He could almost feel the dwarf's cold stern eye judging him. Nonsense, he told himself, you are merely projecting your own doubts outwards. Under the circumstances Gotrek Gurnisson would make the same choices as you. Not that it mattered what the dwarf thought anyway. At the present moment, he was simply another tool to be used to achieve Teclis's ends.

The thought amused him. Perhaps the dwarfs are right to judge us as they do. He considered this for a moment and saw that in this he was the dwarf's superior. No dwarf would ever admit that an elf might be right about such a thing. They were stern, inflexible, judgemental and unforgiving, always had been and always would be.

Still, even that had its uses.

FELIX LOOKED UP at the open sky. At last the swamp was behind them, and the rains had ceased. Even the midge and mosquito bites seemed momentarily less troubling. Ahead of them now lay a range of low barren foothills, rising to huge snow-capped peaks. Down the mountain's flanks ran hundreds of small rivers and streams, transporting the near-constant rains and depositing them in the swamp. Some spears of sunlight had managed to break through the leaden clouds and pierce the gloom. This land had a cruel beauty, he thought, but a beauty nonetheless.

The men of Crannog Mere had fallen silent. They seemed to be nervous now, as if leaving the swamp had the opposite effect on Felix as it had on them. They looked around shiftily like city dwellers suddenly deposited in the middle of a wood. Felix realised that they were leaving the lands they knew for parts more or less unknown, and it was affecting them. Felix had made such transitions so many times now himself that often he barely noticed them. Had it only been days ago he had walked the snow-covered forests of Sylvania? Somehow it seemed much longer. It was amazing how swiftly the mind could accept changes in circumstance when it had to.

He studied his companions. The Slayer looked grim and stolid as ever. Teclis looked quite genuinely pleased to see the sun. He stretched his arms almost in greeting. Murdo looked less nervous than the others, like a man making a journey he had done many times before. Culum simply glared at Felix as if quietly hating him just for being there. Suddenly the day seemed less bright, and the wind a fraction more chill.

They poled the barge across the open lake towards the shore. Felix could see the grey rocks of the bottom. Some were sharp as sword blades and would gut the boat if they hit them. Murdo guided them warily with short terse commands. Ahead of them the mountains loomed. Overhead a single huge eagle stretched its wings to catch the breeze, lazily scanning the land below for prey.

What other things might there be out there, Felix wondered, doing the same? Old powerful magic and Chaos had tainted this land. Surely they had not seen the last of monsters.

THEY BEACHED THE boat, dragged it ashore and into the long grass and rushes where it might be at least partially concealed. Half the men were detailed to watch it. The others would accompany them to the Oracle's cave. Felix was not thrilled to note that Culum would be one of their escorts. Still, at least he seemed to have his hands full carrying the unconscious Dugal.

'We follow the stream to its source,' Murdo said. 'If you get separated from us, find it and follow it. Downhill, it will bring you back to the lake and the boat. Uphill, it will lead eventually to the Oracle's home. Doubtless she will find you, if she wants to.'

The others laughed nervously, making Felix wonder about the role that this Oracle played in the society of Albion. The men's attitude seemed equal parts reverence and fear. He supposed it was hardly surprising if she was a witch. An image of the old hags in the fairy tales of his youth sprang to mind, of bubbling cauldrons and feasts on unhallowed flesh. Try as he might, he could not force it from his mind.

'Keep your eyes peeled for orcs,' said Murdo.

'Orcs?' Felix asked.

'Aye, many have been the sightings of greenskins in these hills in the past few months. Something has stirred them up. And stirred them up badly.'

As ever he looked as if he knew more than he was saying. What secrets are you hiding, Murdo, Felix wondered?

CHAPTER EIGHTEEN

FELIX BREATHED HARD as he walked, and cursed the constant rain. The land sloped upwards steeply. The path was slippery with scree. They followed the curve of the river, and all they saw for many long hours were wild long-horned sheep and some goats. The men of Crannog Mere marched stolidly along, wary now as only men out of their element could be. Gotrek seemed almost happy to be back amid barren hills and distant mountains. The chill breeze did not daunt him, and not even the return of the constant rain dampened his spirits. Teclis seemed preoccupied, concentrating on something far removed from their surroundings. As Felix approached him, he shivered as he noticed that the rain did not touch the elf's garments. Instead, repelled by some invisible shield, it halted a finger's breadth away. Close up it lent the elf a shimmering aura that added to his unearthly appearance.

'What is it?' Felix asked him, wondering if it was wise to interrupt the sorcerer while he concentrated.

'There are currents of magic passing through these hills, deep and old and tainted. Chaos has touched this land deeply, not just on the surface.'

'I have seen much worse,' said Felix, thinking of the lands through which he and Gotrek had once ventured in their search for the lost city of Karag Dum. The elf looked at him and cocked an eyebrow disbelievingly. 'The northern Chaos Wastes,' he added.

'You've been there? And you returned untainted. That is an impressive feat, Felix Jaeger.'

'Not one I would care to repeat,' Felix said. He was sure the dwarf would not thank him for sharing the tale of the voyage of the airship *Spirit of Grungni* with an elf, so he resisted the urge to tell it. Instead he said, 'You say these lands are tainted – in what way? What can we expect to encounter?'

'I think the contamination here runs deep. For some reason Albion has attracted a great deal of dark magical energy. I have heard tales that the Ogham Rings, the great stone circles, attract it and somehow render it harmless. Perhaps that was once true, but I suspect that now they are malfunctioning. All spells eventually wear out, all devices eventually reach the end of their usefulness. Perhaps they still attract the dark magic, but their capacity to store it or purify it has been reduced or lost. Perhaps it has something to do with the opening of the Paths of the Old Ones. Perhaps it is all part of the same great pattern. I do not know. I do know that there is a stone ring nearby and it is bending the flow of magic here, and altering the weather. Perhaps that accounts for the rains. The rains certainly account for why so much of these hills are barren.'

'How so? Everybody knows that rain is needed to make crops grow.'

Teclis shrugged. 'In most cases that is true. But flooding does not help corn grow.'

'It's difficult to flood a hill,' said Felix. 'At least in the way you mean. The water runs downslope. It does not lie.'

'Aye, and if it's heavy enough, it carries the topsoil with it, leaving only exposed rock on which only moss and lichen can grow.'

Looking around them, Felix could see that what the elf had said was true. Near the fast-flowing river there was only stone and rock, nothing grew save for a few hardy plants rooted in patches of soil trapped between boulders. Only away from the river did the green return. Felix considered this.

Some of his natural history professors maintained that the world was shaped by elemental forces – wind and rain and volcanoes and ice – that the lands were as they were because of the way they interacted. Others, and the priests, claimed the world was as it was because the gods had made it that way. What Teclis had said about the Old Ones sculpting continents tended to support that theory. What he said about the topsoil supported the first. Was it possible both were true? Or perhaps the elements were merely the tools the gods had used.

No, that could not be right. It would take centuries, if not millennia, for a river to wear away the bones of mountains. But perhaps the Old Ones' perception of time was different from ours, perhaps for them centuries were but an eyeblink.

'You look confused, Felix Jaeger. What are you thinking about?'

Felix told the elf.

'Perhaps the Old Ones used the elements as you think, but our legends tell us otherwise. They had no need to wait for millennia for erosion and geological forces to do their work. They could cut through tectonic plates with blades of cosmic fire, and level mountains with their spells. And this they did. They sculpted continents the way I might sculpt a statue.'

Felix was not quite willing to give up on his idea yet. 'You speak as if they were artists seeking to create a finished work of art. What if they were more like gardeners? Perhaps they pruned a branch here, irrigated an area there. Planted seeds that would not reach their final form for ages. Perhaps they did not shape the continents exactly to their design. Perhaps they merely put certain forces in motion, knowing that they would eventually one day lead to a certain end.'

Felix expected mockery, but instead the elf looked thoughtful. 'That is an original thought, Felix Jaeger, and one I had not considered. Nor has any elf that I know of. What you say may be correct or not, but you have given me something to think about.'

'I am glad to have been of some service to one of the Elder Race,' said Felix sardonically. 'Let me know when you have finished your deliberations.'

'You may not be alive then, Felix Jaeger. I may not reach any conclusions for a hundred years, if then.'

Felix was a little shocked by the sudden yawning gulf that had opened in the conversation and the glimpse it gave him of his own mortality. In the Empire few men reached the age of sixty. A man of fifty was considered old. Felix might be long in his grave while this youthful-seeming creature still thought upon his words. It sparked a certain resentment in him.

'If you are still alive then. We might all be dead within days.'

THE SLOPE STEEPENED. The going got tougher. They were on a mountain trail now and the rain-slicked gradient was becoming dangerous. Felix breathed in gasps and sweat started to mingle with the rain soaking his clothing.

He looked around. The peaks loomed larger now, and the clouds seemed thicker. Behind them the swamp was a low grim mass of trees and water. He thought he could see the huge stone structure of the Haunted Citadel emerging from the gloom, but it might just have been his imagination.

The land around them now looked gloomier, the rain had leeched even its drab colours. The waters of the river rushed by louder now, boiling white in places where they clashed against rocks and passed through narrow channels. In these last few dying hours of daylight, they had passed a succession of rushing falls whose spray had wet their faces, noticeable even in the rain. Here and there massive rocks far higher than a man flanked the path like sentinels. Sometimes Felix thought they bore some resemblance to ancient statues, their outlines blurred by time, and he was reluctant to put this down entirely to his imaginings.

The men of Crannog Mere all huffed and puffed worse than he. They were not mountain men, and this constant uphill walking was tiring them. Felix knew what a strain it could be to the calves and thighs when you were not used to it. He had walked in the World's Edge Mountains often enough to be familiar with it.

It was getting colder and wetter by the minute, and Felix felt like the chill that had settled in his bones was so deep that no fire would ever entirely remove it. It was like the cold of the grave. Only the dwarf and the elf showed no signs of strain. Gotrek strode along tirelessly like a man out for a summer stroll through an Altdorf park. Teclis was even more annoying – for all his feeble appearance, and his limping walk, he showed not the slightest signs of fatigue. Felix supposed that it must help that the wizard's spells protected him from the wet and cold, but that did not make it any easier to watch him. At least he might throw his shield over the rest of us, Felix thought; the selfish, elvish bastard.

His fingers found the amulet the elf had given him, the one Teclis claimed would shield him from daemons. He was not that selfish, at least not if what he had told Felix was true. Felix had not been troubled by the evil ones, but it had only been a few days so he had no basis for deciding about that. On the other hand, there was no doubt Teclis had rescued them from the Paths of the Old Ones. Even Gotrek had to admit that, albeit through gritted teeth. It was not a subject Felix ever expected to bring up again with the dwarf, at least if he could help it. The dwarf was touchy enough at the best of times.

Footsteps crunched on the scree beside him. He looked up, and was surprised to see Murdo had fallen into step beside him. 'I have been watching you,' said the old man.

'And what have you seen?'

'You do not seem to be under any enchantment that I can tell of, and you fought bravely enough against the spider daemons. I think you are what you say you are, and your companions are what they claim too.'

'Thank you, I think.'

'The problem is that if I accept that I have to accept much o' what else they claim, and that is frightening, laddie.'

'Yes, I suppose it is. We live in frightening times.'

'Aye, the weather has worsened, and the orcs and beastmen have come out of their fastnesses and war stirs across the land. There are rumours of other things, of evil mages abroad in the land.'

'They are abroad in every land,' said Felix sourly. 'Why should yours be different?'

'For in our land, every man and woman who shows a trace of the talent is inducted into a brotherhood, sworn to preserve our ancient ways, watched over by their fellows. I have the talent myself, enough tae ken that yon Teclis there is more powerful than any mage now living in Albion, maybe than any who ever lived here. And he is scared, although he hides it well. That scares me.'

'I think you are wise.'

Murdo nodded his head.

'Why are you telling me this?'

'Because I think maybe we got off on the wrong foot, and that we are all in the same boat and it has a hole in it. And I want you to know that whatever comes, you may rely on the men of Crannog Mere.'

'That is always good to know, but why tell me? Why not tell Teclis or Gotrek?'

'Because you are a man, and it is easier to say to you. And those two are not exactly the sort you can open your heart to.'

Or maybe you are planning treachery, Felix thought, and you think it easier to hoodwink me than them. But somehow he could not quite bring himself to believe that. The old tribesman seemed painfully sincere, and genuinely intimidated by the pair, which was something Felix could understand only too well. He had known Gotrek for years, and he still found him unapproachable, and the elf carried himself with a bearing that might intimidate the Emperor Karl Franz.

Having said his piece, Murdo moved back among his men, as if waiting to see what Felix would do. Felix shrugged. He would mention it to the others when and if the need arose.

Something had been nagging at the back of his mind for a while and it chose this moment to come forth. He had always intended to set down the tale of Gotrek someday, when it came to its inevitable end, but perhaps he should begin setting it down soon, in case something happened to him before it was over. He had seen things worth recounting in these journeys, and met people who would surely leave their names in the histories and legends. Perhaps, if ever he got back to the Empire, he should make a record of his travels with Gotrek and leave it somewhere safe. With his brother, perhaps, or Max Schreiber, assuming the wizard was even still alive. He squared his shoulders and came to a decision. He would do it, and do it soon if the opportunity presented itself.

Another worrying thought occurred to him. Often in the past he had been confronted with the reality of death, his own and other people's. There had been times when he had thought he was going to die, but now, for some reason, in this far distant place, he was confronted by the certainty of it. Perhaps it was his time in the daemon's dungeon, or perhaps it was meeting the ageless elf and talking about time, but something had brought the reality of his mortality home to him.

Even if he avoided all the sword blades, and evil spells and the teeth of monsters, if he did not fall foul to plague, pestilence or accident, some day he would not be here. Death was as certain as tomorrow, just a little further away perhaps, and he now felt as he never had before the urge to do something to be remembered himself, to write his name alongside those of Gotrek and Teclis and the others he had met.

At that moment, he felt he understood just a little of what the Slayer must have felt when Felix had sworn to record his doom. I will record it, he thought – yours and mine and all the others I have seen. There are some things that should be remembered. Assuming, he thought, I am still here to write them down once this is all over. It will not be an epic poem though, he thought. I cannot imagine contriving one of those now. It will be a book or a series of them, setting it all down as it had happened to the best of his recollection. *My Travels with Gotrek*, or *The Trollslayer's Doom*. Something like that, he thought.

He considered this, and all the books he had read as a youth, and as a scholar at the university, and began to think of what he would need to know. Certainly, he would need to record something about Albion, for little was known of it back in the Empire. Here was a chance to add to the sum of that knowledge, and share it – assuming that any survived the coming Chaos invasion or what might happen if what Teclis claimed was true.

He shrugged. He had to assume that someone would. It was a commitment made to the future when times might be better and Chaos might be vanquished. However remote that possibility might seem now, he would proceed on the assumption that it might happen. It was a small, perhaps futile, gesture of faith in the face of events of cosmic malignity. And it was his gesture. Somehow just the thought made him feel a little better, although he was not entirely sure why. He strode back to join the old Truthsayer.

'Tell me about your land,' he said to Murdo.

'What do you want to know?'

As THEY WALKED, the thunder of rushing water grew louder ahead of them. It echoed through the rocks like the booming voice of an angry giant. Felix was worried. Such a sound could cover the hubbub of an approaching army, and visibility was already low because of the clouds, mist and the wilderness of tortured rocks through which they proceeded.

The river was narrower now and moved faster, and several times they had passed gigantic waterfalls tumbling down from above, separated from them as the path wound away and rejoined them later, higher upslope. It was getting dark now, and they were well up the mountainside. Felix tried not to think that mountains were the haunt of orcs, and concentrated on what old Murdo was telling him.

Under normal circumstances, Felix would have been fascinated, for the tattooed man was an interesting speaker, with a fund of knowledge and tales about his land. Felix learned that the men of Albion were divided into many tribes of the highlands and the low. The tribes were interrelated and once, not so long ago, there had been a golden age of peace, but that was before the orcs came, and the other raiders from over the seas. It seemed that the dark elves had found some way to penetrate the eternal mists that surrounded the enchanted island, and so had others. Felix immediately thought of the way he and Gotrek and Teclis had arrived but kept his peace about it. The outsiders had brought war with them. Felix struggled to get his head around the situation.

The orcs had arrived centuries back, few in number at first, as they must have been shipwrecked on the islands. They had bred quickly, swarming everywhere, and only the unification of the tribes under the hero Konark had let men triumph eventually and drive the orcs back into the mountains. The orcs had taken refuge amid ancient ruins in the remote valleys.

Occasional wars had been needed to pen them there. Now it seemed the orcs had multiplied again and something had driven them from the mountains onto the plains. They had even penetrated the great swamp that had kept the folk of Crannog Mere safe for ages. The orcs were bad, but the thought of something wicked and powerful enough to drive them from the mountains was worse. Now the tribes of men needed a leader to unite them once more, or they would be swept away. It was said that in these very mountains a hero by the name of Kron, who claimed to be a descendant of Konark, had done that for a few tribes. Felix gathered that Murdo was helping them because he thought Teclis was capable of discovering the mystery behind the orcs' sudden onslaught, and perhaps even stopping it. Felix certainly hoped so.

He considered what he knew. It seemed no part of the world was immune from its troubles. The great continent of the Old World was being ravaged by Chaos. Ulthuan shook with earthquakes. Albion was plagued by orcs and terrible storms. He would not have been surprised to learn that even in far Cathay, cataclysm had struck. Perhaps all the seers prophesying the end of the world had the truth of it.

He gave his attention back to Murdo. A picture of Albion emerged. It was less advanced than the Old World. The secret of making gunpowder was unknown and armour heavier than leather rare, manufactured by the tribes of the coast who seemed to be the main builders of large towns and cities. Great stone rings, focuses of magical force and energy, and other legacies of the ancients were everywhere. Ruined cities, haunted towers, odd labyrinths open to the sky, whose walls were scribed with mystical runes. Some of these were guarded by monstrous mutated giants, others by strange creatures such as hippogryphs and manticores and other daemonic mutants. Most of the gods of the Old World were known here, but seemed to be regarded more as great spirits than the deities with which he was familiar. Ulric was a wolf spirit of war and winter. Taal, the nature god, was regarded as supreme. In the Empire, there were some primitives who still worshipped the Old Faith, and what Murdo said reminded Felix of what he had read of them. Sigmar was unheard of here, which did not surprise Felix.

Dwarfs were things of legends and old tales. If ever there had been dwarfish cities here, they existed no more. Felix was hardly surprised – Albion was an island and dwarfs were not fond of ships. From what he had gathered from Gotrek, their steamboats were relatively recent developments in a history that stretched back millennia. Elves were known as Dark Ones here and had a reputation for deceit and treachery. Chaos was feared and the four powers of darkness were known but never to be named, whispered Murdo, lest you draw their attention to you. The old man had no idea of the geography of the world beyond his island, had never heard of Araby or Cathay. Bretonnia was a legend of which tales had been brought by shipwrecked sailors. Kislev was an icy island at the north of the world. The Empire was another island, larger and ruled by three emperors who fought constantly. Felix smiled at this distorted notion of history until he realised that his own ideas about Albion would have seemed just as strange to Murdo before he came here. And, he was forced to remind himself, perhaps what the old man was telling him was no more than stories. Certainly he believed them to be true, but he was an uneducated tribesman from a tiny isolated village in a huge swamp in the back end of beyond. It was possible, conceded Felix, that his tale held errors.

Still, on the details of what lay near his home, he seemed sound enough. Felix resolved to keep an open mind until he saw something that contradicted what Murdo said. He pulled his cloak tighter and studied his surroundings. They had emerged onto a wide flat ledge mostly filled with a lake of bubbling water, fed by a huge waterfall that leapt down from overhead to boil and bubble on the rocks below. Massive boulders covered in damp green moss ringed the lake, save where the water poured out over the stone edge to continue to journey to lands below. Spray was everywhere. The roaring was like that of a great wounded beast.

It took him a few moments to realise that there were dead bodies ringing the edge of the lake. It took him a few more seconds to realise that they belonged to women. He rushed over to the nearest one. She had been young and lithe and she had died from a spear in the back. Judging from the bloody foam on her lips, it looked like she had drowned in her own blood. A spear lay near her cold, clutching fingers. Felix noticed the green hand protruding from the water, and the swirl of greenish blood that told him an orc lay dead there.

'Taal's breath,' murmured Murdo. 'That is Laera, who was a chieftain of the Oracle's maiden-guard. There are others nearby – it looks like they were wiped out by orcs.'

Felix looked around. He saw now that some of what he had thought were moss-covered boulders were in fact orcish corpses. The mist and spray and fading light had tricked his eyes.

'Where are the orcs now?' Felix asked.

Stone crunched as Gotrek strode up to the lakeside. He spat on the submerged orcish body casually. 'If they are here, we will find them,' he said.

'Wonderful,' said Felix. 'Can't wait.'

All around the men of Crannog Mere made ready for battle.

CHAPTER NINETEEN

THE MEN OF Crannog Mere stood with weapons ready. Culum had gently placed Dugal on the ground and unslung his stone-headed hammer. Teclis scanned their surroundings warily, as if expecting a horde of ravening greenskins to race down from the surrounding slopes at any minute. Gotrek cackled gleefully and swung his axe a few times, like a woodsman limbering up before chopping down a tree.

'Perhaps they drove the orcs off,' said Felix.

'Nae, laddie. If they had we would be challenged by the maiden-guard. It is the way.'

'Maybe the orcs have left.'

'These corpses are barely stiff, manling,' said Gotrek. 'This fight happened within the hour.'

'Why does this always happen to us?' Felix wondered aloud, and then wished he hadn't. The glances of the tribesmen showed that they were more than willing to suspect that the three companions were somehow responsible for all this. No matter what Murdo said, it appeared that the majority of the men did not trust them. Or perhaps it was just Teclis, he thought, noticing that most of the murderous looks were aimed at the elf.

'Why indeed?' Teclis asked. 'It cannot be purely chance that the orcs struck here mere hours ahead of us, can it?' He gave the impression of one who talked to himself and did not expect any answers from others.

'What now?' Felix asked.

'The Oracle is below, unless the orcs have her. Perhaps her maiden-guard are with her waiting for succour even now,' said Murdo.

'If there's greenskins to be killed, let's get to it,' said Gotrek with more enthusiasm than Felix liked.

'Below?' said Felix pointedly. 'Where exactly is that? I can see no caves.'

In answer, Murdo walked to the edge of the lake, to the cliffs where the waterfall dropped. He seemed to vanish into the water itself, and one by one the men of Albion trooped after him, leaving Dugal in the shelter of the rocks.

Impelled by curiosity, Felix moved forward to where the men had vanished. He could see that there was a clear space wide enough for two people abreast behind where the waterfall fell. A ledge of rock ran there, but there were no men to be seen. Gotrek strode past onto the ledge, ignoring the tons of furious water passing so close, and he too seemed to vanish into the wall. Felix followed and within ten strides found a cave mouth opening to the left. The men were within, along with the Slayer, looking at more dead bodies of women and orcs. Felix found the sight very disturbing. He was not used to looking at so many dead girls. Most of them had been beautiful, too, he noted in passing.

Teclis came behind him and studied the scene. He pushed past Felix and the man felt the spray hit him, repelled by the mage's spells. It seemed a little impolite but Felix was not about to say anything, particularly not since he was already soaked. Teclis gestured and light filled the cave. Felix could see that it vanished deeper into the darkness beneath the mountains.

'Tunnels full of orcs,' he said. 'How can it get any worse?'

'How can it get any better?' said Gotrek. In the strange witch-light cast by the elf, his shadow danced menacingly along the walls.

Murdo fumbled amid the nooks and crannies of the walls until he found torches. Teclis lit them with a word. At first, Felix wondered why they were bothering, since the elf was capable of illuminating their passage, then the thought occurred to him that something might happen to him. It was not a reassuring one.

Gotrek moved to the fore, Murdo looming over him with a lit torch in one hand, spear in the other. It seemed logical in this dark underground space that the dwarf should lead; he was far more at home here than any human or elf could ever be. Felix stood beside Teclis, weapon bared. The tribesmen followed behind them.

Gotrek strode confidently into the gloom. Felix took a deep breath.

'Here we go,' he said.

THERE WERE SIGNS of combat everywhere. Armed warrior women had fought a desperate rearguard action into the depths of the cavern complex. They lay where they had been hacked down, surrounded by the bodies of orcs and goblins. Once, not so long ago, Felix had found something pathetic in the sight of the child-sized corpses of goblins. Not any more. Whatever sympathy he might have had was long gone. Now they just looked like any other small malevolent monster, with their bulging eyes and rows of razor-edged serrated teeth. In some ways they were just as terrifying as their larger orcish kin. They usually attacked in packs. The massive orcs did not need to.

So far the torches and the magelight had proved unnecessary. There were oil lanterns set in niches in the walls, providing a faint flickering illumination. In places they had been tumbled and smashed but the damp floor of the tunnels must have extinguished any blaze. A faint perfume filled the air, from the lantern oil and from some incense that had been added.

He felt the weight of the mountain begin to press in on him, became acutely aware of the mass of stone and rock hanging just above him, ready to crush him. Barely conscious of what he was doing, he listened for the creak of the earth as the mountain settled. He heard nothing but that did not keep him from imagining things. He felt, for instance, that it was getting warmer with every step.

A glance at the elf told him that Teclis was faring little better than he. The elf looked deeply uneasy for the first time that Felix could ever remember. His shoulders were hunched and he stooped, though there was plenty of room even for someone of his height in the tunnel. His gaze flickered everywhere as if seeking threats. Felix knew without being told that the elf was feeling the strain of being underground even more than he was.

Only the Slayer seemed unconcerned. He stood taller and strode with even more confidence than usual. Felix could have sworn that he was even whistling some almost jaunty tune. Nonetheless, Gotrek held his axe ready. Even as Felix watched he paused, sniffed the air and said, 'There are orcs nearby. Lots of orcs.'

THE TUNNELS DEEPENED. The floor became less damp. At first Felix had wondered why anyone would choose to dwell in such a chill, wet place, but now it was warm, and the perfume in the air was almost musky. He could see that all year around, even in the cold of winter, this could be comfortable.

'How does this Oracle live?' he asked Murdo. He was not surprised that his voice came out in a whisper and that the old man replied in kind. He was only talking to cover his nervousness. He knew it was foolish to make a noise when there might be orcs near, but he could not help himself. 'Where do they find food?'

'The tribes bring offerings, and the maiden-guard keep goats and sheep on the higher ground. Perhaps the orcs found those and followed them here, I am thinking.'

'That would seem logical,' said Felix. 'But why would they dwell here anyway? Why not in some more accessible location?'

'This place is sacred, Felix Jaeger. The light has blessed it. The first Oracle communed with the Great Spirits here after wandering lost through the mountains. The gods led her to shelter in these caves in a snowstorm while wolves hunted her. She found the altar of light in their depths and it granted her magical powers.'

For a moment, Teclis looked less queasy and showed a glimmer of professional interest. Felix supposed that any wizard would when matters magical came up. 'It was an ancient artefact?' he asked.

'I do not know, Teclis of the elves. I am not an initiate of these mysteries. I know that in return for taking the sight of her eyes, it granted another sort of sight. And I know that from that first day to this, there has been an Oracle in this place. They come when they are summoned from whatever corner of Albion where they be living.'

'Summoned?' Felix asked. Murdo shrugged.

'They know when it is their time to come here, just as the old Oracle knows when the hour of her dying will come on her. The light grants them this knowledge.'

Felix wondered how much of this was mere superstition and how much truth. He had seen so many strange things in his time that anything seemed possible. It might prove interesting meeting this Oracle, he thought. Under any other circumstances but these.

THE TUNNEL WIDENED out into an area of caves. Felix could see that these had once been occupied chambers. Sleeping pallets lay strewn about the ground. Rent and torn clothing lay everywhere, golden torcs and glittering jewellery caught the light. There were more bodies and from up ahead came the sound of combat. A horde of greenskins packed the entrance of a cave mouth. They seemed to be trying to force their way in against stiff resistance. A dark cloaked figure armed with a stone-tipped spear urged them on.

Gotrek needed no more encouragement, and with a bellowing roar, he raced ahead as fast as his short legs would carry him. The men of Albion followed, overtaking him easily with their long strides. Felix decided to stick close to the

Slayer, and the elf had obviously decided to do the same. He barely seemed to lengthen his limping stride and he was beside Gotrek. As he walked, he spread his arms and chanted. A wall of flame erupted ahead of them, and the screams and bellows of dying orcs and goblins filled the air.

The men of Albion stopped, unable to push their way through the roaring flames. Felix could feel their heat from where he stood. It was like being next to an open furnace. Nothing, it seemed, could live within that incandescent fury.

He was wrong. With a bestial roar, a massive orc burst out of the flames. His clothing smouldered. His greenish skin was seared a sooty black in places, but he came on undaunted. Moments later, another and then another burst through. All of them were huge, bigger than a man and far more muscular. Their yellowish tusks glistened with froth. Massive scimitars gleamed in their huge fists. Their eyes were filled with mad hatred and insensate fury. There were only half a dozen of them, but the sight of them, and the way they had burst through the flames, seemed to fill the folk of Crannog Mere with dismay. Felix understood their feelings only too well. The orcish leader, even more massive than the rest and wearing a helmet of bronze inlaid with bullhorns, grunted something to his fellows in their brutal tongue, and they laughed madly as they advanced.

Felix did not doubt that at that moment the men of Albion would have run had not Gotrek stood his ground. He was sorely tempted to do so himself. Instead, he moved to a position slightly to the left and slightly behind the Slayer, judging this the best place to ward his back. Teclis moved over to the right, a gleaming runeblade clutched in his left hand, the staff blazing with power in his right.

'Steady, lads,' said Murdo. 'These greenskin devils owe us blood for what they did here.'

That was all it took. The men formed up into a fighting line on either side of the three companions. Culum lifted his hammer menacingly. Felix watched the green giants move closer. He was aware of the dryness in his mouth and the beating of his heart. He felt suddenly weak, and everything seemed to be happening much slower than usual. He ignored the sensations, having experienced them in battle many times before, and braced himself for the impact. It was not long in coming.

He saw one orc leap forward and impale itself on the barrier of spears. Undaunted, it drove itself forward, reaching out to snap one man's neck and chop another down with its blade. More spears slammed home into its body. But it fought on, cackling madly, seemingly unkillable by normal weapons, such was its unnatural vitality. Another went for Culum. Sparks flashed as blade met hammer and the big man was driven back by a strength even more prodigious than his own.

Two of the orcs came for Gotrek. He did not wait for them to reach him, instead he strode forward, ducking the sweep of a scimitar and catching the back of an orc's knee with his return blow. The beast fell forward headlong, unable to walk on the amputated stump of its leg. The Slayer's second blow was met by a scimitar and partially deflected. Gotrek snorted with contempt, and aimed another blow that sent the orc leaping backwards, desperately avoiding a stroke that would have caved in its ribs had it connected.

It was Teclis that surprised Felix. Showing no more restraint than Gotrek, he hurled himself forward to confront the orcish leader. The creature was even taller than the elf, and far more massive. Enormous cable-like sinews rippled under its glistening green skin. It snarled something in orcish and laughed when the elf's reply was delivered in the same tongue. The guttural syllables sounded strange in the elf's far higher voice.

'Wait,' shouted Felix, knowing that their situation might yet become desperate if the elf were killed. 'Leave this one for me.'

He moved forward to meet the orc but by then it was far too late. The greenskin chieftain struck with the speed and fury of a summer storm. His blow fell like a thunderbolt, but the elf was simply not there. Moving with a swiftness that blurred sight, he moved around the orc's strike, and his own blade bit home into the orc's upper arm. The creature bellowed with fury and aimed a stroke that would have decapitated the slim elf had it connected. Teclis ducked to one side, executing what seemed almost a courtly bow, and the blade passed above his head. His return stroke was driven upwards with all the force of an uncoiling spring. It bit into the orc's ribs, drawing greenish blood. Only the orc chief's own lightning swiftness had kept the blade from burying itself in his bowels. Strokes passed between the two almost too fast for Felix's eye to follow. The elf gave ground gracefully, moving backward like water flowing over stone. The orc pursued, grunting mightily, until he was almost past Felix. In his fury, his concentration was entirely on the mocking elf who danced away taunting him in his own language and who was slowly inflicting a dozen small cuts on him with his ripostes.

Seeing the opportunity, Felix lunged forward. His blade took the orc in the side, finding its way beneath the ribs and passing right through the stomach. Felix withdrew it, and threw himself back as the orc, striking like a dying scorpion, lashed out at him reflexively. In that fatal moment of distraction, the elf's blade took him through the eye and he slumped to the earth, dead before he hit the ground.

'That was not very sporting, Felix Jaeger,' said Teclis.

'This is not a game,' said Felix angrily, annoyed by the elf's insouciance. 'You can die here the same as anybody else.'

'Is that not part of the thrill of the thing?' said Teclis dangerously. Felix wondered if his ennui could really be that great.

'And who will save Ulthuan if you fall here?' said Felix, turning to enter the battle once more. Even as he did so, he saw the dark cloaked figure had raised his hand. A wave of magical power flowed towards Felix. For a brief moment, he thought he saw the folk around him transformed into daemons. All around he heard the men of Crannog Mere gasp in terror. The irrational urge to turn and flee filled him and he could see the others waver. Looks of horror were on their faces as if they had just seen their worst nightmares materialise in front of them.

The amulet on Felix's chest glowed and a warmth spread through him, dispelling the fear. He heard a cold chill laugh and realised that it had come from the elf. The sound of that dry mirth was more chilling in its way than even the vision of his manifold fear.

'Try your simple sorceries on me would you, man of Albion? I return them to you, redoubled and redoubled again.' The elf spoke a spell and the dark-cloaked figure emitted a high-pitched shriek of pure fear before clutching his chest and collapsing to the ground. The men of Albion steadied and fought on.

Gotrek had chased his orc until it was backed against the wall. His axe flashed once and the creature's chest caved in, entrails exploding everywhere from the force of the impact. Felix looked around to see how the men of Albion were doing. Culum finally saw an opening and aimed his hammer squarely at the beast's head. The force of the impact took the head clean from the shoulders, caving in one side and sending it flying through the air to hit the ground rolling like a ball. It landed at Felix's feet, almost as if the big man had intended it that way, and looked up at him with fierce hatred in the dying light of its eyes.

The other tribesmen had managed to surround the last two orcs and harried them like hounds pulling down a stag. Spears flickered forward, fast as the tongues of snakes, and pierced green flesh. Bleeding and gored from a dozen wounds, the orcs finally went down. They had taken their share of men to hell with them, though, thought Felix. Only half a dozen of the men of Crannog Mere were left.

Gotrek headed towards the opening from which the sounds of fighting had come. Felix followed him into the final caves.

THERE WERE GOBLINS in here, and dead orcs and more dead women. A few of the amazons still stood, battling a scuttling horde of bow-legged goblins. Beyond them was a white-shrouded figure that the women seemed willing to give their lives to protect. Felix raced forward, overtaking the Slayer, and leapt the last few strides that separated him from the goblins.

Wielding his blade with both hands, he hewed about him, taking many of the little monsters before they even knew he was upon them. Their death screams panicked their comrades and they turned frantically to face the new threat, giving the women time to hustle their charge back out of range of the combat.

Excellent, thought Felix, alone against a horde of greenskins. This is where chivalry gets you. He continued to fight though, back-pedalling desperately, knowing that the Slayer could not be too far away. Nor was he disappointed. Within heartbeats, a massive axe flashed past his shoulder and chopped a howling goblin clean in two. Then Gotrek was moving through them like a whirlwind of destruction. Nothing lived that fell within the arc of his blade. His blows smashed through shields, made parries futile for the small creatures. They could no more withstand the Slayer than Felix could have withstood the charge of a bull.

Moments later the men of Albion arrived and the slaughter was complete. That's that, thought Felix, glancing back at the scene of the carnage. He turned around to find himself facing a row of spears, all aimed at his chest.

CHAPTER TWENTY

THE WOMEN WERE armed with spears and small leather shields. They did not look friendly. Felix wondered why they pointed their spears at him so menacingly. Had he not helped save them? Had he not killed orcs? He kept very still anyway. Mistakes get made. Misunderstandings can easily be fatal when there are weapons involved.

'This is sacred ground,' said one of the women. She was almost as tall as Felix and her hair was tied into many locks. Tattoos covered her face and arms and gave her a wild barbaric look.

'I'm sorry – next time I will respect your taboos, and let the orcs slaughter you on your sacred ground.' He could not quite keep the bitterness from his voice. The woman looked as if she was going to attack him. Felix prepared himself to spring clear.

'Be at peace, Siobhain,' said a quavering voice. 'He is a stranger here and he helped save all of our lives. He is entitled to be here.'

'But he is not of our blood,' said Siobhain. 'Any fool can see that...'

Her mouth sprang shut like a steel trap as if she had just realised what she had said. A flush, visible even in the dim light, passed beneath her facial tattoos. A moment later Felix understood why. The old woman to whom she had been talking had eyes of milky white. She was quite obviously blind. The girl gave Felix a glare as if it was all somehow his fault. Felix shrugged.

'You are Felix Jaeger,' said the old woman. Felix kept his own mouth closed with effort. How could she have known his name? Carrier pigeon, a messenger slipped away from Crannog Mere in the dead of night, lots of different ways, the rational part of his mind whispered, but he knew it was wrong. There was magic involved. This old woman was quite plainly a witch of some sort. 'Well met,' said the old woman, her fingers moving through an intricate gesture that might have been part of a spell or a benediction. Felix flinched but nothing happened.

'Well met,' he said back, bowing with as much grace as he could muster. It seemed somehow the right thing to do. He sensed the old woman's attention sliding away from him and took the opportunity to study her. She was a tall woman, sharp faced, but still beautiful. Her robes were of thick grey wool. Her braids were even more complex than Siobhain's. There were tattoos on her face too, but they had faded to near invisibility, like markings on parchment that has been left too long in the sun. How could that have happened, Felix wondered?

'You are welcome here too, Teclis of Ulthuan. You are the first of your kind to set foot in this place for millennia.'

The elf's voice was sardonic. 'As far as I know I am the first of my kind ever to set foot in this place, Oracle.'

'Then you do not know everything,' said the old woman. Her voice had a sharp, brittle quality now. Felix guessed she was used to being treated with more respect. Certainly the tribesmen seemed in awe of her. The expressions on their faces said as much.

'I have been aware of that for more centuries than you have lived,' said Teclis. His own tone was just as sharp. The gods preserve us from the vanity of wizards, thought Felix. A strange smile passed across the old woman's face, almost as if she knew what he was thinking. Gotrek grunted at the elf's words and strode forward.

'I am Gotrek, son of Gurni,' he said, not giving the old woman time to name him. 'Who are you?'

The maiden-guard and the tribesmen bristled at his tone. Hands stiffened on weapons. Gotrek looked supremely unconcerned by the prospect of imminent violence. Felix wished he could share the dwarf's attitude.

'You too are welcome, Slayer.' If Gotrek wondered how she knew what he was, no sign of it appeared on his face. 'I gave up my name when I took the title Oracle.'

The Slayer shrugged. He even managed to make that action somehow menacing. Felix wondered if they had really come all this way just to get into a fight with the people who should have been their allies. Something needed to be done and quickly.

'How did those orcs get here?' he asked. 'This is not the sort of place you just stumble on.'

'They were led here,' said the Oracle.

'Led!' said Murdo. He sounded shocked.

'Aye, Murdo Mac Baldoch, led.'

'What man of the tribes would have led them here? Surely no one could so turn their face from the light?'

'It was more than a man of the tribes, Murdo. It was one of the Council. Siobhain, make yourself useful! You and Mariadh bring the body of the dark-cloaked stranger to us.'

There was silence until the two warrior-maidens returned bearing the body of the sorcerer. The Oracle moved over to it and pulled back the cowl to reveal a lean, pale, tattooed face. The man's features were distorted by terror even in death. Spittle was still on his lips. It looked like he had died of pure fright.

Murdo's face went white. 'Baldurach!' he said. There was both fear and disbelief in his tone. The old man's shoulders slumped and he studied the floor at his feet. 'We are betrayed then, and by one of our own,' he said very softly.

'Some there are who listen to the whispers of the Dark Spirit,' said the Oracle.

'This is not the place to talk of this,' Murdo said, glancing significantly at the three companions. His glance even seemed to take in his own kin, although Felix thought this might have been his own imagination.

'If not here, where?' said the Oracle. 'These three must hear what is said here. Send the others away.' She gestured to her guardians and they began to herd the men out. The Oracle turned and walked deeper into the caves. She did so easily and gracefully, with no hint of the fact that she was blind. Felix felt the hairs stir on the nape of his neck. There are other senses than sight, he told himself. Or perhaps she has simply walked these halls so long she has all the obstructions memorised. Once again something told him that this was not the case.

Gotrek and Teclis fell into step behind her. The elf's mage-light dimmed somewhat but still gave enough illumination to see by. Murdo looked at him with what might have been fear, respect or awe and gestured for Felix to proceed. Felix followed them down into the gloom. The old man's heavy tread told him Murdo was right behind him.

THIS CHAMBER WAS smaller. The walls were carved with more abstract patterns that seemed to map some cosmic maze. In the centre was a massive, perfect stone egg, on which was inscribed similar patterns. Just looking at them made Felix feel slightly dizzy. On the top of the stone egg was a dimple in which something lay.

'Are you sure you want these strangers here?' asked Murdo.

'They are part of this,' said the Oracle. She sat cross-legged in the shadow of the egg and gestured for them to sit likewise. Felix and Teclis joined her. Gotrek lounged against the wall, his axe held nonchalantly in both hands. Murdo glared at him and then he, too, sat.

'What?'

'Dark shadows gather, Murdo. Things long imprisoned will be free. Some of our brothers and sisters have turned from the truth and the light and now serve that which we sought to contain. The ancient brotherhood is broken. A time of schism and chaos is come.'

'Impossible!'

'No, Murdo, not at all. We are mere mortals and it is undying. We are fallible and corruptible. Some have fallen. As was predicted.'

'That it should happen in our time. That the ancient trust should be betrayed.'

'Yet betrayed it is. And orcs found their way into the heart of this sacred place. We should be grateful it was only orcs Baldurach led and not something worse.'

Felix wondered if the elf and dwarf were as confused by this as he. They gave no sign. Teclis appeared to be concentrating hard on everything said. Gotrek merely stared into space as if bored.

'You say they are part of this.'

'Yes. Outsiders have taken over the Temple of the Old Ones. They have opened the ancients' paths. In doing so, they have left an opening through which the ancient enemy can escape.'

'Who is this enemy of which you speak?' Felix asked.

'An ancient spirit of darkness, imprisoned long ago, bound by mighty spells at the dawn of history. It seeks power and the domination of all.'

'It was imprisoned using the power of the paths and the leylines,' said Teclis. He sounded like a physician discussing a case of fever. The Oracle nodded.

'It was the only way. No mortal would have had the power otherwise.'

'And now the flows of power have been disturbed, its shackles have loosened.'

'Yes. Though that is not your problem. Your concerns are more pressing. You seek to prevent the sinking of your homeland, do you not?'

'Yes. How do you know this?'

'Thoughts and visions can pass through the Paths of the Old Ones as well as living beings. I have talked with the same undying ones who talked with you. They told me of your coming. Our fortunes are linked. For you must clear the Temple of the Old Ones and close the paths once more, or your land is doomed.'

'We must do it?' said Felix. 'Why us?'

'For no one else in Albion has the power or the knowledge to do what needs to be done. The temple is in the hands of the fell powers of Chaos. They have driven forth the orcs and bound the god the greenskins worshipped.'

'They have bound a god?' said Felix. 'With all due respect, I think beings who can do that are a little beyond our ability to deal with.'

He did not look around for fear that either the elf or the dwarf might disagree with him. They remained silent.

'It is no true god, Felix Jaeger. It is one of the creations of the Old Ones, a guardian set to watch over their temple and their creations.'

Felix thought about the spider things they had fought back in the swamp. The memory did nothing to increase his liking for the task that was being proposed. 'What sort of monsters are these?'

'One of the giants of Albion, Felix Jaeger.' Felix suppressed a groan. He did not need to be able to see the Slayer to know how interested he was. 'The giants were made long ago, by the Old Ones, to guard their treasures and their secrets. They are near immortal but over the years, it is said, they have become altered, a degenerate parody of the noble creatures they once were. They fell to the worship of Chaos, and other vile practices. They became wicked, predatory creatures, that preyed on all things weaker than they, but still they kept to their duties in an odd way, bound by the geas the Old Ones placed on them. They haunted the old places and made them their lairs, filled them with their ill-gotten treasures.'

This was getting worse and worse – treasures as well as monsters! He was surprised Gotrek was not foaming at the mouth by now. 'And you say one of them has been bound by the forces of Chaos.'

'Aye, Magrig One Eye, mightiest of the giants of old, a slayer of dragons and behemoths in his day, before his brain became clouded and he acquired the lust for manflesh.'

'Oh good, not just an ordinary gigantic monster then,' said Felix.

'No. He is large as a hillock and can smash castle walls with a blow of his club.'

'And now he has been bound to the service of Chaos?' said Teclis.

'Aye, by Kelmain and Lhoigor, two of the foulest and most powerful of all the Changer's servants.'

The old woman gestured and a vision appeared in the glowing mist that sprang up between her hands. It showed two miniature sorcerers, albino twins, one garbed in black, one in gold. Their heads were bald or shaven, their fingers were like claws.

'I know them,' said Felix, unable to keep the surprise from his voice. 'We followed one of them into the Paths of the Old Ones. And they were at Praag with the Chaos horde,' he added hastily, before his words could be misinterpreted.

'Aye,' said Gotrek. 'They were. They advised Arek Daemonclaw and his warlords. They summoned those great living siege engines and the daemons who stormed the walls.'

'They are old enemies of yours?' said Murdo.

'They won't get much older if they come within reach of my axe,' said Gotrek.

'That is good,' said the Oracle, 'for they are evil men and much in need of killing.'

Felix toted up the foes. 'One giant, two sorcerers of great power, what else? Three dragons?'

'The mages have their bodyguards, and every day they bring more and more Chaos warriors through the paths. They plan to use the ancient ways to invade many lands. They either do not know or do not care about the consequences of what they have done.'

'A Chaos army as well then. Good – that seems simple enough. Shall we just walk in and challenge them all to single combat?'

'I do not think you are taking this entirely seriously, Felix Jaeger,' said the Oracle.

'You spotted that, did you? I can see why they call you the Oracle.' Felix seemed unable to keep his mouth shut.

Murdo's hand reached for his knife. 'You will show some respect…'

'Or what? You'll kill me. It seems your Oracle is going to do quite well on that score anyway.'

Felix knew he was sounded hysterical and bitter, but he could not help it. That was the way he felt. It seemed like it was out of the troll's cookpot and into the flames. How could three of them achieve anything under these conditions? It was impossible. There was an army of monsters. There was a giant. There were two of the most powerful and evil magicians on the face of the planet. It did not matter how mighty a warrior Gotrek was or how powerful a sorcerer was Teclis, the odds were very much stacked against them. He shook his head, fighting for self-control. So what else was new? He had faced overwhelming odds before and survived. He and the Slayer had fought their way out of many dark places. This was just going to be one more. He looked at the Oracle.

'I apologise,' he said softly. 'I am just tired and scared.'

'Those are understandable things to be under the circumstances, Felix Jaeger. It does you credit that you know it.'

'For a moment there I just didn't see how we could do it.'

'And you do now?' said Teclis smiling.

'It's simple,' he said. 'All we need is an army to keep the Chaos warriors occupied. Gotrek and I will kill the giant, and you can deal with the wizards. Nothing could be simpler.'

'A good plan, manling,' said Gotrek. Felix thought he detected a hint of sarcasm in the Slayer's voice, but he was not entirely sure. 'And if the elf can't deal with those spellcroakers, I will.'

'I wished I shared your confidence, Gotrek Gurnisson,' said the elf. His manner did not entirely reassure Felix.

'I think parts of what you require can be arranged,' said the Oracle. 'It is only a matter of looking in the right place.'

Excellent, thought Felix, I am going to take advice on how to look for something from a blind woman. He kept his thoughts to himself though. The blind woman smiled as if reading them anyway.

'Now, Teclis of the elves,' she said. 'You must take this, and I will instruct you in its use, and then I will see to Dugal.'

She lifted the amulet from atop the intricate rune-worked egg. Felix could see that it was made of stone, and covered in the now familiar runes. Since it was clear that she intended only the elf to remain, he got up, bowed, and left.

'I hope she is teaching him some powerful magic,' he said, as the sound of murmuring voices faded behind him. 'We are going to need it.'

CHAPTER TWENTY-ONE

FELIX DREW HIS cloak tight about him. The wind blew chill and cold here in the mountains. As they walked over the crest, he could see how deceptive the landscape really was. What looked like a range of high peaks were in fact many intersecting ranges of mountains, and between them lay many valleys and lakes.

Up here, snow lay on the ground still and vegetation was scant. The only wildlife were some high-flying birds, and some wild sheep that bounded warily away when they saw humans. Below them were more pinewoods that rolled almost down to the shores of the lakes in some places. To the north, he could see what looked like a barren valley. What makes one valley fertile and another not he wondered, then shrugged. It was just one more of those questions to which he would most likely never find an answer.

Behind him the tribesmen of Crannog Mere straggled out in a line. At the head of the column were the maiden-guard the Oracle had sent to guide them. The elf mage and the dwarf stood on the brow of the hill, staring around them. It was not the wild beauty of the landscape that held their attention, Felix could tell, but the cluster of circular stone towers that clung to the next ridge top. They were massive brutal structures designed to resist siege. Their only ornamentss were the omnipresent runes that echoed the tattoo patterns on the faces of the warriors. These had been painted in blazing lurid colours on the stonework. Doubtless they held some mystical significance. Perhaps he would ask the elf, he thought.

From the tower a group of warriors had emerged and raced along the ridgeback towards them. There were several score at a rough count, and all of them armed. Felix moved closer to Gotrek and Teclis. He did not doubt that there would be a warm welcome for the Oracle's followers, but he was not so sure how well things would go for strangers. Under the circumstances, he decided, it was better to be on the safe side.

THE FOLK OF Carn Mallog were more bearish than wolvish, Felix decided. They were big men, burly and hard-faced. Their hair was long and shaggy, beards of almost dwarfish length sprouted from their faces, braided and twisted into all manner of fantastic patterns. Tattoos marked their cheeks and sword arms. Huge two-handed swords hung strapped to their backs. Long spears were clutched in their hands. Their clothes consisted of leather jerkins and woollen kilts. Long plaid cloaks covered the shoulders of most. Some had bearskins or wolfskins instead. They seemed to be the men of most importance. They eyed Teclis and Gotrek warily. Their looks made it clear that their reservations applied to Felix as well.

'These men have swords,' Felix said to Gotrek. 'The men of Crannog Mere do not. Why do you think that is?'

'It's hard to work metal in a swamp, manling,' said the dwarf.

'Murdo has a sword,' said Felix, just to be contrary.

'I would guess he traded for it with the mountain men. Mountains and hills are where you find mines and metals, mostly.'

'Why is that?'

The dwarf shrugged. 'Ask the gods,' he said. 'They put the metal there. Dwarfs just dig it out.'

Felix could see he was not going to get any better answer. Teclis returned the men's stares blandly, ignoring their open hostility. Murdo led a huge bear of a man over towards them and swiftly made the introductions. It turned out the man's name was Bran MacKerog, chieftain of the men of Carn Mallog. There was no warmth in the greetings he gave them, only suspicion and perhaps a wary respect.

'I give you thanks for aiding the Oracle,' he said. 'The light watch over her.'

'No thanks are necessary,' said Felix, seeing that his companions were not going to respond. 'We merely did what any men would have under the circumstances.'

As soon as he said it, Felix knew it was not the right thing. He doubted whether Gotrek or Teclis would thank him for comparing them to men. He could see that the thought that neither was human had already passed through Bran's head. For all his brutal features there was a quick intelligence written in those cold blue eyes and that hard-hewn face. Felix doubted that a man got to be chieftain in the mountain tribes by birth alone.

'You will take whisky with us,' he said. Felix was not sure whether it was a request, a command or an invitation.

'We will,' he said quickly in case the others took it the wrong way. They moved towards the towers as night began to gather around the peaks like a cloak.

Teclis limped along with Murdo on one side and Siobhain on the other. They had returned from their talks with the men of Carn Mallog. In the days it had taken them to get this far, both seemed to have accepted him. He supposed it made it easier for them that the Oracle had. Both talked freely and softly in his presence, at least as long as they were out of earshot of the others. Teclis listened with half his attention while his mind pondered the mysteries the Oracle had revealed to him. They had come to him as a profound shock.

'It is bad,' said Murdo. 'The orcs are gathering in the mountains once more. Rumour has it that their shamans have whipped them up to try and retake their valley. Some sort of prophet has arisen among them. It seems they have dwelled there so long they regard it as their own.'

'Is that so?' said Teclis. It seemed his suspicions had been correct. The temple was the key to all of this. It lay at the centre of the vast web of the Paths of the Old Ones, and only from there could those arcane ways be closed once more, although it seemed the price to be paid might be very high. He wondered once more at the other things the old woman had told him. Was it really possible that the Truthsayers had been made privy to certain secrets of the Old Ones that not even the elves had been taught?

'Indeed, Teclis of Ulthuan, it is so,' said the woman. She smiled at him rather oddly, he thought, and touched his arm when she spoke. That raised interesting possibilities if his suspicions were correct.

He smiled and returned his thoughts to their earlier track. Such a thing would certainly be a blow to the vanity of his people if it were true and became common knowledge. According to the Oracle it seemed the formation of the order of Truthsayers dated back to the legendary times when the Old Ones had walked the earth. Why had the elves not been told this? The Old Ones must have had their reasons. Perhaps there were factions among the Old Ones just as with every other race. Perhaps they did not want only one race to possess all magical knowledge. After all, they had given the skill of rune-crafting only to the dwarfs.

'It seems we may face an army of greenskins as well as army of Chaos worshippers,' said Murdo. He looked off at the distant peaks as if he suspected they might be hiding enemies.

'That would not be good,' said Teclis, shifting his attention back to the man. 'We must reach the Chamber of Secrets in the Temple of the Old Ones if I am to do what must be done.'

'I will help you all I can,' said Murdo. 'In any way I can.'

'As will I,' said Siobhain. There was definitely a glint in her eye, Teclis thought. Well, many human women had found him attractive down the ages, but at the moment he needed to keep his mind on other things.

It appeared that the Old Ones had foreseen something of the coming catastrophe, and taught these human wizards to prepare for it. The great stone rings were a means of trapping and controlling the energy of Chaos. If what the Oracle had said was true, then it had not been the elven wizards who turned the tide in the ancient war against Chaos, but the Truthsayers and their stone rings. By draining off the magical power of Chaos at the crucial time, they had blunted its sorcerously driven assault on the world, although at the cost of polluting their own land as the stones' power worked too well.

Perhaps here was the real reason the Paths of the Old Ones had become contaminated. Perhaps it was from magical energy drained from Albion into them. Teclis dismissed the theory. He did not know enough. He reviewed what the Oracle had told him about the temple, and the amulet that now hung from his chest.

It seemed that there were no Truthsayers left with the power to use it as it should be used, so it had fallen to him. He only hoped that he would be up to the task. He touched it with his long fingers. Of course he would. He was Teclis, greatest wizard of this age of the world. If he could not close the paths, nobody could. And that was the most worrying thought of all. If he could not do it...

Ahead of them loomed the first of the great stone towers. It looked like they would arrive just in time for nightfall. Soon he would talk with Bran and the others about the Oracle's plan. And after that... He smiled at the woman. She smiled back at him. We shall see what we shall see, Teclis thought.

'How large an army has your Empire then, Felix Jaeger?' asked Bran. Instantly all the large burly men surrounding him paid more attention.

'I do not know the exact numbers, but many regiments,' said Felix. On the walk to the tower, the mountain chieftain had shown great interest in the Empire and its weapons. War was his business, Felix supposed, and he was merely show-ing a professional interest. Either that or he was pumping him for information with a view to a future invasion. In any case, the questions and the talk always seemed to circle back to the question of military strength.

Felix was not intimidated by the thought. From what he had seen of the men of Albion, the Empire had little to fear. As far as he could tell, they had no knowledge of gunpow-der; they had no organised colleges of battle magic and no access to war machines such as steam tanks or organ guns. Their metalworking skills appeared quite primitive com-pared to Empire men or dwarfs. Still there was something about the mountain chieftain, a naked ambition in his eye that made Felix cautious whenever he spoke.

'Your people are merchants, you say? Not warriors?' The warriors of his bodyguard nudged each other and laughed as if the chieftain had made a joke. Felix was getting a bit tired of this.

'My father is a merchant.'

'That is not what I meant. You say the wealth of your nation is in trade. Is it a very wealthy nation?'

Felix smiled coldly. Bran looked at him the way a robber might size up a rich merchant, or an extortionist a shop-keeper. There was a naked greed in his eye now that was quite obvious.

'Very wealthy,' said Felix. If this backcountry warlord wanted to harbour fantasies of pillaging the Empire, who was he to disabuse him? 'But the dwarfs have even more gold than we...' he added maliciously.

'Aye, but if their warriors are all like Gotrek Gurnisson, 'T'would be hard fighting to take it from them.' Felix saw his meaning at once. He was taking Gotrek as representative of all dwarfs and Felix as representative of the men of the Empire. Felix did not take any offence. The simple truth of the matter was that Gotrek was a lot tougher than he was, although there was something rankling about the assump-tion.

'You might find Felix Jaeger's people harder than you think,' said Murdo, as he fell into step beside them. 'He is.'

Felix was surprised to see him. Murdo had become thick as thieves with Teclis. A glance behind him showed the elf was walking close to Siobhain. Surely what Felix was thinking was happening there could not be happening. Maybe it was. Maybe Murdo was being discreet.

'We will talk further about such things when we get within the brocht,' said Bran. He did not seem to want to continue the conversation with the Truthsayer present. 'Now I must speak with my chieftains. It has been a pleasure, Felix Jaeger. And to see you too, Murdo MacBaldoch.'

As he watched the huge mountain men swagger away, Murdo laughed. 'A good man, Bran is, but greedy and famous as a raider too.'

'So I had gathered,' said Felix.

'A word to the wise,' said the Truthsayer. 'Do not talk to him too much about the riches of your homeland, or he is likely to forget all about the matter at hand and try and talk you into an expedition against your Empire.'

'Are all of your chieftains like him?'

'Unfortunately, most of them are. They would rather raid than rear their own cattle. It's what makes our people so difficult to unite except in the face of a massive threat.'

'Well, you face one now, don't you?'

'That we do, Felix Jaeger. That we do.'

ONCE THE TOWER door was barred, Felix felt like a prisoner. The walls were massive and thick and the place was dim and smelled of unwashed human flesh and animals and wood smoke. Bodies pressed all around in the gloom. It would be all too easy to stick a dagger into someone's back in such circumstances, he realised. Unless they could see in the darkness, like an elf or a dwarf.

There was nothing to be frightened about, he told himself. They had come with the Oracle's blessing and no one would attack them. To do so would be an unforgivable insult to her and to their gods. He smiled sourly to himself. You have only their word for that, he told himself. And had not the ancient seeress herself hinted that there were those who worked against her, and her kind? What exactly were her kind, he wondered?

He felt like he was once again trapped in a huge maze. He did not know his way around here. He could take nothing for granted. The dwarf stomped into view. Well, almost nothing. He could rely on the Slayer to be his usual obstreperous self. He was not sure that was an advantage when you were cooped up in a sealed fortress with a horde of armed men. Against so many, he doubted even Gotrek could prevail.

He studied the place, looking for a way out. There was none that he could see. The place was barbarically simple. There was only one huge room with a massive wooden fire in the centre. The smoke ascended through a series of holes in the wooden floors above to escape through the tower top. The whole place was one enormous chimney, he realised. From what he gathered, each of these massive towers belonged to one family, and all of the families were part of one extended clan. Such was the social organisation of this part of Albion.

From the shadows in which he stood, he could hear voices speaking. One was the booming voice of Bran. 'We have sent messengers to the other clans with word of your coming. They will meet with us at the Ring of Ogh. The greenskins went too far when they attacked the sacred caves.'

'Aye,' Murdo agreed. 'They did.'

'Time enough for a drink,' said Bran. All of the guests were brought to the long table and whisky was produced. All of them were within easy shouting distance of the chieftain. Bran clapped his hands, and fiddlers and pipers began to play as platters of food were brought out. Soon Teclis and Murdo were at work on either ear of the chieftain explaining the situation, answering his probing questions. He seemed to take in the situation very quickly even as he swilled down whisky and chomped on a sheep shank. Felix found his attention drifting – he had heard enough about the paths and disasters to last him a lifetime, and the whisky was leaving a pleasant fire in his belly. Perhaps, he thought, when the others leave this place, I shall stay here. It's come to something, he thought, when that is what qualifies as a pleasant fantasy.

He felt a soft presence wriggle into place beside him. It was Morag, one of the maiden-guard. She was pretty with a freckled face and snub nose and short cropped reddish brown hair. She smiled up at him. He smiled back.

'So tell me about the elf,' she said. 'How long have you been travelling with him?' Felix groaned and began to talk.

The slamming of a goblet on the table brought his attention back to Teclis and Bran.

'No. It is madness,' said Bran. 'I will not lead my people into such a trap.'

There was a distinct vehemence in his voice. 'If you do not show us the high road into the valley the Oracle spoke of, then no one will. The curse will continue on the land. And in part it will be your fault.' The elf's voice was persuasive but Bran did not seem to have much trouble resisting his logic.

'The orcs know of the road. It will be watched. Wait until the clans assemble, then we will force a passage.'

'We do not have time,' said Teclis. 'It will take weeks to assemble an army and we don't have weeks any more. We have days at most.'

Felix suddenly gave the conversation his full attention. This was a new development. He had thought they were going into the valley with an army, but now it looked like the plan had changed. It was nice to be entrusted with such details, Felix thought.

'I tell you the passes will be watched.'

'The greenskins are concentrating their forces on the temple. They will leave only a small force at best.'

'A small force is all it will take to hold us in the passes. Even if I take all my warriors it would be impossible to force passage against determined resistance.'

'I am a wizard of great power. It would be difficult but not impossible, I am sure.'

'I don't care if you wield the power of the gods, I am not going with you,' said Bran. 'Even if you entered the valley, it will be full of orcs.'

'If we can get into the valley, I believe I can conceal us from prying eyes, at least for as long as it takes to reach the temple.'

'And if you cannot? I will join the High King at the Stones of Ogh and we will deal with the greenskins in force.'

'The land may not live that long,' said Murdo. 'If the power within the temple is fully unleashed...'

'No, Murdo,' said Teclis. 'I can see noble Bran's mind is made up. Do not press him. We shall go forward on our own. After all, when we reach the Chamber of Secrets, it will be all the fewer to share in its treasures...'

'Treasures?' said Bran, an entirely new note entering his voice. 'Tell me about these treasures!'

'No. Your mind is made up. Why do you wish to hear about treasure?'

'Why does any man wish to hear about treasure; speak on, elf!' Gotrek gave him a look of disgust but Felix could see that he paid attention too.

The night wore on. Morag drifted away. Felix got drunker and drunker until he could barely keep his eyes open. He found a shadowy spot under a huge wooden support and wrapped himself in his cloak. Despite the sound of drinking, he plunged into an exhausted sleep almost immediately.

CHAPTER TWENTY-TWO

IN THE WAN morning sunlight of the mountain valleys, the events of the previous night seemed like a dream. Felix did his best to ignore his aching head and churning stomach. No more whisky for me, he thought. Still, at least the elf's tales of treasure had done the trick. Felix vaguely remembered roaring drunken toasts being made to the treasures of the Old Ones. He wondered if they really existed or were merely bait for Bran's greed. Did anybody here really think they were going to get their hands on ancient treasures? The odds were a thousand to one against.

He glanced over at the Slayer. Despite the enormous amounts of alcohol he had consumed, Gotrek looked none the worse for the night's drinking. Felix wished fervently that he felt the same way. He glanced back along the path. There were many of the mountain men there, and the swamp dwellers of Crannog Mere, as well as the Oracle's maiden-guard. The elf strode along conversing casually with Siobhain, seemingly completely unaware of the admiring glances of the women, and the jealous glances of many of

the men. Felix began to understand why elves were so disliked. The resentment of the men was almost palpable.

At this point they moved along the side of a sheer drop,
and he was not taking the risk of anyone accidentally pushing him over the edge. They had taken a very narrow path up
the mountainside. It was very cold now and there were
clouds visible below them. Felix squinted sidelong at the
Slayer. He appeared surprisingly jaunty.

Well, why not, Felix thought? We are back in the bloody
mountains, and the prospect of a suicidal quest into enemy
lands is before us. Soon his doom will be upon him most
likely. Felix shrugged. With this hangover, he did not really
care. He continued to trudge wearily up the mountainside,
feeling about a thousand years old.

'WHAT ARE YOU thinking?' asked the woman, Siobhain. She
seemed concerned.

'Many things. None of which I can talk about now,' he
said. She held her peace, although Teclis could tell she was
desperate to know more. Teclis wondered if he was doing
the right thing. This was all going too slowly for his liking.
He could feel the mad raging power ahead of them now. It
seemed so palpable that he was surprised the others could
not, even without his sensitivity to magic.

What he was attempting now was madness. These mountains were full of orcs. The temple was full of Chaos
worshippers and all he had was this small band of barbarians, a dwarf and a reluctant Imperial swordsman. The odds
against success were immense. Still, what could he do?

What were his options? He could leave this small army
and make his own way to the temple. By wrapping himself
in spells of warding and concealment, he could conceivably
make his way through undetected into the heart of the temple complex, but what then?

Kelmain and Lhoigor were both powerful mages, and
would be fighting on a battlefield of their choosing, most
likely woven round with their own protective spells. Perhaps
they might even have subverted the defences of the Old
Ones to their will.

Confident as he was in his own powers, the odds were not in his favour. Unless he could overcome the Chaos mages quickly, their guardians would be able to overcome him physically. All it would take would be one sword blow, and his long life would be over. And it would not just be swords, he knew. There would be all manner of Chaos-worshipping monsters, and this giant of whom the Oracle had spoken. He needed to have physical protection if he were to close the Paths of the Old Ones and battle hostile magic, and that meant more than magic. He needed an army and he needed Gotrek Gurnisson's axe, for the moment anyway.

He considered the pair. The longer he stayed in their company, the longer he saw the hand of destiny at work. Some power watched over them – for good or ill, the elf was not sure, but he was certain that old and powerful forces were at work there, which he could only half glimpse.

He smiled. He was becoming as superstitious as one of the elves of Athel Loren. Fate or chance or the hand of gods, it did not matter. He knew he would most likely need their help before the end. Up ahead, the unleashed energy of the ancients sent billows of power, visible only to a magician, into the sky. He knew just from looking at it that such power could not be contained for long. He only hoped that they would be in time.

He would have given a lot to know more about what his enemies were up to right at this moment.

KELMAIN LOOKED DOWN at Magrig from the stone platform in the side of the ziggurat. The giant glared back up at him with its one good eye. You are not a handsome creature, are you, thought Kelmain, studying the mutated face and huge stinking body? Well, I suppose I would not be either if I had fought as many battles as you. The last one with your late and unlamented brother must have been quite a combat, judging by the fact that you lost your eye, and he lost his life.

'The little greenskins came! Magrig kill many but more will come,' said Magrig in a voice like the rumble of thunder overhead. 'There are many of them and they have powerful magic. Maybe too many even for Magrig to smash.'

'I am sure you will do your best,' said Kelmain. He studied the distant hills with their covering of odd mutated foliage. The swamp smell of the surrounding forest assaulted his nostrils almost as much as the giant's stink. He wondered why the giant seemed so intimidating today. To be sure, he radiated the immense physical power of a being the size of a siege tower, but that was not it – after all, the giant's tiny mind was still firmly under control of the binding spell. He had been ever since they had surprised him in his sleep when they first emerged from the portals into this ancient complex. No, it was not that they were losing control of him.

It took a moment for illumination to strike. Of course: with his squatly massive form, his red matted hair and his one empty socket the giant reminded him of a monstrously huge parody of Gotrek Gurnisson. Was that somehow significant, Kelmain wondered? Was there an omen here? Perhaps he should sacrifice one of the captives the beastmen had brought back and search the entrails for signs. Was it possible the dwarf had somehow escaped from the paths? No. Powerful as he was, the dwarf was no magician. He would be trapped there until the end of the world.

On the other hand, time was getting short. Lhoigor reported that the paths were becoming increasingly hard to control. Some of them vented constant eruptions of Chaotic energy now, and the madness was starting to spread from the Twisted Paths into the unchanged ones. More than one of their acolytes and his warband had failed to return and there were fewer Chaos warriors here than he would have liked with the greenskin tribes massing in the hills. It seemed their awe and fear of Magrig was starting to wear off. Perhaps this had not been such a good plan after all.

Why did our masters put us up to it then, he wondered? Why are we keeping that altar below slick with the hearts-blood of human sacrifices? Why do we keep our acolytes and ourselves working around the clock against whatever odd force it is that is trying to shut down the paths? Was that the work of the accursed elves, he wondered? Or was it something else, some nasty surprise the ancients had left to prevent interlopers using their toys? If so, they would fail. Chaos rules this world, he thought. Nothing will be denied to us. Nothing.

Kelmain could sense their awful greenskin magic being worked up in those hills. Perhaps their shamans have some inkling of what we do here, and are trying to stop us, he thought. Much good it would do them.

'Stay within the temple and smash anything that comes this way!' he told Magrig. 'But come if I call you.'

'I hear and obey, ancient one,' said Magrig.

It pleased Kelmain to be addressed by the title the giant must have used to talk to his creators long ago. Once more he sensed the green flash of orcish magic. What can they be up to, he wondered, as he turned and walked back down the steps and into the heart of the ziggurat.

ZARKHUL WOKE FROM his trance. He was uneasy even though he could sense the comforting mass of thousands of orcs all around and draw power from their presence. They had come from all over the island to be here. Battled their way to join his clans, summoned by the ancient mass instincts of the orcish kind. Something bad was going on. He sensed it. The weather had worsened. Magrig, the sleeping god they had made offerings to for so long, had turned against his people and now his visions spoke of a time and death and hunger for the tribes.

Over and over again the twin gods had shown him visions of the land breaking apart and eating the orcs, of the foul beastmen of Chaos emerging from the temple city like maggots from a corpse, of skies the colour of blood that rained fire and foul warpstone dust. Somehow he knew in his very bones that if they did not reclaim the city and cast the outsiders from its sacred stones then disaster would overtake all of his people. The gods had spoken to him. They had granted him conviction and the mantle of authority that made the chieftains listen to him, even though many of them were his sworn enemies, and had often fought him for control of one ziggurat or another.

Now, like a herd of bison all swinging to face a common threat, the tribes were acting as one. Such things happened to the people when the gods spoke to them. Now they would lay aside their differences and follow him into the great waaargh. They would need to. For in his latest vision he had seen that time was running out and they would need to act soon to avert disaster.

He sensed a tugging at his thoughts and opened his spirit eyes. The spirit of the shaman Gurag hovered before him, invisible to all eyes save his. He spoke with a voice inaudible to all but Zarkhul. 'The men of the mountain are coming along the secret paths. They have allied with elves.'

'Take your force and grind them to a pulp! Gorge on their marrow!' said Zarkhul, speaking in a voice that was not a voice.

'Aye, we will eat manflesh this night, and elf flesh too.' The spirit shimmered and vanished as Gurag returned to his body. Strange, thought Zarkhul, that one so obese in the flesh should see himself as such a proud and muscular warrior in spirit form.

Dismissing the thought, the orc war leader gave his attention to the ziggurats of the temple city below. A lifetime of warfare among their streets against his former rivals had gifted him with knowledge of the best lines of attack, as well as the secret ways beneath the city. With luck the newcomers would not know about those. He would build a mountain of their skulls high as one of the ziggurats as an offering to the Twin Gods. At its peak would be the skull of Magrig and his two strange human familiars. Only when he had made this offering would the gods be appeased. Only then would disaster be averted.

All he needed now was a sign from the shamans to let him know when to begin the attack. He hoped it would not be long in coming.

In the distance lightning flashed and thunder rumbled. Zarkhul wondered if that was the sign. Probably not, he thought. Such weather was too common around here to constitute an omen.

* * *

FELIX STRODE ALONG the mountain paths, not at all reassured by his conversation with the elf. The air was colder now, the weather changing swiftly as it always did in the mountains. Clouds were visible in the valley below them, and slowly they crept up along the flanks of the mountain until they became a mist that reduced even nearby men to blurred shapes. Felix wondered whether this was some doing of the elf's or the work of their enemy, then he realised he did not care.

A squat massive figure appeared out of the gloom before him. He was reassured to hear the dwarf's gruff voice ahead, muttering something in dwarfish. Suddenly thunder rumbled, and in the distance lightning flashed. The flare was diffused by the mist into a brief intense glow and then vanished. Felix wondered whether it was dangerous and lightning might strike him. He felt very vulnerable, as an insect crawling across a window pane where at any time a great hand might swat him.

'Curse this weather,' he said.

'It is strange,' said Gotrek. 'In all my years in mountains, I have never seen clouds come in so fast and thunder so strong.'

'The weather here in Albion is a curse,' said Felix.

'You could be right, manling. Something twists it here, that's for sure.'

Murdo emerged from the mist, silent as a wraith. 'The Stones of Ogham.'

'I take it that has some significance,' said Felix.

'Sometimes. In the areas of the stone rings the weather is often warped. In recent years it has become much worse.'

'These stones hold great magical power then?'

'Aye, they are the work of the ancients.' He looked as if he could say more if he wanted to, but had no intention of doing so. Maybe he did. It was always hard to tell with any sort of wizards. Sometimes they were deep and mysterious because they knew something. Sometimes because they were hiding their ignorance. As a layman Felix was in no position to judge.

'Why have the orcs come here at the same time as us? It cannot be coincidence?'

'Who can tell with the greenskins? Sometimes a mass madness seems to come over them and for no discernable reason they do things in a mass. It's like lemmings throwing themselves off a cliff or the migration of birds. Maybe their gods speak to them. Perhaps the stones are holy to the orcs as well. In places of power it is often easier to attract the attention of the gods and great spirits. '

'Well, tonight would be a night for that,' said Felix. 'This weather is certainly not natural.'

'No,' said Murdo. 'It is not. Perhaps when you have succeeded in your task the world will return to normal, if what the elf says is true.'

'Perhaps,' said Felix.

There was another brilliant flare of light diffused through the mist, then a thunderclap, this time much closer, and the whole mountain seemed to shake. It was all Felix could do to keep from flinching, so sudden and violent was the outburst. He wondered how great the chances of avalanches were here, then decided he did not want to know. The way things were going he knew the kind of answer he would get. A few moments later a drizzle of rain hit his face. It was chill as mountain ice.

'Perfect,' he said. 'Just what I needed to make this day complete.'

The words were no sooner out of his mouth when a scream echoed through the gloom.

'As ever, I spoke too soon,' he said, turning towards its source.

CHAPTER TWENTY-THREE

FELIX RACED THROUGH mist and confusion. Some of the high-land warriors had drawn their huge swords, others brandished their spears as they looked around for the new menace. Howling war-cries emerged from the gloom all around, great bellowing roars that told of the presence of massive bull orcs and the yips and gibbers that spoke of goblins.

Suddenly the clang of weapon on weapon rang through the gloom, followed by the crunch of bone and the screams of wounded men. Felix ran into something big and bounced. It took him a second to realise that he had run smack into the back of an orc. It took him another heartbeat to plunge his sword into its spine. Now was not the time for chivalry, he thought.

The fight was a nightmare. He had only heartbeats to decide whether the shadow emerging from the clouds was a man or a monster. If it was an orc, he struck, if it was a man he tried to hold his blows. He was not entirely sure that he succeeded every time. His flesh crawled. At any moment he expected a blow from some unexpected direction to smash into his flesh and send his soul screaming to Morr's dark kingdom. He knew from the sounds all around him that it was happening often enough.

He needed to move cautiously, for he knew that the edge of the path hung over a vertiginous drop. It would be point-less to avoid the strike of a foe only to plunge to his death in the abyss below. The image almost paralysed him. He stood frozen on the spot for a moment, petrified by the thought of dropping into the gloom below. Somewhere off to his left there was a flash of light, a golden glow that was not lightning, but the casting of an elvish spell. He knew that Teclis was fighting for his life out there in the dark.

Closer yet came Gotrek's fierce bellow. It was followed by the butcher-shop sounds of an axe hitting flesh. From force of habit, Felix made his way towards the noise, knowing that in a wild melee like this, the Slayer's side would be the safest place to be.

TECLIS CURSED THE mist and the strange flows of magic through the mountains of Albion. His ward spells had given him only a heartbeat's warning of the attack. In that instant he had thrown a shield spell around himself.

'Stay with me,' he told Siobhain and drew his sword. It was not pure chivalry on his part. He needed someone to guard his back and he was sure the woman would not plunge a spear into it.

'I am with you,' answered Siobhain.

The flows of magic were sluggish here. Unless he missed his guess, they were currently all being drawn off to the Stone of Ogham, which was most likely the source of this foul weather. He considered trying to channel the winds towards him but decided against it. There was too much chance of some strange feedback effect. The stones distorted magic mightily. This being the case he would need to draw on his personal power and that of the staff of Lileath. Hopefully that would be sufficient.

Swiftly, he wove a web of divination, sending feelers of magic out in a network all around him. They would trip at the presence of orcs and greenskins and warn him of any within about thirty strides. Next he channelled a normal wind towards him, cleaving through the mist. Momentarily it parted the clouds giving him a clear view of the path. Half a dozen orcs raced towards him. He snarled and sent a blast of destructive energy towards them. They bellowed in rage and pain as it ripped through them, boiling flesh from bone like overcooked meat on a joint. One of them, on the very fringe of the spell, was only mildly singed. He leapt forward with eye-blurring speed, his huge scimitar raised in both hands, ready to smite the sorcerer.

Teclis stepped to one side and swung the staff downward, tripping the orc. As it sprawled on its face, he inserted his blade below the flange of its helmet, severing the vertebrae in the neck and cutting the spinal cord like a surgeon. The creature spasmed interestingly as it lost control of its motor functions and began to die. Teclis saw no reason to put it out of its misery and turned to look for a new target. Siobhain put her spear into its back.

A horde of small greenskins scuttled forward. A wave of short spears blurred towards him. There was no time for anything subtle. He spoke a word of command and a wave of flame consumed most of the missiles. He sprang to one side away from the area targeted just in time to hear them clatter onto the stones.

Annoyed by being taken off guard by such crude creatures, he strode into their midst. His blade flickered out, piercing an eyeball here, a windpipe there. The goblins responded with their own weapons, but they were partially deflected by the energy field he had already woven around himself. It was a subtle spell of his own devising which used the force of an enemy's blow against itself. The harder they hit, the more violently their blades were repelled. The danger was that they might strike with enough force to overload the spell. That was why it was best to keep moving and dodge and duck and weave.

Teclis smiled now. In every elf, he suspected, there was a core of bloodlust and what some would call cruelty. In battle this was drawn to the surface. He had seen the mask of culture fall from the faces of too many of his warrior kin not to recognise its presence in himself. It did not disgust him, as it might a human, it was merely another interesting emotion to be catalogued and, if he was honest, enjoyed. Perhaps it was the tainted blood of Aenarion, he thought?

He laughed, and was surprised to see that his laughter elicited looks of horror from Siobhain and the humans around him. Of course, perhaps they did not feel the battle joy flowing through their veins. They were not elves, after all. Nor could they understand what this meant to him personally. He ducked another blow and brought the tip of the staff crunching down on a booted goblin foot. The little creature screeched in pain and clutched its toes, hopping almost comically for the few seconds before he impaled it on his blade.

No, he thought, they could not understand. In his youth, he had been Teclis the weakling, Teclis the cripple, Teclis the pitied. That had been before he had learned to strengthen himself with spells and potions. Now his breath came as easily as any other elf's, and the only sign of his former weakness was a slight limp in his left leg that left him barely less swift and graceful than any other elf. Once these creatures could have overwhelmed him. Once his brother had been needed to protect him from them. No more, he thought, pulling his blade out in a burst of green blood, and then lunging at full extension to skewer another. Now I can look after myself, and enjoy combat as it was meant to be.

His laughter became louder, and the humans looked away. Only Siobhain fought beside him, and even her face showed fear. Thoughts flickered like lightning flashes through his mind. He seemed to be moving so swiftly that he had time to contemplate eternity between blows. It was strange, the only elf he had ever met who seemed to take no pleasure out of this wild battle joy was his brother, quite possibly the deadliest elf who ever lived. Why should that be, Teclis wondered?

'Why should that be?' he asked the goblin that spewed its last meal over itself as the blade took it in the belly. It did not understand elvish, of course, and looked at him as if he were mad. There was something so irresistibly comic in the thought that he simply laughed all the more. He was still laughing as a huge bolt of magical power tore out of the night, and drowned him in a sea of pain.

FELIX HEARD THE cruel hideous laughter ringing out through the mist. What could it be, some orc laughing at the death agonies of its foe, a daemon summoned by one of their shamans? No. There was something familiar about it.

'It's the elf, manling,' said Gotrek from beside him. The dwarf chopped back-handed at a charging orc and cut it in two. Felix threw up his arm to avoid being blinded by the spray of blood and found himself engaged with another huge orc. The force of the creature's strokes numbed his arm. He backed away, parrying as he went, cursing the dim light that made it twice as difficult to concentrate on his foe's flashing blade. He felt something squelch under his heel. He had trodden on a corpse. He fought to keep his balance and had to match the orc blow for blow to avoid being driven back and tripping on the uncertain footing. He heard the dwarf's battle cries recede into the gloom.

It was a mistake. Felix was a strong man but the orc was stronger. Its blows almost sent the blade flying from his hand. He knew that he could not long hold his own in this sort of combat. He needed to take a chance and end this quickly. He ducked, letting the orc's blade pass over his head and then thrust forward with his sword, piercing the orc's belly. The thing roared deafeningly and swiped at him with its massive fist. The force of the impact made stars dance before Felix's eyes. The pain was sickening. He reeled away in one direction, and the orc reeled away in the other to be swallowed by the mist. From all around came the sounds of battle and that hideous piercing laughter.

Concentrate, Felix told himself, fighting to hold down his food, and not simply collapse on the blood-slick ground. It took a massive effort of will to hold himself upright. From all around he heard the sound of scuttling. Small greenish shapes garbed in hooded leather jerkins surrounded him. They cackled and capered as they closed.

This was not looking good, he thought. There was a flash of greenish light and the hideous elvish laughter stopped.

TECLIS FOUGHT TO remain conscious. He knew he was lucky. His magical defences had absorbed most of the impact but still pain surged along every nerve end as he fought to contain and dispel the deadly energy pulsing through him.

Fool, he told himself, his thoughts cold and clear. This is what you get for giving way to the murder lust. You were taken by surprise by a wielder of the power. A crafty one, too. He had shielded himself and husbanded his power until close enough to deliver what should have been a killing stroke. And he had almost succeeded too. Still, almost was not quite good enough.

Now that he had uncloaked himself, the orc shaman was as visible as a beacon burning on a hilltop on a clear night to Teclis's mage sight. He smiled, seeing the greenish-yellow glow of greenskin energy surrounding his foe. It was the familiar magical signature of the shaman. They tapped their energies in some unusual way. The aura brightened as the shaman unleashed another blast. This time Teclis was prepared and his own counter-spell unwove the mesh of alien energy before it had covered half the distance between them. Teclis countered with a bolt of power but the orc's counter-spell was swift and strong. He had the advantage of being fresh and his senses were clear. Teclis still had to deal with the consequences of the shaman's first blast. He hoped that would not prove fatal.

Worse still, his divination web told him that more greenskins were closing on either side; three of them at least and more coming. Where was the girl, he wondered? Lost somewhere in this damned mist, unfortunately. With his attention focused on the shaman he was vulnerable. He could try and defend himself physically and most likely be struck down by the shaman. He could deal with the shaman and take a sword blow for his pains. He could split his attention and fight at less than full effectiveness on two fronts. None of the choices were particularly attractive. Still, he needed to make one and soon. Death stalked ever closer.

FELIX FORCED HIMSELF upright, determined to die on his feet at least. Seeing that their prey was about to put up a fight, the goblins slowed.

'Not too brave, eh?' he said, brandishing his sword menacingly. The goblins in front of him retreated, but others took advantage of his distraction to rush in from left and right. Only the scrape of booted feet on rocks warned him. He swung his blade left and right, driving them back, whirled in case any were coming from behind and then whirled again to face his original attackers who had regained their courage and were closing again.

This was getting him nowhere, he thought. If he stayed here he would die. Acting instantly he threw himself forward slashing with his blade, crashing into the packed mass of greenskins, bowling them over with superior weight and ferocity. He struck left and right furiously, and was rewarded by the jarring of blade on bone, and the agonised squeals of his foes. A moment later and he was clear, back in the main swirl of the battle. He found himself face to face with Murdo and Culum and the men of Crannog Mere.

'I am glad to see you,' he said, joining their ranks as they prepared to face another rush of orcs and goblins.

TECLIS HURLED HIMSELF upwards, invoking the spell of levitation. He strode into the sky at the end of his leap, hoping that it would confuse his foes and get him clear of their blades. There were grunts of dismay from below as the greenskins realised that their prey had eluded them. As he had intended, the mist had covered his movements.

He had not eluded the shaman, though. The nightmarish green glow erupted upwards, a volcanic rush of power that took him all his skill to parry. The deadly sting of the previous blast had gone now and he was free to concentrate on the task at hand. He contained his opponent's spell in an orb of energy and then sent an arc of power crashing down on him. Briefly the shaman's counterspells held out, then one by one they collapsed. Talismans burst in coruscating showers of sparks as they overloaded. The shaman's figure became a statue of molten bronze light in the shape of a monstrously obese orc, then the flesh was stripped from his body, the skeleton vanished and he was gone from the world forever.

Teclis rose above the battle and for a moment stood above the clouds of mist. It was a god-like sensation. He could hear the sounds of battle below, but for the moment he was not part of it. He was free to consider his options.

Not wanting to be taken off guard again, Teclis sent divinatory probes outwards, tendrils of magic designed to alert him to the presence of any enemy mage or spell. It was not flawless, he doubted that such a wide-scale scan could detect the presence of someone under a spell of concealment, but he hoped that he might sense something amiss. It was difficult here in Albion with the flows of magic so disturbed by the presence of the stone rings.

Nothing. That was good. Now he would unleash some power and see what he could do about this attack. Just at that moment something hurtled out of the gloom towards him. He moved to one side and it rocketed by him. The wind of its passage rippled his robes. For a moment, he caught a brief unbelievable glance of what looked like a goblin wearing a pointed helm, and flapping massive leather wings. He shook his head almost unable to believe his eyes. The thing must have been fired from a catapult, that was the only explanation. He could hear its mad giggles as it disappeared out of sight into the clouds and then into the abyss below.

Teclis scanned all around him. From a clump of rocks above he saw more of the goblins and some strange engines that they used to launch themselves into the air. Was it possible, he wondered, that these suicidal creatures had been raining down on the fight all this time, and he had been unaware of it? It certainly looked that way. Even as he watched, several more of them hurtled into the air and vanished into the clouds of mist. Moments later came the sound of screaming.

Now what looked like some kind of leader was directing them to look at him. He could see some of the engines were being realigned in his direction. He lashed out with a storm of light, clearing the ridgetops with blast after blast of pure magical energy. Engines and flyers alike caught light. Once he was sure he had taken care of the visible foes, he asked himself what he was going to do next.

CHAPTER TWENTY-FOUR

FELIX STOOD SHOULDER to shoulder with Murdo and Culum and they began to fight their way through the mass of orcs and goblins. The rock underfoot was slick with condensation and gore. The way it sloped was no help to balance either. The uncertain edge of the path was a cause for constant concern, and in the mist, there was no way to know who was winning.

Felix's arms ached from hacking at orcs. His breath came in gasps. He wondered what had become of the Slayer and the elf. If anything had happened to either of them, his position here was very precarious indeed. He was a stranger in a land of which he knew very little.

The battle became merely a matter of parry, hack or stab whenever a foe came near him. He watched his comrades' backs and they watched his. In the maelstrom of battle, personality and animosities were forgotten. More than once he parried a blow aimed at Culum's back. On several occasions the big hammer-man erupted from the mist to smash the head of an orc attacking Felix to pulp.

Strangest of all were the bat-winged goblins that seemed to descend from the sky, spearing men on their pointed helmets, carrying them off over the edge of the cliffs. The greenskins appeared to have no notion of self-preservation. Froth billowed from their mouths and their wide eyes spoke of some sort of drug abuse. Felix had seen their sort before, in the mountains of the World's Edge back on the boundary of the Empire. It seemed strange to encounter something even vaguely and repulsively familiar so far from home.

Somewhere in the mist, thunder rumbled and golden light flickered. Felix felt vaguely reassured, confident that the elf wizard was still in the fray. More than once he thought he heard Gotrek's bellowed war-cry.

Eventually, after what seemed liked an eternity in hell, the clamour of battle dimmed. The bellows of the orcs grew less and took on a fearful note as they receded into the mist. The shrieks and giggles and wild yips of the goblins faded into the distance. Gradually the voices of men became dominant, and war-cries were replaced by shouts of concern and queries as to the health of brothers and comrades and kin.

Felix found himself looking over at Murdo and wondering if he looked half as bad as the old man. Blood dripped from the Truthsayer's face and arms, the red of men and the green of orc. He had taken a few wounds. A patch of skin on his forehead had been shaved away to reveal pink and bleeding meat beneath. Murdo reached up and muttered an incantation and the wound closed, leaving only a fresh pink scar. Felix noticed that he himself carried a few cuts on his arms and chest but his mail shirt appeared to have preserved him from worse harm.

As if an evil spell had lifted, the mist parted to reveal a scene of awesome carnage. The pathway was covered in the corpses of men and orcs and goblins and even some huge and shapeless monsters of a type that Felix could not name. The men of Carn Mallog had fought bravely but over half of them were down. Only about five of the original war-party from Crannog Mere was left. In the air above them, circled with an aura of power, the elf hovered. Felix could smell burning and saw the flames where strange wooden war engines blazed on the cliffs above.

Gotrek stomped through the shambles like a gore spat-tered daemon of war. He looked grimly pleased with himself and he booted the severed head of an orc chieftain ahead of him like a child playing kickball.

'I see you still live,' said Felix.

'Aye, manling, I do. These were weak creatures and it would have been an unworthy doom to fall to them.'

Felix looked at the piles of dead men and wondered if they would agree with the Slayer's assessment of their foes. Somehow it seemed unlikely. 'Maybe we'll find something more deadly on our quest,' he said sourly.

Gotrek shrugged and glared up at the elf as if annoyed to see that he still lived. Either that or he was considering whether the wizard would make a worthy enough opponent to put him out of his misery. Felix sincerely hoped not. Then he noticed that the elf was gesturing at something.

'I suppose we'd better see what he has found,' Felix said.

BELOW THEM, THEY could see a vast valley, ringed around with mountains. In the middle of the valley, surrounded by boil-ing black clouds, illuminated by lightning bolts, they could see an enormous structure.

'The Temple of the Old Ones,' said Felix.

'Indeed,' said Teclis. 'The Temple of the Old Ones.'

Felix studied the buildings. To be visible from this height, they must be huge. Each was built as a ziggurat, a stepped pyramid with seven huge levels. Each level was marked with runes, and was reached by a ramp from the level below. Strange ramps and tunnels linked the ziggurats running through the trees that seemed to have swallowed the rest of the city. Glowing lights inside indicated that the place was either occupied, haunted or home to some unspeakable sor-cery, perhaps all three.

Gotrek was shaking his head in a puzzled manner.

'What is it?' Felix asked.

'I am reminded of something, that is all.'

'What?'

'The ziggurats of the chaos dwarfs.'

'You think there might be some connection?' asked Teclis.

'I do not know, elf. Nor do I wish to speculate further.'

'As you wish,' said the elf. 'I will tell the others to get some rest. They will need all their strength for the morrow.'

THE PATH WOUND down the far side of the mountains, into the hidden valleys. They all moved cautiously, not quite believing that the elf's spells shielded them as he claimed. They had not seen any orcs this morning, but you never knew.

'Are you sure your magic is working?' Felix asked. 'I can see no difference.'

The elf gave him a strained smile. 'You are within the ambit of the spell.'

'How does it work?'

'It misdirects prying eyes and divinatory magic. Only if someone comes within a dozen strides of us will they notice us. Now if you please, until we are under cover of the trees, I must concentrate on maintaining it.'

As they moved, Felix noticed a change in their surroundings. The air was warmer and there was a foul putrid scent to it, worse than any decay he had smelled back in the swamp. As they descended, it became wetter and there was more vegetation. At first only a few gnarled black trees clung to the mountainside with their roots intermingled with the stone and soil. These proved only to be the first sentries of a vast army of vegetation, a horde of mighty trees and bushes. None of them looked remotely normal. Fungus blighted their branches. Creepers strangled them like serpents. Strange animals scampered along their huge boles. Enormous glistening spiderwebs caught the dim sunlight. Felix felt no urge to see the creatures that had spun them.

Gotrek looked upon them and spat. 'I hate trees almost as much as I hate elves.'

Teclis laughed. 'What have trees ever done to you, Gotrek Gurnisson?' he asked. Felix wondered if the elf liked living dangerously. The Slayer was not someone you provoked lightly.

Gotrek glared back. The men of Carn Mallog moved silently now. A few had shucked their furs as the heat increased. Bran moved alongside Murdo and Siobhain. A faint sheen of perspiration glistened on his face. He looked nervous and slightly shifty. Whatever he might once have thought, it was obvious that he did not like the idea of going any further into this corrupt place. Felix could not say he blamed him, for he had finally recognised the faint tingling brimstone taste in the air.

'Warpstone,' he murmured. 'This is not good.'

'You are correct, Felix Jaeger,' said Teclis. 'It is indeed the bane of the ancients.'

Felix looked at the elf. For once, he knew he was in the presence of someone who could answer his questions, and unlike the Slayer, who seemed to enjoy lecturing. 'What is warpstone?' he asked, aware that he was not the only one listening. His question seemed to have gotten everyone's attention.

'The raw stuff of Chaos,' said Teclis. 'Solidified, congealed, distilled, some combination of all three. It is the pure product of dark magic.'

'I saw a skaven once consume the stuff,' said Felix.

'Then it was a most unusual skaven, for warpstone is very poisonous even to mutants such as the ratmen. I have read that some of the Grey Seers can absorb quantities of a refined form and draw energy from it. If so, I cannot imagine that they would remain sane or healthy for very long, although their sorcerous power would be immense.'

Felix thought of the ratman sorcerer he and Gotrek had so often encountered. The elf's description would easily fit such a creature.

'Warpstone comes from Morrsleib, the Chaos moon,' said Murdo. 'Chunks of it break off and fall to earth in great meteor showers. Such showers regularly land on Albion. Something seems to draw them. Perhaps the stone rings. Perhaps that is their purpose.'

'I do not think so,' said Teclis, but seeing the look of vexation on the old man's face, he corrected himself. 'Let me rephrase that. I believe that Morrsleib may well be made of warpstone, and certainly such meteor showers as you describe have been corroborated by many elvish chroniclers, but I do not believe Morrsleib is the sole source of warp-stone. It is merely a huge, strange astronomical phenomenon. And I do not believe the stone rings were made to attract the meteors, although they may well do so. I believe they have another function.'

'You could well be right,' said Murdo, obviously not wanting to argue with the elf.

'This is all very interesting,' said Felix, 'but I am rather more concerned with the effects that the stuff may have on us.'

'There are only minute traces in the air,' said Teclis. 'And one way or another, I doubt we are going to be here long enough for it to have much effect on us.'

'That's very reassuring,' said Felix. He resisted the urge to point out that while the elf was most likely protected by his magic, the rest of them were not.

The path wound lower down the mountainside. The foliage surrounding them thickened. From the undergrowth came many strange grunts and snuffles and the sounds of huge beasts moving among the branches. Bran's warriors became visibly more nervous. The tension increased. Gotrek's head swung from side to side as he scanned the undergrowth for threats.

'I can see why the giant became corrupt,' said Teclis, 'if this was his dwelling place. A thousand years here would warp anybody's mind.'

'If their mind was not already warped to start with,' said Gotrek pointedly.

'His physical form may well have mutated as well,' said the elf, ignoring the Slayer.

'In what way?' Felix asked, his mouth suddenly dry.

'He will most likely be larger and bear many stigmata of Chaos. He may possess many mutations that will make him harder to kill.'

Felix thought about the troll he and Gotrek had once fought beneath the ruins of Karag Eight Peaks. Someone had chained a bit of warpstone around its neck, and all of the things the elf had described had happened to it. Felix wondered at the depth of the wizard's knowledge. He seemed to

know a lot about many things. I suppose it's one of the
advantages of living for centuries and being a powerful sorcerer, he thought. It would be something worth noting when
he came to write his chronicle of the Slayer's adventures,
though. Some scholars would be willing to pay for that sort
of information alone, although Felix was not sure he wanted
his work to interest those sorts of people. It made the book
of interest to witch hunters and the Imperial censors too.
Perhaps he would just leave it out then, he thought.

The thin layer of earth covering the rocky path thickened
as they descended into the valley, and as it did so it trans-
muted into a horrible blackish-brown mud that clung to
Felix's boots and made sucking sounds as he raised his feet
to walk. Something wet and slimy touched his face. He
shuddered, thinking of the fingers of drowned men or the
tentacles of some particularly obnoxious monster. Instead
he saw it was only a creeper dangling from the branches
above. The branches arched overhead now, forming a passageway through the dense forest that surrounded them.
Felix marvelled at the change in environment. Only a few
hours ago they had been shivering on the misty heights.
Now they were in a warm near-jungle that reminded him of
tales about the Dark Continent he had read as a youth. The
silence deepened. He could hear his own breathing. He felt
certain that something terrible was about to happen.

The long moments drew themselves out, slow as slugs
sliding their way down a wall. He let out a long breath, filled
with his own sense of relief. He walked forward and found
himself on the edge of a huge puddle filled with brown and
muddy water. The edges of the earth came up like those of a
cup to hold it, and there was something obscurely familiar
about the shape.

He shook his head wondering why a massive outline seen
here in the wild back country of Albion should seem familiar to a city boy from Altdorf. Slowly the realisation filtered
into his brain, slowly the enormity of what he was seeing
descended onto his mind. He told himself that it could not
be so. It was merely random chance that had caused the pattern to look as it did.

'It is a footprint,' said Teclis.

'Aye,' said Gotrek with a certain grim satisfaction. 'That it is.'

'It can't be,' said Felix quietly. He paced the side of the mighty tread. It was exactly two of his strides long. If he lay down beside it, it would be almost as long as he was. 'The creature who made it would have to be at least six times as tall as me.'

'And what's your point, manling?' Felix considered what he had just said, realising that he did not want to believe that anything so huge could walk the earth clothed in the shape of a man. On the other hand, just because he feared an encounter with such a creature did not mean it could not exist. In the past he had encountered many huge monsters, why not a giant?

He tried to remember whether any of the noises they had heard earlier might have been the tread of such a monster. How could he tell? What was the point of speculating? Instead he considered the thought of encountering such a creature, trying to scale the thing in his mind. At best he would come up to its calf. Striking it with his sword would be like a child attacking him with a pin. It could lift him one-handed, take off his head with one bite. Hastily dismissing the image from his mind, he turned to Teclis and said; 'I hope you know some spells for controlling giants?'

'The giants of Albion are wilful creatures, and very resistant to magic, so it is said.'

'And yet these Chaos mages control one.'

'Perhaps those reports are incorrect. Perhaps the creature is pacted to Chaos. Perhaps they have access to spells I do not, Felix Jaeger. I am one of the greatest of wizards, it's true, but I do not know everything.'

'This is a historic moment,' sneered Gotrek. 'Perhaps the first time in recorded history an elf has ever admitted that. Be sure to make a record of that, manling.'

'Be sure to make a record of everything,' said Teclis. 'If you survive.'

Somewhere in the distance, something huge bellowed. The cry was answered by the sound of horns and drums.

'Not just giants, it seems,' said Teclis. 'It sounds like orcs and goblins as well.'

'That's reassuring,' said Felix, as they pushed along the path.

CHAPTER TWENTY-FIVE

THE PATH RAN on and on through the stinking forest. The mud grew thicker, but no more massive tracks were visible, a thing for which Felix was profoundly grateful. Instead the forest became more blighted, the trees more twisted, the animals more mutated. A deer with two heads came into view. Spiders big as a man's fist and shimmering like jewels scuttled overhead. They forded a stream of blackish water in which faint glowing particles were visible. Felix guessed that the water here was contaminated with warpstone. His fear was confirmed when Teclis said, 'Pass the word: do not drink of the water or eat anything found here, no matter how edible it might look.'

'I don't think anybody needed to be told that,' said Gotrek.

'You can never be too careful,' said the elf. For once the dwarf did not disagree. The air became thicker and more oppressive with the sort of feel to it that often presages a storm. Suddenly Felix felt nostalgia for the clean air and cold rain of the mountains. He leapt from rock to rock across the ford, not wanting that tainted water to touch even his boots. What are you scared of, he asked himself? Mutated boots? The thought did not seem very funny. He had heard of stranger things in the haunted city of Praag. He cursed to all the gods. It seemed to be his destiny to visit all the worst places in the world. Just once he wished Gotrek's quest would take them to the harem of the Sheik of Araby or the Palace of the Emperor. The way our luck runs, he thought, we would find them overrun with mutants or inhabited by evil mages.

Rain began to fall. It was warmer than mountain rain, and Felix did not like the way it touched his skin. Many of the drops had been filtered through the leaves and branches of those noxious gnarled trees. The gods alone knew what poisons they might contain.

He glanced again. Overhead he thought he caught the glitter of saucer-like eyes. He concentrated. Among the blotched green, he caught sight of a hideous snaggle-toothed face. Before he could say a word, a spear flashed out and smashed into it and a goblin corpse splashed down into the sucking mud.

'I wonder how many more like that there are around here?' he said. Siobhain retrieved her spear from the corpse. The warriors of Albion moved on. Felix had visions of wild-eyed goblin tribesmen peering from the murky undergrowth. It did nothing to improve his mood.

He forced himself to consider what was going on here. It seemed that they were not the only ones with an interest in the Temple of the Old Ones. Did the orcs intend to seize it for their own use, or was there something more sinister afoot?

Teclis shook his head. 'I can see I will have to swathe us in the cloak of unseeing once more,' he said.

'Don't strain yourself, elf,' said Gotrek.

THE LAST BATTERED survivors of Gurag's orcs limped into Zarkhul's camp. He looked at their crestfallen leader. Kur was his name.

'What happened?'

'Gurag was killed by the elf. They made it past us. They are in the valley. They march on the temple.'

Was this the sign he had been waiting for, Zarkhul wondered? Perhaps. All of the tribes were gathered now, they had returned from capturing the stone rings and the shamans had harvested their power. Now seemed as good a time as any for the attack.

'Get your swords out! You can prove your courage to us all. We are going into the city!'

A great roar arose from the gathered horde as his words spread like magic through their ranks. He was certain that even the most distant clans cried with one voice as they responded to his order. At such times as this the orcs would act as one body, could be wielded as one sword, and he was their leader.

AHEAD OF THEM lay the brow of the hill. Felix, Gotrek, Teclis and Murdo made their way up to the crest. They kept to the shadow of the trees and moved quietly although how anything might hear them over the constant lashing of the rain eluded him. At the brow of the hill, they could see that below them, the land cleared. It was wild, open and rocky all the way down to where the temple stood.

The nearest ziggurat was as large as a hill, Felix realised. The temple complex covered an area as large as many human cities. Perhaps only the massive sprawl of Altdorf was larger among all the places he had visited. Over it hung an aura of immense antiquity and strangeness. He could easily believe that no human being had built this place, nor any being remotely man-like such as an elf or a dwarf. Huge glyphs were embedded in the sides; they were rectangular, right-angled mazes which somehow seemed to draw the eye into them. He had to fight to break his gaze away, to keep it from following the patterns. He felt that if he did so, all the way to the end, he might be gifted with strange cosmic insights, but they were not things he wanted. To understand those runes, he felt, might be to leave humanity and sanity behind.

A thought struck him. 'Maps,' he said.

'What, manling?' said Gotrek.

'The runes are maps, of the paths, or of the structure of the paths, or something to do with the...' he let his sentence drag to an end lamely. He realised he must sound like a madman to the others.

'Perhaps you are right,' said the elf. 'It's an interesting theory. Or perhaps they are wards. Symbols can bear within themselves representations of spells. They are patterns of mystical force. Dwarfish rune magic works in this way, I believe.'

'Believe what you like,' said Gotrek. 'But this is getting us no closer to our goal.'

As if in answer to his words, the ziggurats shook. 'And we are running out of time,' said Teclis. 'The power within is starting to run out of control.'

'We go in?' said Felix.

'We go in,' the others agreed. As they spoke, drums thundered around the valley. The orcs too appeared to have come to a decision. Murdo returned and spoke to his men, Bran to his. The maiden-guard hefted their spears and made ready.

Before they knew it, all were engaged in a wild rush downhill, running as fast as they could, using the rocks for cover. Felix was not sure why they did so. Some instinct made them want to cover that open ground as swiftly as possible. The walls of the ancient temple held no promise of shelter or safety and yet somehow they seemed preferable to being caught exposed in the open.

Just the sight of one man running was enough to get the whole nervous crew moving. As they approached the great stone structures he felt as if he was somehow being watched by some vast implacable presence within the temple of the Old Ones, and he wanted more than anything to get himself out from under its gaze as quickly as possible.

He felt almost relieved when he set foot on the first ramp leading up the side of the pyramid. He felt less than relieved when he looked behind him. The whole forest on the hills surrounding the pyramid was suddenly alive with orcs. They emerged from the vile woods in their thousands, whooping and chanting. What have we disturbed here, Felix wondered, knowing that there was no turning back? Against so many there was no chance of returning. Even as they watched, the orcish horde began to rumble downhill, moving with the irresistible force of an avalanche. Perhaps it was the gaze of the orcs we felt, he thought, but knew he was wrong.

'There's a doom for you,' he said to Gotrek, gesturing back towards the mighty horde.

'My doom lies within this pyramid,' said Gotrek, his eyes fixed on the elf's back. Felix was not exactly sure what he meant by that, but it reassured him even less than the sight of all those orcs.

'What now?' he asked Teclis.

'Inside,' he said. 'We are close to the locus of all this power, I can sense it. Our quest is almost over.'

The battle-cries of the greenskins rose behind them. 'One way or another, I think you are right,' Felix said.

FELIX GAUGED THE size of the archway under which they passed. It was ten times the height of a man, large enough to let the giants of his imagination pass through. Wonderful, he thought. As if there was not enough to worry about already.

The place was lit by odd green lights set in the ceiling. They reminded Felix of the ones he had seen in the Paths of the Old Ones. The stonework too was reminiscent of that at the entrance to the paths, although on a far more heroic scale. Why had the mysterious Old Ones felt the need to built roadways so big here? What was it they had taken through from Albion that was so large? Or was his imagination simply too prosaic for the subject? Perhaps the arches were so huge for a completely different purpose. Perhaps there was some mystical significance to their size, shape and form that he simply could not grasp. Perhaps they were part of some sort of rune that could only be read by a god. Not that it mattered much at this hour, Felix thought. If those orcs get their claws on us, all such speculation will be ended. Filled with trepidation, he passed under the arch and into the vast gloomy corridors beyond.

As they did so, the walls shook once more. 'We must hurry now. To the Chamber of Secrets!'

The walls around them shook once more and the lights in the ceiling died. A few of the men let out howls of fear. The dark chamber was suddenly filled with menace. Teclis strode ahead of them, filled with confidence. From the tip of his staff came light to illuminate their way and send things scuttling back away from its circle. Felix caught sight of vast bat-shapes rising into the darkness below the ceilings. Once more he was aware of the huge weight of stones pressing down all around them. He was within the depths of an artificial mountain and something about it oppressed his very soul.

With every step into the ancient darkness he became more certain that the place was haunted. He was not sure what by – perhaps the ghosts of the Old Ones, perhaps the spirits of other long-dead things – but he felt certain that something was there. Very often it seemed to him that just as they entered a chamber, some vast shadow departed, hovering just beyond their sight, waiting and watching with malign intelligence for them to make some misstep or perhaps just to lose their way in the eternal gloom.

Worse yet, the taint of warpstone on the air was getting stronger. There was a pressure in his ears, on the top of his head, within his cheeks, that intensified until it was almost painful. Even his teeth ached. He did not doubt that the elf was right. They were nearing the heart of the most powerful magic Felix had ever encountered. He sensed long-dormant forces coming awake all around them.

Even Gotrek seemed to sense it. His movements were cautious and his head scanned from side to side watchfully. Felix noticed that the runes on the dwarf's axe had begun to glow with their own internal light. That had never been a good sign, in Felix's experience.

Behind them they could hear the echoing shouts of the orcs. The sound seemed to rumble through the old chambers like thunder. The bestial roaring was amplified a dozen-fold until it became the voice of an angry god. In his mind's eye, Felix could picture that vast army of greenskins filing out through the corridors, slowly, inexorably, an irresistible green tide filling up the whole structure.

It seemed unlikely to Felix that they should have got this far without running into some sort of resistance. In his experience, the forces of Chaos never gave up anything they had taken without some sort of fight. Unless of course, it was all a trap. The sudden certainty of it shook him. Were they being lured further into the pyramid to their dooms? Would they be sacrificed in some unspeakable way as part of some dreadful ritual? Had they already been swallowed alive by the vast dark god that was the pyramid itself?

He tried to push the thought from his mind and noticed something else. The amulet the elf had given him was warm enough that he could feel it on his chest. He touched it with his fingers and was surprised by how hot it was, and he saw that the runes on it, written in flowing graceful elvish script, were alight. Something had activated its protective power.

Now in the distance, he heard other sounds, the bellowing of war-cries, the clash of weapon on weapon. Somewhere men or things close to men chanted the names of dark gods. Orcs responded with guttural shouts in their bestial language. So far, on the path they had taken they had encountered nothing. It felt even more like a trap, like walking down the throat of a mighty beast that at any moment might gulp them down into its huge stomach. He gripped tight on his sword as if by holding it tighter he could somehow hold onto his fears as well.

Another thought insinuated itself into Felix's mind. They were not in the body of some great beast, they were trapped in the toils of some great infernal machine, like the engines the dwarfs used to process ore and work metal, only this one processed souls and produced... what? He could not begin to guess. Suddenly he found himself longing for action. His nerves were stretched, his brow covered in cold sweat. Waiting for whatever dreadful doom that was about to ensnare them seemed intolerable. He had to fight down an urge to run towards that distant melee, to throw himself into the mindless carnage, to drown out his consciousness in waves of berserker bloodlust.

The charm grew warmer on his breast. The runes on Gotrek's axe glowed brightly. The auras blazing on

Teclis's amulets almost dazzled him. In the strange glow he could see the faces of the other humans. They all looked strange and bestial, their shadows were the shadows of slouching apes, their features chiselled into expressions of elemental hatred and violence. Culum glared at him malignly. Siobhain's face seemed twisted with insane hatred. Bran looked furtively about as if he feared one of his kin would plunge a spear into his back and claim his crown for their own. They all seemed caught up in some mad dream.

The elf glanced at him and concern passed across his hateful, alien features. 'It's this place,' he said. 'It twists your mind. Chaos and the magic of the Old Ones have intertwined to produce something that mortals were not meant to endure the like of. Be calm. Resist it. Soon we shall be where we need to be.'

As if to mock his soothing words the sounds of violence intensified and the whole pyramid shook as if struck with a giant hammer. The lights flickered to life once more, and a strange keening whining noise filled the air. Felix did not want to consider what could cause such a vast stone structure to quake like a shivering beast. He sensed that forces were being unleashed that might crack the whole world like an egg. He wished he were anywhere but here.

AHEAD OF THEM lay a massive square, open to the sky. That the place had once possessed a roof was evidenced by the fact that huge shattered stones lay everywhere. Mighty stone pillars jutted upwards to support a ceiling that was no longer there. They too showed signs of erosion. Moss had grown on their intricate carved stonework. Tufts of ochre outlined some of the lines and submerged others.

Overhead dark clouds boiled in the sky, glittering redly as if tainted with warpstone dust. Huge thunderbolts lashed down. They must be striking fairly close now. The sight of the open sky increased Felix's claustrophobia rather than the reverse. It reminded him that in another few moments they would plunge back into the stygian gloom. The air here was not fresh. It carried hints of some new corruption. Teclis uttered what might have been an oath in Elvish and moved towards the base of one pillar.

It had been corroded utterly and a white hand stuck out from the rock. Felix moved closer and looking over the elf's shoulder, saw that it was not a human hand. It had only three fingerbones and those were broader and thicker than the fingers of any man. The elf tapped the stonework with the tip of his staff, and rock crumbled to reveal a skeleton that was only remotely human.

It tumbled forward and clattered onto the floor. The elf must have exerted some arcane energy for it did not shatter into a thousand pieces as Felix would have expected. Instead it flipped over as if animated. For a second Felix feared the thing was being returned to some sort of unlife, like the skeletons and zombies he had fought in the ruins of Drakenhof. Others shrank away as well. Only Gotrek and the elf held their ground.

Seeing no immediate danger he moved cautiously forward. The skeleton belonged to a being almost as tall as a man and broader – something about the shape of the head and the disposition of the limbs suggested the batrachian. If a toad and an ape had been crossed, it might have a skeleton like that, Felix thought.

'Slann,' said Teclis. 'One of the Eldest Race, the Old Ones' chosen servants. It was immured here amid these pillars. You would find a similar skeleton at the base of each of these columns. They were entombed alive.'

'But why?' Felix asked.

'As part of some ritual designed to consecrate this place. Their souls were intended as guardians. Maybe they were offerings to whatever it was the Old Ones worshipped. Or maybe the purpose was so alien we could not begin to understand it. Who can tell? Someday when we have more time, I would like to come back and examine this place. Who knows what secrets it contains?'

'This is getting us nowhere,' said Gotrek, raising his axe meaningfully. 'Lead on, elf. Bring us to the heart of this thing.'

Teclis shook himself from his reverie, but paused for a last wondering glance at the skeleton. Felix thought he understood. How long had it been since that creature had lived and breathed and walked in sunlight? Millennia at least. Before the birth of the Empire. Before the first human civilisations arose in ancient Nehekhara. What kind of world had it looked on? What strange marvels had it witnessed? For a brief moment, Felix understood part of the attraction of necromancy. To be able to make such a creature speak and give up its secrets. He shivered and pulled his gaze away, wondering where those dark thoughts had come from. This place really was affecting him, he thought.

As one they passed out of the great courtyard, and back into the bowels of the temple.

FELIX STUDIED THE corridor around him as they marched. At this point it was as wide as a road and the only protective barriers were where support arches jutted out of the walls every fifty strides or so. If there were any chambers leading out of the corridors they had been sealed so cunningly as to be undetectable. Ever since the discovery of the skeleton in the base of the pillar, Felix had suspected that concealed chambers and corpses and secrets were everywhere around them. He found it only to easy to imagine sealed chambers in which legions of batrachian bodies had laid down their lives for their perverse gods, in which sinister engines pulsed with the energies of ancient sorceries.

Overhead the greenish lights glowed eerily. They provided a dim and ghastly luminescence that hid almost as much as it illuminated. Shadows danced grotesquely as the light flickered then surged. They spoke of secret energies ebbing and flowing all around as much as the shaking earth. Once more the image of some huge, complex and ultimately incomprehensible machine struck Felix. But he was prepared to believe that powers that could slowly and inexorably shift continents were being marshalled here.

As the thought struck him, he heard the sounds of battle echo once more through the huge structure.

* * *

THE NOISE OF furious conflict came ever closer. Felix squinted into the distant gloom. Orcs and beastmen fought savagely at the next crossroads. Two mighty inexorable tides of monsters had met and neither was willing to give ground. Felix could not tell who was winning, nor did he care. He wanted merely to be out of this place, and away from the eternal gloom surrounding them.

Teclis raised his hand and gestured for them to stop. All around, men and women readied their weapons, levelling their spears, limbering up their swords. Felix was not sure what use such mighty claymores might have even in these wide corridors. He doubted that there was room for more than two or three men armed in such a way to fight abreast. In a confined space they would prove almost as much a threat to their friends as their enemies.

'No,' said the elf. 'We do not fight. Not yet. We must find another way.'

They waited tensely to see if the battle flowed towards them, but it did not. Instead it receded away from them, flowing into the distance. The small army of humans began its advance once more.

THEY CAME TO another ramp, this one leading down into the depths. From it emerged a foul smell, of stagnant warpstone-polluted water, and old decay. Mould clung to the walls here, a peculiar black stuff that seemed somehow poisonous. It had eaten away at the ancient carvings and formed new and grotesque shapes that hinted at gargoyles and monsters without quite being them.

Without stopping Teclis led them downward into the eternal gloom. Felix looked at the dwarf but he seemed absorbed with his own dark thoughts, his mind appeared to have turned inwards on itself as it often did before moments of extreme and explosive violence.

Even the downward-leading ramp was huge. It descended steeply into a gloom that became ever deeper as the green ceiling lights became ever more intermittent. Felix strode along at the head of the column beside the elf and the dwarf. He found their presence reassuring even here. Then his eyes caught sight of something that left him stunned.

The way ahead was barred by what looked like a huge broken wall of spikes. He strode closer and saw that they were not spikes but bones, part of another, much larger skeleton. A monstrous ribcage loomed above him. He walked along a shattered spine towards a fairly human-looking skull that had been smashed by some titanic blow.

It was the skeleton of a giant. It blocked the entire corridor. Its size was entirely consistent with the creature he had imagined when he saw the huge print in the forest mud.

'I don't think he was entombed here as part of some ancient ritual,' said Felix.

He inspected it for the stigmata of mutation and could see none. The bones were huge, much thicker than those of an ordinary man in proportion to their size, and Felix guessed that the giant had been much broader in life in proportion to his size than a man. Still, there were no horns or claws. A few of the bones from legs and arms were missing but he saw their cracked and broken remains lay close by. It reminded him of the way orcs and beastmen broke bones to suck out the marrow. He suppressed a shudder.

'What could have killed and eaten a giant?' he asked, not really expecting an answer.

'Another giant,' said Gotrek grimly. He strode forward under the huge ribcage and paused to contemplate it for a second as if measuring himself against it. Felix wondered what was passing through his mind. Compared to this huge creature, even Gotrek's mighty axe was less than a child's toy. It was not a reassuring thought. The print they had seen outside was recent and the image of a cannibal giant strong enough to kill even its mighty kin sprang into his mind.

He could tell by the expressions of all the men around him that the same thought had occurred to them. It was with visible reluctance that they continued their trek down into the depths of the pyramid.

CHAPTER TWENTY-SIX

TECLIS STUDIED THE threads of power he sensed all around him. He was close now. Close to the black heart of the mystery he had crossed continents to solve. Close to the source of the dreadful eruptions of power that spelled doom for his homeland unless they were resolved. He felt the flow of vast energies around him, greater even than those pinned down by the watchstones of Ulthuan. Compared to them, this was like measuring a mountain stream against the flow of the mighty river Reik.

There was something wrong here. The flows of energy were not steady. They stuttered. They erupted mightily one instant and faded away to nothing the next, as if someone had invoked their mighty energies but could not quite control them, was in fact battling to contain them. The thought sent fear shuddering through even his perfect self-control. That someone had awoken this sleeping daemon without knowing its true name, had aroused all this power without having the means to completely control it, was almost more frightening than the idea that evildoers had bound it to the service of Chaos.

For if the power that underpinned continents and could shift worlds in their orbit was allowed to raven unchecked then the end of the whole world was perhaps nigh. Certainly the end of this temple and perhaps this island, and as an inevitable consequence, Ulthuan. Worse than that, even the partial control that was going on here was the mark of mighty sorcerers, perhaps more than his equals. He did not relish the prospect of facing them.

His options were scant indeed. They needed to go on, to get to the very core of this, and soon. He led the way downwards into the heart of the pyramid. All around him power surged. All around him battle raged.

THE ROAD ENDED at a mighty arch. Beyond it lay a huge chamber, with many entrances and exits. Felix looked at it. There seemed no rhyme or reason to the place. It was a huge maze laid out according to principles he could not understand. Above them were many galleries and walkways. Ahead of them was open space, and when he went to the edge and looked down, he could see more galleries dropping away beneath them. It was like looking into a huge well.

He was reminded once more of the strange city he and Gotrek and Snorri had gotten lost in during their trek across the Chaos Wastes. Was there some connection between this place and that? Certainly there were similarities between the architecture, but this temple was built on an even more epic scale. In his mind's eye, he suddenly pictured dozens of such places scattered about the world, linked by a web of strange powers, laid out in a pattern just as incomprehensible to a mortal mind as their interiors.

He was distracted from his reverie by the appearance of a horde of orcs on the gallery above and opposite them. Their leader was some sort of shaman, carrying a skull-tipped staff. He shrieked and pointed at them. So much for spells of concealment, Felix thought. Noticing the men below, the orcs raised their bows and sent a wave of arrows hurtling towards them. The distance was great but one could not count on all the force of the missiles being spent. Felix ducked down below the level of the stone banister. Arrows clattered down all around him. A second wave came in and Teclis incinerated them with a spell. Seeing this, the green-skins held their fire and shouted taunts and abuse in their vile tongue. Gotrek answered with a few of his own, and was joined by the human warriors. The elf seemed more concerned with getting them moving again.

The orcs began to surge along the gallery seeking some way to get to their opponents. As Felix watched, beastmen and black armoured Chaos warriors emerged from another entrance and met the greenskins head on. A monstrous melee ensued.

Felix wondered at their luck. Why had they encountered no resistance? Why were the Chaos warriors concentrating on the greenskins? An answer immediately struck him. They were the greater threat. They were, after all, a huge army compared to this small band. Perhaps the Chaos warlords had failed to notice the humans in their midst. If that was the case, Felix thought, it would only be a matter of time before they rectified this oversight.

HIS PREMONITION PROVED true, not a hundred strides from where he had it. The elf led them off the massive balcony along which they marched and into a huge chamber containing more strange pillars. These ones glowed with an eerie green light. Felix could almost sense the power flowing through them. The massive runes glowed along their length. From an entrance at the other end of the chamber, a horde of beastmen suddenly emerged. At their head was a black armoured Chaos warrior on whose chest blazed a glowing Eye of Chaos symbol.

At the sight of the interlopers, the beastmen howled challenges and prayers to their dark gods and threw themselves forward. The warriors of Albion leapt to meet them breast to breast. Within moments a mad melee swirled among the pillars.

'Stay close,' said Teclis. 'We cannot afford to get pinned down here. Time is getting very short.'

'So is my patience,' said Gotrek. Even as he spoke, he hacked down a wolf-headed creature armed with a massive spear, and then split open a goat-head from gizzard to groin. Felix parried the blow of another goat-headed giant and then stabbed over its spear with the tip of his sword. The creature shrieked as it leapt away to avoid being spitted. Its back came into contact with one of the glowing pillars. Immediately, its shrieks intensified and a terrible smell of burning flesh filled the air. As it toppled forward, Felix could see its shoulders and spine were blackened, charred meat. He almost felt like he was putting the thing out of its agony when he cut it down.

Gotrek and Teclis pushed forward, dwarfish axe and elvish blade flickered in unison. Felix could see that Teclis was more than a match for even a master human swordsman, but his prowess fell far short of the dwarf's. For every one beastman the elf cut down, the Slayer hewed down four. Still, Felix thought, for an effete wizard, the elf was not doing at all badly. Every now and again, he stopped and spoke a word of power and gestured. A bolt of energy lashed from his staff to disintegrate his foes.

The three of them formed a spearhead behind which the warriors of Albion chopped their way through their inhuman foes. The dwarf and the elf were unstoppable at least by any power that currently opposed them. The folk of Albion were not quite so lucky. Even as Felix watched he saw the ranks around Bran thinning, clawed down by desperate beastmen. Murdo and Culum went to his aid, hewing their way through the monstrous ranks, bolstering up the hill-king's guard and enabling them to fight their way free of the ruck. Gotrek and the Chaos warrior came into contact. For a few brief moments, starmetal axe clashed with hell-forged black steel, then the Chaos champion was down and his forces begun to retire in disarray.

'Push on, push on,' yelled Teclis. 'We must get to the heart of the pyramid before it is too late.'

Such was the urgency of his tone that not even Gotrek gainsaid him. Once more the pyramid shivered. The glow surrounding the rune-carved pillars grew so bright as to be almost dazzling and then swiftly faded. Where it touched, corpses or living, it burned. Felix hurried on, sensing the elf's desperation and not liking the thought of finding its cause one little bit.

THE DEEPER THEY penetrated into the pyramid, the more difficulty Teclis had in keeping them concealed from spells of prying and warding. Once already his concentration had faltered and they had been seen by the orc shaman. The flows of magical energy were becoming chaotic, partially from the invocation of the powers centred on the temple and partially from the vast surges being unleashed by greenskin shamans and Chaos warlocks. The latter were tiny changes compared to the former, but under such conditions, they introduced uncertainties into the matrix.

Each casting was like a tiny grain of sand shifting in a desert. Of itself it was nothing, but the tiniest piece of extra weight and pressure it created could cause a whole dune to tremble and fall into a new pattern. So it was here. Perhaps one day, if he lived, he would set his theories about this to paper. At the moment, he had other concerns.

In order to avoid contributing to the maelstrom, he was drawing on the power contained in the staff, and his own personal energies and these were tiring in the extreme. He possessed certain powdered roots and herbs that would aid him, but preferred not to use them unless he absolutely must. The price to be paid for renewed energy was a loss of concentration and intellectual sharpness, and at the moment, he needed all his wits about him.

His force was too small to risk it being caught up in another melee. Time was growing short. He needed to find the safest path to the heart of this labyrinth and confront the sorcerers at work there, and he needed the blades of the men and dwarf to shield him. He knew he was going to have to risk a spell of his own, and trust to the fact that any other mage present was most likely too caught up in the intricacies of battle magic to notice something as subtle as he was going to attempt.

He gestured for the others to wait, closed his eyes and murmured the spell of All Seeing. At first, as always, there was no change, then slowly the frontiers of his perception began to expand outwards like a slowly inflating bubble. Suddenly he was able to stand outside himself and look down, seeing in three hundred and sixty degrees. He felt dizzy as his mind struggled to adjust to perceptions it had never been intended to deal with, to see things from a perspective no mortal normally viewed from. Had it not been for decades of practice and the discipline of centuries he doubted he could have done so. As far as he knew no human had ever achieved the mental flexibility needed to perform this ritual without the use of potent hallucinogenic drugs. Even then, he doubted the spell was very useful to them. Only elves it seemed could perform this, and the Old Ones who had taught them it, of course. Perhaps the slann could as well, but who could tell what that strange batrachian race were capable of?

He realised that he was becoming distracted, as his mind sought to escape the pressure to which he was subjecting it. He breathed deeply, stilled his racing heart with a thought and let his consciousness continue to balloon.

He became aware of all the corridors radiating away from his current position. He saw most were empty, but that in some beastmen raced and orcs moved stealthily. It seemed that nearby the battle for the pyramid had reached a new phase, of stealthy stalking, as each side sought to take the other by surprise. Outwards his perceptions raced like the ripples from a dropped stone racing towards the edge of a dark still pool.

He saw pockets of savage conflict where orc and beastman battled. He saw shamans cast spells with wands of bone and warlocks respond with spells of subtle Tzeentchian intricacy. He felt the tearing of the fabric of reality these caused like a pain inside his skull.

Onwards and outwards his vision ranged until he saw the whole pyramid as a vast seething ant-heap of violence and conflict filled with hordes of monsters bent on doing each other harm. He saw huge trolls and monstrous dragonogres. He saw bizarre limbless pit-bred monsters, all mouth and eyes, bouncing into battle with shrieking goblins on their backs. He saw harpies flap among the galleries and

Giantslayer 283

descend on bellowing black orcs to claw at their eyes with
razor-sharp talons.

There was much he could not see. Certain areas were
shielded by strange runes. Others were blocked from his
sight by dazzling swirls and flows of cosmic energy which
blinded him when he attempted to concentrate on them. He
forced his mind to drink in what it could and memorise
what it must, and then he focused his attention on what he
sought, the strange vast vortex of power that lurked deep in
the heart of this mad structure.

This part was easy. His attention was drawn to it like a
moth to a flame or a drowning swimmer to the centre of a
whirlpool. He saw the spells of warding set up to protect it.
They were potent and strong but they lacked the subtlety and
power of the slann wards. With luck and skill and concentration he could avoid them. He sent his consciousness
flowing along the intricate patterns, avoiding the mystical
tripwires and pitfalls, trying not to set off any of the alarms.
It felt like agonisingly slow, painful work, but he knew that
in reality he was still caught in the moment between one
heartbeat and another. In passing he saw the warriors who
waited at the centre and the huge thing that stalked the heart
of the pyramid, he sensed its primordial rage and hunger.
Then at last his mind found what it sought: the central chamber, the heart of the madness, the place where the power
flowed out of the world beyond and into the mortal realm.

He saw a massive structure that somehow suggested a sac-
rificial altar slicked with blood and the controls of some
intricate machine. He saw the piles of corpses that had been
offered up to the gods alone knew what. He saw giant pillars
at either end of the hall through which all the condensed
and collected magical energy was focused, and he saw the
vast and intricate web of forces that radiated out from this
place and into hundreds of others. Here was one of the great
nexi of the Paths of the Old Ones, perhaps the greatest, save
for that vast abyss that gaped at the northern pole.

He could see now where all the Chaos warriors and beastmen were coming from. They were entering through the
Paths of the Old Ones and emerging here. Even as he

watched, a burst of energy told him of the arrival of another warband. He watched them immediately take orders from the wizards who controlled this place, and race outwards to do battle.

Here then, at last, were the beings who had worked to open this place – near identical albino twins of vulpine aspect. One was clad in spun gold and the other in deepest black. He could sense at once that they were mages of vast dark power. Something linked them, a tie of blood and magic that reminded him of the one that linked himself and his twin, only greater. He sensed their malice and glee as they worked and realised that they were in no sense sane. They did not care if they destroyed this island or this world. Perhaps they would be glad. There was no way he could persuade them to stop, so that slim chance was gone. Two such as these were going to have to be overcome by force. He only hoped he possessed enough to do the work.

Even as he watched he could see that one of them was working spells similar to his own to guide the forces of Chaos against the orcs. The other supervised the engine at the chamber's heart, seemingly unaware or unconcerned that he had woken forces beyond his power to control.

Teclis cancelled his spell and his consciousness immediately flowed back into the vessel that was his body. He shook his head and checked the spells of concealment he had laid over the party. Now more than ever they were needed. If one of those mages sensed them before they reached the innermost sanctum, he could throw enough of the Chaos warriors and beastmen forward to overwhelm them. He believed that his weaves were tight and effective. At the moment his greatest fear was that they would be reported to the wizards by one of their lackeys. Against that, haste was the only defence.

CHAPTER TWENTY-SEVEN

ZARKHUL PUSHED ON into the heart of the pyramid. He led
his bodyguard out into this, the heart of the largest ziggurat. He was close to his goal. Soon he and his warriors
would slay the interlopers who defiled the temple. They
would cleanse this place in blood. He summoned the spirit
power of his people and his gods and brought his blessing
down on his warriors. Now, he thought, there would be a
reckoning.

KELMAIN SENSED A disturbance in the wards. He thought he
had sensed one before but he had not been sure. The tides
of power here were so turbulent that it had been hard to tell.
This was different. This bore the imprint of greenskin magic
and it was close, very close and immensely powerful.
Somehow it seemed the orcs had found their way into the
heart of the city. There were too many of them to be resisted,
at least until reinforcements could be summoned. They
needed time to calm the seething energies of the paths and
bring them back under control, then once more they could
summon aid. He needed all his remaining forces here to

guard the Chamber of Secrets until that could happen. He
cast the spell of summoning that would draw Magrig to
him.

FELIX GASPED FOR breath. The elf had led them at a fast trot
through the labyrinth. Felix was not sure how he found his
path and kept to it, but it seemed to be working. As they
descended into the depths, they managed to avoid any more
marauding bands of beastmen or orcs. Their way was clear.
From the pressure in his head, he could tell they were getting
closer and closer to their goal. Powerful evil magic was at work.

From up ahead now, he could see a strange pulsing glow.
It blazed brighter then receded almost to invisibility. More
than ever he felt like a bug crawling through the chambers
of some huge creature's house. The scale of the corridors was
oppressive. Large enough for even the dead giant to have
moved through. What had been brought here, he wondered? Why did these ways need to be so large? Had the Old
Ones brought ships down here? Or were they giants themselves? So many questions and so few answers.

Suddenly from close by, he heard the sound of insane
enraged bellowing so loud that it was almost earsplitting,
and so terrifying he almost froze on the spot. Only a creature far larger than a man could have made that much noise.
Only a giant. Moreover, even as he listened the screaming
came closer, bringing with it the sounds of battle.

Felix exchanged looks with Gotrek and Teclis. They knew
what was coming too. The elf looked calm. Gotrek looked
angry. His beard bristled and he ran his thumb along the
blade of his axe until a bead of blood showed. The men of
Albion looked poised for flight. This horror looked like it
might prove the final one for their shattered nerves. They
looked ready to break and run in a moment.

What happened next happened almost too quickly for the
mind to comprehend. A huge shadow appeared far down
the passageway, blocking out the ceiling lights with its bulk.
From all around it came a whirlwind of screams and war-
cries. These seemed like the reedy piping of swamp birds
compared to the bellowing of the huge monster.

Carried by its huge stride the giant was on them almost before they could react. Felix got a quick glance of the thing. It had once looked like a man, but that time had been long ago. Now it was warped hideously. Its proportions were almost dwarf-like. Its shoulders were immensely huge. Its legs like the boles of massive trees. The comparison was an easy one to make, for in one hand it held a club that was little more than the branch-stripped remains of a tree. But it was the face that Felix would remember in his nightmares.

Once perhaps, it had borne the features of a nobly proportioned man, albeit one with a monumentally huge jaw. Now those features had run like melted wax, so that flabby jowls hung down almost to the creature's chest. Idiot fury and pain filled its one good eye. Drool dribbled from between teeth the size of tombstones. The smell was appalling. It reeked like a legion of beggars who had spent all day trawling through a sewer for the vilest refuse. Felix started to gag.

All around the creature were orcs and Chaos warriors, fighting with it and each other. The giant did not care. It lashed out with its club, reducing them to jelly-like smears. The force of its blows was irresistible. One would have been enough to smash a warship to flinders. As it moved, it stamped on the small creatures surrounding it, like a man might crush vermin underfoot.

It took them in with one glance, casually smashed a dozen of the men of Albion to paste and passed on into the depths of the pyramid, leaving them trapped in the furious melee.

'Quickly,' said Teclis. 'We must follow it.'

'You're joking,' said Felix, blocking the blow of a massive orc, a second before Gotrek's axe chopped it in two.

The elf shook its head. 'It is heading into the depths to the axis of power. It is being drawn there or summoned.'

'Summoned?' said Felix. 'What could summon that?'

'I do not know,' said Teclis. 'But I am sure we will find out.'

Even as the elf spoke, the dwarf surged past him, hewing frantically, desperate it seemed to get on the trail of a monster worthy of guaranteeing his doom.

Felix followed. There was nothing else to do.

* * *

AND SO THEY came to the heart of the temple, to the secret chambers where the ancient engines of the Old Ones had been reactivated by the dark sorcery of Chaos. They emerged into a huge chamber where a dozen portals had opened. Through two of them emerged the warriors of Chaos, beast-men, minotaurs, harpies, iron-collared daemonic hounds, all the nightmare creatures Felix had hoped never to meet again. All around them were piles of dead bodies, both greenskin and beastman.

Standing atop a huge altar were Kelmain and Lhoigor. One of them manipulated the energies by passing his hands over the controls of the ancient machines. The other appeared to be frozen. The giant loomed before him, listening to the seductive voice of evil. Immediately Felix saw why the creature had been summoned. Hordes of greenskins flowed through several other entrances to the huge chamber, enough to overcome even those temporarily guarding it. How they had got there Felix had no idea, but according to the men of Albion the greenskins had been at home here for centuries before being driven out, so perhaps they knew some secret way. Not that it mattered. It looked like he and his companions were going to be caught between the hammer of Chaos and the anvil of orcdom. There were thousands of foes in this chamber, and two of the deadliest sorcerers he had ever seen along with their enthralled gigantic servitor. He offered up a last prayer to Sigmar. He knew he was not going to survive this.

Even as the thought passed through his mind, the walls shook. The runes along the walls glittered. The face of Lhoigor twisted as he tried to control the mystical backlash. Even to Felix's untrained eye, it was obvious that he was not able to do it.

Suddenly he understood what was going on and why there were so few Chaos warriors. The mages had unleashed forces they could not control. Through the open portals, Felix could see a seething sea of energy. It was slowly advancing through the portals, as inexorable and irresistible as lava. There would be no more reinforcements from the Chaos Wastes, Felix realised. They had most likely been swallowed by raw stuff of Chaos that flowed within the paths. He could not find any sympathy in himself for such creatures.

Another thought passed through his mind. The orcs could win here and their victory would be as bad as that of Chaos. For unless the ancient engines were shut down, the forces unleashed would tear apart Ulthuan and Albion and eventually perhaps the world.

'What are we going to do?' Felix said.

'Guard me,' said Teclis. 'I must reach that altar.'

'Typical of an elf,' said Gotrek, his tone almost humorous. 'The world is ending and all he is concerned about is his own safety.'

Still, when the elf moved, the Slayer followed, and Felix went with him.

THEY BATTLED THEIR way across the chamber, the human warriors forming a tight knot around the elf. They had no idea what he was going to do but they seemed determined to defend him in any case. All around them orc fought with beastman and Chaos warrior.

Felix could see that this worked to their advantage. Only rarely did their foes make anything like a concerted rush towards them. At those times the fighting became hot and deadly and men and women died. Felix ducked the sweep of a Chaos warrior's blade, lashed out a counter-blow against the cold black metal armour. His sword almost dropped from fingers numbed by the force of impact. The ancient magical blade cut through the enchanted vambrace and bit into the Chaos warrior's arm. Another stroke took him through the gorget and buried the blade deep in his throat.

Up ahead Gotrek and Teclis fought like daemons, chopping down anything that got in their path. Man or monster, beast or orc, nothing withstood them. The destruction they wrought was immense. They were almost halfway to their goal when it all went horribly wrong.

Teclis knew it was only a matter of time before the Chaos sorcerers spotted him. His spells had prevented them from being detected by wards as they had moved through the pyramid, but they would be visible to magesight now. One of the twins was busy, trying to control the immense flow of power through the master altar. The other appeared to be feeding him strength while at the same time guiding the forces of Chaos. Teclis could sense the summons going out to every part of the pyramid. He did not need to understand the language to know that it was urging them to return to this chamber by the swiftest route possible.

Once the spell was complete the black-clad albino opened his eyes and gazed around. Their eyes met. Teclis felt the spark of recognition pass between them. Each knew the other for what they were immediately – a master sorcerer. The Chaos mage smiled evilly and bellowed something in an ancient half-recognisable tongue. Teclis ducked the sweep of an orcish blade, frantically trying to make out what his foe had shouted through the din of battle. He felt certain it was not a spell. The next thing he chanted was though – a moment later an enormous arc of power smashed outwards towards him and the Slayer. Desperately Teclis prepared a counter-spell. Even as he did so a monstrous shadow passed over the elf.

Felix looked up. His gaze travelled up enormous columnar legs, along a mighty misshapen body and came to rest once more on that hideous gigantic face. Everyone around him stood as if paralysed. He did not blame them. The sheer ferocity of the giant's howl was enough to unman most people. For a moment, all was silent. All around them, nothing seemed to move.

Felix was not sure whether this was really the case or if it was an illusion. Often in the past, in moments of crisis, things had seemed to freeze or move with extreme slowness. Perhaps this was one of them.

A moment later he was certain of it. The huge monster raised its club and brought it down in a sweeping arc, designed to reduce the elf to bloody sludge. Felix's thoughts raced as he tried to work out what to do. Nothing came. He could not block the blow. He began to move forward, thinking perhaps that he could push the elf to one side, then he noticed that with painful slowness the Slayer appeared to be doing exactly that.

One of Gotrek's ham-sized hands thrust the elf out of harm's way, then the Slayer bounded aside himself. Such was the force of the Slayer's blow that the elf was hurled from his feet and sent rolling away. Felix suspected that the dwarf had most likely enjoyed doing that. A heartbeat later there was a thunder-crack as the club connected with stone. The impact hurled chips of gravel everywhere. One caught Felix on the face, gashing a bloody weal across his cheek.

Undaunted by the enormous size of his foe, Gotrek bounded forward. His axe smashed into the giant's ankle. Blood flowed from an enormous cut. The dwarf's mad laughter rang out as he hacked once more. The runes on his axe glowed ever brighter as it bit into the giant's Chaos-tainted flesh. Was it possible that he might succeed in bringing down even this titanic beast, Felix wondered?

Behind the giant, he noticed the Chaos mage launch another spell. Felix knew it boded nothing good. He glanced at Teclis to see if the elf mage was doing anything but he was still flipping himself to his feet. A second later a sphere of glowing red left the mage's hand and, rotating as it came, flickered towards the Slayer, leaving a glowing blood-red contrail in its wake.

Gotrek did not hesitate. His axe flashed upwards to intercept it, and this proved to be his undoing. The moment the sphere touched the axe, it disintegrated in an enormous flash of light. A second later the Slayer reeled backwards, moving awkwardly, obviously blinded. The Chaos mage bellowed something again, in some obscure language.

The giant gave an idiot giggle, bent down and grabbed Gotrek in one enormous hand. Felix momentarily expected to see the fist close and reduce the dwarf to a bloody mess and now he was too far away to do anything to help the Slayer.

TECLIS PULLED HIMSELF to his feet. His ribs were sore from the blow the Slayer had landed when pushing him out of the giant's way. He did not know whether to be grateful or enraged. It felt as if some of his ribs were broken. Not only that, his pride was hurt. He would not have believed it possible for anyone to landed a blow on him unawares, and yet the Slayer had. It said much for the dwarf's prowess. The thoughts flickered through his mind as he pulled himself clear of the struggle between dwarf and giant. He felt fairly sure that this time even Gotrek Gurnisson had bitten off more than he could chew. Regrettably, Teclis was in no position to help him. He had another, even larger problem – how to overcome the Chaos sorcerers and close the Paths of the Old Ones before the tide of Chaos overran this temple, and undermined the whole geo-mystical pattern of the Old Ones' work, sinking Ulthuan and ravaging the lands of men.

At the moment, the roaring giant cut them off from his sight. He bounded off to the right, chopping down a beastman who came too close, parrying a blow from a goblin spear as it rose to impale him. Murdo was at his back, his spear flashing. The elf had no time to be grateful.

'You must stop them!' the old man bellowed. Teclis did not reply to this redundant statement. He was too busy concentrating on how to do it. Seeing himself ignored, the old man muttered a prayer. Runes burned along the length of his spear and he cast it directly at the black-robed mage. It flew with incredible speed, like a thunderbolt, so swift that even Teclis's sight could barely follow it. He was surprised when it was only partially deflected by the mage's protective spells, slashing his side like a sword-blow. Even more impressively, the spear swerved in flight and began to return to the old man's hand. It seemed that the magic of men was still capable of surprising him.

The Chaos sorcerer was not best pleased. He gestured, and a polychromatic sphere of light flickered around his hand. He gestured again and a geyser of the raw stuff of Chaos appeared – hurtling towards Murdo. The Truthsayer sprang to one side. The stuff hit two of the men behind him and they fell apart as if hosed down with acid.

A bellow of pain somewhere to the left and behind them told Teclis that against all odds Gotrek Gurnisson appeared to be alive and keeping the giant occupied. Knowing that the dwarf could not last much longer Teclis decided he'd better make his move while the monster was still distracted.

Gathering all his strength, he prepared to act.

SOMEHOW, SINEWS BULGING, Gotrek resisted that enormous force. His axe arm was outside the giant's grip and still flailed away, drawing blood with every swipe. The giant raised him to the level of its mouth. Felix watched, horrified, knowing what was coming next. The creature's mouth was so huge it could take the Slayer in one bite.

At the last second, just before his struggling form was stuffed into the thing's mouth, Gotrek shook his head and appeared to regain his sight. His situation was awful. Even if he freed himself, he could do nothing except fall to his death on the hard stone below. As if realising this, the dwarf bellowed defiance and chopped down with his axe, slicing through the giant's fingers. The giant's grip came free and Gotrek leapt forward, pushing himself off the giant's palm with his feet, burying his blade right into the middle of the giant's enormous forehead. Magrig let out a bellow of pain that almost burst Felix's eardrums.

Hanging from his axe like a climber using a pick to hold onto the face of a mountain, Gotrek reached over and stuck his hand into the giant's plate-sized eye. Felix winced as he reached under the lid and tugged the remaining eyeball free of the socket. The giant spasmed and tried to swat at the dwarf. Gotrek tugged his axe free and let himself drop, still clutching at the ball of jelly that had once been an eye. Felix thought he would drop to his doom, but was surprised to see a cable of veinous substance come loose behind the eye. It occurred to him that the Slayer was swinging from what remained of the giant's optic nerve. The giant's blow slapped into its own head with enormous force. It had dropped its club now as it howled and raged in its agony. It stopped and shook its head as if that would somehow get rid of the pain. Of course, it only increased it.

Gotrek swung backwards and forwards like the pendulum on a clock, dropping ever lower as the giant bent double. Blood and brain fluid were starting to leak through the enormous wound on the giant's forehead. At the lowest point of his orbit, Gotrek reached up and slashed the nerve with his axe, falling the last dozen feet to the ground and rebounding to his feet. He was an awful sight, covered in gore, blood leaking from the corners of his own mouth, but still he refused to slow down. He lashed out with his axe once again, catching the giant behind the ankle, cutting a tendon the size of a ship's cable. The giant teetered on its feet, unable to see or control one of its legs. Slowly, like a huge tree falling in the forest, it began to topple. Felix was already moving, throwing himself clear of the monster as it collapsed. Many of the orcs and goblins were not so lucky. They fell crushed beneath its huge weight, never to rise again.

Still, the giant was not finished. With an awful vitality it rolled and flailed at anything around it. Perhaps it could still hear movements, perhaps it was merely lashing out at random. Felix did not wait around to conclude his investigation at close range. He backed away swiftly. Gotrek did not. Moving with startling speed considering his wounds, he raced in closer, under the arm of the flailing giant.

Felix paused in his flight to watch what happened next. The Slayer struck twice. One blow opened the giant's windpipe, the other its jugular vein. A torrent of red flowed forth, billowing upwards like a geyser. At the same time a hideous gurgling rasping sounded, as the giant tried to fill its lungs, while air wheezed out through the incision the Slayer had left. Had that been deliberate, Felix wondered, an act of malicious cruelty, or had the Slayer merely missed his first stroke? He doubted he would ever find out.

Even as the Slayer jogged clear, the giant lashed out frantically, desperate to avenge itself on its tormentor. One of its massive arms caught the Slayer a glancing blow and sent him hurtling across the room as if launched by a giant catapult. The last Felix saw of his semiconscious form was as it descended into a horde of screaming goblins who let up a horrible shriek of triumph, and turned to tear their prey to pieces.

CHAPTER TWENTY-EIGHT

TECLIS INVOKED THE spell of levitation and marched upwards
into the air, determined to put himself above the melee. At
the same time he invoked multiple overlapping shields,
reinforcing those created by his charms and amulets. A brilliant golden sphere surrounded him. The din of battle
decreased as the warding spells blocked it out. Even so, the
giant's screech of pain was almost deafening, as was the
thunderous crash at it fell to the ground. What was going
on, he wondered, unwilling to take his eyes off the Chaos
mages? Surely the Slayer could not have killed the giant? It
was a feat that beggared belief.

Naturally a golden glowing figure hovering over the battle
chamber attracted the attention of other foes. In a sense he
had made himself a very attractive target. Spears and rocks
rose to greet him and angled away, repelled by the power of
his wards.

A smile twisted the face of the black-robed Chaos mage.
Teclis noted that the wound along his flank was already sealing itself, as powerful regenerative magic went to work. He
had expected something similar. This pair would have all

manner of devious protections. Now was the time to start testing them.

Teclis gestured and invoked the name of Lileath. Power sang in his veins as he forged a spell of awesome power. Spheres of destructive energy danced on his fingertips and left comet contrails in the air as he directed them towards his foe. The Chaos mage raised his staff in a barring gesture and a barrier of pure power shimmered into being in the air between them. The golden spheres hit it and exploded, sending shock waves rippling outwards from the point of impact. The force of the blast sent men, mutants and orcs to their knees. It caused the outer layer of his wards to flare into incandescent brightness as it neutralised them.

His opponent was both swift and skilled, that much was clear, but his speed was no match for an elf's. Even as his foe began to shape an offensive spell, Teclis unleashed another attack. Wave after wave of destructive energy rippled out from him, a torrent of power that could have reduced a castle wall to so much slag.

A black aura sprang into being around the Chaos mage as his own talismans and wards sought to protect him. They blazed ever brighter as he strove to neutralise the ever-increasing amount of energy the elf mage brought to bear. More than that, they had bought Kelmain time enough to abort his offensive spell and begin to invoke protections of his own. Teclis gritted his teeth and threw ever greater amounts of power at him, confident that eventually he would be victorious.

At that point, he sensed a bolt of colossal energy scything towards him from the direction of the altar. It was too late for him to do anything but pray that his wards would hold. It seemed that the other Chaos mage had decided to abandon trying to control the portals and entered the fray.

INSIDE THE CENTRAL chamber Felix saw all was chaos and carnage. Towering, grotesque shadows danced everywhere as the mages fought like angry gods overhead. The gore spattered giant, blinded, throat cut, hamstrung, raised its hands and tried to staunch the flow of gore from its neck. All around goblins, orcs and beastmen filled with blood-lust pranced and shouted and stabbed, like daemons tormenting a fallen deity in some nether hell. Unable to endure the torments, the giant lashed out with its fists, crushing a few of its tormentors, sending the rest shrieking away. It ended up sprawling in a spreading pool of its own blood. A few of the beastmen, too berserk to retreat, were crushed as it thrashed about.

Briefly, Felix lost sight of the Slayer as he sought to avoid joining them. Out of the gloom emerged a few of the men of Albion and the last of the maiden-guard, led by Siobhain. Murdo was with them too, a strange glow surrounding his spear, and black corrupt-looking mist evaporating from its point as if he had stabbed some evil thing with acidic blood.

'By the light, it does my heart good to see you yet live, Felix Jaeger,' said the old man. 'We shall make a last stand here worthy of the heroes of old. We must slay those foul wizards or die in the attempt.'

The others brandished their weapons and formed up around them. Felix was less interested in heroic last stands than he was in finding Gotrek. He knew that with the Slayer down, his chances of escape from this hellhole were exactly nil. And he was not at all sure that a last-ditch attempt to kill the wizards would do any good. With the sorcerers defeated, the forces they had unleashed here could raven out of control. Still, that was what Teclis was here for, he supposed.

'We must find the Slayer,' he bellowed. Seeing the looks of the men of Albion, he added, 'his axe can slay those spell-casters.'

At that moment, out of the corner of his eye, he caught sight of the goblins. They seemed to be swarming over something. Not waiting to see if the others followed, Felix charged towards them. A dozen strides and he bowled over the first of the little greenskins and skewered another on his sword. Two swift strokes beheaded another pair. Noticing their new attacker, they turned to face him. Momentum carried Felix forward over another goblin. He lashed out with his boot and sent a greenskin flying like a kicked cat and stabbed another through the chest. Taking his sword in both

hands he hewed like a woodcutter at those in front of him
and found himself face to face with Gotrek.

The Slayer looked done in. He bled from a dozen small
wounds, he leaned on the shaft of his axe for support, and
the corpse of a goblin dangled from his fist, hanging there
like a rabbit with a broken neck. Others lay trampled underfoot.

Gotrek gave him a dazed uncomprehending glance, which
was hardly surprising considering the amount of punish-
ment he had taken.

'You,' he said. 'You have come to record my doom, then.'

'Some doom,' said Felix, hoping to snap the Slayer from
his trance. 'Overwhelmed by a horde of snotlings.'

'These are not snotlings, manling. They are too big.'

Murdo arrived beside him.

'You have healing magic – do something!' Felix snapped.

Murdo nodded and gestured to the others. They formed a
circle around him and the Slayer. The old man began to
chant. Felix hoped the spell would work, for the way things
were going, they desperately needed the Slayer's axe.

Overhead, the golden figure of Teclis blazed with light;
attacked on both sides by the two Chaos wizards it looked
like his defences were starting to fail. The brimstone stench
of warpstone filled the air as the raw stuff of Chaos started
to emerge from one of the gates. The temple shook as if hit
by a giant hammer. The earth bucked and shook beneath
their feet. Felix did not need to be a wizard to know that the
end was very close.

TECLIS CURSED HIS overconfidence as agony wracked his body.
He had gone from attack to desperate defence in a heartbeat.
Secure in the knowledge that he could overwhelm Blackstaff,
and certain that the Chaos mage's twin would be kept busy
trying to control the energies he had unleashed, he had not
reckoned on him abandoning the task to come to his
brother's aid. In doing so he had made the situation doubly
desperate, for unless something was done about the swiftly
unravelling nexus of forces around them, disaster would
overwhelm them all. Unfortunately at the moment, all Teclis

could do was try to shore up his defences and endure, hoping against hope that some miracle would happen to give him the advantage over his foes before death took him.

He forced his lips into a smile that had as much agony in it as mirth. Whatever happened, he would go down fighting. If worst came to the worst he would unleash all the energies in his helm and staff in one final cataclysmic strike. In his own death he would take this pair down with him. But who then will save Ulthuan? The thought nagged away at the back of his mind, but he had no answer to it.

'ENOUGH, OLD MAN, enough,' said a familiar gruff voice. 'Any more of your spells and my head will explode.'

Felix glanced around to see that the Slayer looked better. Not exactly well, but capable of thought and movement. His blood-caked form was a grim sight but his grip on the axe was firm, and his stride was sure. All around came the sounds of battle as the last of the folk of Albion held their ground against the oncoming hordes. Felix's arm was tired from swinging it at orcs and beastmen.

'There's sorcerers to be killed,' said Felix.

'Is one of them an elf?' said Gotrek.

'No.'

'Too bad – but I suppose those Chaos-worshipping swine will have to do.' The Slayer barged forward through the line of men, and like a swimmer casting himself from a high crag into deep water, dove into the battle once more. Felix was right behind him.

LHOIGOR LAUGHED AS he summoned more and more energy to throw at the elvish wizard. He was surprised that the mage still endured. He and his twin had thrown enough power at him to have killed a daemon, or levelled a small mountain. Amazingly, their foe still lived, although now Lhoigor could sense him weakening. In a few more heartbeats he would be done. Just as well really, considering how close the nexus point was to erupting. And if that went, this temple, the whole island, and a fair chunk of the continent would go with it.

Lhoigor smiled. Would that be such a bad thing, he asked himself? Granted, they would no longer be able to move the armies of Chaos through the paths. On the other hand, the lands of men and elves would suffer such devastation as they had not endured in millennia. The cities of men would be overthrown. The survivors would be thrown back into barbarism and be easy prey. The hordes of Chaos would sweep over them. The survivors would grovel before the idols of their new gods, before offering up their weeping souls on the blackened altars.

Of course, there was the little matter of the fact that he and Kelmain might die as well, but even that might be avoided. There were still means of escape along a few of the Old Ones' open routes. They could kill the elf and withdraw, leaving their followers and their attackers to their fate. The more he thought of it, the more this appealed to Lhoigor.

At that moment, he saw a familiar dwarfish figure coming towards him through the press of battle. Even more astounding than the fact that the elf lived was the fact that Gotrek Gurnisson was still alive. That decided him – there was no way he was remaining to face that axe if he could help it. So be it, he thought. Let these fools fight to the death. They could kill the elf and make good their escape.

FELIX DODGED A massive chunk of fallen masonry that had crashed down from the ceiling. As he advanced through the melee, he reeled like a drunk man on the deck of a storm-tossed ship. The tremors were getting worse, he knew, the smell of brimstone more intense. Of them all, only Gotrek moved easily, keeping his footing with the sureness of a cat.

Panic spread through the battle. Even the ferocity of the orcs and the rage of the beastmen could not maintain itself in the face of the collapsing temple. The dying giant in the middle of the battle had cleared a space for itself. Already many of the combatants were starting to flee, hoping to escape the imminent destruction of the temple. Where they thought they were going to hide eluded Felix. If the structure collapsed, as seemed all too likely, there was nowhere safe to go.

A few of them, in their fear, were throwing themselves into the open portals. Some were swallowed up by the oncoming waves of Chaotic matter. Others vanished into the shadows. After his own encounters within that alien extra-dimensional labyrinth Felix did not envy them. The panic created a different problem. Now they had to fight their way forward through a press of bodies determined to escape at any cost. Goblins scrambled over the shoulders of orcs, beastman and greenskin ran shoulder to shoulder, their animosity overwhelmed by the magnitude of the impending catastrophe.

Felix followed in the wake of the Slayer as he hewed a path through the press of bodies. Everyone present seemed to have been caught up in the wild panic. All of them shared the same sense of impending doom. Felix stabbed out at anyone who looked like they would get around the Slayer, and so at last, they came to the great plinth atop which stood the altar.

Enormous whips of dreadful energy leapt from it to lash the floating form of the elven mage. The shields of light protecting him seemed to dim by the second. Felix knew that if they did not save him soon, they would be too late.

Gotrek vaulted onto the plinth and raced at the golden-robed Chaos sorcerer. The vulture-like man sensed his presence and raised his staff, the smell of ozone and brimstone filling the air as a gigantic bolt of energy arced towards the Slayer. Gotrek raised his axe. The runes blazed so brightly their after-image was engraved on Felix's field of vision. He half expected the Slayer to be incinerated but no, Gotrek stood although his hair and beard were singed. If anything this seemed to goad him to a berserk madness. Dwarfs took harm to their facial hair very seriously.

The Slayer charged forward and as he did so, Murdo's spear hurtled over his shoulder to embed itself in the sorcerer's flesh. A look of panic crossed his face. Felix knew he would never forget that expression. He looked more stunned than in pain, as if he could not quite believe what was happening to him, then Gotrek was upon him.

The sorcerer raised his staff to parry the axe. Gotrek laughed dementedly as he brought the axe down in a glittering arc. It impacted on the staff and broke it asunder. Brilliant energy burst forth explosively but the axe continued inexorably and clove the mage in two. Not content with this, Gotrek chopped his corpse into smaller parts. Small lightning bolts earthed themselves from the body as if many spells were being discharged into the altar.

The second Chaos mage screamed as his twin died. He turned to look at the body and for a second terrible pain, all the agony his brother seemed to have avoided, was written on his face. His concentration lapsed and at that moment a river of molten elvish power descended on him. For a moment, he stood silhouetted in its blaze. Felix saw small lines of darkness unravel within the glow, and then the Chaos mage was gone. The river of power lashed over the corpse of his brother cleansing the earth of its foulness.

Felix found himself standing with the survivors of the men of Albion atop the great plinth in the central chamber of the Temple of the Old Ones. Teclis descended from above to join them. They stood in what appeared to be an island of sanity as Chaos erupted all around.

'What now?' Felix said.

'I must unravel the work of these madmen,' said the elf. 'You must go before this place is destroyed.'

'An idea I am all in favour of,' said Felix, 'but how do you propose we do it?' He gestured to the crowds of fleeing enemies and the walls that seemed ready to collapse all around them.

'There is only one way,' said the elf. He pointed to the still open portals that led down into the Paths of the Old Ones. Several of them appeared clear of the Chaos contamination. Felix shook his head. 'Oh no,' he said. 'I am not going in there again.'

'There is no other way,' said the elf.

'We don't know how to find our way through the paths. There are daemons in there.'

'Not all the paths are twisted. I know the way,' said Murdo. 'I know the rituals. I can get us out.'

'Very good,' said the elf. 'Now get going. I have work to do here.'

'Are you sure you can do it?' asked Murdo.

'If I cannot, no one can,' said the elf. 'Go.'

'Is there anything I can do?' said Murdo.

'Pray,' said the elf. 'Now go!'

Murdo led the pitiful band of survivors to the opening in the wall. He glanced at the runes on the archway and gestured for them to pass through it. Gotrek watched the elf as he turned towards the altar. He paused for a long moment, as if about to say something, and then turned on his heel to follow Murdo. He seemed to realise that this was work for wizards and there was nothing he could do here.

Felix touched the elf on the shoulder. 'Good luck,' he said.

'And to you, Felix Jaeger,' replied the elf. 'Be careful. In the paths those things might still come for you.'

Felix reached the arch.

'I hope he succeeds,' he said to Gotrek.

'If he fails there's one good thing about it,' said the Slayer.

'What?'

'One less elf in the world.'

They moved down into the ancient darkness that led to the Paths of the Old Ones. Behind them, the elf began to sing a spell.

CHAPTER TWENTY-NINE

TECLIS STOOD ATOP the ancient altar in the Chamber of Secrets. All around him were signs of imminent catastrophe. The walls shook and huge chunks of rock descended from the ceiling, crushing greenskin and beastman alike. The giant still moved and thrashed, albeit slower now, and its howling was audible even over the shattering of fallen masonry and the panicked screams. The sulphur stench of warpstone and Chaos filled the air. To his mage sight vast interlocking patterns of energy shimmered and danced.

He touched the amulet the Oracle had given him. Now was the time to use it. Briefly he considered following the others, and seeking refuge within the paths. The scale of the task daunted him. He had minutes at most to shut down the vast network of magic the Old Ones had created. There was no option. There was no place for him to run if he failed anyway, and he would not let down his people. He must do what the Oracle had sent him to do. He must awaken the guardians of the Old Ones.

He offered up a prayer to Asuryan and took a deep breath, seeking to clear his mind, then he turned to confront the altar. It was a vast square block covered in familiar-looking angular runes. Most of them glowed. All of them represented something. At first they were bafflingly alien, but he realised that somehow his former foes had managed to activate them, and this meant they were not beyond his ability either. Particularly not when he held this ancient talisman. He held it up to the light and recited the spell he had been taught. Instantly power was drained from him into the amulet. Cords of energy seemed to flow out of it to the altar, binding him to it. The runes glowed ever brighter. The earth shook like a frightened beast.

It was pointless trying to understand the runes themselves. They were merely symbols anyway. What he needed was to comprehend the forces they represented. He opened his mind, bringing all of his mystical acuteness to bear on the problem. One rune was as good as any other for his purposes, so he chose one he recognised as having been present on every portal he had seen, and focused his mage sight on it.

As his point of view zoomed in, he saw that it was a work of breathtaking delicacy. The rune itself was connected to all the other runes by a vast web of interlocking forces. It was virtually a universe of them in itself. As above, so below, he thought, wondering if by manipulating the rune he could manipulate the forces themselves. Now was not the time to experiment though. Swiftly, working between one heartbeat and another, he allowed his consciousness to flow through the talisman and expand outwards to encompass the whole vast mystical lattice as earlier he had struggled to understand the layout of the pyramid.

Everything he saw tended to confirm his suspicions. The altar was the fulcrum of a vast system; its pattern held a deeper meaning and there was something about it that was oddly and hauntingly familiar, although at the moment he could not quite put his finger on what.

The pattern shimmered and started to fade. He saw that the whole thing was on the verge of disintegration and his heart hammered against his ribs. The plinth shook beneath his feet. More stones were dislodged. The giant's death howls set his teeth on edge. For a moment, he realised that the whole vast intricate web was about to explode and there was nothing he could do about it. The whole unstable system was about to unleash all its energy in a final destructive torrent. He waited for the end to come, knowing that he was at the very epicentre of the coming destruction.

A moment passed and then another. Nothing happened. He breathed again, and considered what he had witnessed. He knew now what the pattern reminded him of. Seen from certain angles it was almost identical to the map inscribed in the Haunted Citadel. Swirls of Chaotic energy were moving through the whole structure. The complex of energy represented by the runes was nothing less than a map of the Paths of the Old Ones and the whole complex system of tectonic forces they were interlinked with. He saw how the whole system had its roots in the realm of Chaos, that other space of infinite dangerous energies. He saw how it lay halfway between this world and the realm of daemons. He saw in one sudden blinding flash of insight all the nodal points through which power pulsed.

He saw too that the system was corrupted now, infected by Chaos, the ancient safeguards destroyed, perhaps by some colossal cosmic accident, perhaps by malevolent design. No matter, he thought. Unless he did something soon it would be too late. But, great though his understanding of sorcery was, whatever was controlling this whole vast world-spanning net of magic was beyond him. There was no way he could hope to understand it in the very limited time he had available. That would be the work of a lifetime, and even then he was not sure mortal minds could comprehend the thing in its entirety. So far he had found no sign of the guardians. He had expected them to come in response to his summons, but there was nothing. Perhaps they had passed into death.

Frustration and fear gnawed at him. He had come so far and done so much and it looked like he was a lifetime too late. He and all his people were the butt of some vast cosmic joke. He had been brought all this way merely to witness the final doom of his people. He stifled a curse. There must be something he could do. There must be some way to save the situation. If only he could find it.

FELIX FOLLOWED MURDO down into the bowels of the earth. His mouth felt dry and his hand returned constantly to the amulet the elf had given him. He did not want to go any further. He realised that he had never feared anything as much in his life as he feared returning to the Paths of the Old Ones. His feet felt like they were encased in boots of lead. It was a massive effort to take one step further. I would rather die than pass into that eldritch other world one more time, he thought.

And that's exactly what will happen if you don't. If you stay you will be buried alive at best, or swallowed by the oncoming tide of Chaos at worst. But if you pass through the portal you may lose even your soul. There had to be another way. Perhaps he could find a way back through the tunnels. Even as the thought occurred to him, he knew it was madness. There was no way he could cover that whole vast distance before the temple collapsed. And even if the gods smiled on him, and he did manage it, he would be in a huge haunted forest surrounded by the survivors of the Chaos army and the greenskins and hundreds of leagues from home. There was no chance of escape that way. He felt like a rat cornered by a cat. He wanted to lash out and hit something, but he knew it would do no good.

Ahead of him Murdo had stopped at a familiar-looking ramp. Beyond it lay a shimmering portal filled with many shifting colours. Felix thought he could see daemonic forms taking shape in there but told himself it was just his imagination. The old Truthsayer had begun a chant and a change took place in the glistening surface. It began to dim and solidify and Felix thought he saw himself and the others reflected as in some vast dull mirror. What was going on? At least it seemed like the old man had not been lying when he claimed to know something of the secrets of the paths.

The walls shook once more. The odour of warpstone increased. Felix felt that if he stayed here he would be suffocated by it. It seemed that the elf had failed in his task. The quakes came more swiftly now.

Murdo spoke to his people. One by one they stepped through the gate and vanished. Felix looked at the Slayer. Gotrek strode forward, axe held ready as if to smite some foe. Felix moved to join him. He felt a hand on his shoulder.

'I have opened the way, lad. It is safe – have no fear. I must return now and help the elf.'

Felix paused, half grateful for the interruption, half desperate to get the ordeal over with. 'Are you sure? He wanted to do it alone.'

'There are some things that cannot be done alone, and this is one. I go now. May the light watch over you.'

'And you,' said Felix, watching the old man limp back up the corridor. 'Good luck.'

Then he strode forward into the vortex. Cold slithered over him. Panic filled him. There was a sudden sensation of tremendous acceleration.

TECLIS DESPERATELY SCANNED the great rune map, looking for something, anything that would aid him. He knew his task was all but hopeless, but he refused to give up. In heartbeats he scanned the outer limits of the paths, and found nothing useful, so he returned his attention closer to home, to the pyramid itself. It was the centre of all this. Surely there must be something here. The ghosts of the Isle of the Dead would not have sent him here otherwise.

Another memory flickered through his mind: the pillars containing the skeletons of long-dead slann. He did not know why that thought came to him at the moment, except perhaps the idea of ghosts was in his mind. Perhaps the trapped sorcerers had sent the idea to him. It did not matter. He sought the glyph that simulated the mystical structure of the great ziggurat and let his attention flow to the hall of the pillars. Yes, he thought, there was something there. Something faint, but still present. He reached out with a faint tendril of magical essence and activated the pillars.

At once, he sensed another presence reaching out to touch him, through the intricate network of energy. At first he was wary, wondering if this was some sort of trap, whether a daemon was making its presence felt through the disintegrating Chaos-contaminated system. He shielded his mind but the presence was persistent and it did not have the feel of Chaos. There was something slow and alien and cold about it. A sense of power and baffled intelligence, of some great cold-blooded creature awakening from a long sleep.

Who are you? The thought was not in Elvish and he could not quite grasp its full range of meaning, but the gist was clear. *Why have you wakened us?*

'I am Teclis of the elves, and I seek your aid in averting disaster.' He pictured what was going on in his mind and projected it outwards.

Ah, you are one of the young races, the ones we helped teach back in the days of life. Your race has changed a great deal in a very short time.

Teclis smiled ironically. That was not what the elves thought. They thought themselves conservative and unchanging with a civilisation that had lasted ages.

An eyeblink in the time of the Old Ones, the Great Ones.

'Who are you?' asked Teclis.

We are the wardens charged by the Old Ones to oversee the great design. We gave our lives so that our spirits might remain and watch over the work but something went wrong and we had to close the paths to avoid catastrophe. We have slept and our power has been leeched away and now catastrophe looms. Others have interfered with the pattern, moulding it to their own designs, and they have caused great harm.

Images flickered into the elf's mind. He saw his own people building their watchstones and siphoning off power. He saw the ancestors of the men of Albion, tall and proud and far more advanced than the men of today, build their great stone circles. He saw how, well-intentioned though they might have been, they had distorted things. More images flickered though his mind and he saw further back in time, to the opening of the great warp gate and the havoc that wrought on the pattern magic of the Old Ones.

Ah, there is the cause. Alas, even had we our full strength, undoing that would be beyond us. Undoing that would be beyond the power of gods.

'Then there is nothing to be done?' queried Teclis. 'The work of the Old Ones will be unravelled and my homeland will be destroyed.'

No, young one, if you are willing, there is a way. You have great power and with it we can perhaps close the paths and seal them, at least temporarily.

'Any respite would be good, but how long?'

Heartbeats of the Great Watcher. Ten cycles of the world around the eye of heaven. Perhaps twenty.

Teclis considered this. 'Not long.'

Not long, and there is a price.

'Name it,' stated Teclis.

One of the pillars was shattered. One of our souls was lost. We need a replacement to make our pattern complete once more.

'You are talking about death, a living sacrifice. Myself.'

Yes.

Teclis took no time to reach his decision. 'I accept. What must I do?'

That will not be necessary, elf, said another voice. Teclis recognised it as belonging to Murdo. He knew the old man was standing at the altar now, hand on his shoulder, linked to him by contact, at once there and in this netherspace.

I know more of this than you do, continued Murdo. *My people have studied the mysteries of the patterns. My ancestors were taught by these cold-blooded ones. I have a better chance. Also I am old and must pass from this world soon. You have centuries yet.*

'Only if we succeed,' replied Teclis.

We must succeed.

'Very well. Let us proceed.'

FELIX FELT AS if his head was going to explode. Something had gone very wrong. Thousands of images coruscated through his mind. He saw visions of many things, of places and worlds and bubbles within the paths. The moment seemed to stretch forever. He sensed hungry things coming for him and knew the daemons were once more on his trail. He felt like he was tumbling endlessly down the corridors of infinity at fantastic speed. Somewhere far off he sensed power pulsing through the Paths of the Old Ones, as if something long dormant had woken. The hungry things came ever closer, and there was a terrifying sense that it was him and him alone they were after, that somehow they sensed his presence, and wanted to feast on his soul.

Suddenly up ahead was another vortex. He wondered whether he could possibly reach it in time.

GUIDED BY THE spirits of the ancient guardians, Teclis went to work. Knowledge flowed into him. He began to understand the huge complex of energies that flowed through the paths. He saw how every part was designed like a finely constructed machine. Now the machine was broken, and the fact that it still partially functioned was leading it to disaster, like a chariot still being dragged along an open road even though its axle was broken. What he needed was to close the portals so that they would not draw on those ravening runaway energies.

He opened his eyes and looked around the main chamber. Murdo lay now atop the altar. Teclis considered what he was going to do and was repelled by it. His whole life had been spent thinking that the sacrifice of sentient beings was a barbarous act. That they performed such things was what separated the dark elves from his own people.

He told himself that Murdo had volunteered for this, that he was giving up his life willingly and for the greater good, just as the ancient slann masters had done millennia ago. Doubts assailed him. Murdo was not a slann, perhaps the ritual would not even work, how could he hope to join with those ancient ghosts of an alien species? Teclis knew he could perform the sacrifice and it might all still be in vain. There was a very good chance of it. And even if they succeeded the solution would only be temporary. Decades at the most. The old open wound at the northern gate would still be there. The paths would be forced open once more. To an elf like himself, a decade was not a huge amount of time. What was the point?

He tried to shrug off his despair. The point was that they would buy more time. In a decade he could learn more, muster greater forces, return here with greater knowledge and more power. It was worth taking the chance, worth buying the time. If they succeeded.

'Ready?' he asked Murdo. The old man nodded. He clearly wanted to speak but could not. Despite his bravado, there was fear in his eyes. Teclis considered his own doubts and found them small compared to those that must assail the Truthsayer. He lay spreadeagled on the altar in the position they had been directed to by the slann, with his head and feet aligned with the ancient mystical poles of power.

Teclis spoke the words that he had been taught, his throat twisting as he struggled to spit out the alien syllables. Only centuries of practice in the arcane tongues allowed him to do it. As he spoke the words, he found his inner vision twisting, comprehension and power flowed through him. He had no sacred knife, as the old mage priests had, but his sword would do in its place. As he reached the climax of the ritual with the temple shuddering around him like a frightened beast, and the smell of warpstone and decay in his nostrils, he plunged the blade home, ripping open Murdo's chest and pulling out his heart, spraying the altar with blood. He winced at the pain in the old man's eyes. Yet part of him, hidden and dark, half felt only by himself, felt a secret satisfaction. The gap between even the highest of high elves and the darkest of dark was not so great after all, he thought, with a thrill at the sickness of his satisfaction. Blood flowed outwards, emptying itself over the altar, flowing through the ancient runic channels.

Teclis waited for a sign. Nothing happened. After all that, nothing. Murdo had given up his life in vain, and Teclis had violated the laws of his people for nothing. He stifled a curse, and controlled the urge to unleash a powerful bolt of energy at the altar. He studied it with his eyes and his mage sight and still saw no difference. Blood continued to gush, the light passed from the old man's eyes. Still nothing.

Wait. From the corner of his eye, he thought he saw the runes begin to glow in a new configuration. He felt a tug of power, through the spell that linked him with the altar, and fed it more. The blood-drenched runes began to glow. He saw Murdo's spirit drawn from his body, and dragged downward into the altar. While his lips chanted, and his own heart still beat, he freed his own spirit to pursue it. Once more his vision was drawn into the infinite maze of energy. He saw the old man's spirit, young-looking now and bathed in light, draw towards twelve others. They looked like great upright toads, but there was a suggestion of intelligence about them, and nobility and power that impressed even Teclis. He joined with them, filling a gap in their ranks, and at once began to work their great spell. Teclis joined in, feeding them his own power, performing the role that in ancient times living mage priests would have performed, providing a link between the world of the living and them.

There will be pain, the voice in his head told him. It did not lie. As he became one with them, he realised that they were one with the great pattern of the paths, and they could feel the corruption within them as purest agony. The polar warp-gate was indeed a wound to them and one that gave them great pain. Worse, it was one they could do nothing about. Teclis could understand now why they had closed the paths and retreated into dormancy. Enduring ages of such pain would surely have driven them mad.

Instead they concentrated on the rune markers of the paths, the things that drew power from the realm of Chaos. Closing the way was not going to be easy here. The raw primal power of the daemonic realm was forcing its way through the gaps the runes provided, like lava erupting through the crust of the earth.

He felt agony increase as they exerted themselves to shut the paths down. It was a pressure well nigh unbearable. He forced himself to concentrate, draw on the deepest reserves of his being and focus on the spell. Somewhere very far off, his body still chanted. He wanted to retreat into it, make the pain stop, just for an instant, but he knew that would be fatal – if he left the circle now before the spell was complete, all would fail.

Teclis kept chanting as one by one the runes were sealed. The pain mounted. He wondered if it would ever stop or if he would die of his agony and his spirit would be trapped here forever.

A small still part of his mind prayed that the others had gotten clear. It would not be a good thing to be trapped within the Paths of the Old Ones when the way was finally sealed. Pain mounted in his mind, searing at him. Blackness hovered at the edge of his mind. Desperately he tried to hold onto consciousness, as they made one final effort.

FELIX FELT AN enormous wave of pressure pass over him. He was not sure what was happening, but his speed seemed to be falling. At the same time, the sense of evil presence increased, as if the things stalking him were closing the distance. He willed himself to move faster but nothing happened. In the back of his mind, he thought he heard daemonic howls of triumph. He knew he was doomed if he fell into their clutches. Teclis could not save him now, and Gotrek was nowhere to be seen.

Feeling claws reaching for him, he stretched out, reaching for the vortex. It was close now, but perhaps not close enough, he thought he felt phantom fingers on his cloak. He reached further, stretched himself to the utmost. Almost there. He was certain something touched him now. Gossamer fingers that grew stronger and scalier. The howls of triumph were loud in his mind. An eternity of torture loomed.

Then something changed. Some power shifted within the strange extra-dimensional labyrinth. The vortex up ahead seemed to swirl slower, its energy draining away. The howls of triumph turned to shrieks of fear. Something had scared his pursuers. He sensed them retreat, moving off into the distance as if desperate to reach sanctuary before some dreadful event occurred. Perhaps the elf had succeeded. Perhaps he had closed the Paths of the Old Ones to Chaos.

Another thought struck Felix. Perhaps he had closed the paths to everyone else too. If that was the case he would be trapped in here. Along with the daemons, if they did not make good their escape. Desperately he twisted, throwing himself towards the vortex. It was smaller now, weaker, closing rapidly. He aimed himself like a diver and prayed to Sigmar to preserve him. For a long moment, nothing happened, then somehow he was through, falling back once more into the world he knew.

He landed sprawling on his face on hard stone. He lay there gasping. When he looked up, the Slayer was standing over him. Over the dwarf's shoulder he could see the human survivors and a slice of blue sky. The air smelled of salt and sea water.

'What kept you, manling?' Gotrek asked.

'You don't want to know.'

'Where's Murdo?'

'He won't be joining us, and neither will Teclis is my guess.'

'No great loss there.'

'Do you think they succeeded?'

'Well, so far there's no sign of the world ending, but maybe we had better wait a few days to be sure.'

Felix rose to his feet and limped towards the light. They had emerged halfway up a chalk cliff, looking out to a misty sea. Gulls called, and watery sunlight filtered down through the thick cloud. Siobhain and Culum glared at him but he would not let their hostility get to him, at least not right now. He felt like a man granted a new lease of life, and he intended to enjoy it.

Even as the thought occurred to him, it began to rain.

TECLIS FELT AS if he had been beaten very thoroughly with a large wooden club. His bones ached, his muscles ached, his head throbbed as if a goblin were using it for a drum. The air was foetid and smelled of warpstone and death. Near the altar the dead giant's corpse stunk worse than a cesspit. He was thousands of leagues from home with no means of transportation in the tumbled-down remains of an ancient haunted temple, most likely surrounded by orcs and beastmen.

He let none of this bother him. He was still alive and the Paths of the Old Ones were closed. The threat of continent-shattering doom was temporarily withdrawn. They had succeeded. He looked down at the corpse of Murdo and gently closed the wide-staring eyes. He wondered where the old man's spirit was now. Trapped in the stones along with the slann? Without his own pillar it would inevitably decay, and with it, the spell they had woven.

Teclis knew that he would need to return here and see what he could do about that, probably with an army and a host of mages, but right now, he was tired and a long way from home, and he needed a place to sleep. Leave tomorrow's problems for tomorrow, he told himself as he limped off in search of a safe spot to recover his powers and begin the long journey home to Ulthuan.

More Warhammer from the Black Library

The Gotrek & Felix novels
by William King

THE DWARF TROLLSLAYER Gotrek Gurnisson and his long-suffering human companion Felix Jaeger are arguably the most infamous heroes of the Warhammer World. Follow their exploits in these novels from the Black Library.

TROLLSLAYER

TROLLSLAYER IS THE first part of the death saga of Gotrek Gurnisson, as retold by his travelling companion Felix Jaeger. Set in the darkly gothic world of Warhammer, TROLLSLAYER is an episodic novel featuring some of the most extraordinary adventures of this deadly pair of heroes. Monsters, daemons, sorcerers, mutants, orcs, beastmen and worse are to be found as Gotrek strives to achieve a noble death in battle. Felix, of course, only has to survive to tell the tale.

SKAVENSLAYER

THE SECOND GOTREK and Felix adventure – SKAVENSLAYER – is set in the mighty city of Nuln. Seeking to undermine the very fabric of the Empire with their arcane warp-sorcery, the skaven, twisted Chaos rat-men, are at large in the reeking sewers beneath the ancient city. Led by Grey Seer Thanquol, the servants of the Horned Rat are determined to overthrow this bastion of humanity. Against such forces, what possible threat can just two hard-bitten adventurers pose?

DAEMONSLAYER

GOTREK AND FELIX join an expedition northwards in search of the long-lost dwarf hall of Karag Dum. Setting forth for the hideous Realms of Chaos in an experimental dwarf airship, Gotrek and Felix are sworn to succeed or die in the attempt. But greater and more sinister energies are coming into play, as a daemonic power is awoken to fulfil its ancient, deadly promise.

DRAGONSLAYER

IN THE FOURTH instalment in the saga of Gotrek and Felix, the fearless duo find themselves pursued by the insidious and ruthless skaven-lord, Grey Seer Thanquol. DRAGONSLAYER sees the fearless Slayer and his sworn companion back aboard an dwarf airship in a search for a golden hoard – and its deadly guardian.

BEASTSLAYER

STORM CLOUDS GATHER around the icy city of Praag as the foul hordes of Chaos lay ruinous siege to the northern lands of Kislev. Will the presence of Gotrek and Felix be enough to prevent this ancient city from being over-whelmed by the massed forces of Chaos and their fearsome leader, Arek Daemonclaw?

VAMPIRESLAYER

AS THE FORCES of Chaos gather in the north to threaten the Old World, the Slayer Gotrek and his companion Felix are beset by a new, terrible foe. An evil is forming in darkest Sylvania which threatens to reach out and tear the heart from our band of intrepid heroes. The gripping saga of Gotrek and Felix continues in this epic tale of deadly battle and soul-rending tragedy.

GIANTSLAYER

A DARKNESS IS gathering over the storm-wracked isle of Albion. Foul creatures stalk the land and the omens fore-tell the coming of a great evil. With the aid of the mighty high elf mage Teclis, Gotrek and Felix are compelled to fight the evil of Chaos before it can grow to threaten the whole world.

Inferno! is the Black Library's high-octane fiction magazine, which throws you headlong into the worlds of Warhammer. From the dark, orc-infested forests of the Old World to the grim battlefields of the war-torn far future, Inferno! magazine is packed with storming tales of heroism and carnage.

Featuring work by awesome writers such as:

- **Dan Abnett**
- **Ben Counter**
- **William King**
- **Robin D Laws**
- **Graham McNeill**

and lots more!

Published every two months, Inferno! magazine brings the grim worlds of Warhammer to life.